Maggie co‎_____ ‎was; she knew she was dying. "I‎_____ ‎to die."

"Look at me," Simon commanded. "What is your decision?"

I want to be with him, Maggie thought suddenly. *Nothing else matters.* She managed to lift up her hand, and caress his face softly.

Simon put his arms around her, then kissed her fiercely. The sickness faded beneath the passion Maggie felt. *I never wanted anything as much as I want him,* she thought hazily.

"You're beautiful," he whispered. He ran his hands lightly across her body, fingertips barely touching her. Maggie moaned, aching with desire.

"Tell me who I am," he ordered while thrusting into her.

"My master."

"And you'll be mine forever?"

"Forever."

Simon sank his teeth deep within the wounds on her neck again. Maggie moaned, digging her nails into his back. The rapture she now felt made her prior ecstasy pale in comparison. She felt wave after wave of intense, unbearable pleasure as he drained the blood from her. Maggie felt him growing harder within her as he drank her blood. It seemed to go on forever, making love while he drank her blood. She didn't want it to ever stop. . . .

CRIMSON KISS

TRISHA BAKER

PINNACLE BOOKS
Kensington Publishing Corp.

http://www.pinnaclebooks.com

PROLOGUE

March 17, 1998

Unobserved, Meghann O'Neill entered the dark hospital room after the relatives holding vigil over the dying old woman departed. She felt her throat close with pity when she stared at her oldest friend, who was moaning and writhing in agony on the narrow hospital bed. Bridie Fraser was beyond the reach of the drugs her doctors had prescribed; they could do nothing to ease her pain.

But I can help, Meghann thought, and reached out to take Bridie's skeletal, clammy hand. Meghann closed her eyes and focused all her energy on the old woman's mind, as her mentor had taught her to do. "Be still, Bridie. The pain is gone."

Meghann felt the tension in the hand she grasped ease as a numb lassitude not unlike the effect of Novocain banished her friend's pain. Bridie leaned back against her pillows, whispering, "Who . . . Who are you?"

Meghann waved her free hand and the harsh fluorescent overhead lights came on, illuminating the small room.

Bridie Fraser gasped; her watery blue eyes were wide with shock. "Maggie!"

Meghann smiled down at her best friend. "Hello, Bridie."

"B-but . . . ," the old woman stuttered. "It's not . . . you can't . . . Maggie, you haven't changed at all! Are you a dream?"

"I'm real," Meghann assured her. There was a reason she hadn't aged in the fifty-four years since she'd last seen Bridie, but she couldn't share the truth with her old friend.

Bridie Fraser smiled, and Meghann saw her pretty young friend for a moment in the eyes of the old woman. "Maggie . . . Maggie, you've finally come back. You . . . You're an angel now, come to take me home."

Meghann gave her a crooked smile. "Not exactly an angel, Bridie. But if you are ready to die, I can help you."

"Oh, Maggie," Bridie whispered. "I missed you so much. Why did you disappear like that? Was it that man? Did you really run away to marry him?"

Meghann's hand tightened over Bridie's until the old woman cried out in pain.

"Oh, Bridie—I'm sorry. I didn't mean to hurt you . . . now or then. Will you forgive me?"

"Just tell me you were happy, Maggie."

Meghann blinked rapidly, holding back tears. "Of course I was happy. Were you?"

"I had forty years with my Henry. And—oh, Maggie! I wish you could see Paul—he's such a handsome, smart boy. What about you, Maggie? Did you have children?"

Meghann couldn't take much more of this; hearing about the sweet, happy life Bridie had led made her realize how cursed her own had been since the night Simon Baldevar walked into it. "Bridie, if you want the pain to stop forever, I can help. But this must be your decision."

"There's no decision—what I've been doing since I got this cancer isn't living. Help me, Maggie. Take me home."

Meghann grasped her friend's hand. "Listen to my voice." She began talking to Bridie about their childhood memories: the old days of cheating on a math test in Sister Mary Margaret's sixth-grade class, their first school dance, drinking ice-cream sodas and reading movie magazines, waiting on line at Radio City Music Hall to see *Gone With the Wind.*

While she talked, Meghann wrapped her power around Bridie's heart, the stubborn heart that was still beating in the cancer-racked body. The strain of keeping her voice upbeat while she concentrated her entire will on holding Bridie's heart still made her tremble; small beads of perspiration formed on the ivory skin of her forehead, but she did it—she used her skill to help her friend.

Meghann leaned over and closed the sightless, staring eyes. Even after fifty years, she was uneasy around death, particularly when she caused it. "Good-bye, Bridie."

Good-bye as well to the last person who remembered Maggie O'Neill—the bright-eyed, happy undergraduate she'd been before she met Simon Baldevar.

Was it thoughts of her dead master that made Meghann feel weak and sick or had she expended too much energy helping her old friend? She collapsed into a chair by the bed, trembling and nauseous. She didn't need a mirror to tell her how awful she must look—she had to have blood right away.

"Thank you."

Meghann looked up at the white-haired old man who had entered the room. She really was sick if her senses hadn't warned her of the mortal entering the room. How much had he seen?

"I don't know who you are, but thank you for helping my wife."

Before Meghann could shake the gnarled hand in front of her, a team of doctors and nurses stormed into the room, responding to the flat, loud beep on Bridie's heart monitor.

"Flatliner!" one of them barked. "Code Blue!"

"No," Henry protested. "Don't you bring Bridie back—she's at peace now."

An arrogant doctor took control. "This man is hysterical. Get him out of here."

Meghann forced herself out of the chair and walked over to the doctor. She put a restraining hand on him. "Doctor, I believe you should defer to the wishes of the family in this matter." The doctor found himself unable to protest when he looked into the young woman's eyes. Without another word, he left the room, the others trailing in his wake.

Meghann was shaking now. Commanding the doctor had depleted her strength. *She had to get blood.* She found herself walking toward Henry Fraser.

No! She ran out of the room, ignoring Henry, who was yelling, "Wait! Come back. . . ."

Meghann rushed through the hospital corridors. She should have known helping Bridie would leave her weak.

As she hurried through the emergency room, she crashed into a tall, muscular man. He snarled, "Bitch! The word is excuse me!"

Meghann whirled around. "Watch who you call a bitch."

The man took a step back in shock. He simply could not believe what stood in front of him—a young woman with bright red hair that made her pale, colorless skin look even worse. He thought a ghost was glaring at him. The worst part was her light green eyes; they blazed with power and hatred. They made him want to run, but he found he couldn't move.

Meghann felt his fear, and relished it. She felt the darkness rising within her, and didn't even try to stop it. She simply grabbed the man's arm and propelled him toward a nearby empty staircase.

"Please, miss," he whimpered, "don't hurt me. I'm sorry. . . ."

Meghann's grin made his heart stop cold. "It's too late for sorry, friend. Now kneel before me." This was a minor trick she'd learned from Simon—seeing someone's pain and humiliation made their blood taste better.

Meghann leaned down and sank her blood teeth into the man's jugular vein. He screamed, but Meghann barely heard him. How good the blood was, strong and hot. It filled her mouth and she wanted to drink down every precious drop. Each mouthful pushed her anxiety and hurt further away. Her skin regained color; the shaky, queasy feeling vanished. Still, Meghann went on sucking the man's blood, enjoying the feeling of total control she had over him. She wanted to drink forever. . . .

It wasn't until the man passed out that Meghann returned to her senses; she looked down at the unconscious man. What the hell had she done? She heard Alcuin lecturing her: "You never have to kill or frighten your hosts. A small amount will sustain you. . . ."

She cursed and put her fist through the wall. Didn't it ever get better? Fifty years she'd been a vampire, and she still couldn't control the depraved impulses inside her.

Meghann was appalled. It had been years since she'd given in to blood lust like this. And now she was aware of a slight giddiness she felt. She looked at the man's arm; it was covered in track marks. A heroin addict—no wonder the blood tasted so good. Well, at least the punctures could be explained away. He'd assume he tried to fix through the vein in his neck.

Meghann put her hand to the pulse in the man's neck. It was there . . . somewhat weak but steady. At least she hadn't killed him. Meghann focused on his blood flow. . . . No, she hadn't infected him either. Meghann decided she would leave him here; he would assume that he had nodded off and forgotten or been attacked. But first she focused her will on his mind, commanding him to forget meeting her and being bitten.

Meghann looked down at herself. The white blouse she was wearing with the black suit was soaked in blood. She took it off and used it to wipe excess blood from her mouth and chin. She put the blazer of her black suit back on; it barely covered her breasts. Her blood teeth had retracted; she could be seen in the mortal world again.

Meghann reached into her purse and withdrew several hundred dollars from her wallet. She placed it in the pocket of the unconscious man's jeans. Leaning over him, she whispered, "I'm sorry."

A pathetic offering, but the only one Meghann could make. She was truly disgusted with herself. All those years of good behavior down the drain with one feeding. If she was going to behave that way, she might as well have remained Simon's consort.

Meghann left the staircase and headed for her car, a 1958 Cadillac convertible. She got behind the wheel and lit a Camel cigarette. She started the car, and laughed grimly at the thought that these cigarettes had just killed her good friend Bridie.

That's one thing, whatever happens I'm not going to die of lung cancer, she thought.

* * *

Since returning to New York, Meghann had bought a large Victorian house in Rockaway Beach. She loved the ocean, and had good memories of the place. Of course there were horrible memories too, courtesy of Simon Baldevar.

When Meghann crossed the Veterans Memorial Bridge, she felt a change in the air. A nonmortal presence near . . .

Alcuin! Meghann smiled at the thought that her mentor was here. Of course it was a surprise, but she wanted to see him. She reached out with her senses to pinpoint his location, and found herself driving the car to a secluded area of beach near Breezy Point.

On the boardwalk, Meghann saw a hooded figure by the shore. She hurried toward him. "Alcuin!"

"Meghann!" he said as he picked her up and whirled her around. Then he sobered. "Tell me what happened tonight."

Without a word, Meghann reached into her bag and handed him the blood-soaked blouse.

Alcuin put it to his face and sniffed. "Why?" he asked simply.

Meghann looked out at the black sea, wishing that just once she could see the sun dance on the water again. "I went to visit Bridie . . . and I just left there feeling so angry and cheated. Damn it! Why the hell has this happened to me? It should have been me there, ready to die after a long, good life. I don't mean I want to die in that kind of pain—but I'm not supposed to appear at a friend's bedside as the goddamn angel of death. Why the hell do I have to live like this? And then that stupid man got in my way . . ."

"Banrion." Alcuin soothed her with his special name for her, the Gaelic word for queen. "I wish I had known

you were planning to visit a mortal friend; I could have warned you."

"Warned me about what?"

"Exactly what happened tonight. Meghann, you aren't the first vampire to visit someone from your mortal lifetime. It's always a shock and a bitter moment when you realize what could have been. Charles had the same reaction."

"You mean Charles . . ."

"Yes, he went to visit a young man with whom he'd fought in the war. When he saw him being tended to by his wife, Charles was wild with fury and grief. Do you remember what I told you? Those two emotions make you most vulnerable to the darkness. Put it behind you, *banrion*. You didn't kill the man, and you did your best to make amends. Now for your penance, don't feed for one fortnight. Spend the time keeping the Perpetual Adoration and meditating upon your sins."

Meghann felt absolved—after all, Alcuin had been a bishop before he'd been transformed.

Alcuin smiled when he saw the relief on Meghann's face. "Now, *banrion*, let's talk of more pleasant matters. You received your doctorate?"

Meghann smiled back, linking her arm through Alcuin's as they walked back toward her car. "Oh, yes— and I see patients now . . . mostly abused partners referred to me by the university counseling center." Meghann was a psychologist.

"How wonderful—and what a gorgeous car." Alcuin admired the black paint, and patted the rocket fins that had been embossed with flames. "I believe car making became an art form in the fifties and sixties."

Meghann put the top down—the cold wouldn't bother her and Alcuin the way it would mortals. "I don't think you came to America to congratulate me on my degree or my car."

Alcuin nodded. "Would you mind if I drove, Meghann? I have some very unpleasant news."

"I didn't know you knew how to drive."

"It would be a bit ridiculous to live seven hundred years and refuse to keep up with modern innovations."

Meghann handed him the keys, and got in on the passenger side. "What happened? Is it Charles?" Charles Tarleton was one of Alcuin's other apprentices, and the vampire who'd introduced Meghann to Alcuin's circle.

"Charles is fine," Alcuin told her as he started driving. "But, Meghann . . . I don't know how to tell you this without upsetting you. Just listen calmly and remember . . . You've become a very strong vampire in the past thirty years and you'll never be without my protection."

Meghann's heart started beating rapidly. "Why would I need your protection?" she demanded.

Alcuin busied himself with watching the traffic, avoiding Meghann's eyes. "I have evidence that Simon Baldevar is alive."

"No!" Meghann screamed immediately. "He can't be. . . . Alcuin, I killed him over forty years ago!"

When they arrived at Meghann's house, Alcuin shut off the engine and took one of her ice-cold hands. "Meghann, you know you were never completely sure that you killed him."

Meghann simply could not believe this—she could not feel secure in the world if she thought Simon was still alive. He would kill her. . . . No, wait. He would torture her horribly and then he'd kill her.

Meghann racked her brain for any rationalization to refute Alcuin's statement. "But," she said wildly, "forty years have gone by. Why would he suddenly resurface?

Why would he go underground for all that time? It's not like him."

"*Banrion,* I never told you this because there was no point upsetting you, but Simon has disappeared before. . . . The last time was for seventy years. He spends the time developing his strength."

Wonderful, she thought grimly.

She looked up at Alcuin. "What proof do you have that he might be alive?"

"Photographs—I'll show them to you inside."

Meghann nodded. "I want Jimmy to see them too." Jimmy Delacroix was a mortal Meghann had trained to hunt renegade vampires who refused to live by Alcuin's dictate that vampires not murder or torture the mortals they drank from.

"Of course."

When they entered the living room, Jimmy's eyes widened in disgust and fear at the sight of Alcuin, whom he had never seen before.

Damn, Meghann thought. She'd been so rattled by Alcuin's news that she completely forgot how shocked poor Jimmy would be when he saw Alcuin. Her mentor might be one of the wisest vampires alive but was also hideously deformed. A vampire of a different bloodline from Meghann's had transformed him. As a result, he had no hair or eyebrows and had viciously long fangs that curved past his jawbone and were permanent fixtures (unlike Meghann's, which retracted when she wasn't feeding). His skin was translucent, and all his veins stuck out prominently.

Meghann knew Alcuin understood Jimmy's shock and rage when he looked at him. Eight years ago, a vampire of Alcuin's type had murdered Jimmy's wife and three-year-old son.

"Jimmy," she said softly, "it's all right. This is Alcuin. I told you about him."

Jimmy pulled himself back from the horrifying memories, plastering a bitter grin on his face. "Sure," he slurred, swigging from a half-empty decanter of bourbon he plucked from the coffee table. "How are you doing, handsome?"

Of all the nights to drink, did Jimmy have to pick the time Alcuin visited? Meghann decided to give him time to pull himself together.

"Jimmy, please ask our guest if he would like any refreshments."

Jimmy glared at Meghann, who stared back. With a put-upon air, he asked Alcuin sarcastically, "Would you like any refreshments, my lord?"

"Some water, please."

"And what about you, my vampire queen?"

"Some coffee would be nice. And make enough for yourself," Meghann said pointedly.

Jimmy thought about responding to that and then lurched off to the kitchen.

"Didn't you say Mr. Delacroix had given up drinking?"

"He has . . . for the most part," Meghann answered, "but we had a disagreement last night."

Alcuin did not ask if the disagreement was part of a lover's quarrel. He knew the vampire-hunter had lived with Meghann for six years, but he had never asked her what their relationship was. You'll face a difficult decision, *banrion,* he thought, love between a mortal and a vampire rarely comes to a good end.

Meghann went to the kitchen to see if Jimmy needed any help. "So I don't have to serve Count Dracula by myself? You're not going to show me off as your pet Renfield?"

Meghann laughed as she got some coffee mugs and

a water glass from the cupboard. "Now, Jimmy, you know I don't go around making humans my slaves."

"Yeah, I guess that was more in your old boyfriend's line of country," Jimmy said, referring to Simon Baldevar.

"Funny that you should mention him."

"Why?" Jimmy took a closer look at her.

Meghann bit her lip and wrapped her arms around her body. "Alcuin thinks Simon might still be alive."

"Jesus Christ!" Jimmy exploded, bringing Alcuin hurrying into the kitchen. He turned on him. "How the hell can that son of a bitch be alive? Maggie killed him forty years ago!"

Meghann put the coffee and water on a tray. "Jimmy, let's continue this in the living room. Alcuin said he has some photographs to show us."

Alcuin took the tray while Jimmy went over to Meghann. The jolt of fear he'd received when Meghann told him about Simon had knocked the alcohol out of his system. "Maggie, I thought you said you killed him."

"I thought I did," she told him while they walked back into the living room. "I mean, the last time I saw Simon Baldevar, he was lying on a rooftop with a stake through his heart that I had impaled him with. He couldn't move; I thought daylight would take care of him."

"No doubt he had an ally you weren't aware of come and remove the stake," Alcuin told her.

"Let's not jump the gun," Jimmy said. "We still aren't one hundred percent sure he's alive."

Alcuin reached into his cloak and handed Meghann a flat brown envelope. She sat down on the ottoman and inspected the photos, with Jimmy looking over her shoulder.

The pictures made Meghann feel physically ill. Since

becoming a vampire, Meghann had witnessed many terrible things. These photographs, with their shocking and pathetic images, were one of the most devastating things she had ever seen.

The photos appeared to be of some sort of nursery or orphanage. With the exception of five women in nun's habits, an elderly priest, and two women in plain clothes, the victims in the photographs were all children. The youngest corpse looked to be about two years old, and the oldest child was probably twelve. Altogether, the photos showed ten dead children.

Each corpse had been brutally slashed. Some were nearly beheaded from the wounds inflicted. Some were cut on their wrists. It did not escape Meghann's notice that each wound was on a vein or artery.

Meghann's eyes fell on the priest. She first she saw the terror and pain on his face. Then she noticed . . . Dear God!

Jimmy snatched the picture when it fell out of her hands. "What the hell?"

Alcuin looked as uncomfortable as Meghann. "The priest was found with an ornate Russian Orthodox cross inserted into his anus."

Jimmy was disgusted. "Why the hell would someone do that?"

Meghann answered. "If Simon committed these murders, I can explain the priest. I saw him do the same thing in Cuba. It is my guess that the priest entered the room and saw Simon's blood teeth out. If he grabbed the cross and held it up for protection, screaming that movie foolishness about standing back in the name of Christ, then Simon yanked the cross out of his hands, bent him over, and . . . Well, Simon's sense of humor did run to such things." She could still see the young Cuban priest moaning and crying. It wasn't the physical pain that made him cry; it was the desolate knowledge that his God could not protect him from the evil fiend that had violated the sanctuary of the small island church.

Meghann felt bile in her throat. She went to the small bar in the living room and poured a tumbler full of absinthe—one of the few substances that could intoxicate a vampire. Grain alcohol worked too, but it was even viler tasting than absinthe. Meghann noticed Jimmy eyeing her glass, which would probably kill him if he drank the whole thing.

She took a large mouthful to steady herself and asked Alcuin, "What are these pictures of?"

"St. Paul's Home for Abused Wives and Children in San Diego. The church takes in women and children with no place to go until the women can find a job or family members willing to help them. The cops think the attack took place between eight and nine P.M. They say it could have been far worse. There are usually fifty families and thirty nuns there. The rest were at a bazaar. These children were sick, and they couldn't attend."

Although the children were simply slashed, the cross was mild compared to the atrocities visited on the poor women in the pictures. Some of the dead were forced into a kneeling position. These corpses were facing other standing corpses in a crude simulation of oral sex. The victims were kept in position by wooden stakes that impaled them, and were then ground into the floor.

"The coroner said they died after they were impaled . . . not before."

Meghann could have guessed that by the pain and horror in their open, staring eyes. She also thought, from the fright on the children's faces, that they had been forced to watch the carnage before they were killed.

"How do you know this is the work of vampires?"

Jimmy asked. "It could have been the work of psycho-paths. Even the cross could be the inspiration of some crazy kids."

"That's precisely what the cops believe," Alcuin re-sponded. "They think this is the work of some satanic cult. However, what they cannot explain is the fact that there was almost no blood at the crime scene. When the bodies were examined by the coroner, he said they had been bled dry."

"Besides," Meghann told Jimmy, "look at the stab wounds. You'll notice very subtle puncture marks im-bedded in the slashes." She looked up at Alcuin. "This is definitely the work of vampires, but how can you be sure it's Simon? He's not the only vampire to resent the whole crucifix business."

"Yeah," Jimmy echoed.

"Meghann, take another look at that picture of the nun by St. Joseph's statue."

Meghann looked, and dropped the photograph. "My God . . . the pendant!"

The picture was of a nun wearing only her veil, with her legs wrapped tightly around the statue. That was not what had disturbed Meghann. At the foot of the statue was a gold pendant from the fourteenth cen-tury—a gift from Simon. Meghann had left it behind on the night she thought he died.

Alcuin reached into his cloak and withdrew the pen-dant. "Charles was able to bribe one of the cops and get this for you. . . . I thought you might want it back."

Meghann eyed the object with distaste, and then thought she should have it—perhaps it could be used in a binding spell against Simon. She sat silently for a few moments, twirling the pendant in her hands before she spoke. "Simon is neither careless nor stupid. He left that pendant behind as a calling card."

"It's more than that," Alcuin told her. "It's an invitation."

"To what?" Jimmy asked.

"To me," Meghann answered tonelessly. "He knows that I became Alcuin's apprentice. . . . He wants to confront me and Alcuin for taking me in. The priest was a direct taunt to Alcuin. Simon is telling us that he considers us no threat." Meghann realized something else about those pictures. Her panic-stricken eyes met Alcuin's. "How could I have not seen it before? It was no accident . . . choosing a home for battered wives and children." Meghann leaped up from the chair, her eyes wild and her face pale. "Alcuin, he knows! He knows I became a psychologist, and I spend my life trying to help people like that! Dear God, he's mocking me twice. He must have been around me or found out enough to know what I do and now he's saying he can spit on that, destroy it . . . and me completely!"

Meghann collapsed on the couch. She couldn't make herself say the rest out loud. Simon had another reason for killing children. She had killed him (or thought she had) when he threatened the life of a child. Now Simon was telling her that one life meant nothing. She could almost hear his loathsome voice: "Look long and hard at those pictures, my sweet. Could you have stopped the slaughter this time?"

"Meghann," Alcuin said gently, interrupting her thoughts. "You're right. . . . He will try to destroy you completely. He's always despised me, but what he feels for you is a different matter. That monster thinks he was in love with you. You not only spurned what he considers to be love, you escaped him. In the process, you nearly killed him. Very few vampires have been able to do what you, his protégée, managed. Please be aware that what he did to those poor souls is mild compared to what he must have in mind for you."

Meghann shivered, remembering what Simon had done to her the night before she left him. Jimmy went over to the couch and put his arms around her. She looked up, smiling slightly.

Alcuin looked grave. "Meghann, you don't know how much I wish I could protect you from this threat."

"Why the hell can't you?" Jimmy snapped. "I mean, you're older than he is; Maggie says you're powerful. Why can't you just take care of him?"

"Don't be so rude," Meghann scolded. "And the only way I can see Alcuin protecting me from Simon is to shadow me every minute of the night. Do you think I want to live that way—never able to go anywhere or do anything without looking over my shoulder?"

Stung by the rebuke, Jimmy replied, "All I was saying is maybe he could find Simon. . . ."

Meghann finished the poison in her glass; she poured more. "Jimmy, if we're fortunate, Simon will think the same way you do. He'll expect me to be scared—to hide behind Alcuin's protection. After all, he never gave me credit for being anything but his little concubine." Fear lessened as anger and thoughts of vengeance took its place. She turned to Alcuin. "But he'll be surprised, won't he? With your help, I'm strong enough to confront him. And I want to do this—I owe him for ruining my life, staining my soul with the evil he made me do. I want to see him again—so that I can kill him the way I thought I had forty years ago."

Alcuin smiled at the change in her. She was holding her head high and thrusting her jaw forward in determination. The regal way she held herself, no matter what the situation, was the first thing he'd noticed about her; it was why he called her *banrion*. But he could not allow her to be reckless or overconfident. "Meghann, I have lived for seven centuries and the thought of a confrontation with Simon Baldevar worries me. He has tremendous power, and when you add to that his feelings toward you . . . we must proceed with extreme caution. Now we must start to plan for his attack."

Alcuin glanced at Jimmy, who frowned. "What?"

Alcuin spoke carefully—not wishing to offend the mortal. "Jimmy, we have a small chance of defeating Simon. You, on the other hand, have none. We will offer you our protection, but you will not be involved in this battle."

Jimmy's mouth dropped open. He leaped off the sofa and would have attacked Alcuin if Meghann had not held him back. "Not be involved?" he yelled. "Who the fuck do you think you are? Some fucking vampire killed my wife and kid and you're telling me I won't be involved? Fuck you! What did you think—while Maggie has to wait for this asshole to come get her, I was just going to sit here and knit?" Outraged, he was trying to break the iron hold Meghann had on him.

Alcuin observed the thrashing vampire-hunter and sighed. Seeing the way Jimmy reacted over the thought of Meghann being hurt left no doubt in his mind that these two were lovers. God help you, young man, he thought to himself, for Simon will have no mercy on any man who receives from Meghann what she denied him—love.

Meghann spoke softly. "Jimmy, calm down." She looked at Alcuin. "Obviously, we can't send him away for fear that Simon will find him. Who knows how much he's found out about me? Let Jimmy be involved—we might be fortunate enough to find out where Simon sleeps. If we did, Jimmy's aid would be invaluable." Her eyes pleaded with Alcuin to go along.

Alcuin knew what she was truly asking—that he not make her mortal lover feel insignificant. The man needed to feel he was doing all he could to protect her.

At a slight nod from Alcuin, Meghann released

Jimmy. Alcuin came over and shook his hand. "We welcome your assistance."

With that settled, Jimmy hit Alcuin with a barrage of questions concerning his plans.

Meghann wandered over to the back window, not really paying attention. She was staring out at the sea, remembering the past—Simon Baldevar and how she became a vampire.

ONE

April 21, 1944

When Maggie O'Neill came home after pitching for the Hunter College varsity softball team, she saw that her roommate, Bridie McGovern, was putting away the cleaning supplies.

"About time," Bridie grumbled at her. "Did you deliberately pitch slow so that all the cleaning would be done when you got home?"

"Fair is fair, Bridie. Didn't I agree to do all the cooking and dish washing next week if you'd clean the house today? And I went into the USO at eight this morning to help with the blood drive. Besides, you're in very good company. I read somewhere that Joan Crawford cleans her Hollywood mansion on her hands and knees."

"Big deal," Bridie grouched.

"Anyhow, don't be mad—look what I brought home." Maggie reached into the brown paper bag she was carrying and removed four bottles of beer.

Bridie's mood immediately improved. "Great! I'll get the bottle opener; you get some glasses. Did you bring home any cigarettes? I'm all out."

After the girls were seated on the couch, Bridie asked, "How's the blood drive going?"

"Not bad—I must have called everyone in Manhattan to come out and give blood on Monday."

Bridie eyed Maggie. "And will the donors include yourself?"

"Of course," Maggie said indignantly. "I've never *not* given blood. I just have a little trouble with the needle."

Bridie snorted. "A little trouble? I never saw anyone over the age of five make such a fuss about needles. Anyway, how was the game?"

"I pitched a shutout," Maggie said gleefully, opening the second bottle of beer. "You should have seen the looks on the faces of those Barnard snobs."

"Good—then maybe my news won't bother you too much."

"Is something wrong?" Maggie asked.

"I can't go with you to Pauline's tonight." Pauline Manchester was a wealthy girl Bridie and Maggie had met at the USO. They weren't really close, but Pauline had invited them to one of her mother's society parties. They'd gone to a few in the past and both girls had been looking forward to the party.

"Why can't you go? Is something wrong?"

"The hospital called." Bridie was a student nurse at St. Vincent's Hospital. "A bunch of girls called in sick. They need me to work the midnight-to-eight shift all weekend."

"That's too bad."

"Are you still going?"

"Of course."

"What will Johnny think?" Johnny Devlin was Maggie's fiancé. He'd been wounded in France and had come home three weeks ago.

Maggie frowned and lit another cigarette. "I don't

have to answer to him. And anyway, who says he has to know I'm going by myself? He's up at Harvard this weekend on an admissions interview."

Bridie opened her second bottle of beer. "Maggie, is there something wrong between you and Johnny?"

Maggie took a strong pull of her cigarette before answering. "I don't know. It's just that he's different now. Since he came home, sometimes it feels like we've got nothing to talk about."

"Are you getting cold feet about the wedding?"

Maggie hadn't wanted to think about this, but now that the question was in front of her, she felt she had to answer it. "I think I am. But I don't know what to do. Should I break off our engagement?"

"Give it a little more time," Bridie advised. "It could just be that you have to get used to each other again."

"Maybe," Maggie replied. "Let's talk about something a little more upbeat—like what I'm going to wear tonight." Maggie didn't want to think about Johnny anymore. She just wanted to go to Pauline's party and have some fun.

When the butler opened the door to admit Maggie to Pauline's three-floor Fifth Avenue apartment, the first person she saw was Pauline's mother, Evelyn Manchester. "Maggie, how nice to see you again!" Evelyn swooped down and kissed the air in front of Maggie in that curious fashion rich people had. "You look wonderful, darling."

"Thank you." Maggie knew she looked pretty tonight. She was wearing a violet gown that had lace shoulder straps, a fitted waist, and a full-skirt that was four layers of rayon and purple taffeta. Maggie thought the color went well with her flame-red hair, which she had put up in a French twist.

Maggie looked around the party. "Where is Pauline? I don't see her anywhere."

Evelyn rolled her eyes. "Oh, she's in love with my guest of honor, and got so tongue-tied she ran away to hide in the parlor. You know how bashful Pauline is."

"Well, if she likes the fellow, shouldn't she be down here talking to him and not cowering in some room?"

"I couldn't put it better myself. Maggie, be a dear and go upstairs and drag my daughter back down here."

When Maggie opened the door to the parlor, Pauline looked up and wailed, "I'm in love!"

"So I heard," Maggie said wryly. "Who is he? Your mother said something about him being the guest of honor."

"Oh, he and Mother have some sort of business deal. He's new to the country and she's throwing this party to introduce him to New York society. Oh, Maggie, I've never seen such a gorgeous man in my life!"

Maggie started lifting pillows off the chintz sofa and bibelots off the mantel. Pauline frowned. "What are you doing?"

Maggie turned around and lifted her hands up. "Pauline, I don't see any gorgeous guys around here."

"Well, he's downstairs."

"Really? Then shouldn't you be there too? For all you know, some other girl is downstairs with him while we're wasting time talking. Come on, let's go!"

"I can't," Pauline whined. "I got so nervous when Mother introduced us that I couldn't say a word. I just can't go back downstairs."

"I know what you need," Maggie told her.

"What?"

"Booze! I'll go back downstairs and get you a drink to take the edge off—something strong. We'll have a

drink and then you'll go back downstairs before your
mother has a heart attack. Deal?"

"Well . . ."

"Great!" Maggie said. "Now, what do you like to
drink?"

"Martinis."

At the bar, Pauline's cousin Kippy Greenwood ac-
costed Maggie. He had lank black hair, pimples, and
was too skinny. He had been coming on to Maggie for
two years without success.

"Hey, Maggie," he slurred, "you gonna have a drink
with me?"

"Buzz off," she replied disinterestedly. "And how
many have you had? You smell like a distillery."

"What's the matter with you?" Kippy demanded.
"Rich, good-looking guy like me comes on to you . . .
a girl should be flattered."

"A girl *would* be flattered if a rich, good-looking guy
came on to her. . . . You're another story."

"What makes you think you can talk to me like that?"
Kippy put an expression of aristocratic disdain on his
face. It did not go at all well with his obvious state of
inebriation. "You're just some cheap Mick girl my
cousin invited to a society party."

Maggie got the drinks from the bartender (a martini
for Pauline and a scotch on the rocks for her), thought
about leaving, and then decided to give Kippy a piece
of her mind. She didn't notice the man who was watching their argument with a great deal of interest.

"There's nothing wrong with being Irish, you lout,"
she told Kippy. "But there's plenty wrong with using
your money and connections to cop a four-F while the
real men are fighting overseas."

Kippy flushed and grabbed her arm. "Take that
back."

"Let go of me!"

Kippy smirked. "What are you going to do about it?"

Maggie drove her spike heel into his toe. Kippy yelped in pain, grabbing his injured foot. "You little . . ."

A man grabbed his arm from behind. "Apologize to the young lady."

Kippy and Maggie looked at the stranger. Maggie thought she had never seen such a good-looking man in her life. He was tall, with broad shoulders, and elegantly dressed in a tuxedo. He had tousled chestnut-brown hair and his amber eyes seemed to pierce through Maggie. What mesmerized her most was his presence. He made everyone else at the party fade into the background. It was almost like the rest of the people were black and white, but he was in Technicolor.

Kippy said petulantly, "Make her apologize. She stepped on my foot."

The man turned Kippy around very slowly, and said in a soft whisper that seemed laced with iron, "Young man, I do not ask people to do things twice."

As Kippy stared at the stranger, he lost all the color in his face. He turned around and mumbled, "I'm sorry, Maggie."

Maggie simply nodded her head.

"Now leave us," the man commanded and Kippy responded like a dog fresh out of obedience school.

After Kippy left, Maggie found her voice again. "Thank you."

"There's no need to thank me—now I have you all to myself." The man smiled at Maggie. His whispery voice sent shivers down her spine. He has a strange accent, she thought. Maybe British, but something about the way he speaks is a little odd.

That remark made her uneasy—it did not come across as flirtation. "I have to leave," she told him.

As she turned to leave, she felt his hand on her shoulder. "Aren't you forgetting something?"

Maggie looked back at the bar and saw her drinks. She grabbed them.

"Are you sharing those drinks with a sweetheart?" the stranger asked her.

"Well, no, with a girlfriend, but I do have a, um, sweetheart—but he's not here now." Maggie was babbling. "I have to go. Maybe I'll see you later." She left the bar, cursing herself for sounding like some simpering fool. What was wrong with her? She'd met plenty of handsome men, and she hadn't behaved like some simpleminded idiot. But there was something very compelling about that man. . . .

Maggie reached down and gulped her scotch to soothe her nerves. When she reached the stairs, she turned around and saw that the stranger was still staring at her. Maggie turned around quickly and hurried up the stairs.

When she got back to the parlor, Pauline asked, "What took you so long?"

"Oh, that moron of a cousin of yours tried to put the make on me . . . again. Here's your drink." Maggie put the martini on a marquetry table near Pauline.

"I'm sorry, Maggie. I've told him to leave you alone."

"Don't worry about it. You might, however, want to warn him to lay off the sauce. He got fresh and some guy nearly punched him out."

Pauline's eyes became as big as saucers. "You mean two men fought over you? How romantic! You're so lucky."

Maggie rolled her eyes. "I wouldn't exactly call it fighting—more like the second fellow was just being a gentleman. As for lucky—if you want men to duel over you, honey, you're going to have to leave this room and attend your very own party. So finish that drink and let's go downstairs."

"But, Maggie," Pauline whined, "you don't understand. I'm scared I'll look like an idiot in front of this fellow I like."

"Look, Pauline, just flirt with the man."

"How do you flirt?"

Maggie restrained herself from sighing. Pauline was the classic wallflower. She had dull dishwater-blond hair, plain features, and was gangly and flat like a boy. Plus that frumpy gown she had on! It was black rayon with a straight A-line cut that did nothing for her. You would think with all her money Pauline could buy better clothes. To top it all off, the girl had no personality.

Maggie chose her words carefully. "You saw *Gone With the Wind,* right? When you're with this man, just pretend you're Scarlett O'Hara. Laugh at his jokes, tell him how wonderful he is, and make sure you dance with him. When you're dancing, tell him he's the best dancer you've ever known and make sure you gaze into his eyes."

Pauline looked doubtful, and Maggie had to admit it was a stretch. Still, what was she supposed to say? If this guy is anything to look at, he's not going to give a stick like you the time of day. Maggie gave her a reassuring smile. "Come on, enough dillydallying. It's time to go downstairs and sweep this man off his feet."

"Maybe a cigarette first," Pauline suggested timidly.

"No," Maggie said firmly. "If you want a cigarette, get the guy to light it for you."

On the way downstairs, Maggie asked Pauline, "What's your fellow's name?"

"Lord Baldevar."

Maggie raised an eyebrow. "Lord Baldevar? So when you get married and become Lady Baldevar, can I still call you Pauline?"

Pauline giggled. "Oh, Maggie . . ." Then she stopped and blanched. "Oh my God, there he is!"

Maggie looked, and her heart dropped into her shoes. Pauline's Adonis was the man who had rescued her from Kippy. He noticed Pauline staring, and walked over to them.

"Pauline, you must tell your mother what a wonderful party this is for me." Lord Baldevar kissed Pauline on the cheek. "Won't you introduce me to your beautiful companion?" he said, gazing at Maggie intently.

Pauline pouted. "This is Maggie O'Neill," she said gracelessly.

Lord Baldevar grinned slightly. "Miss O'Neill and I have already met," he said, reaching for Maggie's hand. Automatically she put it out, and he kissed her hand. When his lips made contact with her hand, Maggie (to her disgust) shivered. Her reaction did not go unnoticed by Pauline, who glared, or Lord Baldevar, whose grin widened. Maggie thought he looked like the Cheshire cat.

"When did you meet Maggie?" Pauline demanded.

Before he could reply, Maggie told Pauline, "We met at the bar before."

"Oh." Pauline seemed slightly mollified. "You know, Maggie's engaged to a war hero."

Maggie had to grin at that pointed bit of information. The band started playing a waltz.

"A waltz!" Pauline shrilled. "I just love waltzing!" She looked at Lord Baldevar expectantly. Maggie winced. Didn't the girl have any sense of timing?

"I'm sure you can find someone else here who shares that desire," he replied, not taking his eyes off Maggie.

Pauline flushed, and her lip quivered. Before she could say anything, her mother came by.

"There you are, Simon. Girls, I'm afraid I must steal

him away for a few minutes. I want him to meet Senator Hale."

Once Lord Baldevar and her mother were out of earshot, Pauline turned on Maggie. "How dare you!"

Maggie frowned. "How dare I what?"

"You're trying to steal Simon away from me. I saw the way you were looking at him!"

Did you see the way he was looking at me? Maggie mused to herself. "Watch yourself, Pauline," Maggie warned.

"No!" Pauline shrieked. "I think you should leave!"

Who did Pauline think she was talking to? Maggie decided that Pauline needed to be taught a lesson. She gave Pauline her sweetest smile. "I'll be happy to leave—after one dance." Maggie brushed past Pauline, and headed over to Lord Baldevar and the senator.

Maggie tapped Lord Baldevar on the shoulder. He turned around and his eyes seemed to light up at the sight of her. "Yes?"

Maggie's heart was pounding and her throat was dry. "Would you like to dance?" she asked bluntly—no use beating around the bush.

Lord Baldevar bowed low—an old-fashioned, courtly gesture. "I would be honored," he told her. "Please excuse me, Senator." He took Maggie's hand and led her to the dance floor.

Fortunately, the band left off the boring society music and started playing "It Had to Be You."

After they danced for a few moments, Lord Baldevar told Maggie, "You're breaking my heart."

"What?" She was startled.

"Are you only dancing with me to spite Pauline?"

Maggie glanced over to where the thunderstruck Pauline was watching them. She caught Pauline's eye and grinned wickedly. Then she turned back to Lord Baldevar. "You must admit it's a pretty good reason."

He pulled Maggie a bit closer to him. "Tell me how

you met Pauline. You don't seem to have much in common."

"We both volunteer at the USO—dance with soldiers, organize blood drives, that sort of thing."

"Poor soldiers." Lord Baldevar sighed. "Risk your life defending your country and your reward is a dance with Pauline Manchester."

Maggie giggled. "That isn't very nice, Lord Baldevar. True, but not at all nice."

"I insist that you call me Simon."

"If you'll call me Maggie."

"No."

"Why not?"

"Maggie doesn't suit you. Is it your full name?"

"Well, no. My name is Meghann, for my mother. But everyone has always called me Maggie."

"I am not everyone. Meghann is perfect for you—beautiful and a bit unusual. But, Meghann, I'm still a bit disappointed in your reason for asking me to dance."

"What would you like it to be?"

Simon smiled and pulled her very close to him. "For the same reason I am dancing with you—that you find me utterly irresistible."

Maggie had no reply for that. Instead, she looked up and wondered what was happening. She'd never felt like this. She'd never danced with a man and wanted to put her hands through his hair or wanted to stroke his face. . . .

"If you keep looking at me like that, I won't be responsible for my actions," he warned.

Maggie flushed, dropping her eyes.

Simon tilted her chin up with his hand. "I didn't want you to stop."

The song stopped, and went into a rumba. Simon

pulled her off the dance floor. "Don't you find this a rather dull party, Meghann?"

"Exceedingly," she told him. "But I'm leaving now. I'm persona non grata, you see." She inclined her head to where Pauline was tearfully complaining to her mother. Evelyn Manchester glared pure daggers at Maggie.

"Then I must leave too. I'm certainly not letting you out of my sight," Simon told her. "Take me on a tour of your city."

"Now?"

"Why not?"

"You're the guest of honor," she protested.

"At a party that is boring me to tears. That is the privilege of extreme wealth, Meghann—I may do whatever I please. Shall we?"

Before Maggie could say yes, no, or maybe, Simon had already pulled her down the stairs, and retrieved his coat and her purse from the maid.

"B-but," she stammered while they waited for the elevator. "I-I'm engaged and . . ."

Maggie was standing against the wall, and Simon put his arm on the wall above her. He was leaning dangerously close to her. "I am rather saddened to hear that you are engaged. Soon the time for an adventure like tonight will be long gone for you. Wouldn't you like one adventure before you're married?"

Maggie heard herself say yes.

"Wonderful," Simon told her. "Now, tell me where you're taking me."

"To the ferry."

"Where?"

"The Staten Island Ferry," Maggie explained. "When it pulls away from the city, you can see the skyline. Of course a lot of the buildings are observing the dimout, but there are still plenty of lights and it looks beautiful at night. And best of all, it only costs a nickel."

"I assure you money is no object, Meghann. But the ferry does sound intriguing. Let's hail a taxi!"

TWO

I can't believe I'm on a date with an English lord, Maggie thought as the cab made its way downtown. *What about Johnny?* Then Maggie decided that there was really no need to call this a date—she was simply being friendly. Hadn't she been friendly to all those GIs at the USO dances? This was the same thing. Simon was new to the city and he'd asked her to show him around. There was nothing wrong with that.

Sure, her conscience told her snidely. *Tell me another one.*

Oh, be quiet, she replied. *I haven't done anything wrong.*

Yet, it told her.

Stop that, she said firmly, and turned to Simon. "What do you do?" she asked him.

"So it's true," he smiled. "Americans are utterly pre-occupied with occupation."

"Well, that's what happens when you have to earn a living," she retorted. "We aren't aristocratic, idle rich who sit around inheriting money and doing nothing."

The cabdriver laughed. "She got you there, Mac."

"So she did," he replied. "While I am not 'idle rich,' I'm afraid I'm a rather boring businessman. I own some factories, land, make acquisitions—that sort of thing."

Maggie really hoped she had only imagined the way he looked at her when he said "acquisitions."

"And you, Meghann? How do you spend your days?"

"I volunteer at the USO, but I already told you that. Let's see. I work at a munitions plant. They let me have tonight off. And I also take classes at Hunter College. I'll probably transfer to Radcliffe in the fall," she stated with a touch of pride.

Before Simon could inquire further, the cabdriver piped up. "What do you need college for? You're a girl."

"Is there some reason *women* shouldn't go to college?" she demanded to know.

"Of course there is—they should be at home."

"And who has been running this country—the factories, the banks—during the war?" she inquired heatedly.

"Listen, that's only while the men are away. No soldier's gonna want to come home to some broad who wants to wear the pants."

"Why does the thought of a woman having an education or a job threaten you?"

"It doesn't threaten me, but who needs some ball breaker, excuse my language," he said hastily at a dark look from Simon, "some . . . ah, woman . . . who wants to compete? I don't need that. And neither does any guy with sense."

"I see," Maggie told him. "I guess you need a woman to be completely dependent on you in order to be able to function with her."

"What the hell do you mean by function!"

Fortunately, the cab had arrived at the Staten Island Ferry Terminal. Simon paid the driver and told him, "My young companion has some nonconformist ideas."

The cabbie seemed ready to continue the argument

until he looked at the money in his hand. Then his face lit up like a sunrise. "Gee, thanks! And don't worry about her ideas. She'll grow out of that. At least she's pretty."

Simon pulled her away from the taxi before she could tell the hack exactly where to put his archaic, unsolicited opinions. "How much did you tip that philistine?" she demanded. "What a patronizing, old-fashioned, boorish . . ."

"Meghann, don't be so hard on the poor fellow. On one point, he was quite right."

"About women staying home?" she asked in a viper's tone.

"About you being beautiful," he replied, caressing her cheek.

Flustered from both the compliment and the caress, Maggie muttered, "He didn't say I was beautiful. He said I was pretty."

"Then I say you're beautiful." Simon noticed the hateful blush coloring her face. He turned her toward him. "Hasn't anyone ever told you that you're beautiful? You seem so bashful when I compliment you."

"Well, s-sure," she stammered, "but they never said it as . . . uh . . . as, um . . . extravagantly as you do."

"That," he said softly, looking deep into her eyes, "was their mistake. I do not intend to repeat it."

He was leaning toward her. Maggie stepped away hastily, telling him, "I'll go see what time the next ferry leaves."

As she walked away, she acknowledged to herself ruefully, Face it—this is a date. Now if you had any brains at all, you'd leave this minute. That was great advice— too bad she felt completely incapable of following it.

"We're in luck," she told Simon, who had walked over to her. "The next boat leaves in a few minutes."

Simon looked around the circular, cavernous room

with its ugly yellow-tiled walls. "The view does get better?" he asked hopefully.

"Don't be silly," she giggled, "of course it does."

While they waited for the boat to dock, Simon asked her how old she was.

"Eighteen," she told him. "I'll be nineteen in July. How old are you?"

Something about her question seemed to amuse him. "I'm thirty-three," he said.

There weren't very many people on the ferry. She and Simon stood by the rails, staring at the activity by the Brooklyn Piers. Ships filled the port, and men were busy unloading cargos. "Does your city never shut down?" he asked her.

"Nope, there's always something going on." Taking on her role of tour guide, she pointed out the Brooklyn Bridge and the Manhattan Bridge, the lights from the cars twinkling in the dark.

As the boat pulled away from the dock, they were able to see more of the city skyline—including the Empire State Building.

Simon took in the well-lit buildings. "Did someone forget to tell New York about the dimout?"

"A lot of people ignore it," she told him and gestured to some of the dark buildings. "But some people observe it—normally you see a lot more lights—and the Empire State Building used to be lit up on top."

"You seem to know the skyline very well."

"I love it," she told him. "On the night before my . . . fiancé"—she stumbled over that word a little—"was called to duty, we went up on my dad's rooftop and got dr . . . uh, intoxicated. Then we watched the sunrise over the city."

"Why didn't you marry before he left?"

"Well, I was only seventeen and my father said that was too young to be married." She wasn't going to add

all the unflattering remarks her father made at the
time—ranging from his dislike of Johnny Devlin to
Maggie being too young and silly to know what she was
doing.

"Then I owe your father my thanks." Before Maggie
could recover from that remark, he asked, "Do you live
with your parents?"

"No, Daddy knew how angry I was about him not
letting me marry Johnny. So his graduation present to
me was that I could live in an apartment in the city
with my best friend, Bridie McGovern. See, she'd been
accepted to nursing school and I was going to Hunter.
Since we were both going to be in Manhattan all the
time, he said it made sense for us to live there on our
own. He knows the guy who owns the building we live
in." Maggie gestured to the passing sites. "Look, there's
Ellis Island and the Statue of Liberty. Hey!" she said
indignantly. "You're not looking!"

"I'd much rather look at you." He put his hands on
her hair.

Maggie yelped when he started taking out the hairpins. "What are you doing?"

"Be still," Simon ordered, and she stood quietly
while he took her hair down. He didn't hurt her at all
when he took the pins out, but his touch was making
her feel queasy and warm . . . and weak. She found
herself gripping the ship's rail.

When the last hairpin was out, Simon fluffed her
hair around her shoulders. Keeping his hands in her
hair, he tilted her face up to him. "Titian hair . . . You
look radiant in the moonlight."

His hands were keeping her hair from blowing into
her face. He leaned down to kiss her—it should have
been a romantic moment. But the wind from the river
was cold, and Maggie hadn't bothered to wear a coat
to Pauline's. When she started shivering, Simon took

his tuxedo jacket off and wrapped it around her shoulders. "Shall we go inside?"

There was hardly anybody inside. She and Simon were able to sit by themselves on one of the wooden benches by the windows. Maggie started to sit on the bench, but Simon grabbed her without a word and placed her on his lap.

"Do you mind?" His tone seemed to imply that it wouldn't matter if she did.

"No," she told him, "but you really can't see much from here."

"I'm seeing all I wish to see," he said. Then he started stroking her arms. "You have a rather strong right arm."

"I pitch for the softball team at school."

Simon's eyebrows shot up. "I thought baseball was a man's sport?"

"Not entirely," she replied. "A lot of girls like it—but when you're the youngest child and you have six brothers, I guess you grow up as a tomboy."

"Ah, so that explains why you go around stomping on toes and arguing with strange men without any thought of consequence."

Maggie laughed, feeling quite comfortable on Simon's lap. "Well, they taught me how to throw a punch, climb a tree, and hit a ball. Do you know I never had any dolls or tea sets? My dad just never thought to buy me anything like that. Instead, I had my brother's old baseball cards and old footballs to play with."

"You only mention your father. Didn't your mother try to stem this masculine upbringing?"

Maggie looked down. "Well, she died when I was five. She had cancer."

"I'm sorry. Do you remember?"

Maybe it was the fact that they were practically alone on the boat. Or maybe it was Simon's soft amber eyes making her feel so protected, but she found herself telling him things she'd never told another person before. He never interrupted; he simply stroked her hair while she told him of the sketchy images she had from that time.

"I don't really remember my mother at all. All I remember is my brother Frankie telling me one day that he was going to take me to school because Mommy was too sick. And then I remember waking up late one night." Her voice got a little shaky. "I heard someone moaning in pain, so I went to the door of my bedroom. My father was in the hallway, outside his bedroom. He saw me and shouted, 'Maggie, go back to sleep! Everything's okay.' And then in the morning, my mother was dead. Daddy didn't let me go to the funeral—he said I was too young. So Brian—one of my other brothers—he stayed with me. I remember him crying."

Someone came over. "I'm sorry, but you have to leave now. This ship isn't leaving for a half hour."

Simon looked up at him. "Is there some reason we couldn't wait?"

The man seemed about to shake his head, but then he said uncertainly, "Well, sure. I guess it's not a problem." He wandered away.

Maggie forgot her sadness. "How did you do that? They almost always make you leave."

"I've been told I can be quite persuasive. Are your brothers overseas now?"

"Four of them are. Frankie, the oldest, is a cop and has three kids. They haven't taken him yet. And Paul was wounded in North Africa, so he came home."

Simon took in her gown and makeup. "What did you tell me? That you grew up as a . . . tomboy? But obviously, someone taught you other skills."

His look flustered her again. What was wrong with her? "Well, Frankie got married when I was twelve, and his wife, Theresa, took an interest in me. She taught me all about dresses, lipstick, and high heels. And then there was Bridie. We pretty much learned a lot together . . . from the makeup counter at Woolworth's and the movie magazines. Wait a minute! I'm being so rude." She castigated herself, and smiled. "Here I've been talking my head off and I never asked you anything."

"I want to know more about you. Tell me what young people do in America. How do you entertain yourselves?"

Maggie thought about that. "We go to movies and ice-cream parlors. Sometimes we go on dates to the nightclubs . . . but usually my boyfriends don't have the money for that. And then in the summer we go to ball games, the beach, and Playland."

"The beach?" Simon questioned. "You're very fair, Meghann. Doesn't the sun burn your skin?"

"Oh, sure," she replied. "If I'm not careful. I have to keep remembering to put on the suntan lotion or I get burned. And I also wind up with a million freckles. I don't mind, though. I love the sun." Maggie took a look at Simon. If he had one flaw, it was that his skin was too pale. "What about you? You don't like the sun?"

"No," he told her flatly. "I don't."

"Then what do you like?"

"You." He smiled.

People were coming onto the boat again. Maggie stood up. "Come on," she told him. "I promised you a tour of the city. And you're getting one whether you want it or not!"

"I hardly dare argue. You might do grave injury to my toes."

"Kippy deserved that," she protested.

"He deserved far more, but at the time I was more interested in meeting you. You knew the young man?" They walked back outside.

"He's Pauline's cousin. I bet anything they'll get married someday—no one else is going to want them."

"How catty, Meghann—I like that."

They were both quiet on the way back, staring at the moonlit water. Maggie thought she'd never forget this night, or the man she was with. Was this what people meant by shipboard romances? She had asked him how long he was going to be in New York, and he told her a few more days. What harm could there be in seeing him? He'd be gone soon. She was sure Johnny must have had a few girls while he'd been in Europe.

They were coming back into Manhattan. With a sense of mischief, Maggie showed Simon the old fort on Governors Island. "That's where the colonists fired on the hated British ships when they came into the harbor."

Simon raised an eyebrow. "Hated British, is it?"

"Hated," she said firmly. "Absolutely despised. Who could like anything about such a loathsome race?"

Simon picked her up and swung her around. She giggled and demanded to be put down. "Not until you take back those slurs on my ancestry."

"No way!" she laughed. "So I guess you'll just have to hold on to me forever."

"I suppose I shall," he said, bringing her very close. "Or do my very best to persuade you to look on at least one Englishman with favor." He tightened his arms around her, and kissed her very softly on the lips.

Maggie could not understand how one small kiss could make her feel so weak. "Please put me down," she murmured.

He released her immediately, and they left the ferry. "I feel terrible about such a cheap date, Meghann. Didn't you mention before that some of your beaux didn't always have enough funds to entertain you in

style? Tell me someplace you've never been that you've
always wanted to go."

"The Stork Club?" she suggested.

Simon hailed another cab, and admonished her,
"No arguing this time."

"Do you think women should stay at home?" she
asked before he opened the car door.

He pulled her close again. She shivered and he
smiled very softly. "If I wanted a woman to stay at home,
I would make sure she enjoyed the time there."

"This place is wonderful," Maggie said enthusiastically after they walked through a small lobby and she
had her first glimpse of the elegant supper club. Its
posh barroom was on her left, with a long mirror above
it; everything was illuminated by a soft, rosy light.

"I'm glad you like it."

In truth, Maggie was more spellbound by Simon Baldevar than the Stork Club. She reflected ruefully that
her other dates (including Johnny Devlin) had behaved
like country bumpkins compared to him.

Sometimes they had taken her to nightclubs . . .
places that were cheap rip-offs of the Stork Club or El
Morocco. Even there, the boys had been cowed by the
condescension of headwaiters, not knowing how one
got a table that was not right next to the kitchen.

Simon certainly didn't have any problems with headwaiters, she thought, watching a captain greet him ef-
fusively. There was something about Simon that made
people jump to do his bidding, Maggie observed as the
fawning captain opened a thick glass door and led them
into a huge room paneled with mirrors that reflected
the tuxedo-clad men and fashionably attired women
dancing, drinking, and chattering at the tables.

Maggie glanced at one of the mirrors and then

blinked in confusion. Either she had dust in her eyes or someone hadn't cleaned the mirror properly because Simon's reflection was all blurred . . . nearly invisible.

Simon gave her arm a gentle tug, and they continued to follow the captain past the main room and into a small oak-paneled room.

"This is the Cub Room," Maggie whispered excitedly after the captain seated them at a small banquette table. "I read about it in Winchell's column all the time!"

"That gossipmonger," Simon scorned, but he gave her a smile.

The waiter returned, bearing the bottle of Dom Perignon 1911 Simon ordered.

Maggie had never had champagne like this. Even the stuff at Frankie's wedding tasted like cheap seltzer compared to this dry liquid that went down her throat like silk.

"This tastes great," she enthused, starting to rummage through her purse for a pack of cigarettes. She was eager to be able to tell Bridie she'd used one of the famous Stork Club ashtrays, dipped her ashes right onto the stork wearing a black top hat.

"Don't," Simon said, putting his hand over the unopened pack of Lucky Strikes.

"Why not?" Maggie was surprised; she hardly knew anyone who didn't smoke.

"I dislike the taste of tobacco."

"But if I'm the one who's smoking, how will you taste—oh!"

Simon grinned and extended his hand to her. "Would you like to dance?"

"One O'clock Jump!" Maggie glowed when the horns started thumping out the infectious, lively beat.

Tuck in, throw out, change places, sugar-push, do a tight whip . . . Simon performed all the steps with a grace and agility that made Maggie feel like she was dancing on air. What a marvelous dancer he was! Was there nothing this man couldn't do?

When they linked hands to trade places, Maggie felt his eyes on her and looked up, puzzled. It was almost like he was trying to come to some kind of decision, she thought while her feet pounded out the swing steps without missing a beat.

For the next song, the orchestra started playing "It Had to Be You."

"Much better," Simon whispered into her ear.

"What do you mean?"

"This time, you're not dancing with me for spite." He nibbled her ear, and she felt like she would have fallen if he weren't holding her up.

"You shouldn't do that," she protested in a soft voice that probably would encourage him to do more rather than less.

"Why not?"

Because it made her want more. Because it made her feel like she was melting, like she wanted him to peel her clothes off and kiss her like that all over. . . .

Jesus Christ! She felt her cheeks turning red again. Maggie had never had thoughts like that, ever! She looked up into Simon's arch grin, and thought it was almost like he knew exactly what she was thinking.

"This . . . this could be our song." Why did her voice sound so tremulous?

"What does that mean, sweetheart?"

"Well, when people, uh, go together, they're supposed to have a song—something they'll always remember each other by. And since we've danced to it twice in one night . . ."

"I hardly need a song to remember you by, Meghann. But I rather like the idea of 'going together.' " He pulled her very close, kissing her neck.

"Please stop doing that," she whispered.

"Don't you like it?" Simon kept her close. "I thought you said you were engaged."

"Well, Johnny never did anything like that." Her prim words completely clashed with the new, sultry purr she heard in her voice. What was this man doing to her?

Simon raised an eyebrow in disbelief.

"Well, we're Catholic," she explained defensively. "Everything is supposed to wait till you get married."

Simon laughed. "Ah, yes . . . No pleasure, purely procreation. Is that right?"

"Well . . ." It did sound kind of silly when put that way. Why hadn't Johnny done any of this? She liked it a lot.

Simon looked down at her quizzically. "You are aware of what happens when people marry? Or has the church decided knowledge has to wait until after marriage too?"

"My sister-in-law told me when I got engaged."

"And what did she tell you?"

"That it's a cross to bear."

Simon laughed so hard he wasn't able to keep dancing. A few people turned to stare out of curiosity while Maggie turned an interesting shade of magenta. What had possessed her to say that?

He got himself under control, and they walked back to their table.

"I'm sorry, Meghann—I shouldn't have laughed like that."

"It wasn't that funny," she sniffed.

"Not at all—it would be tragic for you to have such a dim view of marriage." Before they sat down, he lifted her chin and kissed her. "Was that a cross to bear?"

"No," she whispered, thankful for the chair she was able to sink into before she fell.

For a while, Simon kept her laughing with his sardonic descriptions of Pauline Manchester and some of the other ill-favored guests at the party. Then a rather stout gentleman who had his arm around a stunning, tall blonde passed their table. The blonde took in Maggie's hair streaming down her shoulders in a disdainful glance. Maggie glared back, refusing to look embarrassed.

"You shouldn't have taken my hairpins out," Maggie complained to Simon. "I look like I don't know how to dress for a night on the town."

"You look beautiful," he replied. "Don't let the woman's jealousy get to you."

"Jealous?" Maggie questioned in astonishment. "Why should she be jealous of me?"

"You did see the gentleman she was with? Perhaps she envies you for not having to entertain old, ugly but wealthy gentleman to buy all the finer things in life. You don't think she'd like to go out with someone rich and handsome?"

Maggie was tired of feeling flustered and ill at ease. She decided to tease. "Whoever told you you're handsome?"

"Meghann! You're wounding my pride." He sighed in mock resignation. "But if you do not find me attractive, perhaps I should ask that man," he said, indicating the blonde and her toadlike companion, "if he would like to trade dates?"

Maggie looked at the other table, and shuddered. If you looked as good as that girl, why should you have to bother with some ugly man?

"Why are you looking so wistful, Meghann?"

"I was just thinking how I'd love to look like that— tall, blond, and willowy."

Simon took her hand. "You mean you'd trade away

that beautiful fire-red hair and verdant eyes to look like a thousand other women?"

"Well, all girls want to look like her. . . ."

"You have no reason to envy her. She should envy your unspoiled beauty and sweetness."

Maggie blushed again, and Simon told her briskly, "Not that you deserve any compliments. As I recall, you informed me I was not at all handsome."

"I didn't say that—I just asked you who told you that you're handsome."

Simon's eyes trapped hers. "Am I handsome, Meghann?"

"Yes," she told him softly.

To lighten the mood, Simon continued to ponder the relationship of the other couple, saying that the blonde's interest in the man couldn't possibly be financial—no, she must be attracted by his stunning physique.

"You have a forked tongue, Lord Baldevar," Maggie admonished him.

"And who had nothing but deprecatory remarks about Pauline this evening?"

"Not me," Maggie said innocently while he poured her another glass of champagne and then turned the bottleneck up in the ice bucket. Although Maggie was feeling no pain, she thought it didn't look like the alcohol had affected Simon at all.

"In fact," she said wickedly, "I think you and Pauline would make a lovely couple."

"My dear, you shall pay for that remark."

"How?" she challenged laughingly.

"However I see fit."

The waiters were informing the remaining customers that unfortunately the Stork Club was closing now in compliance with the wartime curfew.

"Oh." Maggie was downcast. "I like it here."

"We can come back," Simon told her. "Assuming I forgive you for attempting to burden me with Pauline."

They were outside now, and the cold air was sobering Maggie up. "Where would you like to go now, Meghann?"

Home, she thought to herself, *before I manage to get myself into trouble with this man.* She remembered how it felt when he kissed her.

"I have to get up early tomorrow," she lied.

"Then I shall have to see you home. You said you live nearby? Would you like to take a cab or walk?"

Maggie looked up at the sky filled with stars, and the full moon. The air was crisp but not cold. "Walk."

On the way to her apartment, Maggie was in a quandary. What was going to happen? Would he expect her to ask him upstairs? And if she did, what would happen?

Maggie dismissed from her mind the notion that this man might simply neck with her and leave. So what was she going to do? She couldn't go to bed with him. Even putting Johnny aside, the fact remained that Maggie was Catholic enough to believe that sex before marriage was a mortal sin. Plus terrible things could happen. . . . She could wind up having a baby. Her father would kill her.

Okay, she told herself firmly when they arrived in front of her apartment house. *I'll just go upstairs, and I'll forget I ever met this man.*

"Thank you for walking me home." Maggie started to walk away, trying to ignore those golden eyes before they tempted her into doing something she'd regret.

Silently Simon turned her toward him. He put his hand under her chin, leaned down, and kissed her. At the first contact of his lips, Maggie felt her knees buckle; Simon embraced her to keep her from falling. She put her arms around him, and kissed him back hungrily, all her reservations forgotten. Maggie had never been kissed like this. The tip of his tongue licked her lips, causing her to tremble. At some slight pressure on her lips, she opened her mouth to receive him. His tongue explored her mouth slowly but thoroughly. It felt like he wanted to possess her.

And I want him to possess me, she thought. *God, how I want it.* She felt like she was going to melt.

Simon broke off the kiss and stroked her hair softly. "Meghann, I want to come upstairs with you. May I?"

At that moment, Maggie could barely remember Johnny's name. All she could think of was that Bridie wasn't home, so there was nothing standing in the way of her inviting Simon upstairs.

"Yes," she said simply.

What in God's name am I doing? Maggie thought, giving Simon a sidelong glance as she fumbled with the keyhole. Was she really going to give her virginity to this stranger standing beside her? All the reckless passion she'd felt when he kissed her had vanished during the short walk to her third-floor apartment; now her only emotion was cold, quaking fear.

Tell him to leave, the voice of common sense hissed at her, but Maggie couldn't push any words past the leaden lump in her throat. Besides, the only thing worse than her fear of what would happen when she finally opened the door was her mortification at the thought of backing out now, of having to tell Simon she'd chickened out.

"Damn!" she cursed when the key fell from her trembling hand and clattered to the floor. Maggie bent down and then felt a large, warm hand on her shoulder. Looking up, she saw Simon hunched down next to her.

Smiling, he tucked a stray lock of hair behind her ear and plucked the key up off the tiled floor, placing it in her outstretched palm. When their eyes met, Maggie felt an odd sense of serenity fall over her, dissipating her panic. Calm restored, Maggie inserted the key into the lock with no further difficulty.

"Please come in," she said, ushering him into the small apartment she shared with Bridie. Anxiously Maggie's eyes wandered toward the bedroom and her cheeks flooded with color while her heart began to pound so loudly she was sure Simon would hear the hectic drumbeat. Surely, she wasn't supposed to just lead him into the bedroom! No, there must be other steps . . . amenities. . . .

"Drinks!" Maggie screeched, and Simon turned toward her, though the apartment was too dark for her to make out his expression. Maggie stepped away from him, turning on a small lamp on an end table by the couch, continuing to jabber nervously. "I . . . I could make you a highball. . . . Do you like ginger ale? Or I can make some coffee . . . I really make very good coffee. . . ."

Simon started walking toward her and Maggie backed away involuntarily, stumbling against the arm of the couch and falling onto the cushions in an undignified heap.

Hastily reseating herself, Maggie blushed furiously, not looking up when she muttered, "I'm sorry" to Simon as he took a seat beside her. Quick tears stung her eyelids and she blinked them away, feeling like an utter fool, sure she was doing everything wrong and Simon couldn't feel anything for her now but pity and disdain.

"You have nothing to apologize for, little one," Simon said and reached out to draw her into his lap. Maggie peered up at him hopefully, warmed by both the new endearment and the tender, husky tone of his voice. Maybe she hadn't ruined everything after all. "Now what's the matter, sweetheart?"

It actually took her a moment to remember, so lulled did she feel by the warm, soft lap cushioning her and the strong but gentle hand stroking her hair. "I . . . I don't know what I'm supposed to do."

At first shocked by her own candor and uneased by the way this man compelled her to tell truths she'd have kept from anyone else, Maggie felt a rush of relief when Simon simply smiled. He revealed a dimple in his left cheek she longed to kiss, and he started twining fiery strands of her hair around his fingers to bring her closer to him. "Meghann, you don't have to 'do' anything but enjoy the pleasure I so want to give you."

Maggie started to say something else, but it was blotted out forever when Simon started to kiss her. The firm lips over hers banished her anxiety completely, bringing back all the knee-weakening desire she'd felt downstairs. Her hands reached up of their own volition to wrap around his neck and she pressed her body against him, feeling the hand around her waist tighten almost painfully.

God, this was wonderful, Maggie thought, overwhelmed by the dizzying sensations she felt as Simon continued to kiss her; his touch became more demanding as she became less restrained.

"Delicious," Simon murmured, attaching his lips to her neck. Eagerly Maggie pushed his head down, reveling in the heat that coursed through her as he kissed and licked the soft flesh of her neck. Then she thought she felt something hard and disturbingly sharp at the hollow of her throat, but Simon pushed her away abruptly, standing her on unsteady legs.

Giving her a quick smile, he took off his black bow tie while his eyes wandered over her body. He ran a finger under her chin; his fingertip made a slow, lazy path until it stopped just over her left breast. "I want you to take off your . . . shoes."

Maggie giggled at the mischievous twinkle in his eyes and kicked her silver mules off, returning his bold gaze with a saucy grin. "Is there anything else I should take off?"

"It appears that nervous maiden of a few moments ago has vanished. . . . Good riddance to her," Simon said with a grin. Almost leering, as he spun her around.

"Oh," Maggie gasped when he unzipped her violet gown. Wordlessly she stepped out of the dress, bemused when she realized she was standing before a man wearing little else besides her lavender slip.

"Pull your hair up," Simon commanded and Maggie obeyed, using both hands to gather her shoulder-length hair into a haphazard upsweep.

"Good girl," he murmured and ran his lips down the nape of her neck, making her skin break out into tiny little shivers of gooseflesh. "Now keep your hands up until I tell you otherwise."

The directive proved harder than Maggie would have thought when Simon's hands reached up to cup the curve of her breasts. With exquisite slowness, Simon began to run his fingers in wide circles around her breasts, slowly spiraling toward her nipples while he planted soft kisses on her neck and ears. Maggie sagged against him, feeling an unfamiliar throbbing start to build inside her when she felt the hard, solid planes of his body pressed against hers.

"Oooh." Maggie heard herself moan when Simon's teasing fingers turned her nipples into hard little points, and unbearable warmth pulsated through her, making it almost impossible to stay on her feet. Startled by the open lust in her throaty moan, Maggie stiffened abruptly. What on earth was she doing? A decent girl wouldn't . . .

"No," Simon said and whirled her around. Maggie felt mesmerized by the demanding gaze that seemed to penetrate to the depths of her soul. It was his eyes that kept her against him far more than the imprisoning grip on her forearms.

"No," Simon said again, and she shivered at the intensity in his voice. "Don't ever feel shame for anything we do together, Meghann."

"I'm not ashamed," Maggie said, and she wasn't. The brief embarrassment fell from her just like the gown she'd shed moments before. "It's just . . . I . . . I never felt anything like that before. . . ."

"Of course you didn't," Simon said, giving her a voluptuary grin before his mouth encircled her breast.

"Oh, yes," she whimpered at the hot, soft tongue she felt through the thin silk of her slip, clinging to Simon as he stood up and carried her toward the bedroom.

"What could you know of passion?" Simon whispered and deposited her on the double bed with the rose-patterned quilt. At that action, one puzzling thought pierced her nervous though eager anticipation: How did Simon know which bed was hers and which was Bridie's without asking her? Maybe he'd simply made a lucky guess.

"Those fool boys you've been exposed to would never be able to rouse you; their fumbling, oafish gestures would leave you thinking lovemaking was something distasteful," Simon said, beginning to undress. Maggie quickly forgot her pique over the beds as his elegant clothes fell to the floor; she'd never seen a naked man before and her wide eyes devoured him with a virgin's curiosity.

"May I touch you?" she asked shyly, and he grinned broadly.

"You can do anything you want," Simon told her and lay down on the bed beside her.

At first timid, Maggie rapidly gained confidence

from Simon's utter stillness as her hands roamed over his pale, almost hairless body. She eagerly ran her hands over the sloping, bulging muscles in his arms while her eyes feasted on the wonderful breadth of his broad shoulders. She compared the hawkish, unmistakably aristocratic features of his face to the lean powerful physique of his thickly muscled chest, flat stomach and strong masculine legs his stylish clothes had hidden away. She thought Simon looked just like the dashing knight adorning the cover of one of her library lending novels . . . nobility mixed with uncompromising strength.

"Don't be shy, little one," Simon murmured when her hands made an abrupt halt at his navel; her eyes bulged almost comically at the hard, swelling flesh a scant inch from her hand. Gently he grasped her hand and wrapped it around him.

"I didn't know it would be so warm," Maggie whispered, hardly aware of what she was saying as her hand instinctively tightened around the quivering, jerking flesh.

"Did I do something wrong?" she inquired anxiously when Simon groaned, and he laughed softly as he pulled her toward him.

"You can do no wrong with me, Meghann," Simon assured her, slowly pulling off the rest of her clothes. "Glorious." Simon sighed when she lay naked beneath him, and he started to caress every inch of her. Maggie moaned at each new touch and stretched eagerly to meet the roving hands and mouth that gave her pleasure she'd never even imagined.

Beyond reservation now, Maggie simply spread her legs for the tender but demanding hand that stroked warm, secret flesh she'd never even touched herself. She heard herself making deep, almost feral sounds in her throat as she felt a delightful pressure begin to build inside her. It escalated rapidly into a pulsating rush of feeling that made her scream out like a woman possessed. "Oh, yes, yes, yes, yes!"

Then she felt Simon's hand withdraw and he positioned himself between her legs before driving into her with one firm thrust that made her cry out from the unexpected pain.

The mouth that descended on hers again cut off her startled cry and she felt the sharp ache start to recede as Simon remained motionless, allowing her body to adjust to him. Then, with infinitesimal care, he began to move about very slowly, only increasing the tempo when Maggie's hips rose up to meet his thrusts, instinctively matching his rhythm.

"Oh," she cried softly, feeling a yearning, a *need* start to build as Simon moved inside her. She didn't understand what it was she wanted, what made her writhe and arch, what caused choked little cries to issue from her closed lips. She only knew Simon could somehow ease the burning pain inside her.

"Yes!" she finally screamed out, sinking her nails deep into Simon's back while her body shuddered from the force of her climax. She'd never felt anything like this sudden electrifying jolt that made her cry gratefully, "I love you! I love you so much!"

At her words, Simon's expression became wry, almost pitying, and he plunged deeper inside her; his movements so hard and fierce she actually became dizzy.

"Please stop," she gasped, but Simon refused to give her any respite. Though her body continued to respond, Maggie began to grow nervous, even a little frightened. The amber eyes locked on hers no longer seemed tender and loving—now Simon's eyes had a harsh, avid glitter that made Maggie try to pull away from him. Why did he look like that . . . like he was a miser about to enter a room full of gold, like a ravenous animal smelling meat?

"Please," she whimpered again as the world spun around her, and she had to shut her eyes to stop the lurching sensation that made her feel like she was trapped inside a Ferris wheel. The darkness swirled around her and the only thing Maggie was truly aware of was the ecstasy of climax after climax as Simon continued to thrust into her until a brutal, ripping pain pierced the thick fog of pleasure blunting her senses.

"No," she tried to say, but she couldn't seem to open her mouth or even her eyes to see what had hurt her so badly. She couldn't tell where the pain began, only that first there was a sharp, invasive pain like a stab wound, but then it lessened as a peculiar lassitude spread through her, making it harder and harder to stay awake.

Finally, with a supreme effort, Maggie managed to open her eyes and smile weakly at the gold eyes shining down at her. She saw the harshness that had frightened her was gone, replaced by love and something that resembled deep surprise, almost shock. She started to try to speak, to ask Simon why he looked so startled yet happy, but before she could open her mouth, Simon started to kiss her, leaving a vaguely metallic but not unpleasant taste in her mouth.

This can't be real, Maggie thought hazily when Simon entered her again and she felt the deep pleasure and half-terrifying, half-wonderful pain reclaim her. There couldn't really be a driving stranger with burning gold eyes possessing her like a wild, wonderful storm. It just couldn't be happening; it had to be a dream was Maggie's last coherent thought before she collapsed against the pillows, unconscious.

THREE

Bridie came home around nine A.M., feeling exhausted and irritable. She thought she heard retching sounds coming from the bathroom. "Maggie, are you okay?" When she didn't get any response, she hurried over to the bathroom.

Maggie, dressed in a ragged white cotton nightgown, was crouched beside the toilet, trying to hold her hair back while she vomited. Bridie got a washcloth from the hall closet, and started running it under the cold water in the bathroom.

"When did you start feeling sick?" she asked Maggie.

Maggie was still retching. Finally she pushed herself back and looked up. Bridie gasped in shock at her friend's appearance. Maggie was terribly pale, and she had purple circles under her eyes.

"I look that bad?" Maggie croaked, her voice hoarse after hours of vomiting. Bridie noticed that Maggie had her arms wrapped around herself tightly—like she was trying to keep warm. She was also sweating.

Bridie reached down and put the cold cloth on her friend's forehead. "When did you start feeling sick?" Bridie watched in alarm as Maggie started vomiting again.

Oh, God, Maggie thought, when is this going to stop?

Her throat was on fire, and her ribs ached. And her head—she'd never had such a skull-splitting headache; it hurt to think, to keep her eyes open. But the worst was the cold—she felt like she'd never be warm again.

When Maggie was done, she answered Bridie's question. "I don't know. I woke up around six, I think, and I felt so nauseous. I barely made it to the bathroom . . . and I've been here since then."

"You've been vomiting like this for the past three hours?" Bridie didn't like that. If Maggie didn't stop soon, she was likely to get dehydrated. She reached into the medicine cabinet for the thermometer, and stuck it in Maggie's mouth. "I want to get your temperature. I'll be right back." Bridie went into the kitchen and filled the huge soup pot with some water on the bottom. Then she placed the pot by Maggie's bed.

Maggie was still shivering, and her skin was cold and clammy to the touch. Bridie thought her friend simply had a bad stomach virus. She took the thermometer out of her mouth. "One hundred two degrees! Come on, I'm going to run a bath. We need to get that temperature down."

Bridie began running a lukewarm bath for her friend. She handed Maggie two aspirin with a glass of water to cut the fever down. Maggie swallowed the aspirin, and immediately vomited them up. She began gulping the water thirstily. "Hey, drink that slowly—no use having it come back up," Bridie cautioned.

Maggie sipped while the tub was filling up. Cold water seemed to be the only thing she wanted.

When Maggie came out of the tub, Bridie gave her a quick alcohol rub, then handed her a towel and a fresh nightgown. "Why don't you try to get some rest now?"

Maggie had to lean heavily on Bridie to manage the

short distance from the bathroom to the bedroom. "Why are you limping?"

"My left leg hurts," Maggie replied. "I think I was lying down on it in the bathroom."

Once Maggie was settled in bed, Bridie took her temperature again. "One hundred . . . that's a little better. I'm going to get some more aspirin. See if you can keep them down this time."

Bridie brought the aspirin along with a glass of ginger ale. This time, Maggie managed to keep the aspirin down. Now all she wanted to do was sleep; she'd never been so tired.

"Bridie?" she asked sleepily.

"What?"

"Can you pull down the shade. The light is bothering me."

Bridie looked outside. It was actually an overcast day. But she knew that anything could bother people when they were sick. "Did you start feeling sick at the party?"

"What party?" Maggie muttered before she fell into an exhausted sleep.

When Maggie woke up, she felt much better. It was almost like she hadn't been sick. She looked at the clock on the nightstand—six P.M.! "Bridie, why did you let me sleep so late? Now the whole day is gone."

Bridie came into the bedroom, thermometer in hand. "Obviously, you needed the rest. Now let me see your temperature."

"But I'm fine now," Maggie protested.

"Who's the nurse here? You or me? I'll tell you if you're fine or not." Truthfully, she thought Maggie looked a lot better. Those awful circles were gone; she was just a little pale.

Bridie took the thermometer out. "Normal. I guess

it was a twenty-four-hour bug of some kind. You think you got it at the party?"

"Party?"

Bridie rolled her eyes. "That's the second time you've said that. Come on, Maggie, the party last night at Pauline's. How was it?"

Maggie frowned. The last thing she remembered from last night was the butler opening the door for her; everything else was a blank. The fever must have really scrambled her brains. "Okay, I guess."

"Just okay?"

Maggie shrugged noncommitally, and got out of bed. "Can I shower, Nurse?"

"Sure, it's a good idea. Your dad's coming over. He said he got us some steaks off the black market."

Maggie's stomach started growling at the thought of food; she was roaringly hungry. When was the last time she'd eaten?

When she came out of the shower, she threw on a brown knitted-wool sweater and a black box-pleated skirt that was knee-length. She wasn't going to bother with a slip or socks; it was only her father coming over. She pulled her hair back from her face with a black ribbon.

"Did Johnny call today?" she asked Bridie.

"Not yet," she replied as the doorbell rang.

Maggie's father, Jack O'Neill, was a huge bear of a man. He boasted a shock of white hair and startling green eyes that he'd passed on to his daughter. He gave Maggie a quick hug, and shoved a large brown paper bag into her hands. "Here, go broil these beauties. And how about a highball? How are you, Bridie?"

"Great, Mr. O'Neill. Maggie, I'll get your dad a drink; you can wash the meat."

"Okay." Maggie took the bag into the kitchen, cut

the string on the butcher's bag, and stared at the three large steaks lying in a pool of congealed blood.

She turned the water on in the kitchen sink and started to put the meat underneath it. Then she was seized by a bizarre urge when she looked at the blood. *I can't do that,* she thought, but it was nearly a compulsion.

She glanced out of the kitchen to see if Bridie was coming yet. Then she went back to the meat and quickly lapped the excess blood from the bag and the raw meat. It gave her a turn of disgust, but she couldn't stop herself. When she heard Bridie walking toward the kitchen, she hurriedly wiped her mouth and washed the meat with water.

Bridie got out the broiling pan. "Are they ready?"

"Here." Maggie put them in the pan.

Bridie put the pan in the broiler, then looked at Maggie. "You must be feeling a lot better. You've got some color back in your cheeks."

"Thanks." Maggie did feel better, but she couldn't understand why she'd wanted to drink that yucky, congealed blood. If she were married, she would've thought she was pregnant. *Oh, well,* she told herself while she took some potatoes out of the Frigidaire, *I guess everybody gets strange cravings from time to time.*

"Very good, Maggie," her father said approvingly after they were done eating. "It's about time you learned to make steak rare. I keep telling you that you destroy the vitamins when you cook it too long."

"Thank you, Daddy."

She and Bridie started clearing the table. "How's Johnny?" her father asked.

"Not bad. You know he's up at Harvard this weekend."

"Yup, planning to move my little girl to Boston." He glanced at Bridie. "Maggie tell you her crazy plan?"

"I don't know if 'crazy' is the word I would use, Mr. O'Neill," Bridie said diplomatically.

Maggie removed the used tablecloth. "Daddy, there is nothing crazy about a woman being a psychoanalyst."

"But that means going to medical school, doesn't it? Becoming a doctor?"

"Yeah," she shouted from the kitchen. She and Bridie were doing the dishes together.

Jack came into the kitchen. "But, honey, you hate the sight of blood. When you had to dissect that frog in high school, you fainted dead away." He asked Bridie, "Who wants a squeamish doctor?"

"Daddy," Maggie said patiently, "I'm not going to be a GP. I'm going to be a psychiatrist. That means working with people's minds, not their bodies."

"But how are you going to get through medical school? Don't they make you open up dead people?"

Maggie paled at that thought. "Well, Johnny will help me. He wants to be a surgeon."

"I'll believe it when I see it," Jack answered. "Why don't you make some coffee? I have some time to kill before I leave."

"You have plans?"

"A movie date." Jack grinned sheepishly, adding, "With Mrs. Moore."

Maggie smiled. Mrs. Moore had been widowed a year. "Don't do anything I wouldn't do."

"Don't be fresh," he replied, laughing. "I think I'll go see if there's any news." He went back into the living room and turned on the radio.

"He's right," Bridie remarked.

"Who's right?" Maggie asked. "About what?"

"About you and med school, Miss The-Sight-of-Blood-Turns-My-Stomach." Bridie raised an eyebrow, splashing Maggie with the soapy water in the sink. "Or were you planning on me coming with you—and doing all the science work like I did all your homework for you?"

Maggie rolled her eyes, splashing Bridie back. "Listen to Miss High-and-Mighty. Or maybe you've forgotten all the English papers and history papers I wrote for you?"

"That was nothing."

"Ha!" Maggie replied. "You'd still be in high school if it weren't for me."

"Oh, would I?" Bridie made a huge splash, and managed to soak the right side of Maggie's hair.

Maggie responded by dumping a cup of water right on top of Bridie's head.

Both girls were laughing so hard they could barely stand up. Bridie brandished the broiling pan full of water threateningly when the doorbell rang.

"Are you expecting anyone?" Maggie gasped.

"No," Bridie replied, giggling. "It's probably Old Lady Scanlon complaining that we're making too much noise. It's your turn to deal with her."

"I'm going, I'm going." Maggie was still laughing when she opened the door to Simon Baldevar.

Holy Mother, she had gone to bed with this man! Maggie thought the fever would have to give her brain damage to forget something like that. The memories of last night were putting her in a state that went far beyond shock—it had never occurred to Maggie that she would lose her virginity before her wedding night. Why, she was no better than a whore to sleep with a man she hardly knew. She couldn't even bring herself to look him in the eye.

"Hello, Meghann," he said in that low purr that made her knees weak.

As she stared at him, she realized he was much taller

than she had thought last night. Without her heels on, she barely came up to his shoulder. The matter of heels reminded Maggie that she was standing in front of him barefoot, with no makeup, and dish soap clotting in her hair. *I must look like a hag*, she thought.

She guessed Simon didn't mind her appearance because he leaned down to kiss her. She backed away, and told him, "My father's here."

On cue, Jack O'Neill came to the door. He gave Simon the same menacing stare he'd given everyone she ever went out with. "Who's your friend?" he growled at Maggie. Bridie, who had come out of the kitchen, looked greatly interested in an introduction too.

Simon introduced himself since Maggie had lost the power of speech. "I am Lord Simon Baldevar. I came over to thank your daughter for showing me the town last night." He extended his hand to Jack.

Pointedly ignoring the hand, Jack kept his thundery gaze on Maggie. Her red face had not escaped his notice. "Exactly what did you show him, Meghann Katherine O'Neill?"

"The ferry," she replied weakly.

Always a good friend, Bridie came to Maggie's rescue. "I need help with these dishes."

Maggie leaped at any excuse to escape her father's gaze. "Sure, be right there. Uh, excuse me," she said to Simon. "Please come inside." She dashed for the kitchen before her father could say anything.

"I guess you should come in," she heard Jack say grudgingly to Simon. "So where did you meet my little girl? Did she tell you she's got a brother on the force?"

In the kitchen, Maggie started wiping the soap out of her hair, and Bridie dried her own damp hair. "Maggie, you rat! How could you meet a gorgeous fellow like that and not tell me? Where did you find him? What about Johnny? Does he have a brother?"

"I met him at Pauline's, and he hasn't told me whether he has siblings."

"And I thought the party was just okay," Bridie said sarcastically. "Fink! Tell me everything."

"Nothing to tell," Maggie muttered, looking at the floor.

"Ha! I saw the way he looked at you—and so did your dad. And what was that business about the ferry? Now talk."

Maggie gave her friend a fairly truthful version of the events of the previous night—only leaving out the fact that they'd gone to bed together. Bridie was her best friend, but Maggie didn't intend to tell anyone, not even the priest at confession, about that.

"So what about Johnny? And why is he here?"

"I don't know why he's here. And I don't know about Johnny either. Oh, my God, the coffee!" Maggie managed to save it from being overboiled.

"Maggie," her father bellowed from the living room, "get in here!"

Oh, God, what's happened now? She didn't think Simon would tell her father anything, but he could have guessed. . . .

Maggie rushed back into the living room, with Bridie behind her, and could not believe her eyes. Her father, who had never liked anyone she brought home, who despised the English, was happily chatting away with Simon. He had even offered him one of his cigars.

"Jesus, Maggie," Jack scolded, "you have a guest and you disappear into the kitchen? This fellow is gonna think I never taught you any manners. Why don't you get out that cognac I gave you girls for Christmas? You do have snifter glasses, don't you?"

"Actually, we prefer to drink it with a straw in the bottle." Maggie went to the bureau in the living room for the glasses.

"Always with that fresh mouth. Why don't you show your new friend your knuckles—how often the nuns rapped you for your wise remarks?"

While Bridie and Maggie brought out the coffee, liquor, and utensils, Jack continued with his embarrassing tales of Maggie's childhood. If he didn't happen to be her father and outweigh her by a hundred pounds, she could have cheerfully strangled him.

"I swear," he told Simon, "almost every day the nuns whacked her for her mouth."

"The nuns hit everybody every day," she interjected.

"I have never cared for nuns," Simon put in, smiling at Maggie in sympathy.

"Neither did Maggie," Bridie said. "That's why she got in so much trouble."

Maggie glared at Bridie, and poured the cognac for her father and Simon. "I don't recall being alone when I got into trouble." She took a sip of cognac and began to choke.

"Maggie!" Bridie started pounding on her back. "Are you okay?"

"Fine," she rasped. "It was just too . . . strong. I guess I'm still a little under the weather."

"You don't feel well?" Simon asked.

"I was sick before, but I'm a lot better now."

"I'm glad." He smiled at her.

At least we're off the subject of my childhood, Maggie thought. She let her father and Bridie do most of the talking. Bridie had asked her why Simon was there, but Maggie had no idea. She had eavesdropped on enough of her brothers' conversations to know that there were always girls around who "gave in." But you didn't visit those girls and talk with their parents. Had he come over because he expected her to sleep with him again? He was obviously rich; maybe he was going to ask her to be his mistress. Well, she would certainly set him straight if he did. Last night was just a mistake.

As Maggie started following the conversation, something bothered her. Her father and Bridie . . . It was so odd, but they almost seemed controlled. Jack especially—he never was so warm to any of her boyfriends, but he was treating Simon like a favorite son. Maggie had the strange feeling that they were characters in a play . . . doing exactly as they were told. But who had written the script?

She kept quiet, unable to get last night out of her head. How could she have done such dirty things? Nice people didn't do stuff like that; she was sure of it. Then she looked over at Simon—his strong, muscled body, his compelling eyes—and she wanted more than anything to do every single one of those things again.

Simon caught her stare and smiled softly. Unless she was mistaken, he was thinking about last night too.

Jack caught the looks his daughter was giving her new friend. It made him uncomfortable, and then he understood why. She didn't look like his little girl when she looked at Simon Baldevar—she looked like a woman. And what have you been doing to make her look like that, he felt like asking the man. Then again, the fellow didn't seem to be just looking for a good time. If Jack wasn't mistaken, this rich lord seemed to be in love with Maggie. Well, he'd have to ask him what his intentions were.

"Maggie, you should go do the coffee dishes before they dry up." That was not a suggestion. It was given in the tone she'd recognized since childhood as an ironclad command.

Maggie raised her eyebrows at Bridie, and they vanished into the kitchen.

"So what about Johnny?" was the first thing out of Bridie's mouth while they did the few dessert dishes.

"I don't know," Maggie told her honestly. "But isn't he gorgeous?"

"I can't say I'd blame you for throwing over Johnny for a fellow like that. But how do you know he's serious about you? Doesn't he have to go back to England?"

That's exactly what Maggie was frightened of—that she'd slept with an attractive stranger who was going to forget all about her. He probably had a lot of girls after him, so why pick little Maggie O'Neill?

Bridie saw Maggie's brow crease and hastily put in, "Well, anyone can tell he likes you. And he did come over here tonight."

Maggie brightened. "That's true." Then she crept over to the kitchen doorway. "Aren't you dying to know what Daddy threw us out of the room to tell him?"

Both girls tried their best to peek outside without either man seeing them. Simon and Jack seemed to be engaged in an intense discussion. Jack looked almost grim until Simon leaned over and said something that put a wide grin on his face. Then Jack got up, and the girls scampered back to the dishes. Jack entered the kitchen to find the pair drying up the dishes. They hoped they had completely nonchalant expressions.

Jack pinched Maggie's cheek hard. "I guess it's time for me to head over to the movie. Why don't you tag along, Bridie?"

The girls turned to each other with identical expressions of bewilderment. Maggie's *father* was suggesting she spend time alone with a fellow? Had hell frozen over?

"Sure, Mr. O'Neill," Bridie replied haltingly. "Just let me change into my nurse's uniform."

While Bridie changed, Jack proudly displayed a photograph of Maggie wearing pigtails and holding her mitt. Her brother Frankie had an arm around her.

"Maggie was fourteen and her brother had her pitch

two innings for his team," Jack bragged to Simon. "This little girl struck out six men. She's got a better fastball than a lot of guys I've seen."

"Daddy," she said good-naturedly, "you always make it sound like I pitched against the Yankees. Those guys were so drunk by the seventh inning they probably didn't even remember how to hold the bat."

Bridie came back, and they said good night. Maggie was still stunned, and that feeling of acting in a play came over her again. This was unreal—her father leaving her alone with some man he didn't know. She was tempted to call them back.

What the hell are you doing? Maggie asked herself. You should have asked Simon to leave—the way your father damn well would have if he knew what happened last night. Now he'll expect more of what you gave out last night, you tramp.

"What did my father say to you?" she asked curiously when she came back into the living room.

"He said, and I quote, 'English lord or not, if you get my little girl in trouble or break her heart, I'll mop the floor with you.' "

"Oh, God, I'm sorry." Maggie was so embarrassed— and uncomfortable—at the thought her father might have to make good on that threat in nine months.

"Don't apologize. It was touching to see your father's concern. I believe I put his mind at ease."

"How?"

Simon took her hand and kissed it. "By assuring him my intentions were completely honorable. I told him he need not worry about me breaking your heart—the only heart that might get broken is mine. Are you happy to see me again, Meghann?"

"Very," she replied, barely able to remember Johnny's name.

"Good." He inspected a large wooden crucifix hanging by the bookcase. He turned to Maggie. "I take it you're a Catholic?"

"Didn't I tell you I was last night? Anyway, what else would I be with a name like Meghann Katherine Agnes O'Neill?"

"Agnes?"

"It's what I chose for my confirmation name," she explained. "Agnes was the first bride of Christ. She chose to be beheaded rather than marry a rich but mortal noble."

Simon gave her that slow, arching smile that made her knees weak. "And did you choose her name because you wanted to be a bride of Christ, Meghann—by keeping your body pure and serving the Savior?"

"N-not exactly," she stammered. "I admired her faith in God. I think it's amazing that some people believe so strongly in an ideal that they're not swayed by the thought of death or torture."

"Personally, I think it's rather foolish." Simon touched the cross again. "You don't find an object like this to be a garish show of devotion?"

"Not at all," she told him. "That cross belonged to my mother."

"Ah." Simon sat down on the couch. "Tell me, how devout a Catholic are you?"

Why was he so interested in her religious feelings? "Apparently not very devout at all," she said tartly. "Otherwise, I wouldn't have condemned my immortal soul to hell by sleeping with a man I'm not married to."

Simon roared with laughter and Maggie blushed. What possessed her to say things like that around Simon? She was usually blunt, not reckless.

"Would that all forms of condemnation gave such pleasure," he said, extending his hand to Maggie. "Come closer, my pretty heretic."

Maggie remained where she was and Simon arched his left eyebrow. She said haltingly, "I don't want you to get the . . . uh . . . wrong idea. Um, last night . . . It's just I've never done anything like that. . . ."

"Meghann, there's no need to tell me what I already know. Now come sit with me, please." Despite his soft voice, Maggie felt like he was commanding her. And she walked over and sat next to him with no thought of refusal.

Simon reached into his suit pocket and pulled out a small black jeweler's box. He kissed Maggie on the forehead and put the box in her hands. "Open it. I've been waiting all night to see if you like my gift."

Maggie opened the box and saw a beautiful gold pendant on a fine gold chain. She fell in love with it immediately. The pendant was shaped like an acorn and it had emeralds and pearls interspersed throughout the gold hoops. Four letters were dangling down from the pendant. "A-M-O-R," she read out loud.

"*Amor,*" Simon told her. "It means love."

"I know. But I thought *amour* was spelled with a u."

"Not in the fourteenth century," he replied. "This is an heirloom, darling, its been in my family for centuries."

"Then I can't take it," she protested. "It's too valuable."

Simon opened the clasp on the chain and placed the pendant around Maggie's neck. "What you gave me last night was far more valuable. This is just a small token of appreciation. I won't take no for an answer."

Maggie was touched. No one had ever given her anything so valuable. "If you won't take no for an answer, I guess all I can say is thank you." She leaned over and kissed him on the lips.

What she'd intended to be a quick peck turned into more when Simon embraced her and eased her body back into the sofa. Without breaking off their kiss, he removed her top and she felt his hand on her thigh. Maggie reached up and started unbuttoning his shirt.

When the phone rang, Maggie felt like someone had thrown a bucket of cold water over her. She looked with dismay at the state of undress she and Simon were in. *What is wrong with me? Why can't I think straight when he touches me?* Maggie untangled herself from Simon and hurried over to the phone. "Hello?"

"Hi, honey, are you okay? You sound funny."

Maggie felt guilt mixed with rising shame. "Oh, hi, Johnny. No, I'm fine. I was just a little sick today."

"I hope I didn't wake you. It sounded like you were out of breath."

"No, no. How are you? How's Harvard?"

"Great," Johnny replied enthusiastically. "The dean loved me. He said it's gonna be a snap for me to get into the premed program. And guess what? He also introduced me to the dean of admissions at Radcliffe. Sure, he wants to meet you, but he thinks it should be no problem for you to transfer in the fall."

That news was enough to make her almost forget Simon Baldevar. "Radcliffe?" Maggie squealed. "Johnny, are you kidding me?"

"Nope," he said happily. "I told them all about you—the softball and how you've made Phi Beta Kappa every semester that you've been at Hunter. They said you'd probably even get a scholarship. So think about it. With a scholarship and the GI Bill paying my way, plus if our folks chip in a little, we can get married and get a small apartment up here in September. What do you say?"

Maggie thought he sounded like the old Johnny again—full of plans and enthusiasm. "I say that's wonderful, fantastic. . . ."

She broke off because a bare-chested Simon stood in

front of her. *How can I make plans to get married when I'm sleeping around with a perfect stranger?* Simon knelt down in front of her and started kissing her legs with light, feathery kisses. Maggie moaned and nearly dropped the receiver.

"Hey, are you all right? You sound like you're in pain."

Maggie couldn't think with Simon kissing her like that. "Uh, Johnny, I'm feeling sick again. I have to go. Call me tomorrow—I should be better by then." She hung up the phone and told Simon, "I think you should leave, I'm engaged."

In reply, he picked her up by the waist and pushed her against the wall. Then he kissed her hard. Maggie felt a shot of pure desire rush through her. She wrapped her legs around him and kissed him back hungrily.

"I don't think you would have made a good bride of Christ." With a lusty grin, he told her, "And I don't think you'll make a very good bride to that young man either. Will you think of me on your honeymoon, sweetheart? Will you hunger for me?"

"Don't . . . ," she began, but he put a finger to her lips.

"Be my bride, Meghann." He kissed her again and carried her into the bedroom.

When he put her on the bed, she asked him, "What do you want from me?"

"You needn't sound so plaintive. I want nothing that you do not wish to give me. Shall I leave, Meghann?" He ran one finger lightly from her chin to her navel.

This was it; all she had to do was tell him to go. Her life would return to normal. She'd keep this encounter a secret and marry Johnny Devlin. Maggie looked up, ready to tell Simon to leave. But the words died on her lips when she looked into his eyes. Why did she feel like she was drowning when she gazed into his eyes?

Simon saw the invitation in her eyes and leaned down. "I believe you've made your choice, my sweet."

Maggie kissed him with no thought of consequence, no thought for anything but the almost primal desire she felt at his touch.

"Beautiful," Simon murmured after he undressed her. Maggie felt almost caressed by the slow, sweeping gaze that roamed over her body. Then Simon lay down on the bed and positioned her so she was straddled across his body. "Make love to me."

"What?" Maggie said in a breathy whisper so far removed from her normal voice that it was like hearing a stranger speak. What was happening to her? This sensuous woman, with her husky voice and bold hands and lips, who confidently explored the lean, hard body beneath her . . . Could she really be Maggie O'Neill?

"Make love to me," Simon repeated, and grasped her hips tightly, bringing her down on top of him.

This felt even better than last night. Maggie arched her back, delighting in the strong hands that guided her hips, pushing her up and down in a rhythm that caused unbelievable pleasure to course through her.

Emboldened by the new position, Maggie began to move independently of Simon. Seeming delighted with her new assertive behavior, Simon removed his hands and allowed her to set the pace for their lovemaking. It was a long, lovely pace she set until the sweet tension building inside her became an unbearable need and she brought them both to a shuddering, gasping finale.

At least this time I remember making love, Maggie thought afterward, her head comfortably nestled by Simon's heart. How bizarre that she'd forgotten last night and all the divine things they'd done until Simon showed up on her doorstep. Then Maggie frowned, realizing her recollection of the night before was still fragmented; she still had no memory of Simon leaving the apartment after they made love. Maybe she'd fallen asleep and Simon let himself out. Well, she certainly couldn't ask him. How insulting that would be—oh, by the way, I totally forgot going to bed with you, could you please refresh my memory?

Maggie felt Simon stiffen and she looked down, frowning at the suppressed mirth twinkling in his eyes.

"What's so funny?" she demanded, thinking it was almost like he was laughing at what she'd been thinking . . . her inability to remember the night before.

"It's not amusement," Simon said, and brushed his fingers across her cheek. "I'm simply very happy."

"Oh." Maggie smiled and said softly, "I'm happy too."

"Truly?" Simon questioned, reaching up to wrap his arms around her so she was pressed tightly against him. "Happy enough to remain with me for eternity?"

"Eternity?" Maggie squealed. She got her arms free so she could hug him close and kiss his lips with a resounding smack. "Oh, Simon! Are you asking me to be your countess?"

Simon laughed, a clipped sound that made Maggie frown. "I am asking a great deal more than that. I want you to belong to me utterly."

Belong to him? What a strange way to put it—why didn't Simon ask her to marry him, tell her he loved her and wanted her to love him back? "I don't understand."

"Of course you don't." Before Maggie could say anything else, Simon rolled around so she was lying under him. Then he grabbed her hands and pinned them above her head. Simon was looking at her with the strangest expression, great tenderness mixed with something . . . predatory. Yes, that was it! He was looking at her like he wanted to own her. "I don't want to hurt you." The intensity in his eyes almost frightened her. "Promise me you'll remember that—no matter what happens, I never want to hurt you."

Maggie was confused. Who are you? she almost asked. Why are you here? Then she looked into those beautiful golden eyes and felt so protected, so loved. "I think I'm falling in love with you," she heard herself say.

Simon offered her a lopsided grin before he started kissing her breasts with such slow, teasing caresses she almost screamed. "I should hope so," he murmured, not raising his head. "Because I am already in love with you."

"Oh, God," she whimpered, shocked by the ache filling her at his touch. They'd just finished making love and she felt like she'd die if he didn't enter her again. What was Simon doing to her? "Make love to me!"

Simon looked up and smiled in triumph. "What will you do for me in return?"

"I . . . what," Maggie panted, unable to concentrate on anything but the hot, almost unbearable throbbing building inside her. "Any . . . anything you say!"

"Sweet little Meghann," Simon said almost sadly, teasing her nipples unmercifully with casual flicks of his tongue. "You don't know what anything is."

"Then tell me," Maggie pleaded. "Just tell me what you want and I'll do it."

Her appeal brought nothing but a cynical grin to Simon's face and he still refused to enter her. "Please," she mewled, close to hating him for the way he was making her grovel. Hadn't he just said he loved her? Why was he treating her like this?

Simon placed one finger inside her and started moving it around in a maddeningly slow, circular motion. "Oh, God," she answered with a sigh.

"Meghann, I want you as I've never wanted any other

woman. But if I take you, it's forever. I'll only be satisfied if I have all of you . . . body and soul. That means no one—not your family, not your friends or any interest—comes before me. You give yourself to me completely or not at all. Will you agree to that?"

In the years that followed, Maggie realized exactly what she gave Simon that night, but at that moment, she was too filled with lust to be able to think. Hardly aware of what she was saying, she screamed, "Yes— body, soul, everything! Just take me! Please!"

"Oh, I intend to," he whispered as he thrust deep inside her, making her scream again. Maggie felt the world fade away as the now familiar haze of lust and fierce, insatiable need enveloped her. Nothing mattered but the mouth devouring hers, the clever hands that brought her to such a feverish pitch, and the wonderful, driving force that made her dig her nails into Simon's back and beg for more. In her blissful abandonment, Maggie barely heard Simon when he said, "Don't worry, sweetheart. I intend to make you mine before this night is over."

FOUR

Maggie smelled something awful under her nose. She jerked away and opened her eyes. Dr. O'Shea, the family doctor, was standing over her with a small brown bottle.

"Thank God, you're awake!" Bridie cried.

Dr. O'Shea saw Maggie looking at the bottle. "Smelling salts, banshee. You fainted." Dr. O'Shea called her "banshee" because of the way she used to scream when he had to use a needle.

"When did I faint?"

"An excellent question. Do you think you can help us with the answer? But first, I have some questions of my own. How many fingers am I holding up?"

"Three."

"Very good. Now what time is it?"

Maggie didn't want to answer any more questions. She was tired. All she wanted to do was sleep. She glanced at the window, and then she moaned. The light was hurting her eyes. "Why don't you tell me?" she asked Dr. O'Shea sleepily.

"Five P.M."

"Five," Maggie murmured in that same drowsy voice, "but that means I've been in bed the whole day."

"Maggie, I was so scared when I came home and I

couldn't wake you up," Bridie said. "You were so pale and . . ."

Dr. O'Shea noticed the anxiety on Maggie's face and said mildly, "Let's not get upset here. The important thing is my favorite patient is awake now, so she's going to help me figure out what's the matter. Now, Daddy tells me you weren't feeling so good yesterday either? When did you start feeling sick?" Maggie saw her father sitting on the edge of the bed.

"I guess yesterday morning," she told Dr. O'Shea while he examined her eyes. "I woke up sick. . . . I was throwing up a lot and I was really cold." She yawned; she didn't even have the strength to sit up.

"Chills? Was there a fever?"

"Yes, but it went away last night."

"What else do you feel? A little tired, maybe?"

"Yes," Maggie answered, "very tired . . . like I could sleep all the time."

"Well, we can't have that. What would all your boy-friends do with you sleeping all the time? Anyway, what's the number up to now, brat . . . twenty boy-friends, thirty?"

Maggie giggled. "Just one."

"Do you mean Simon?" Bridie asked.

Maggie sat up with a start; she felt her cheeks turning red. Bridie had just reminded her that she'd slept with him again last night. And she felt something ominous. She remembered making love, but she couldn't remember him leaving. What the hell had happened? Why was her heart going a mile a minute? Wait . . . something Simon had asked her. Yes, some foolishness about bodies and souls. It was probably his way of being romantic or something. This sickness was God's way of punishing her for sleeping with a man who wasn't her husband. "He is *not* my boyfriend."

"You didn't have a fight?" her father asked. He

hadn't looked that upset when they found out Johnny Devlin had been wounded.

"Calm down, Daddy. I just meant he's an . . . acquaintance."

"Acquaintance?" Dr. O'Shea questioned. "All men should make acquaintances of pretty young girls like you. Does it hurt when I do this?" He started pressing down on her abdomen.

"No more than the rest of me hurts," Maggie told him. "That's another thing. . . . It's like my bones hurt."

Dr. O'Shea looked at her with new concern. "Bones hurt? Open your mouth, banshee."

Maggie opened, and he probed for a few minutes. "Okay . . . now tell me. You notice any bruises lately that won't go away?"

"No."

"And you're tired a lot? Let's get a look at your blood pressure."

Bridie took her blood pressure. While she was applying the cuff to Maggie's arm, Maggie asked her, "When did you come home?"

"At four. They made me work a double shift. When I think of you here by yourself, sick . . . ."

"Look, Bridie, I'm not on my deathbed or anything. Am I, Dr. O'Shea?"

He raised his shaggy white eyebrows. "Deathbed? Do me a favor and save the dramatics for the movies." He took a look at the blood pressure reading and frowned. "Bridie, do the reading again, please."

Bridie did so. When she was done, Dr. O'Shea said, "Eighty-eight over sixty . . . This blood pressure is too low, hon." He shot Bridie a glance to keep her quiet. "Tell me when you first started feeling sick."

Maggie told him about how she woke up with the chills and vomiting the day before. And how she woke up the previous evening feeling better, and how the steak made her feel fine. When she was done telling him, she started feeling exhausted again.

Dr. O'Shea noticed and said, "Lie back. Bridie, get a few pillows to prop up her legs, please. And a quilt. I don't like these blue lips and fingernails. You have a mild case of shock. A few more questions and you can go back to sleep. So the steak made you feel better? Maybe Daddy could get you some more steak? And some liver too?"

"Of course," Jack said. "By when?"

"The sooner, the better. Sweetheart, I want you to go to the hospital tomorrow." When Maggie started protesting, he said, "No ifs, ands, or buts about it. If today weren't Sunday, I'd admit you tonight. I need some tests to figure out what we're dealing with."

"What do you think it is?" Maggie asked.

"I'm not so sure. I'm going to draw a little blood." Maggie paled. "Banshee, you're still scared of needles? You give blood to all those handsome GIs and not a drop for your old friend Dr. O'Shea? Have you told your friend what we did in the old days when you needed a shot?"

Maggie turned to Bridie while Dr. O'Shea swabbed a bit of alcohol on her upper arm. "I was such a baby. . . . Poor Dr. O'Shea had to put on a show and get me laughing so hard I didn't notice the needle."

Dr. O'Shea prepared the needle. "Do you remember your favorite one?" He grabbed a sheet off the bed and wrapped it around his shoulders like a cape. In a hideously terrible imitation of Bela Lugosi, he cried, "I have come to suck your blood!" Maggie and Bridie started laughing. While Maggie was laughing, Dr. O'Shea quickly inserted the needle in her arm and started drawing blood. "Just like the old days, hmmm?"

Maggie had never liked needles, but she started shaking. She could feel the blood being taken from her and she wanted to scream out, *Stop it! Leave me alone!* She felt so violated. Maggie started to yank the needle out with her other hand, but Bridie grabbed her arm. "What's wrong with you, Maggie?"

Maggie was sweating and trembling. "I don't know . . . I just felt like . . . I don't know. It wasn't the needle. . . . it was more like I had a memory of somebody doing something terrible to me. I can't explain it—maybe I just had a bad dream or something. I'm sorry, Dr. O'Shea."

"No harm, no foul," he answered. He removed the needle from her arm and put the blood sample in his black medical bag. "Why don't you try and rest, Maggie? Daddy and I are going to have a little talk outside."

"I'm an adult," Maggie protested.

"Of course you are—but right now you're a sick one. Now relax a little while . . . I'll be back tomorrow and we'll chat as long as you want to."

Maggie curled up while Bridie, Jack, and Dr. O'Shea went out to the living room.

"What's the matter with her, Doctor?" she heard her father ask. Was he shouting? Maggie thought. She could hear him as clearly as though he was still in the same room with her.

"I'll be honest with you, Jack. I'm concerned. But we have a nurse here. What do you think is the matter with your friend?"

"I'd guess anemia, Doctor." *Why did they go outside to talk about me if they're going to be so loud?* Then Maggie realized that even though she could hear them clearly, there was a muffled quality to their voices—like they were whispering. *So why can I hear them? Every thing else about me is falling apart, but I've suddenly got incredible hearing.*

"She has all the symptoms of anemia," Dr. O'Shea

answered. "The pale skin, listlessness, low blood pressure. But the onset is a little sudden—especially with the shock. Bridie, when did she last give blood?"

"Two months ago, Doctor."

"Two months? Well, I don't think she has internal bleeding. Of course, we'll need some X rays to rule it out completely. But it's almost like she's suffering from severe blood loss. And she has other symptoms that bother me—that fever and the bone ache."

"What could that be a symptom of?" Jack asked worriedly.

Dr. O'Shea sighed. "Now, Jack, I don't want you getting excited. It's very likely that all she has is anemia or maybe some sort of virus. . . ."

"Spit it out, Doctor. What do you think she has?"

"Jack, there's a very small chance this could be leukemia."

Leukemia! Maggie's heart started beating rapidly. Holy Jesus Christ! People died from that. *I can't die,* Maggie thought desperately. *I'm supposed to get married in a month; I'm only eighteen years old.*

"But she's missing a lot of the major symptoms," Dr. O'Shea was saying. "No sores in her mouth, no bruising, and the liver and spleen don't seem enlarged. But we have to be alert for symptoms like that. Now I've taken the blood sample, so we should know in a few days what we're dealing with. Tomorrow I want Bridie to bring her by the hospital—we're going to do a complete set of tests. In the meantime, we're going on the anemia theory. Jack, get her that meat tonight if you can. I want her eating steak and liver morning, noon, and night. Bridie, I want you to go out and get some castor oil. I'm also going to write you a prescription for iron pills and some tranquilizers in case Maggie gets a little restless tonight. I want her to get as much sleep as she can. You can get it filled at the hospital."

Bridie and Jack came back into the bedroom. Jack kissed her on the cheek and left. Bridie propped her legs up with some pillows, put an extra quilt on the bed, and asked, "Do you want anything before I go out?"

"Maybe something to read. I'm having trouble falling asleep." She couldn't fall asleep because she'd been anxious since Bridie mentioned Simon's name. What was that all about?

Bridie brought her some movie magazines. When Maggie frowned, Bridie told her, "No getting involved in a novel and forgetting to sleep. Those magazines are just what the doctor ordered." Bridie turned on the lamp by the bed, and started to leave.

"Bridie, tell me the truth. Am I really sick?"

"Honey, the doctor has to run some tests before he knows what's wrong." Bridie fluffed her pillows. "Now, you heard Dr. O'Shea—try and get some rest."

Maggie noted that Bridie hadn't answered her question. *Wait,* Maggie thought desperately. *Don't leave me by myself; I'm scared.* Then her common sense challenged her. What did she have to be scared of? And what could she tell Bridie? *Don't go; I'm scared. I'm scared Simon will get me.* Wait a minute—what left field had that thought come out of? *I'm sick,* she told herself firmly, *my mind is playing tricks on me. Next I'll see pink elephants on the ceiling.*

Maggie tried to read the magazines but couldn't concentrate. She was frightened that when Dr. O'Shea put her in the hospital tomorrow, she'd never leave. What if it turned out she did have leukemia? And she couldn't get rid of that nameless anxiety that was making her hands shake. It seemed like it was getting worse as the sun set farther in the sky. *What am I so scared of? I'm a little old to be scared of the dark.*

Maggie's left leg, which still hurt, was starting to itch

terribly. *Damn,* she thought to herself, *I forgot to tell Dr. O'Shea about that pain in my leg.* Maggie started to scratch but felt something odd. It was almost like two holes in her skin. Could she have cut herself somehow? Maybe all she had was some sort of infection.

Maggie threw the bedsheets off and pushed her nightgown up. The cuts were on the inside of her left thigh, and difficult to see. Maggie bent down and tilted the lamp so that it illuminated her leg.

That's strange, she thought, getting a better look at the marks. That was the only word she could think of for them . . . "marks." They were two jagged, somewhat circular holes with dried blood on them. She put the lamp back on the nightstand. How the hell did that happen? Maggie thought. Had something bitten her?

The second the word "bitten" went through her mind everything fell into place. Maggie leaned back against the pillows, her heart galloping and her body shaking. Even her lips were trembling. Maggie remembered now. She remembered how those two nights with Simon Baldevar ended. He made love to her, and then with long vicious fangs, he bit into her thigh and sucked her blood. And she had given him permission to do it.

"No!" she screamed out loud. NO! NO! NO! It can't be true, she told herself, and it's insane to even think it. Are you saying Simon is a vampire? That's ridiculous. Vampires don't exist.

But she looked at her shaking hands, and a part of her knew it was true. Look at those marks, a voice told her. What else could have made them? And have you ever seen Simon Baldevar during the day?

Wait a second, she told herself firmly. *It doesn't mean anything that I haven't seen him during the day. I've only known the man for two days; maybe he was busy during the day.* But she knew somebody who should have seen him during the day.

She put her legs over the side of the bed and felt dizzy. It took her a full minute to get over the attack. She made it to the kitchen dragging herself along the wall and walking very slowly.

She grabbed the phone, but her hand was shaking so hard it took her a few minutes to dial the number correctly. "Pauline?"

"I'm not talking to you," the girl told her petulantly. "After you tried to steal Simon from me . . ."

"Look," Maggie cried out, "I'm not interested in him. If you want him, have him. I need to know—"

"I do have him," Pauline said in triumph. "We have a date in a half hour for dinner at the Plaza."

Maggie glanced out the window. Damn! It would be completely dark in a half hour; Pauline's date wouldn't prove a thing. Maggie poured every ounce of charm and persuasion she had into her voice. "Pauline, you're right to be mad."

"I know I am. And I'm hanging up."

"No!" Maggie screamed. "Please, don't. Pauline, I'm really sick. Please, I need your help."

"Jesus, Maggie. You scared me to death . . . screaming like that." Pauline relented. "Anyway, now that I know Simon likes me, I'm not so mad. What's the matter?"

"I just want to know one thing. Have you ever seen Simon during the day? Or maybe your mother met him for lunch?"

"What kind of off-the-wall question is that?"

"Just tell me," Maggie pleaded.

A gloating tone entered Pauline's voice. "Is he giving you the runaround? Too busy to see the great Maggie O'Neill during the day? I know you're not used to fellows putting you off."

"Yes, fine, whatever you want," Maggie said desperately. "Just tell me if you or your mom has seen him when the sun was in the sky."

"Maggie, whatever you're sick with, I think it's gone to your head. You have to understand that someone like Simon is very busy during the day with business arrangements. . . ."

"Your mother is engaged in a business deal with him. Has she ever met him during the day?"

"What is so important about seeing him during the day?"

"Pauline!"

"All right, already. Anything to get you off the phone." Pauline considered. "They had dinner yesterday . . . and he came to the party . . . a few days before that they met for drinks. Hmmm, guess what, Maggie? We've only seen him at night. Satisfied?"

That was not what Maggie wanted to hear. She wanted Pauline to tell her they met for lunch all the time so that she could put her insane thoughts to rest. But those marks and now no one had seen him during the day . . .

"Pauline?"

"Now what?"

"Maybe you should cancel your date."

"I knew it! I knew you were jealous! How does it feel to have the shoe on the other foot for a change? Get used to it, Maggie. Simon prefers me to you and hell will freeze over before I cancel a date with him." Pauline hung up.

Panic had made Maggie's mouth dry. She decided to go into the kitchen and get a glass of water. *Simon will be here for you soon, now that it's dark,* that same voice told her.

"Shut up," Maggie said out loud. At least leukemia was rational. People died young; she'd learn to accept it if she had to. But she was not about to go around having warped fantasies about some man she hardly knew being a blood-sucking vampire.

As Maggie was filling the water glass, a new thought occurred to her, and she went limp with relief. Maybe this was all psychosomatic! Yes, that made perfect sense. She'd learned all about psychosomatic illness in that psychology class she'd taken last semester. She examined the facts. Each time she slept with Simon she woke up horribly ill the next day. Of course! She felt guilty and the guilt was manifesting itself in physical symptoms. After all, what she'd done went completely against her upbringing. And she'd betrayed her fiancé. Now she was punishing herself with fever and delusions. Maybe she needed to see a psychoanalyst.

Maggie took the water back into the bedroom, her head throbbing miserably. She saw that Bridie's lipstick had fallen off the vanity table. Maggie reached down to pick it up and place it back on the vanity. She moved too quickly when she straightened up; another dizzy spell attacked her. She grabbed the vanity table for support, and took several deep breaths. When she looked up, she was staring directly into the mirror above the vanity. What she saw made her gasp.

Maggie could find a rational explanation for the marks on her leg and her memories. But there was nothing rational about the hellish thing she saw staring back at her in the mirror.

Maggie wasn't casting a full reflection. Her image in the mirror was see-through. Through her body, she could see the bed behind her.

"No," Maggie whimpered. She put a trembling hand up and watched it go through her face.

That half image made it impossible to deny what was going on. Maggie kept staring, then found the voice to scream and scream and scream again. She kept scream-

ing until a merciful blackness descended on her consciousness and she slumped to the floor.

Maggie woke up, and felt the nubbles of the rug
against her cheek. She opened her eyes and saw a pair
of polished black shoes in front of her. Maggie pushed
herself up on her hands and saw Simon Baldevar in
front of her. He held out his hand to her, and Maggie
saw the two huge fangs sticking out of his mouth. She
started screaming. . . .

Still screaming from the dream (memory?), she
found herself on a strange bed. She tried to jump off
the bed and found that she couldn't. Her wrists were
chained to the bedpost.

"Oh, God," she whimpered. Maggie looked at her
arms. Each wrist had a gold manacle on it that was
attached to heavy gold chains secured to the bedpost.
Her arms ached; she must have been tied up for a long
time.

Maggie started struggling wildly, tearing at the
chains. She yanked and yanked to no avail. And the
effort was making her feel dizzy.

*Oh, Jesus, where am I? Why am I not at home? Did someone
kidnap me? Am I going to be raped? Murdered?*

Tears started falling down her cheeks, and Maggie
was sobbing hysterically. *What's happening to me? I don't
cast a reflection anymore and now I've been kidnapped. What
else can happen?*

As though some malicious force wished to show Maggie exactly what could happen, Simon Baldevar appeared in front of the bed. How else could she describe
it? One minute he wasn't there and the next minute
he was there—like magic. She thought a shadow might
have been there for a split second before he appeared.

Maggie gaped at the apparition in front of her, the

shock cutting off her sobs. What in the name of God was Simon?

"God has very little to do with what I am, sweet child," Simon said, and reached over to caress her cheek.

Maggie moved her face away, and Simon yanked her hair, hard. He kept his other hand on her cheek. "Don't ever attempt to move away from me, Meghann."

Bound, her scalp stinging from the pain, Maggie stared into his eyes. This was not the same man who'd taken her on the ferry and chatted with her father. That had just been an illusion. Now she was with something else, some evil creature with eyes blazing with a hard, bright, unholy light. They made Maggie feel utterly helpless. There would be no way for her to plead with this . . . thing.

"Don't think of me as a thing." Although Simon's tone was pleasant enough, there seemed to be menace underlying it. He released her hair. "I am known as a vampire."

Maggie found her voice again. "You can read my mind?"

"I can read any mortal."

That meant that every minute she was with him, her thoughts were as clear as though she'd shouted them. Outraged at the thought of being so violated, Maggie spat in his face.

Ruthlessly Simon grabbed Maggie's hair so hard her head tilted backward. Two fangs extended from Simon's mouth. As Maggie watched in horror, he bent over her extended neck and bit down hard on her jugular vein.

Maggie's body spasmed, and she heard herself scream. Oh, how it hurt! She'd never felt pain like this—a hot, stabbing sensation that was quickly replaced by a dull ache as Simon began sucking on the wound. Those sucking noises were hideous and the pain was the least of it. Maggie had never been so cold, and she could feel the strength leaving her body as Simon drank her blood.

Abruptly Simon raised his head. Nauseous and dizzy, Maggie fell against the pillows, shivering and moaning. If the cold didn't stop, she would die.

"It doesn't have to be an unpleasant experience, Meghann," Simon told her. "Look at me. Do you want me to hurt you?"

Maggie opened her eyes, and felt even worse at the sight of her blood on those unspeakable fangs. "No," she whimpered.

"No, what?" Simon asked softly.

Now Maggie remembered what she'd called him last night as he drank her blood. If she weren't so weak, she would have been disgusted with herself. With a great effort, she kept herself from saying what he wanted.

"No, what, Meghann?" he asked again as he bent his head toward her neck.

Maggie couldn't take that agony again. As his fangs began to sink into her flesh, Maggie screamed out, "No, Master! Master, please don't hurt me!"

Simon put a red handkerchief in Maggie's hand. He indicated the saliva on his face and said, "Wipe it off."

Maggie did as she was told. What was going to happen now? What did Simon have in mind for her?

When she was done, Simon put his hand over the wound in her neck. "You'll feel better now."

In a moment, Maggie did feel better. The cold, the pain, even her fear, vanished. Now that she wasn't afraid, she could think clearly.

Removing his hand, Simon sat down on the bed. He said nothing, but stared at her intently.

Maggie forced herself to ask what she feared most. "Are you going to kill me?"

Simon laughed. "Quite the opposite, my dear."

"Why are you doing this to me?" she demanded to know.

"Because we belong together," Simon told her as he leaned over and kissed her.

Why does this feel so good to me? Maggie wondered as she found herself kissing him back. *I should hate him, but I crave his touch so badly.* She couldn't believe how she felt, warm and eager. How could she desire this fiend? What was wrong with her?

Simon gently kissed the wounds on her neck. "Don't be afraid, my love."

Maggie didn't feel frightened when he began drinking her blood again. It felt so different this time—it was almost like making love. She felt waves of pure lust and grabbed his hair, pushing him closer to her neck. He responded by pulling her into a tight embrace. It felt incredible. Maggie wrapped her legs around him; she never wanted him to stop. There was no pain, no cold . . .

"No," Maggie whimpered in protest when Simon raised his head. *Why does he have to stop? And why am I thinking like this?* the still sane part of her asked.

Simon untangled himself from Maggie. Smiling softly, he arranged her hair to hide the marks on her neck. "It would be impolite to continue in front of company, sweet." He picked up a red cloth from the nightstand by the bed, and used it to wipe Maggie's blood from his mouth and chin.

"Company?" was all Maggie had time to say before the huge wooden door to the room crashed open.

Pauline Manchester stood in the doorway. Her hair, which had been arranged in a blue snood, was askew. The navy suit she was wearing emphasized her skinny, narrow build. Even from the bed, Maggie could smell the gin fumes emanating from her.

"You truly surprise me," Simon told her coldly. "I would not have thought you could be any less attractive—but then, I'd never seen you disheveled and intoxicated."

Pauline stumbled over to him. "Listen, you sonofabitch," she slurred. "I waited for you at the Plaza for three hours and you're here playing degenerate games with some whore." Pauline craned her neck to see past Simon, and her eyes widened when she realized who was on the bed. "Maggie! How could you do this to me? Liar! You said you were sick."

"Pauline, Simon's a monster!" Maggie screamed. "Get the hell out of here!" Waves of dizziness overcame her, and she collapsed against the pillows.

"Don't tire yourself," Simon ordered sharply. He leaned over and whispered in her ear, "You didn't appear to find me monstrous a few moments ago, sweet." When he turned around, he asked Pauline, "What is wrong, my dear? Are you upset that I do not choose to play games with you? You are far too plain and spiritless for my tastes." Simon grinned at Pauline in a way that made Maggie's blood run cold. *Why doesn't Pauline try to get away? I just warned her.* Then Maggie saw the slightly glazed look in Pauline's eyes, and realized Simon was controlling her in some way. *Dear God,* Maggie thought. *He can control us both like puppets—the same way he controlled Bridie, Daddy, and me last night.*

"You can't talk to me that way!" Pauline cried. Simon grabbed her wrist and she screamed. "Let me go, you bastard! My mother will have you killed!"

Simon's evil, vicious laughter made both girls flinch. "Why are you here, little wren? Do you want to take Meghann's place in my bed?"

Maggie, whom Simon seemed to have forgotten

about for the moment, gasped as he forced Pauline to her knees.

"Poor little rich girl," Simon said softly. "All that money, yet you are so drab. No wonder your mother has been unable to purchase a husband for you."

"Please stop," Pauline whined, squirming and trying to break his hold on her wrist.

"I have no desire to please you. And I find it amusing that you're so jealous of my Meghann."

"I'm not jealous of her," Pauline denied, tears appearing in her eyes as Simon applied more pressure to her wrist.

"Don't lie to me," Simon said in a menacing whisper. "You're jealous of her and every other pretty girl you've ever come into contact with. You can't harm the debutantes, but why don't you tell Meghann about Sara?"

"No one knows about Sara."

"I know. You won't tell Meghann? Very well, I shall. Sara was a kitchen maid. An undesirable job, but how you envied her golden blond hair and bright blue eyes. When it became too much to bear, seeing what no amount of your mother's money could ever give you, you went to your dear Mama with a tale that Sara stole your emerald earrings. Sara was fired, of course, and you, my ugly duckling, had a new ruby brooch to comfort you." Maggie heard a crack, and Pauline screamed. Her hand was in an unnatural position—Simon must have broken her wrist. He still did not let go, even with Pauline crying in pain.

Simon grabbed her injured hand tightly, and Pauline screamed in agony. "Let her go!" Maggie shouted.

"Be silent. She would never speak up on your behalf. Would you?" he asked Pauline.

"No," Pauline choked out.

"Why not?"

"I hate her!" Pauline screamed.

"Of course you do," Simon soothed. "Do you want to trade places with her?"

Pauline didn't respond, and Simon applied more pressure to her wrist. "Answer me."

"Yes, yes!" Pauline howled. "She doesn't deserve to be in bed with you—I do!"

"Then so be it," Simon said.

If Maggie weren't seeing this with her own eyes, she would never believe it. Simon had just broken her wrist, not to mention her spirit, and Pauline was looking at him with an expression near ecstasy as he bent toward her. Her happiness changed to unease when he lifted her off the floor with one hand under her chin.

When Pauline's neck was level with his mouth, Simon's fangs extended from his mouth. Pauline opened her mouth in horror as his fangs sank into her neck. She tried to push him away, but her feeble effort halted as the sucking sounds grew louder. Only when her body was completely limp and her eyes rolled into the back of her head did Simon fling her to the floor like so much garbage.

Walking over the lifeless heap that had been Pauline Manchester, Simon stepped into the open doorway and bellowed, "Trevor!"

Within seconds, a middle-aged man appeared in the doorway. "Sir?"

"Cut her head off, then throw it in the furnace," Simon ordered. "Throw her body off the docks. If it washes up on shore, the police will assume some fiend murdered her."

Without a word or a glance at Maggie tied up on the bed, Trevor picked up Pauline's body and left the room.

Simon shut the door, and then turned to Maggie.

Before Simon could do anything, Maggie spoke up.

"Pauline wouldn't have gotten past that man unless you wanted her to."

"Correct."

"Is he a vampire too?"

"Trevor?" Simon laughed. "No, merely a devoted servant. There are far too few of them in your century."

"Why did you kill Pauline?" Maggie demanded.

"A boring business matter."

"Business?"

"Pauline's mother owns some land in England that I desire," Simon explained as he used the scarlet cloth to wipe Pauline's blood away. "She set a ridiculous price. I believe she kept dickering with me in the hope that I would become attracted to her plain albeit beloved daughter. When she finds out that Pauline's been murdered, she'll be a broken women. It will be child's play to take advantage of her grief and obtain the land."

"You killed Pauline to close a business deal?"

"Never mind," Simon said shortly. "I'd much rather discuss pleasure than business." He stroked Maggie's fiery hair.

Maggie shivered. "Do you mean it gave you pleasure to kill Pauline?"

"Killing always gives me pleasure, but I was referring to you, sweetheart. You are my pleasure. If you choose to be, Meghann."

Maggie was afraid again. "You said you're not going to kill me."

"Unless you ask me to. Will you stay with me, Meghann? Or do you want to leave this room as Pauline did?"

"Stay with you?" Maggie asked. "Do you mean you'd make me a vampire?"

"It's already started. You noticed today that you didn't cast a reflection."

"Couldn't you just let me go home?" Maggie pleaded. "I know you can make me forget tonight—like you made me forget you biting me before. Let me go home, please."

"Home?" Simon questioned. Maggie's heart stopped at the black look on his face. "I offer you eternal life . . . and you beg for release into a mundane existence. Perhaps I should kill you."

Maggie started crying. "Then kill me, you vile beast! I'm not Pauline . . . I won't beg you. If you want to kill me, then do it! I want to go home. I want my father. I wish I never met you, whatever the hell you are!"

Simon undid the restraints on her wrists. "You are free to leave."

Maggie sat up, and nearly passed out from blood loss and shock. *I won't let him see me faint,* she thought grimly, and struggled to put her feet on the ground. She had to lean on the nightstand to get up from the bed. Once she was standing, another dizzy spell attacked her, but she managed to stay on her feet. *Now all I have to do is walk.* Maggie took one step away from the nightstand, and fell on her face.

Simon picked her up and put her on the bed. He lay down and held Maggie close to him. "I admire your spirit, Meghann."

Maggie tried to push herself away from him, but she was too weak. "If you can read my thoughts, you must know I hate you."

"You don't hate me. You're confused and I frightened you. I apologize. I forget how young you are and how strange this must be to you."

"Can't you let me go?" Maggie pleaded again.

"You saw how frail you are. Meghann, if I don't complete the transformation, you'll die within a few days. Your life can never return to what it was."

Maggie knew he wasn't lying. She could feel how

weak she was; she knew she was dying. "I don't want to die."

"Look at me," Simon commanded. Maggie raised her head, wincing at the pain in her neck. "What is your decision?" he asked.

I want to be with him, Maggie thought suddenly. *Nothing else matters.* She managed to lift up her hand and caress his face softly.

Simon put his arms around her, then kissed her fiercely. The sickness faded beside the passion Maggie felt. *I have never wanted anything as much as I want him,* she thought hazily.

"You're beautiful," he whispered. He ran his hands lightly across her body, fingertips barely touching her. Maggie moaned, aching with desire. Pauline had already been forgotten.

"Tell me who I am," he ordered while thrusting into her.

"My master." She didn't feel any regret or embarrassment for calling him "my master." *I want to belong to him,* she thought while she writhed beneath him.

"And you'll be mine forever?"

"Forever."

Simon sank his teeth deep within the wounds on her neck again. Maggie moaned, digging her nails into his back. The rapture she now felt made her prior ecstasy pale in comparison. She felt wave after wave of intense, unbearable pleasure as he drained the blood from her. Maggie felt him growing harder within her as he drank her blood. It seemed to go on forever, making love while he drank her blood. She didn't want it to ever stop.

They climaxed together and Simon withdrew from her. He raised his wrist to his fangs and bit down. When the blood appeared, he held his wrist to Maggie's lips and told her to drink it.

Maggie drank deeply, then gagged. It tasted horrible, like vinegar and some indefinable sour taste. When Simon pulled his wrist away, she felt the sickness return—ten times stronger than it had been before.

Simon put the restraints back on her wrists. "I'm sorry, love, but transformation is a painful, shocking process. I must restrain you, or you might hurt yourself."

Maggie barely heard him. The only thing she could concentrate on was the pain. It was terrible, and it was all over her body. She felt like her bones were melting, like the skin was being peeled off her body. Dimly she heard herself screaming, and felt her body convulsing. Now it hurt too much to scream; she was breathing in short, shallow gasps. It was like there was an iron clamp on her bones, and someone kept tightening it. Just when Maggie thought the pain couldn't get any worse, she would be assaulted by a fresh wave of agony. And it was cold! If only someone would stop the cold. Cold and pain, cold and pain—it was a repetitious drum in her mind. Maggie couldn't think; she became a screaming, crying, shivering thing with no focus on anything but the pain and the cold.

At some point, she thought she saw her father's face. "Oh, Daddy, please make it stop," she tried to say. Then she saw other familiar faces, but the pain made them leave her. *Come back,* she thought incoherently. *Why are you leaving me? Come back and make it stop.* As the pain worsened, Maggie curled into a ball as much as the restraints would allow her. In delirium, she thought, *Can't anybody take this away? Help me, help me.*

Then a voice answered her. The voice said it was her master, and he could make the pain stop. "Focus on my voice," her master told her.

"I can't," she heard herself say.

"Yes, you can. The pain isn't your master. . . . I am. Heed me, and the pain will stop."

Yes, Maggie thought, nearly insane from agony. *My master can make the pain stop; I must listen to my master.* Gradually, through the long horrible night, Maggie was able to listen to her master. When the pain nearly drove her to the brink of insanity, her master forced it to recede.

As her master banished the pain, he told Maggie certain things in a soft, hypnotic voice. She must always obey him, or the pain would come back.

"I'll always obey you, Master." Yes, if she obeyed her master, the pain couldn't get to her—he'd make it stay away.

Finally the pain snapped. Maggie—no, her master preferred Meghann—opened her eyes. Simon was by her side, and he took off the restraints.

"It's time to rest, darling. It's nearly sunrise." He stretched out on the bed beside her.

"Am I a vampire now?" Meghann asked drowsily.

"Almost," Simon answered, and gathered her into his arms. "First you must feed. But now we both need to rest. Sleep, my love."

With that, Meghann fell asleep in her master's arms, unaware of the horror he had in mind for the next evening.

FIVE

"It's beautiful, isn't it?"

"I love it," she replied. "I love you." Maggie never got tired of watching the sun rise over the skyline. It brought the cool, gray buildings to life. But why did she feel so cold? Johnny had been called to active duty in July—it was summertime. "Johnny, I'm cold."

Johnny chucked her playfully under the chin. "Sorry about that, Raggedy Ann," he said, using the name he'd teased her with when they were children. "That'll teach you to go around sleeping with strange vampires."

"That never happened," she assured him. "If it had, I wouldn't be here. Vampires can't stand sunlight."

"Maggie, you have to help me with the blood drive." Pauline Manchester was standing in front of Johnny, her navy blue suit soaked in blood.

"Go away, Pauline; I can't help you. Simon took all my blood."

"Maggie, you have to help me. It's the least you can do after you let Simon kill me."

"No, I'm watching the sunrise. It's the last time I'm going to see Johnny for three years." It's freezing up here. Maggie started shivering. And why was Johnny's uniform covered in blood? Had he been wounded?

The rooftop went dark. Maggie looked up at the sun. It had turned black. And the skyline was drenched in blood.

"That's your life now," Johnny told her.

"No!" Maggie shrieked. "Take it back. I don't want it! I don't want it!"

She felt a pair of hands shaking her. "Meghann, wake up."

She sat up with a start.

Simon stroked her hair. "You were having a nightmare, darling."

Meghann threw the quilt over her in an effort to keep warm. "I still am," she moaned. "Everything hurts and I'm so cold."

Simon used a cloth to wipe her clammy forehead. "Do you feel anything else?"

She became aware of another sensation—almost a craving. It was like being hungry, but worse. She felt like her body was being pulled toward something—some magical thing that would make all this misery go away. But what was it that she wanted so badly?

"Blood," Simon told her.

Blood! Yes, that was what she needed; she was going to die if she didn't have it. Meghann clutched at Simon. "You said you're my master," she said wildly. "You have to help me; tell me how to get blood! Help me, please! I don't know what to do. Help me!"

Simon plucked her hands from his shoulders. "Shhh, little one," he soothed. Even through the pain, Meghann was able to perceive that there was something wrong with his comforting. It was masking something else. She thought she saw a nasty gleam of anticipation in his amber eyes. "I know you don't know what to do. Of course I'll help you. As your master, it's my duty to teach you. I'm going to get you someone to feed off right now. Are you ready?"

The pain was making her double over. "Yes," she

gasped. "Please bring me blood." With a small grin, he kissed Meghann and left.

"Don't leave me," she started to plead, but then she thought better of it. Let him leave if he was going to bring back blood. She watched the door anxiously. How long would it take for him to return? The craving was tearing her apart. Meghann was trembling from head to foot; every part of her ached and screamed for blood.

She heard dim sounds outside, like screams. Then she realized that she was hearing a man scream curses at Simon. *Oh, no,* she thought with the beginnings of dread. *I know that voice. It's . . .*

"Johnny!" Meghann gasped when the door flew open.

Simon was holding Johnny by the hair; he had him a few inches off the ground. He did not seem to be expending any more effort to hold on to the struggling, thrashing man than someone would to hold a newspaper. Once he had the door shut, Simon threw Johnny on the floor. Johnny started to scramble toward Meghann.

"Maggie, thank God! You're alive," he started to say, but his relief was replaced with horror when he got a good look at his fiancée. He could barely recognize this woman as Maggie O'Neill. Her skin had no color. She was wearing an ivory gown that looked nearly yellow in comparison to her pallid, corpselike skin. Even her freckles were gone and her lips were chalk white. Her shoulder-length hair fell past her waist. And her fingernails! They were so long that they curved. "What the hell happened to you?"

She saw how the joy on his face died when he looked at her. Now he was looking at her with a mix of pity and disgust. "What's wrong with me?" she cried.

"There is nothing wrong with you," Simon told her.

He grabbed Johnny's right arm and twisted it behind his back. Johnny tried to ram his other elbow into Simon without success. "Be still or I shall break your spine," Simon told him in a tone that left no doubt to his sincerity or his ability to carry out the threat.

He looked over at Meghann, who was praying that the growing suspicion she had was wrong. *No*, she thought in abject horror, *he wouldn't make me . . .*

"Come feed off him," Simon commanded Meghann, confirming her worst fears.

"No!" she gasped.

"Are you disobeying me?" he asked her softly, so softly you could almost miss the menace in his voice.

Meghann's eyes widened and she nervously backed two paces away. Then the pain attacked again, and she cried out.

"Is the pain getting worse?" Simon asked in a grotesque parody of concern.

Meghann couldn't keep from crying out. "Yes!"

"Goddamn it, what's wrong, Maggie?" Johnny cried.

"I told you to be still." Simon shattered his kneecap. Johnny turned nearly as pale as Meghann and crumpled to the floor silently.

"You bastard!" Meghann shrieked at Simon. "Don't you hurt him!"

Simon crossed the room so rapidly she did not even see him move. He loomed over Meghann, who had sunk to the floor, unable to stand, the pain was so terrible. "You are very fortunate that I choose to be amused rather than angered." Casually Simon took her left hand and broke the index finger. She screamed as the new agony reverberated all the way from her injured finger to the base of her spine.

"You will never," he said in that same terribly soft but monstrous voice, "speak to me like that again. Now apologize for the grave insult you have given your master, wretched child."

The agony in her body faded a little besides the absolute terror Meghann felt when she glanced up at Simon. Any thoughts of protest were gone when she saw his eyes glare down at her. "I'm so-sor . . . I'm sorry," she stuttered, so scared her teeth were chattering.

He grabbed her hair. It didn't hurt, but it frightened her. "You're sorry, what?"

Belatedly she remembered. "I'm sorry, Master."

"I accept your apology," Simon told her, tightening his grip on her hair. "Now drink his blood."

Meghann pulled herself onto her knees. "Please, Master," she cried, beyond pride. "I'll do anything else you ask. But please don't make me drink his blood."

Simon laughed softly. "Anything else," he mimicked cruelly while he slapped her face. "Have you any idea how many before you have used that pathetic entreaty with me? It means I'm sorry but you've asked something of me I have no desire to do. But keep asking and perhaps I'll find something I don't mind doing."

Simon yanked her off the ground and pulled her up until she was on eye level with him. "In my time," he said slowly, each word as emphasized as a pistol shot, "people did not give their word lightly. Only last night you swore you would obey me as your master. Yet tonight you curse me, defy me. It would disappoint me greatly if you were merely being flippant, if your vow meant nothing to you."

Meghann was shaking from head to toe in pain and fear. "I meant it," she whimpered.

"Then do as I bid you." Simon let go of her. She stumbled but didn't fall down because he started dragging her by the hair toward Johnny. Tears were streaming down her face, but she didn't dare protest.

Johnny had woken up; he was moaning incoherently.

"Why are you crying, hon?" he mumbled when he saw Maggie above him.

He's only semiconscious, she thought.

"We can't have that." Simon put his hand on Johnny. He became fully alert, screaming from the pain. "Maggie, what the hell is going on?"

"I'm sorry," she started to tell him, but she became distracted by a new aroma in the air. It was subtle but very pleasant. The scent was coming from Johnny; Meghann looked at him with new interest.

Johnny nearly fainted again when he saw the look on her face. It combined intense speculation with a sort of detachment. It was making her pale green eyes glow in the deathly pale skin. Johnny thought she looked inhuman.

Simon noted the change in her demeanor. "It's his blood you smell. Just the smell of blood is making you feel better, isn't it? Drink his blood, sweet. All your agony will vanish the second you sink your teeth into his flesh."

The need for blood was becoming unbearable. Meghann started to lean forward. Her mouth was nearly on Johnny's neck when he whimpered, "Please, Maggie." She fell back, shocked at herself. Was she really about to drink her fiancé's blood? She would have moved away, but Simon grabbed her by the back of her neck and kept her locked in place.

"He's not your fiancé anymore," Simon said in a soothing, low voice. "Look at him. He looks at you with revulsion. He won't love you, sweetheart. He thinks you're a monster now. Don't pity him; use him. You need his blood. You'll die without it."

Meghann didn't really hear him. She heard a new voice inside her that was a thousand times more persuasive than Simon Baldevar. It screamed at her to take the precious blood, pleaded with her not to spare another second.

"That's the blood lust. Listen to it, darling."

She put her hand on Johnny's neck. At the feel of his strong pulse beneath her hand, she felt a brief pain when her blood teeth tore through her gums.

Johnny saw his fiancée looming over him with fangs hanging out of her mouth, and he lost consciousness again.

There was no more room for thought. Meghann was consumed with the desire for blood. She never saw Simon's cruel smile of victory when she leaned down and buried her new teeth in Johnny's jugular vein.

The blood filled her mouth, and Meghann swallowed it down greedily. She'd never forget the first time she tasted blood. She sucked down every drop, loving the rich copper taste. It was healing her; the sickness was fading. She was able to feel her index finger knot back together. There was no pain now and she was warm again. In place of the pain, she felt a power she never imagined existed flowing through her. The blood was giving her Johnny's strength, his life force, and vitality. Meghann kept drinking, reveling in the rush the blood was giving her.

She looked up when she heard a tearing noise. Meghann saw that Simon had cut Johnny's wrist open. He extended the wrist toward her, inviting her to drink with him.

Eagerly she abandoned Johnny's neck and stretched out besides Simon. Together they drained Johnny of his blood. How wonderful to share the blood with her master. Why had she fought him before? He was right; she'd never have to be cold or hurt again. Not as long as there were humans to drink from. . . .

When Johnny was dead, Simon turned to Meghann and started licking the excess blood off her lips and neck. She moaned, and started licking the blood off him too. Before long, Simon pushed the gown up around her thighs. He'd barely entered her before Meghann started to climax, crying out, "Master, I love you! I love you!"

In response, Simon yanked the lacy, silk strings on her bodice apart and attached his mouth to her breasts, sucking and pulling on her tender flesh with the same avid need he'd just devoted to Johnny's wrist. Wide-eyed, Meghann watched Simon lap up the small trickle of blood flowing from her nipple. There was a momentary pain, but it vanished quickly; in its place was a bliss so powerful it made Meghann cling to her master, begging him to drink more of her blood.

"I love you, Master," she cried again. Yes, she loved him—loved the dark, exciting feelings that came alive within her at his lightest touch. She loved how he felt inside her, iron and steel driving into her and filling her with some of his amazing strength. She loved the delicious languor that crept through her while Simon drank from her, and she loved the firm, hard lips on hers that blotted out all other thoughts but taking from him all the satisfaction he could give.

"Good girl." Simon bit down viciously on her neck, sending another pang of desire through her. "You're learning to be a vampire—to devote yourself to pleasure and take from others all you desire. Take all the love you want from me and all the blood you need from them," Simon said, and waved a casual hand at the corpse next to them. "Take and take and take again, Meghann—it's all yours."

"Yes!" she rasped, her green eyes blazing with the same unholy light that had filled them when she first smelled mortal blood. "It's all mine and you gave it to me! I love you, Simon. I love you so much!"

"Show me," Simon said, and Meghann did, matching each forceful thrust with one of her own, unmindful of the lamp that crashed to the floor beside them or the uncomfortable hardwood floor her back slammed against as she and Simon tore into each other with ferocious need.

Afterward, with Simon still caressing her slick, sticky form, she looked down at her breasts, bemused to discover for all of Simon's harsh treatment there wasn't so much as a faint bruise on her creamy white skin.

Maybe I can't be scarred or bruised anymore, Meghann thought, and pulled the laces on her negligee together, trying without success to keep her eyes away from the dead body a few feet from her. The ecstasy of sex and drinking blood faded when she looked down at Johnny's corpse. *What have I done? I murdered my fiancé and then had sex a few inches from his dead body. What have I become?*

A vampire, Simon told her without speaking.

"I heard you," she told him out loud.

"Of course you did. Telepathy is just one of your new gifts."

"Telepathy?"

"The ability to hear thoughts," Simon explained.

Meghann considered that as she looked at Johnny's body again. *Did I kill the man I was supposed to marry and drink his blood so I could hear thoughts?* Meghann was shocked by how little she felt. *What is wrong with me?*

Simon gently pulled her away from the corpse. He sat down on the bed, placing her in his lap. "Darling, why are you pushing yourself to feel something utterly useless? He was a mortal; we don't owe them anything. Humans are a source of nourishment to us, nothing more."

Meghann glared at him. "Was that all I was to you at Pauline's party—a source of nourishment?"

Simon's mouth twitched. "Silly child, I would not

have transformed you if I felt that way. I'm in love with you."

Meghann looked back at Johnny. *Can I regard people as nothing more than the means to an end, a way to satisfy my needs?*

"Don't think that way, sweetheart. Look at yourself and tell me what you feel."

Meghann looked down at herself. Her skin had color again—it looked like cream. And apart from her uncertainty, she felt wonderful. All the weakness was gone; she felt a sense of strength and euphoria.

"You look breathtaking," Simon told her. "You were beautiful before, but now you dazzle me." He pushed her hair away from her face.

"What's going to happen to me now?" she asked him.

"What do you mean?"

"Well, I can't go home."

"You are home, my love. Your home is with me."

"Why are you doing this?"

"I told you—I love you."

"But you hardly know me."

"I know all I need to know." Simon stood up and took Meghann's hand. "Now let's go out—I'm finding this room oppressive."

"Out?" she said dumbly.

"You didn't think you were going to spend eternity in this room, did you?"

"No, but . . ."

"Then let's go."

"Wait a minute," she snapped, and felt nervous again when he raised his eyebrows at her tone. "Please? I have more questions."

"Very well, you may ask me a few more questions." Simon lounged against the door.

"Have you done this before?"

"Transformation? Of course, and I made the people who accepted my gift pay for it with everything they held dear."

"How am I supposed to pay?" she asked.

"That is what makes you unique, darling." He took both her hands in his, and searched her eyes intently. "All I want from you is love. Will you find that so difficult?"

I don't know, she thought. *What do I know about this man? That he's capable of the most amoral, evil kind of behavior. Inflicting pain at will. That he's made me into something I barely understand. He does terrible things, yet he can be loving a second later. And I feel so safe and happy when I look in his gold-brown eyes.*

That gave Meghann a very disquieting thought. "Simon," she asked hesitantly, "are you making me love you?"

He howled with laughter and sank to the floor. "Precious child, I have been accused of lacking scruples before, but I assure you I have standards. I have cast no evil spell over you. I promise you your feelings are your own." He took her face in his hands. "Now tell me what those feelings are."

Meghann stroked his hair and thought the eager but cautious look in his eyes almost made him seem vulnerable. It was seeing that brief softness that made her lean over and kiss him softly.

He kissed her back and murmured, "I knew you wouldn't disappoint me. Now let's leave this room. Come along, I'm sure you'll want to bathe."

Meghann followed him, stepping over Johnny's corpse without a second glance. She was more interested in what Simon had just said. "Bathe?"

"Were you planning to go out like that?" He took in her unwashed, tangled hair and the drops of blood on her neck and chest.

"Of course not, but I didn't think vampires bathed."

"How did you think they kept clean?"

"I never really thought about it."

"I don't imagine you did." He led Meghann up a flight of stairs into what she assumed was the living room. Whatever flaws he has, the man has excellent taste, Meghann thought to herself.

The room had a high ceiling, with a softly lit chandelier. She admired the Oriental rug, sconces, and sumptuous furnishings. Meghann was drawn to a tapestry of two knights fighting that hung over the fireplace. She pointed to it. "Is that authentic?"

"Of course it is. French—done in the late 1300s. Do you like my home?"

"It's beautiful." She wandered over to the massive floor-to-ceiling bookcases, teeming with books. It was plainly a room decorated with wealth and taste, so much more interesting than Pauline's elegant but cold home.

"Evelyn Manchester did not decorate that house. Like most nouveau riche, she allowed a decorator to tell her what to do. The result is a home with no personality. I'm glad you have taste enough to discern the difference." Simon pulled her away before she could start reading some of the titles in the bookcase. "You may admire your new home to your heart's content later. For now, I'd like you to get dressed—I made reservations for nine-thirty."

Meghann glanced at him. "Do you always assume things will go your way?"

"I don't assume. I know." Trevor groveled up to Simon, who issued a few curt orders concerning Johnny's body. The servant immediately headed downstairs to carry out his bidding.

"Is that man your slave?" she asked Simon.

"Don't be silly. I told you he is my servant, and I pay

him a substantial wage for his services." Simon directed her upstairs to shower and dress. "I told Trevor to buy everything you would need."

The first thing Meghann did was cut and file the claws on her hands into manageable nails. Then she brushed her teeth vigorously, trying to get the taste of blood out of her mouth. She ran a cautious hand over her gums. She felt two slight bumps; she assumed these were her new blood teeth.

In the steaming shower, Meghann considered the events of the evening. Her foremost thought was that this man she hardly knew, Simon Baldevar, held her life in his hands. She couldn't go home to her father or Bridie—that meant she wasn't just depending on Simon to explain what being a vampire meant; she needed him for basic necessities like food and shelter. What would happen if he grew bored with her or if she did something to offend him?

Why me? Why did he make me a vampire? He says he loves me, but I don't understand it. She knew she was pretty, but if she was honest, there were girls who were a lot prettier. There were models and showgirls; with his looks and apparent wealth, he certainly could have as many of those girls as he wanted. *So why me?*

She stepped out of the shower, and eyed the black-marble tub. How much money does he have, anyway, she thought as she brushed her hair with a gold-backed brush. She caught a glimpse of her half reflection in the mirror above the long marble sink counter. It was just as well that Trevor hadn't included makeup—there was no way she could apply it.

The dressing room made Meghann feel like she'd died and gone to heaven. A walk-in closet was stuffed with clothing and furs. When did he buy all this stuff? A full-length mirror with wings that closed to display a medieval love scene of a lady leaning over a knight, who looked up at her in adoration, a vanity table, and cream damask silk with green accents covered the walls.

"Do you like it?" Simon entered the room, fully dressed. He held out a floor-length spring-green dress with a matching cape. He also gave her black satin strap sandals and stockings. Where did he find those? They hadn't been available for years.

"The room or the dress?"

"Both."

Meghann sat at the dressing table, and stared down at her long hair in bewilderment until Simon came to her and expertly gathered it into a chignon. "Soon enough you'll learn to groom yourself without a mirror. After all, blind mortals do it with ease. Now, do you like your suite?"

"It's lovely." She put on the dress, and ran her hand over her neck. The wounds had vanished.

Simon took in her appearance. "The dress matches your eyes."

"Trevor forgot makeup."

"No, he didn't. It's a pity you can't see your face clearly—you're breathtaking. You have no need of cosmetics. Are you ready to leave?"

She turned to him. "Why am I see-through in the mirror?"

He took her face in his hands. "Because you are no longer human. Vampires do not cast full reflections, nor can they be caught on film."

"But why?" She hesitated and forced herself to ask, "Is it because we're evil?"

"Evil is a matter of interpretation. Certainly, in the mortal world, you would be considered an evil creature, if someone could force themselves to believe you existed. People refuse to acknowledge our existence; they relegate us to the world of myth."

"So I can't go in the sun, I don't cast a full reflection,

and to people, I'm an abomination. What do we have to make it worthwhile?"

"Unquestioned dominion over the night, freedom from death and disease. Meghann, when we step outside—I have given you the night forever. No one can harm us at night; we are invincible. You will have power you never dreamed of over people—to hunt, to make them do your bidding. All we give up is the sun—in a few years, you'll barely remember it. As for your reflection, don't let it cause you sadness. It is undeniable proof that you are a supernatural creature." Simon pulled her up, and kissed her. "And you, precious child, have something no other vampire does."

"What is that?"

"My love. Now let's leave this place so you can see the new world I have given you."

When Meghann stepped outside with him, the lights and noise of the city assaulted her. The worst was that she could hear the thoughts of everyone who passed by. . . . She felt like she was going to pass out.

Meghann, Simon's voice cut into the chaos in her head. *Can you hear me?*

Yes, she answered silently.

Imagine a radio. Now look at that radio and find the volume. Turn the volume all the way down.

It took her a few minutes to hold the radio image in her mind long enough to turn the volume, but when she did, the noise was cut off abruptly.

"It's gone," she said in wonder.

"Very good," Simon told her. "Few novices learn so quickly. You're going to make an excellent vampire, my love. For now, concentrate on me. It's easier to ignore the noise of mortals' thoughts when you're focused on something else. If it comes back, imagine the radio again."

He hailed a taxi, and directed the driver to the Waldorf.

Simon ordered red wine, a bottle of 1924 Mouton Rothschild—impressing their waiter.

"Bela Lugosi never drank wine," she remarked when the waiter left.

Simon's mouth quirked. "I guess this is the right time for a discussion on vampire myths. Is your knowledge of vampires limited to Hollywood movies?"

"I read *Dracula*," she answered with a sniff.

"Even worse. Well, ask your questions, sweetheart. What do you wish to know?"

"Do I have to sleep in a coffin now?" she questioned.

Simon laughed so loud a few of the diners turned to stare. "Did you sleep in one last night?"

"Well," she said, floundering, "I wasn't exactly a vampire then."

"But I was. Do you recall me vanishing to find my coffin filled with the dirt of my burial place to keep my powers strong? What a macabre notion." Simon shook his head in distaste. "No coffin, darling. The only thing you must do is make sure you sleep in a place that allows in no sunlight. The sun will destroy a vampire. What other notions shall I disabuse?"

"Well, the bit about crosses can't be true," she said half to herself. "You touched my mother's cross. What about garlic—can that hurt you? Can vampires turn into mist or bats?"

"Why would I want to turn myself into a filthy, rabid creature like a bat?"

The waiter came to take their order, temporarily postponing vampire discussion. Simon advised Meghann to have steak, and he ordered lobster for himself.

As the waiter wrote down their order, she heard him

say, "Lucky fella. How come I don't get to sit here with a pretty piece like that?"

Startled, she started to ask what the hell was the matter with him when Simon put a restraining hand on her wrist.

You heard his thoughts, Meghann—like you're hearing mine right now. That can happen when a human thinks something with a great deal of force.

After the waiter left, she asked, "So you don't hear everything people think?"

"The dreary, stumbling, mundane thoughts of most mortals are of no interest to me. I hear what I want to hear."

She thought about the food he had just ordered. "We can eat?" she asked.

"You must eat. Forget that *excuse me, I already dined* foolishness of fiction." Simon laughed briefly and then buttered a roll. "I always thought that a rather ridiculous presumption. If we were dead, why should it matter what we ingested? And if food was a hazard, mortals would not need crosses—they could kill us by forcing a chocolate bar down our throats. Listen carefully, Meghann. You are not undead, or any of the other precious phrases your movies have taught you about vampirism. In some ways, you'll find your life unchanged. You'll eat, drink, and groom yourself as you always have. As far as garlic goes, vampires are sensitive creatures. We are alive to sensation in a way that mortals cannot comprehend. In time, that will provide you with great pleasure, but for now, you are vulnerable. Garlic would overwhelm you . . . the same way that cognac did the other night. Keep your palate simple for the time being, Meghann."

Simon leaned back and sipped some wine. "Excellent. As I said, you are not dead. What you are is, quite simply, supernatural. You are no longer human. When the sun rises, you will sleep—that is not something you can control. You will find that when the dawn comes later tonight, you will start to feel very tired and weak. It is imperative to get to a resting place before the sun comes up. When the sun sets, you will wake up. Actually, vampires usually rise about an hour before the sun sets—during dusk."

"Besides sunlight, what can kill a vampire?"

"What a morbid question. Well, the books are right about a stake through the heart, but that doesn't kill you right away. It takes a few hours—agonizing hours. Sunlight, on the other hand, will kill you in a matter of minutes."

The food arrived, and Meghann tore into the steak, quite relieved that vampirism didn't mean giving up her favorite foods. She looked up, then asked, "What are the new gifts you said I have now?"

"Well, you just asked me if I could transform into a bat. I can't, but I could certainly convince mortals that I had turned into a bat before their eyes. A vampire's greatest gift is the power of mind. You can use your will to make mortals do or think anything you desire."

"So you just used your will to make me forget you'd bitten me?"

"Until I wanted you to remember—it's a bit like hypnosis. You can also read mortal thoughts; you have superhuman strength and an incredible ability to heal yourself. If I were to reach across the table and smash your adorable nose, it would heal in a matter of minutes. A gunshot wound could not harm you, nor could poison—"

"Can you fly?" she interrupted. "Do you live forever?"

"I'll give you a lesson on 'flying' later. As for immortality, you will live as long as you have the will to live. I know of vampires who have lived over a thousand years.

Then, when they were tired or too lonely, some died simply because they wished it. Others have greeted the sunrise to end their lives, or had a human servant expose their sleeping bodies to the sunlight."

"Servants." Meghann was horror-struck. "What about that man . . . Trevor? Couldn't he just decide to expose you to the sun during the day?"

"The room where we shall rest is impenetrable. No one may enter once I lock it."

Meghann ate silently, considering all Simon told her. None of it—her reflection, killing Johnny Devlin, sitting in the Oak Room having this insane conversation—seemed quite real. She felt like she was stuck inside a dream. *So when am I going to wake up?*

Over dessert, Simon reached into his jacket and withdrew a small black box.

"Another gift?" Meghann asked as she opened it.

"More than a gift, sweet," he told her softly.

The box held a gold signet ring that had an emerald on each shoulder, with the inscription *"nul si bien"* on the bezel. "None so well," she translated.

"How did you know that, Meghann?"

"Medieval history class," she told him.

She held the ring up to the light, admiring the fiery sparks in the dull gold. "Was that your family's motto?" she asked.

"Yes. What else did you learn in this class? Why would a man give a woman a ring with his family's insignia?"

Meghann realized the significance of the ring. "For marriage," she said softly. "Is this a wedding ring?" she asked him.

Simon took the ring from her, and picked up her left hand. "It is," he replied. "With this ring, I pledge my worldly goods, my love, and my solemn promise to teach you all you need to know as a vampire. Do you accept?"

"What do I pledge in return, Master?" she said, not taking her eyes off his.

"Love, obedience, and loyalty. Can you give me those things?"

"Please tell me why you chose me," she implored. "I was thinking before—there are so many girls in the world, and plenty of them more beautiful, richer, smarter than I am. Why me?"

Simon took her other hand. "Yes, there are many beautiful women in the world. And I have enjoyed the attentions of thousands of beautiful women. Most, I drank their blood and killed them. You are asking me how you are different?"

She nodded.

"Beauty is not enough to hold my interest. As for wealth, I have more than enough—I do not need to transform a woman to gain more. I fell in love with you, Meghann. I fell in love with the hectic energy and supreme confidence I felt within you—and witnessed when you asked me to dance with you. I suspect part of that is your origin—New Yorkers have a zest for living others lack."

Simon paused, then looked away. Meghann noticed that his hands were trembling a little. "I have never been in love before. Do you know how many years I have longed for someone like you? Someone with beauty, intelligence, and an inner fire to match my own. I have never loved anyone else—never wished to share my life, never wanted to love and protect a woman the way I long to love and protect you. Will you let me do that?"

Whatever she came to think of Simon Baldevar in later years, in that moment she loved him. His words and the simple, earnest look in his amber eyes pulled on her heart. She forgot the terrible things she'd seen him do. For that one moment, they were nothing more than a man and a woman in love.

"I pledge to you my loyalty, love, and . . . obedience," she said in a soft but clear voice.

Simon put the ring on her finger. "I had Trevor get it sized for your hand. Unless you break the ring or your finger, it's not coming off."

Meghann admired the ring. "I don't want it to come off. Who else has worn it?"

Simon narrowed his eyes, and went from a love-struck boy to a hawk. "What do you mean?"

"Nothing," she said, startled by his change of mood. "It's just that you said this is a family ring. I thought maybe your mother or other relatives must have worn it."

"Forgive me for snapping at you, sweet. I thought you were implying that I had given it to other women— which I have not. As for the ring's lineage, be patient, Meghann. In time, I shall share my history with you— and the history of my family."

He smiled again, erasing the harsh look from his face. "Shall we go? I would like to give you some lessons before tonight is over."

SIX

"Write a letter to your father," Simon instructed her. He'd taken her to his study, where he guided her to the huge black leather chair behind his massive oak desk.

Meghann looked in bewilderment at the blank parchment and fountain pen before her. "What am I supposed to write? What should I tell him?"

"That you are sorry for abruptly disappearing last night, but you and I have decided to elope. You don't want him to worry about you. Tell him that due to a pressing business engagement, we had to leave the country immediately. You are not sure when we'll be back in the States, but you'll keep in touch." Simon kissed Meghann lightly, and started to leave the room. "I'll be back in a few minutes, darling."

"Dear Daddy," she started to write, and the room swirled alarmingly. Writing "Daddy" broke down the protective state of shock she was in. *Maggie,* part of her soul cried out to her, *this is wrong! Simon Baldevar is evil; why am I here?* Then another, younger part of her screamed, *Get me out of here! I want this to end; I want my daddy!*

Meghann started to sob, and pushed the paper away. The thought of never seeing her father again was break-

ing her heart. *What have I done?* she thought. *I'm scared.*
She had seen enough to know that Simon could go
from a sweet, tender lover to a callous madman in a
matter of seconds. *Dear God, what would he do if he came
in right now and saw me crying?*

That thought cut off her tears like a slap across the
face. *I can't ever even think unhappy or disloyal thoughts; I
must control myself around him. Never give him a reason to
hurt me like he did Johnny and Pauline.*

Meghann, a new cold part of her whispered. She recognized that voice—it was the blood lust, the part that
begged her to drink Johnny's blood. *Meghann, be sen-
sible,* it advised. *Even if you despise Simon, right now
he's all you've got. Do you honestly think your father
would want to see you the way you are now? Would he
open his arms to you if he knew that you killed Johnny?
Write that damned letter, and don't ever think of the
past again. Think only of Simon.*

She knew the voice was right; this was a matter of
survival. Like a sleepwalker, she picked up the pen and
managed to write the letter without really thinking
much about it.

April 24, 1944
Dear Daddy,
    I know you must be worried to death about me.
I'm so sorry that I didn't call you last night, but
everything has happened so quickly I've hardly
had a chance to think.
    Lord Baldevar proposed, and I accepted. I
know I should have waited to tell you, but he has
pressing business in London. I know that sounds
vague, but it has to do with the war effort and I
really cannot tell you any more than that. I will
write soon, to let you know where I am, and when
we will visit America again.

Please tell Johnny Devlin how sorry I am. That is the coward's way out, making you tell him, but I can't stand the thought of writing a Dear John letter. Please give my love to Bridie, Frankie, Theresa, Paul, Peter, Brian, Seamus, and Patrick.

Daddy, I love you so much. No girl could have had a better father.

Love,
Maggie

There, Meghann thought to herself grimly. *That's the last time I think of myself as Maggie.* Maggie brought to mind an innocent, happy girl with no thoughts more serious than baseball games, dances, or cramming for an exam she'd ignored. Maggie had nothing to do with the creature Simon had created.

Simon came back in, holding a pile of clothes that he put on an armchair. "Done already? Very good, let me see it."

Meghann handed him the letter without comment.

He read it quickly, and smiled over the letter. "Wonderful touch, Meghann—that bit about your fiancé. Well done. Trevor will deliver it to your father tomorrow."

"What if he wants to see me?"

"We won't be here, pet. We have a seven o'clock flight to Cuba."

"Why Cuba?"

"I own a casino there. You'll like it, Meghann. A very fertile ground for vampires. Speaking of which, would you like to learn to hunt now? It will distract you from your sadness."

Surprised that he knew she'd been crying, she looked at him. Was he angry with her?

He turned the chair around, and knelt before Meghann. "Sweet, I am not an ogre. I know that you're bemused by all that has happened in the past few days; I expect that there would be some grief and confusion."

"You're not mad?" she asked timidly.

He kissed her on the lips. "However sad you are, the fact remains that you chose me. That is all that matters. Your uncertainty will fade when you realize what lies before you. Particularly when you feel the exhilaration of the hunt. Are you ready?"

She felt some anticipation at his words. She nodded.

"Put these on." He handed her the pile of clothing.

Meghann examined them with distaste. There was a long black skirt that was far too tight; it clung to her body like a second skin. Then there was a pair of cheap red shoes with five-inch heels, and an off-the-shoulder red top that came dangerously close to exposing her breasts.

"I can't wear red," she protested. "It's going to look horrible with my hair."

Simon stroked the long red hair. "You have beautiful hair, darling. But I think you'll wish to disguise it when you hunt for prey—it's far too distinctive." He handed her a long, frizzy blond wig.

She put it on, careful to make sure her real hair was completely covered. "I look awful!" she wailed. "Cheap and tacky—like some streetwalker!"

"Precisely the effect I was looking for—and you could never look awful." He eyed the costume with amusement.

She wobbled on the precarious heels for a few minutes before she was able to walk normally. "It's not enough you made me a vampire—now you're going to turn me into a hooker?"

Simon chuckled. "What an amusing creature you are, Meghann. And I would never turn my pretty little consort into a hooker—but you're about to find it an invaluable disguise."

Simon escorted her to the Times Square area, where several women had on outfits that made Meghann's look conservative. With her newly improved vision, she also spotted several hard-looking men lurking in dark corners, keeping an eye on the garishly dressed women.

"Are those pimps?" she asked Simon.

"I would imagine so," he replied. "Their merchandise leaves much to be desired, in my opinion."

"Will they bother us?"

"No one bothers me, sweet." As though he was illustrating the point, one of the pimps started stalking over to Simon, widened his eyes, and then retreated back to his corner.

"What did you do?" Meghann asked.

"I put a vivid image in his head of what can happen to mortals who bother the wrong person—something you will learn how to do in time. For now, I want you to focus your entire attention on one person—try that man over there." Simon pointed to a rotund gentleman standing under a streetlight a few feet from them. "What did I tell you about the radio?"

"To turn the volume all the way down."

"Now you are going to look at him and turn the volume up a tiny bit."

Meghann looked at the man and imagined turning the volume up. Immediately the noise of the street assaulted her. Myriad thoughts—*I need a fix; he'll kill me if I don't get a john; my feet hurt*—rushed through her head. She staggered, and would have fallen if Simon hadn't grabbed her by the shoulders.

"Steady," Simon whispered. "Concentrate, Meghann. Center your entire attention upon him. . . . No one else exists."

Meghann opened her eyes and looked at the man again. She was standing at least four feet from him, but with her new senses, she could make out every detail.

She smelled the cologne he wore; she observed that his gray suit was a good cut but ill-kept. There were small wrinkles and a minuscule food stain on the lapel. His grossly fat stomach had caused two buttons to pop on his white shirt.

As Meghann stared, she cautiously raised the volume by a fraction. This time, it worked; she received his thoughts without interference from anyone else on the street.

She turned to Simon, delighted with herself. "It's working!" she shouted in triumph. Several people turned to stare, but they looked away when Simon waved his hand. He grinned at Meghann, and silently told her to lower her voice.

"His name is Arnold Greene," she whispered. Simon nodded in encouragement and Meghann went on. "He's sixty-two years old, and married. He's a corporate attorney, and he makes a lot of money, but he's here tonight because . . . because . . ." Meghann got the full thrust of his thoughts and snapped, "Oh, that's disgusting!"

"I suppose it is distasteful when you take the fellow's appearance into account. But how can you turn his desire to your advantage?"

"What do you mean?"

"He wants a pretty young girl to satisfy desires his wife finds repugnant." Simon raised his eyebrows. "Don't you fit the bill?"

Now Meghann understood the purpose of the hooker garb. What an ingenious way to find men, get them alone, and drain their blood!

Simon saw understanding bloom on her face. "Go to him, sweetheart. There is a cheap motel a block away. He'll take you there, and you'll take his blood." He saw some slight anxiety cross her face. He patted her awful wig for support. "Don't be frightened. I'll be nearby if anything goes wrong. But I have a feeling it won't—I think you're going to pass this test with flying colors." Without warning, Simon disappeared. No one seemed to take any notice. *When will he show me how to do that?* Meghann wondered.

Taking a deep breath, she walked over to Arnold Greene, ignoring the baleful stares of the whores.

One grabbed her arm, and hissed, "This is my corner, sister!"

Meghann pushed her. She thought it a slight nudge, but the woman flew off the ground and crashed into a row of trash cans. None of the other hookers bothered Meghann.

She tapped Arnold on the shoulder. He turned around, and she smiled sweetly. "Hello, would you like a date?"

Arnold stared at her, mouth slightly open.

Come on, she thought impatiently. *Ask me how much.*

"How much?"

My God, she thought. *All I have to do is think something, and people do what I tell them.* This new mental ability combined with the physical strength made her look at vampirism in a new light. Maybe this is a good thing, after all. Meghann was so electrified by the thought of her new power that she almost forgot about the man in front of her.

Since she hadn't responded, the man plowed ahead. "Look," he said, poking her shoulder to get her attention, "I'll go five dollars and the price of the room. Take it or leave it."

"Fine."

Arnold Greene smiled, exposing several missing teeth. "Let's go."

He escorted her to a seedy-looking hotel that had several disreputable characters lolling around in the dimly lit and foul-smelling lobby. He paid the clerk and got the key to a small, dark, tacky room that had an ancient scarred wooden dresser and a sagging metal-frame bed. With her new hearing, Meghann heard a man beating a woman with a belt in a room several doors down; she also heard roaches scurrying through the walls. That sound made her shiver—she hated bugs.

"You're awfully pretty," Arnold told her, tearing off his suit. "Have you been doing this long?"

"No. Actually, you're my first," she smiled.

"Oh, yeah?" he questioned, vanity puffing him up. "Well, I tell you what—we'll start you off light, honey. Just give me a blow job."

"A what?" she asked blankly. She wouldn't look into his head for clarification—that sounded thoroughly repulsive.

Arnold pushed his pants down around his ankles. "You know—put it in your mouth and suck me off." He gestured impatiently to his penis. "Come on, honey, get on your knees. I'm paying you good money." He placed a $5 bill on the dresser.

Meghann resisted an urge to giggle. How ironic. She'd been transformed into a vampire, drank blood, and she still could be shocked by the thought of a previously unknown sex act. She was about to object when she remembered a most interesting fact from biology class: *During an erection, the penis fills with blood.*

No, she couldn't do that . . . could she? Well, why not? Hadn't she murdered her own fiancé to satisfy the blood lust several hours before? If she could kill Johnny, the boy who gave her her first kiss, whom she fully expected to marry before the end of summer . . .

A rough hand on her shoulders yanked Meghann out of her reverie. "Get on your fucking knees."

"Get your filthy hands off me!" Meghann snarled, and the mortal backed away so fast one would have thought her skin had turned to fire beneath his hand.

"I don't want any trouble," Arnold whined, and started to shuffle nervously toward the door, hampered by the pants still pooled around his feet.

"Come on, baby," Meghann cooed. She gave him the most enchanting smile she could muster, and hastily unbuttoned her top to expose her breasts. "Don't leave when I haven't had a chance to show you a good time yet."

She didn't know if it was her conciliatory tone, her half-naked body that enticed him, or maybe the mortal simply couldn't resist when Meghann told him not to leave. He came away from the door and hurried toward her.

Meghann obediently fell to her knees and gave him a wanton leer before taking the stubby, little penis into her mouth. If Arnold had left, she thought, God only knows what Simon would have done to her.

"Oh," Arnold panted, and mashed her head against his fat stomach. "Yeah, that's good . . . hey!" Pangs of pleasure changed to paroxysms of pain when Meghann sank her blood teeth deep into his penis. Arnold spun around wildly, trying desperately to wrench himself away from the inexorable grip of her teeth. "Stop! Oh, God!" he gasped. His hands on her shoulders weakened, and he sank to the floor, moaning in agony. His penis seemed alive with nerves, each one aching as she sucked the blood from him. He began praying to die, anything to escape the horrible torment this witch was inflicting on him. His last thought was that he would be found in this motel, everyone knowing his shame.

Meghann found an exhilaration she never dreamed existed as Arnold's blood flooded her mouth. This was even better than the neck or wrist—it provided so much blood, so quickly. Why had blood repulsed her when she was mortal? It was wonderful, the strength she gained from feeding. She felt like she could knock down buildings single-handed, and she felt her mind expanding. There was a feeling of great superiority to the man she was feeding off. What was he? Nothing, Simon was right, they were only food. Oh, how alive and invigorated the blood made her!

When Arnold died, his penis went limp and Meghann's blood supply was cut off. She gazed at the man dispassionately. He was completely pale, and his sightless eyes were looking at her with an expression of pain fixed there for eternity. She leaned over and shut them, wondering what she was supposed to do next.

She looked up at the sound of applause. Simon stood in the open doorway. "Darling child," he said, gesturing to the mutilated penis, "you have a talent for depravity I never guessed at." He shut the door and came into the cheap room.

Meghann wiped the blood off her mouth with the filthy sheet from the bed. This time, she hadn't gotten any blood on her body or clothing. "Well, when he asked me to do that . . . you know," she explained, coloring slightly, "it occurred to me that it would be a perfect way to take blood and—"

Simon picked her up and swung her around. "What a sweet child you are . . . to be embarrassed by what that swine asked of you. And you were right—it is an excellent manner of feeding. Not one I would choose to use, but very effective for a female vampire. One thing, sweetheart." He put her down, tilting her chin up to him.

"What I have taught you tonight is an excellent ruse to lure prey. But you are never, *never* to sleep with any man you feed off. I would consider that infidelity. Do you understand me?"

She stood on her tiptoes and kissed him hungrily. When she broke off, she asked him softly, "Why would I want to sleep with them?"

Simon looked down at her, desire darkening his eyes.

"Have you any idea how much you please me?" Then he reached into his blazer and handed Meghann a straight-back razor. "But your lessons for the evening are incomplete." He took her back to Arnold's corpse. "Eradicate the puncture marks with the razor. When you feed, you cannot leave behind any hint that the death could have been caused by a vampire. Now, when the body is discovered, the overworked coroner will assume that a particularly vicious whore killed this man and robbed him. You may also want to consider using a weapon like this from time to time instead of your blood teeth." Simon took Arnold's wallet and pocketed the cash, leaving his identification intact. Then he threw the wallet to the floor and leaned against the peeling, water-stained wallpaper; his expression was one of keen interest as Meghann glanced uneasily between the razor in her hands and the dead man's penis.

Hadn't she just killed this man and felt nothing but contempt for him while she did it? So why was she unable to do as Simon ordered and slash through the incriminating marks so no one would suspect Arnold Greene's true cause of death?

Just do it, Meghann told herself, and brought the shiny steel tip of the razor to the flaccid penis, but then her eyes fell on her victim's wallet. It had landed faceup, exposing a black-and-white photo that made Meghann suck in her breath and blink hard at the tears filling her eyes.

The picture, yellowed from age and crumbling at the edges, showed a smiling Arnold Greene wearing a striped polo shirt with his arm around a little girl Meghann guessed to be about seven or so. The child was no beauty, but she had an enchanting gap-toothed grin and she clutched a huge panda bear almost as big as she was. In the background, Meghann saw the gargantuan, brightly lit Wonder Wheel at Coney Island.

That's his daughter, Meghann thought, and she flung the razor from her, picked up the wallet, and ran her hand gingerly over the picture. *I bet he won that panda for his little girl; just like my daddy won so many toys for me. Oh, this is so wrong—what is this poor girl going to do without her father? What have I done?*

"Enough." Simon moved to grab the wallet from her, but Meghann tightened her grip and screamed "No!" at the top of her voice.

"Give me that wallet, Meghann," Simon ordered, seeming unaffected by the high-pitched screech that put a crack in the wall beside him. Simon's icy, inhuman whisper, combined with an expression that hinted no end of misery was in store for her if she didn't obey, made Meghann reluctantly place the wallet in her master's hands. Her expression was wary and tense when she glanced up at him.

"Leave me alone!" she shrieked when Simon's hand inched toward her. Panicked, Meghann glanced at the straight-back razor and it trembled violently on the floor before it rose up and flew into her hands.

"You have such promise, little one," Simon said, and Meghann turned her astonished gaze toward him.

"I did this?" she questioned hesitantly. "But how?"

"It's called telekinesis," Simon said, and crouched down next to her. "It's the ability to move objects with your mind."

"You're saying my mind made that razor rise off the floor and into my hands?" At Simon's nod, Meghann protested. "But I didn't tell it to do that at all. . . . Really, I didn't. I wouldn't try to hurt you."

Simon laughed lightly and planted a quick kiss on her temple. "But you were afraid I was about to hurt you for disobeying, weren't you?"

"Are you going to hurt me?" Meghann asked uneasily, and Simon laughed again, placing his hands over hers.

"Hurt you? What on earth for?" Simon slipped the razor from her hands, holding it up to the light of the single bulb in the ugly room. "I merely meant to help you finish your work, but in your fear, you thought I'd harm you. It was that fear that brought this new power to life inside you. . . . Your mind put the weapon in your hands so you'd be safe. Would you like to try again?"

"You mean move something else? Oh, yes!" Meghann said, her brief remorse for what she'd done to Arnold Greene utterly forgotten.

Simon arched his hand back and flung the razor at the wall. His aim was accurate and the blade sank half-way through the crumbling plaster wall.

"Get it out of the wall, Meghann, and back into your hands."

Meghann stared at the protruding blade and held her hand out, imagining the blade sliding out of the wall and into her hands. Before she knew what was happening, the thing flew right at her and she ducked to avoid being slashed in the face.

"Simon," she gasped when he handed her the razor after she finally sat up. "I did it—I really did it! I thought something and I made it happen! This is wonderful!"

"Indeed it is." Simon smiled and gestured to the dead man. "Don't you see, darling, that you and I are far, far above our prey? Don't waste your emotions on them or feel shame. Simply do what you need to do and don't give them another thought."

"It's not him I'm concerned with." Meghann tried to explain her sentiments; she picked up the wallet again. "It's just—Simon, can't you see? I feel bad for his family."

"Why? Did you tell Arnold Greene to venture into a dangerous area and satisfy his base urges with some cheap harlot?"

"Well, no, but—"

"There's no but, Meghann. Was he not a grown man, fully aware of the risk he was taking? It is he who has brought shame and grief to his family by choosing to come here this evening, not you. You merely did as any intelligent vampire does and took advantage of the situation. Aren't you happy with the power you gained by draining him?"

Meghann nodded, thinking not only of the fascinating telekinesis but that absolute rush of power and almost unbearable exhilaration she felt when she drank blood.

"If you want to keep experiencing that pleasure without drawing very unwelcome attention to yourself, you must cover your tracks. Now go on, sweetheart. Use that razor as I taught you. That thing on the floor is not your equal or worthy of your guilt."

Simon's right, Meghann told herself firmly, and brought the razor down, slashing through a sizeable chunk of the man's penis to eradicate the wounds. All the while, she swallowed the bile in her throat and drowned out her outraged conscience's protest by repeating over and over, *It's okay. He's not equal to me, not anymore, not ever again. . . .*

"There now," Simon said when she was done, hugging her close. "You'll see how easy it gets with time. And you don't always have to do this. There's drowning, setting fire to the corpse, all sorts of ways to hide our presence from mortals."

Meghann nodded and buried her face in his shirt so she wouldn't have to look at the mutilated corpse, but she pulled away immediately, offended by the cloy-

ing scent of cheap perfume clinging to Simon's clothing.

"Where were you before you came in here?" she
demanded, and the corners of Simon's mouth quirked
at her suspicious tone.

"Why, I had to feed too, little one. I used the young
lady you shoved into the trash cans. Needless to say,
she is on her way to hell as we speak."

"Did you sleep with her? After everything you just
said about infidelity and how I'm never supposed to
sleep with anyone I feed from . . ."

Meghann thought her heated words would anger
him, but Simon only stared into her mutinous eyes,
smiling gently. "What did you just ask me? Sweet, why
would I want a drug-addled, passably pretty but well-
used whore when I have you? If my clothing reeks from
her, it is simply because her body was pressed to mine
when I fed from her. Now erase that scowl from your
pretty face—you need not fear I'll be untrue. I only
want you, darling."

"Oh, Simon," Meghann cried, falling down on the
sagging bed with him. "I only want you too!" Eagerly
she returned his impassioned kisses, feeling an almost
savage delight when she thought this darkly exciting
creature who could have any woman he desired only
wanted her.

I love you so much, Meghann said telepathically so she
wouldn't have to break off the kiss that was becoming
more urgent and full of need. *You make me so happy. I
never knew I could feel like this, feel so free and alive!*

"No more tears and pining for your mortal existence?" Simon inquired with a slight smile.

Meghann shook her head. "I'm not going to cry anymore. I don't need my fam . . . I don't need anyone
from my mortal life as long as I have you."

She thought she saw Simon swallow hard before he

took her into a bone-crushing embrace, feverishly kissing her eyes, cheeks, and lips. "Sweetheart, I was so
hoping you would say that. I knew when you saw what
I had given you, all your pain and longing for the past
would fade. I love you too, my precious child." Then
he sat up, scowling at the gray, sticky sheet on the bed.
"I want very much to make love to you, but I'll be
damned if I'll do it in a horror of a room like this. Do
you remember asking me if vampires could fly?"

"We're going to fly now?" she asked eagerly.

"Not exactly. Have you ever heard of the astral plane,
Meghann?"

"No."

"The astral plane," Simon lectured, "is the field, or
realm of the spiritual world. Some believe that is where
your soul goes when you dream. There are many mortals who believe that their souls can travel on that plane.
A few can—after a period of intense meditation. Their
souls leave their bodies temporarily and go 'traveling.'
It's also referred to as astral projection. People have
done it to observe others, to gain spiritual power, to
warn a loved one they cannot reach through normal
measures of imminent dangers. As vampires, we can
travel the plane quite easily, but we do not have to leave
our physical bodies behind. Vampires can travel on the
astral plane with body and soul intact."

Meghann listened in fascination. "And you're going
to teach me how to do that now?"

"No, sweet. It will take a great deal of time for your
powers to develop to the point where you are capable
of traveling the plane by yourself. However, you can
travel with me. I should also tell you that there are a
few rules involved. You cannot travel somewhere you've
never been before, and it only works on distances of
up to thirty miles. Now, I want you to close your eyes,

and empty your mind of all thoughts. Whatever you do, do not open your eyes."

Meghann closed her eyes, and Simon picked her up. She tried to keep her mind clear.

Suddenly she felt a terrific gust of wind and heard a high-pitched moaning sound—almost a keening. It was terribly cold, and she thought she felt something try to grab her.

"All right, darling."

Meghann opened her eyes cautiously; they were standing in the bedroom where Simon transformed her. "That's all?"

"It goes by very quickly," Simon told her.

"I thought I felt something grab me."

"The astral plane can be quite dangerous to a novice," Simon warned. "There are many . . . forms there you have no desire to come in contact with."

Meghann shivered. Was he talking about demons?

"Don't be frightened, sweet. As long as you travel with me, you are perfectly safe. In time, you'll learn to do it yourself."

Meghann examined the room they were in. She had been too overwhelmed before to take any notice of her surroundings.

The room was entirely decorated in shades of red and gold. The walls were covered with the same silk that decorated Meghann's dressing room—except it was vermilion instead of cream. The polished wood floor had red and gold throw rugs scattered haphazardly about. The only furniture besides the bed was a huge dark wooden armoire. The bed was a wonderful antique-brass affair with a gold quilt and four scarlet and gold pillows. The ornate brass headboard was carved into the shape of cavorting imps and fairies. Meghann noticed that the gold manacles that had imprisoned her last night were still attached to the head-board.

Simon ran a hand over one of the fairies. "That is what you remind me of, little one." He reached over and snatched the wig off her head. Then he slowly removed the hairpins just as he'd done on the ferry.

"I think of you as a wood nymph—a divinely beautiful, impish creature I would expect to encounter in an enchanted forest."

Meghann giggled at his flowery speech.

He raised an eyebrow in mock anger. "I try to woo you and you giggle?" Simon eyed the red blouse. "You look awful—that top clashes with the copper in your hair."

She reached out to slap him playfully, and he used her hand to fling her on the bed. "You would strike your master?"

"If he says I look awful." She laughed seductively—her family quite forgotten.

"Why don't we simply remedy the situation?" He climbed on the bed, and removed the top.

"Meghann?" he questioned. "Do you remember what that coarse man asked of you?"

"Of course." Hesitantly she asked, "You're not going to make me do that, are you?"

Simon kissed her neck until she relaxed against him. "I won't make you do anything. But I promise you it can be quite enjoyable . . . especially for the woman."

"For the woman? Oh, my!" The thought made her start throbbing with desire.

"Well," she told him huskily. "I can certainly try."

Meghann considered the task before her and decided to go about it the same way she licked Popsicles in the summer—slowly, savoring each taste. That worked wonderfully well—Simon moaned and dug his fingers into her hair. Her lover's response gave

Meghann a feeling of triumph. For the first time, she was in control—not Simon. Sex gave her power over him.

Meghann hadn't even completed that thought when Simon reached down and hurled her onto the bed. He attached the manacles, then started making love to her. "I never lose control, Meghann."

He was thrusting so hard her head banged painfully against the headboard, but it still felt good. "I didn't mean it that way, Master," she gasped out before the familiar heat ignited inside her. Once again, she was arching her back to meet every delicious lunge. Without thinking, Meghann stretched her hands, wanting to feel Simon's thick chestnut hair entwined in her fists, and the restraints snapped in half.

Stunned, Meghann barely registered the limp gold chains dangling from her wrists before Simon tore the now useless manacles off her wrists. The rippling muscles in his arms did not even flex—let alone strain—from the effort. Then he grabbed both her wrists with one hand and forced them above her head while he kept thrusting into her.

"Break this hold, little one," Simon invited in an almost taunting whisper, clamping down on her wrists until she was sure he'd break her bones just like he'd broken Pauline's the night before.

Bully, Meghann almost said, but the menace in Simon's expression forced her to hold her tongue. So she cast her eyes down and pretended submission, though she despised herself for this new timidity that was so foreign to her forthright, strong-willed nature. What was happening to her that she'd lie here so passively while her supposed lover held her down, all but raping her? Maybe Pauline had been the lucky one . . . She'd only had her spirit broken once, but it looked like it might be an every-night affair for her.

Abruptly Simon tilted her chin up with his free hand and leaned down to kiss her. Expecting him to be forceful, Meghann was surprised by the almost delicate touch of his lips on hers. The contrast between the cruel hand pinioning her wrists and the light, tender kiss first startled her, but then it had her moaning and writhing eagerly beneath him, her miserable thoughts forgotten. But just as she was about to climax, Simon withdrew from her and rolled onto his back, his expression showing obvious amusement at her distress. "I wouldn't want to break your spirit, Meghann."

Oh, no . . . She wasn't about to apologize for not wanting to be brutalized during sex! Ignoring the unsatisfied ache inside her, Meghann shrugged and said with a feigned nonchalance, "If you're through, I think I'll go upstairs and get something to drink."

As she started to slide off the bed, Simon grabbed her around the waist and pulled her back toward him. "I'd say you're far from broken, little firebrand." Before Meghann could reply, Simon hooked his fingers behind her knees and brought them up around his shoulders.

"What are you doing?" Meghann started to ask, but her words sharply halted when Simon buried his tongue between her legs.

"Didn't I tell you what a pleasurable experience this can be?" he murmured, tongue and mouth exploring her with swirling, lazy strokes that made her whimper with pleasure while her heels dug into his back.

"Uh-huh," Meghann managed weakly as that knowing tongue found every secret, intimate crevice, leaving a path of burning, pulsating heat in its wake. Then Simon found her center and Meghann screamed out her joy, pushing herself closer to him, craving the tumultuous release she knew he could give to her. But he withdrew again at the last possible second, peeling her legs off his shoulders and staring down expressionlessly while Meghann looked up at him with mute entreaty.

Please, Meghann started to say, willing to beg, willing to do anything as long as Simon would satisfy the voracious, screaming need inside her. As she opened her mouth, the gold eyes moved to her wrists, and Meghann understood what her master wanted, what she'd have to do before he'd touch her again.

A long silence passed between them and then slowly Meghann raised her trembling arms, crossing her wrists and putting them over her head. Her eyes filled with tears because she finally realized Simon, with his impenetrable strength, ruthless ways, and mastery of her body had the power to demolish her pride and make her his slave.

His face was a mask of outright victory as he grabbed her wrists, but then Simon surprised her, uncrossing her wrists and kissing her palms gently before he placed her hands by her sides. Then he kissed her softly on her forehead, lips, neck, and breasts, his lips finally reaching the flesh he'd so cruelly abandoned moments before.

Only after Meghann reached a climax so strong it plunged her into a whirlwind of sensation and made her cry with relief did Simon enter her, rapidly building the fire inside her to a fever pitch, but this time there was no teasing withdrawal. She now felt Simon relax his iron control over himself and then plunge them both into a world of reckless, unbridled passion from which they emerged limp and gasping for breath.

"I shouldn't tease you so," Simon finally said, and Meghann made the effort to open her eyes and raise her head from his chest.

"I have no desire to crush your spirit or make you a mindless slave," he confided, plucking hair turned dark and wet with perspiration off her breasts. "Forgive me for forgetting I've taken a rather naive young girl and introduced her to games she might find a bit shocking before realizing how much pleasure they bring."

"All of that was only a game?" Meghann asked, not sure if she liked games where she had to beg, even if the end was quite delicious.

"Don't look so uncertain. I'll never do anything that makes you scared or uncomfortable," Simon assured her, but when she smiled her relief, his expression changed and the saffron eyes were full of power. He said intensely, "Just as I won't harm you, I'm sure you'll never again make the mistake of assuming you can use desire to manipulate your master."

"Of course not," Meghann said immediately, swallowing nervously when she realized how careful she'd have to be not only to not *say* anything that might displease Simon but also not to *think* anything that would make him angry.

Part of her cried out at such oppression, but Meghann suppressed the dangerous thoughts, thinking instead her situation wasn't so terrible at all. She was the chosen consort of a handsome, wealthy creature who was a terrific lover. He'd given her immortality, the ability to dominate anyone with her mind, and the unimaginable pleasure of drinking blood. The one thing she must be careful of was to never make him angry or displease him. So she bowed her head and told him, "I'm sorry, Master . . . if my thoughts made you angry."

The stern expression melted into a pleased grin, and Meghann knew at once she'd done the right thing. "I wasn't angry, Meghann. I just wanted to make sure you understood your place with me." Then he embraced her again and Meghann forgot his momentary displeasure—unaware he'd just set the pattern for their relationship.

SEVEN

December 14, 1957

Meghann gathered her hair into an elegant but happenstance upsweep that she knew Simon liked. Then she went over to the large walk-in closet to try to decide what to wear for the evening ahead.

While she was inspecting and discarding gowns, she felt two hands descend on her shoulders and a soft kiss on the nape of her neck.

She turned around and admired her lover. He looks so elegant in a tuxedo, *she thought,* he's still the best-looking man I've ever seen.

"Thank you, sweetheart. And your negligee," he commented, eyeing the half-slip and stockings appreciatively, "makes me want to ravish you, but I suggest you get dressed. It wouldn't do for the host and hostess to be late."

Simon examined the dresses and tossed her a moss-green silk gown with a plunging neckline. He pulled it over her head, and smiled at her appearance. "It will match your gift."

"What gift?" She followed him to the sitting room where he was pouring champagne into two Baccarat flutes. "And you still haven't told me what this party's for."

"I wanted to surprise you, darling. I finally found a buyer for the hotel."

"That's wonderful! Who is it?" Since 1953, after the failed Fidelista attempt to seize Moncada, Simon had wanted to sell his interests in Cuba.

"A foolish man who cannot read the writing on the wall. He is unable to understand that the Fidelistas will prevail— Batista cannot hold the tide forever. And when Castro gains control, he is not going to be interested in catering to casinos and tourism."

"I hope the Fidelistas do gain control," Meghann remarked. "Look at the brutal conditions most of the Cubans live under. What good is a thriving gambling industry if it doesn't improve the lives of the people?"

Simon caressed her cheek. "Since when have you developed an interest in the lives of mortals, my little proletariat?"

"Shouldn't you have some interest in human affairs?" she asked. "If Castro gains power, business will suffer. If they had helped the people, given them good-paying jobs instead of slave wages, then Castro wouldn't be able to gain support and people like you wouldn't have to sell."

"The gain isn't enough to interest me. Let humans work out their own muddled affairs, Meghann. At worst, we find ourselves suffering through minor inconveniences like war before they manage to patch up their problems for a while. And why should mortals' lives concern us when all that we need is their blood?"

Meghann kept quiet, but she was finding herself lately more and more interested in people. It gave her a turn of disgust when she saw the tourists gaily drive by a group of ragged, hungry children. But Simon was right. Why should it matter to her?

Simon handed her a flat black box with an old-fashioned clasp. "Perhaps if you've decided to embrace socialism, I should take my gift back."

Meghann eyed the box curiously. "What's the occasion?"

"Valentine's Day, sweet."

"Oh!" she cried in dismay. "I forgot to get you anything."

Simon pulled her into his lap, kissing her slowly. When his lips wandered to her neck, she arched back—and then he set her firmly on her feet. He did that sometimes, leaving them both in a state of arousal all night. "You're here with me— that's all I want. Now open your present."

As Meghann fiddled with the lock, she reflected on how thoroughly Simon Baldevar had spoiled her over the past decade. Couture clothing, fine wines, trips, jewelry, furs—anything she wanted he gave to her. The man certainly wasn't tightfisted. She got the box open, and gasped. Lying in black silk was a gorgeous emerald necklace set in antique gold, with matching earrings. It was beautiful—the bronze gold setting against the sparkling gems. "Where did you get this?" she asked.

Simon put it around her neck. "An auction—more and more fine names are going downhill. I suspect the problem is spoiled, inept generations who have no idea how to keep a fortune intact." He stepped back to admire her appearance. The emeralds looked sensational against the backdrop of her fiery red hair and pale skin. "Let's go downstairs, pet. It's time for your surprise."

"What surprise?" she asked. "I thought selling the hotel was the surprise."

"You'll see," he told her with an enigmatic smile.

He guided her through the casino—where she found prey and liked to gamble sometimes—to one of the smaller supper clubs in the hotel. It could only hold about fifty people. The sign on the gold door read, CLOSED FOR PRIVATE PARTY.

When Meghann entered the room on Simon's arm, all the assembled guests turned to look at them. Meghann was used to that—Simon tended to turn heads, and she guessed she did too. But there was something very different about this group— she couldn't read them very easily. They had a very different aura, almost like . . .

"These are all vampires!" she gasped.

Simon grinned. "Surprise, darling."

"*But why—*"

"*You always complain that I neglect this part of your education. Consider this party a small step toward amends.*" The crowd swelled forward, and Simon started making introductions.

It didn't take a genius to figure out that all these vampires were beholden to Simon in some way, she thought while she smiled and extended her hand to be kissed. They were all quite polite and more than a bit subservient. She reflected that this party was probably like when some corporate big shot showed up at the Christmas party. Everyone was very courteous and respectful, but who can really let their hair down in front of the boss?

And their attitude toward her had the same courtesy, but she felt something underlying it. Aside from introductory pleasantries, no one really talked to her—they just stared at her.

"*I feel like I'm on display,*" she complained to Simon.

"*You are, my sweet. They are all quite curious about my consort—no one has ever enjoyed my undivided attention the way you have.*"

So that was it, she thought sourly. Come meet the bride of Dracula. Meghann didn't like it at all. It was damned strange to be gawked at like you were some museum piece or oddity.

Only one young man actually looked her in the eye, as opposed to the sidelong glances she was getting from everyone else. He was nice-looking, with dark black hair and eyes. He caught Meghann's glance and bowed slightly. She smiled at him, and he smiled back—a bit uncertainly.

Simon followed her smile, and scowled. " '*Who dares to mock our solemnity?*' " he said softly.

Meghann looked at him questioningly, and he told her, "A quote from Romeo and Juliet, *sweet. It means—*"

"*I know what it means,*" she told him tartly. "*You don't have to treat me like some silly piece of fluff. Tybalt said it to Lord Capulet when Romeo's friends crashed his party. Are you trying to tell me that young man is an uninvited guest?*"

Simon pulled her into an empty alcove. "I don't care for your tone."

Meghann blanched at his sharp voice. Simon could spoil and cosset her, but he was equally capable of very harsh treatment if she displeased him. A long time ago, she'd learned how to placate him, and even managed to convince herself she didn't mind what she was doing.

She widened her eyes, and let her lip quiver slightly. "I'm sorry, Master," she said in a low, penitent whisper.

He gave her a sweeping look, but she kept her eyes—and thoughts—completely humble and sweet.

Finally he smiled and stroked her cheek. "I forgive you," he told her, and she worked hard at not seething from the thought that she had to beg forgiveness simply for speaking her mind. It was getting harder to do. "And yes, that young man is not my guest."

"Are you going to throw him out?"

"There's no need to ruin the night for everybody. And I have a feeling he'll be leaving soon." Simon pulled her onto the dance floor—at least she wouldn't have to talk and possibly offend him.

When the clock struck twelve, Simon left Meghann at the edge of the dance floor—by the doors that led to the beach. "I have to make an announcement, darling."

He walked over to the raised dais, and dismissed the mortal band. Meghann noticed the young man from before edging over to her. Why didn't Simon like him? She did. She thought he was the only vampire here she might like to talk to. All the rest seemed like a bunch of sycophants.

Simon was addressing the guests; the overeager, anxious looks on their faces repulsed Meghann.

"I apologize for my neglect—but you must understand I've had other thoughts on my mind for the past few years." He looked at Meghann lingeringly, and the crowd tittered.

She narrowed her eyes. Did she have to be treated like some little doll of Simon's?

She heard a low voice behind her. *"Don't worry about what these fools think—or what that madman up there thinks of you."* Meghann gasped at such a description of Simon. She turned to the young man, intent on asking him who he was, but Simon hadn't finished speaking.

"I have arranged for a diversion tonight—a small gift for you." Meghann shivered at the new atmosphere in the room—fifty or so vampires, all with blood lust in their eyes. What was going on here?

Trevor came in the room with a group of twenty young men and women. Actually, Meghann didn't think they were men or women—they seemed too young, none of them could be over eighteen. They were all naked—with superb, oiled bodies. And they had heavy gold chains around their necks. They seemed drugged and quite docile. Meghann's heart started thumping. What was Simon doing?

With a malicious laugh, he told his acolytes, *"Let the festivities begin."* He leaped off the dais and grabbed two of the young women. He began drinking from both of them simultaneously—one from a vein in her breast, the other from her wrist.

Meghann was appalled. Especially when a beautiful blonde joined Simon and his young prisoners. Soon all the vampires were hungrily tearing into the captives. Meghann was sickened by the sound of so many fangs lunging into flesh, and all the vampires feeding with abandon.

The captives were no longer mute—they were screaming in pain. The sound of vampire laughter chilled Meghann—she had to get away from this blood bacchanal. Without another thought, she ran out of the room, onto the beach.

The air felt so good after the oppressive atmosphere of that hellish room, with the odor of blood and fear heavy in the air. Dear God, what kind of sick mind enjoyed that kind of public feeding? Meghann thought it was distasteful. You should drink blood in private. And there was something else . . . She was sorry for those poor young people, their agony. What was *happening? Why was she different from the others? Why was she no longer able to take pleasure in people's pain?*

She felt a hand on her shoulder, and turned around. It was the young man. Like Meghann, his clothing was immaculate—he had not taken part in the "festivities" either.

"Would you like to take a walk, Meghann?"

"Who are you?" she asked.

Then she felt another hand on her shoulder—a much stronger touch. With a sinking feeling, she turned to Simon's impassive stare.

"You were not invited," he told the young man. "And it is time for you to leave."

The young man did not appear frightened. He bowed to Meghann and told her, "Till we meet again."

Meghann awoke in her usual abrupt manner—sitting up with her eyes wide open. She lay back for a few minutes, thinking about the dream.

That party had taken place nearly ten months ago. After the mystery guest left, Simon had simply escorted Meghann back to their suite. To this day, he had not said anything about her leaving the party—or talking to the young man. And Meghann was too frightened to risk his wrath by asking questions.

That was really annoying her—the way she had to tiptoe around Simon and kowtow to him. She was so tired of always curbing her thoughts, and behaving like the sweet, vacuous mannequin he expected her to be. But he had ways of making her behave . . .

Well, Meghann thought to herself with some cheer, *at least I don't have to worry about it for five days.* After a tour of Italy and France, Simon had abruptly deposited her in New York City. He said he had some business to take care of, and left Meghann by herself for the first time since he transformed her.

She didn't care what his business was—she was thankful for the freedom. Tonight was her first night on her own. This was also the first time she'd been back in New York since becoming a vampire.

Meghann went upstairs to dress, trying to wrench her thoughts away from the tension between her and Simon, and her increasing melancholy. Ever since that wretched party, she'd felt depressed. The only respite came when she fed. Lately she found herself feeding two and sometimes three times a night to escape the constant sadness. But the exhilaration of drinking blood rarely lasted more than a few minutes. And if she wasn't sad, she was angry—which was downright dangerous. Every time her temper rose, she worked furiously to suppress it. But she was so tired of being at Simon's beck and call, having to call him "Master," and constantly worry that she might inadvertently offend him. . . .

Stop it, she told herself firmly. Are you going to fritter away your holiday by moping around? As an open act of rebellion, Meghann threw on a pair of jeans and a black turtleneck. One of Simon's many rules was that she be elegantly dressed at all times. He abhorred casual clothing, and he forbade her to wear black. This clothing (along with her album collection) had been stealthily purchased, and then stuck all the way in the back of her closets.

When she got downstairs, she saw a sight to lift her spirits. Trevor was comfortably ensconced in an Eames chair Simon favored, with a glass of scotch at his side and a cigarette between his lips.

He opened his eyes and saw Meghann. Immediately he stubbed out the cigarette in a Waterford ashtray and threw himself out of the chair. "Oh, please, miss," he whined, "don't tell the master. I . . . I was going to clean up—I swear. I'm terribly sorry. . . ."

He's scared to death of Simon, she thought. All things considered, that was a very healthy attitude. She smiled, and Trevor was taken aback. He'd never really allowed himself to look at her, but he thought she was the most beautiful . . .

Meghann saw where his thoughts were going and said briskly, "Don't worry, Trevor. You can sit down. It's OK." He looked a bit doubtful but sat down again. "I'm not going to tell Simon . . . on one condition."

He was wary. She wouldn't get him in trouble with the master, would she? "What is it?"

She extended her hand. "Let me have a cigarette."

Dumbfounded, he handed her the pack of Lucky Strikes and his lighter. "I didn't think vamp . . . I mean, I never saw the master smoke."

Meghann hadn't smoked in thirteen years, but since Simon hated smoking . . . She lit up and then inhaled. The first puff made her choke, but then it tasted fine.

Trevor watched her uncertainly. He had no idea what the master's woman was all about.

Meghann took a sip of Trevor's drink, and grimaced. "This is rotgut, Trevor. If we're doing 'While the cat's away, the mice will play,' let's do it right." She walked over to the small bar and pulled out a bottle of Glenfiddich. Vampires didn't become intoxicated, but she liked the taste of a good scotch. So did Simon.

"Miss!" Trevor exclaimed. "That's the master's private stock."

"So I'll tell him I drank it," she said shortly. "Trevor, my name is Meghann—*not* miss. And do me a favor—don't call Simon 'master' in my presence."

Meghann gave him the drink, but he was pale and trembling. "What's the matter?"

"Please," he whispered, "don't make me call you by your first name. If I got used to it, and the mas . . . if he heard me do it, he'd tear my tongue out."

Meghann thought the man probably wasn't exaggerating. "OK, just leave off the master bit."

For a while, they smoked and drank in silence. Meghann was very curious about the man she privately thought of as Simon's Renfield. They'd never talked much—minor household details that Simon expected her to handle. She thought wryly about her mortal dreams—being an independent career woman. She would have bashed Johnny Devlin's head in if he'd suggested her being a boring housewife. And yet—if you stripped away the wealth and vampirism, wasn't that precisely what she had become? A prim little chatelaine? Certainly, she had no career—she depended on Simon for everything; she had no money of her own. Meghann frowned, and poured more scotch. Why couldn't she get falling-down drunk? Maybe then she could forget how unhappy she was—being treated like a mindless toy.

"Trevor?" she asked suddenly. "Why do you work for Simon?"

"For the money," he replied, too startled to lie. "I get fifty thousand a year and one million dollars after twenty years."

Meghann was outraged. He kept the secret of what Simon was and cleaned up after him—only for money? Trevor certainly would have fit in well at the death camps—*just keep the cash coming and I'll forget all about the poison-gas showers.* But who was she to judge Trevor? He only buried the bodies; she and Simon were the ones who killed people.

She was getting restless. She had to do something, get away from Simon's house, from any reminder of him. In fact, she wanted to forget she was a vampire—for one night. She wanted to be Maggie O'Neill again.

She stalked over to the hall closet. She pushed past the furs (lately they made her feel like a kept woman) and took out a khaki raincoat.

"Miss?" Trevor questioned.

"What?"

"Where are you going?"

What harm would it do to tell him? "To visit my father."

Trevor's jaw dropped open. He dropped his eyes, but not before Meghann saw his disconcertment.

She started to feel apprehensive. "What is it?" she demanded.

"I can't tell you," he mumbled. "The master—"

"He's not here," Meghann snapped. "Now tell me what's wrong!"

"He'll kill me—"

Meghann yanked him out of the chair and banged his head against the fireplace. "I'll kill you if you make me ask you again. Tell me!"

Trevor was scared out of his mind. The master did not lose control—there was no telling what this creature would do. She yanked his head so that he was staring into her green eyes. He could not resist the force he saw reflected there.

"Your father's dead," he said quickly.

He fell to the floor. Meghann stared down at him, shock and denial all over her face.

"When did he die?" she whispered.

"The master made me promise." He grunted as her foot connected with his ribs. Now he could barely breathe; he thought she might have broken his ribs.

Meghann picked up the fireplace poker. She hadn't lived with Simon Baldevar for thirteen years without picking up a thing or two.

"Trevor," she said in a calm tone that belied the fury he saw in her eyes. "I will take this poker and ram one of your eyes out if you don't start answering my questions. Then I will eat that eye in front of you. Now, when did my father die?"

Oh, God, help him—why had the master left him

alone with her? As the poker entered his eye, Trevor cried out, "He died six months ago! A box came here from your brother."

"Get the box," Meghann ordered.

Trevor tried to stand, but found he couldn't stand straight from the pain. But he'd do anything to keep this woman from hurting him. He hobbled away, returning in fifteen minutes with a large cardboard box. Why hadn't the master gotten rid of it?

Meghann snatched the box from him, and tore it open. She saw several effects—photo albums, pictures, a large wooden cross, her mother's lace tablecloth, and a plain envelope marked MAGGIE. She tore it open, and read it.

July 30, 1957
Maggie,

Daddy wanted you to have these things. If it were up to me, I wouldn't give you a goddamned thing. How could you stay away like this? Ignore all Daddy's letters? At the end, in the hospital, he wanted you there so bad. All he did was cry out for you, and you never came. What's the matter with you? You married some rich guy and forgot you have a family.

Well, I've done what Daddy asked. But as far as I'm concerned, I have no sister.

Frank

She was standing so still Trevor almost thought she had died standing up. There was no animation. She simply stared down at the letter like she had been turned to stone.

"Miss," he begged, "it wasn't my fault."

Meghann turned to him, and he screamed shrilly.

Her skin looked like paper—with great emerald eyes blazing grief and cold fury.

"Not your fault?" she questioned venomously. Then she threw herself on him and started beating him furiously. "How the hell can you tell me it's not your fault?" She screamed expletives and insults at the top of her lungs between blows. Her voice went through him like a knife—all the glass in the room shattered. "You despicable, vile lapdog—it's all your fault! You work for that evil man for money! You snake . . . you loathsome shit! I hate you! You can walk in daylight. . . . If you had any balls, you'd put a stake through his black heart!"

Meghann threw herself off him, and he touched his face gingerly. He knew he had a black eye and a bruised lip. And it felt like he'd lost several teeth.

Meghann picked up a shard from the liquor bottle and put it to his neck. "Tell me how long my father was sick."

"Two years," he mumbled through the blood.

Two years. Her brother was right to hate her—but that was because he didn't know better. He didn't know where the blame truly belonged. Oh, God—the grief hit her strong. *My father's dead.* Meghann dashed for the door—she had to get out of here before she went mad.

"Miss?" Trevor moaned. "Where are you going? If the master calls—"

"You tell that miserable cocksucker he can go to hell for all I care!" And she slammed the door so hard the stained glass shattered.

Trevor thought grimly that she could give the master a message like that herself if she wanted to. He dragged himself off the floor—he had to get to a hospital.

Meghann walked the streets, hardly noticing where she was. It was building up, all that sadness. She couldn't control it anymore, and she was so scared to let loose and really feel again. . . .

Ruthlessly she tried to repress her memories of her father. How could he be dead? It wasn't right; he was only sixty-seven. None of this was right—she looked up at a Christmas display window. Her miserable see-through-image sickened her. *It isn't right. Why am I like this? I want to see the sun; I want my daddy.* . . .

No, no, no! If she thought Daddy, she'd start bawling. *No, I can't. I won't cry. Blood,* she thought suddenly. *That will make it better. I'll drink blood and forget.* . . .

She ran into an alley, and saw a bum curling up in a doorway, trying to keep warm. She grabbed him and started drinking frenziedly.

The blood poured down her throat, and it made no difference. The pain wouldn't stop. Then, out of the corner of her eye, she noticed another derelict by the fence. He hadn't seen Meghann. He was too absorbed in the needle he was trying to stick in his arm.

With a small cry, she dropped her victim. *My God,* she thought dully, *I'm no better than a common drug addict. That junkie . . . we're doing the same thing, trying to kill the pain with a drug. That's all I've done for thirteen years is try to push the pain away. And I was drinking blood while my father was dying.*

Meghann gave in to the pain, and started sobbing. The force of her tears was so strong she was soon kneeling on the floor next to her prey. She cried for everything—herself, her father, Johnny, all the innocent people she had killed to stay alive.

She had crossed the line into hysteria, weeping so hard she couldn't breathe. For thirteen years, everything had been repressed—now it was coming out. She cried and cried; still, the hard lump in her throat didn't lessen. She wept for all the things she'd lost—the sun, the children she'd never have, Sunday picnics, Dodger games with her daddy. . . .

Most of all, she cried for Jack O'Neill. *Daddy, I'm almost glad you're dead. What would you think of me? I'm a monster, an evil freak. Why did this happen? Why? Why?* Suddenly she couldn't stand it anymore. She put her sharp nails on her face, intending to tear her face and body to ribbons, to pay for what she'd done.

"No!" Strong hands grabbed hers before she could maul her face.

She looked up, still weeping wildly. She saw two black eyes regarding her with concern.

"I know you," she sobbed, "you're that vampire who left Simon's party."

"I'm the *other* vampire who left Simon's party," he corrected gently. "You didn't stay either."

"Of course I didn't!" she yelled, beyond caring who he was or why he was there. "I can't stand it anymore. I won't kill, I won't!"

"You don't have to." He dropped her hands and put his hands on Meghann's victim. To her complete shock, the man got up and walked away.

"He's not dead," she whispered. She could not have been more stunned if she'd been at Lazarus's grave when Christ resurrected him.

The young man smiled. "Of course he's not. We don't kill to feed."

"Who's we?" she asked, starting to recover her wits. "And who are you? Why are you here?"

The young man studied her with grave concern. "I am Charles Tarleton; please don't be frightened. You couldn't sense my presence because your pain blocked out everything else. Please, I don't mean to pry, but I know part of the reason you're upset. You can't stand killing . . . or life with Lord Baldevar. Am I correct?"

She nodded. She didn't know why, but she trusted Charles implicitly. She felt like she'd always known him.

"But," he said quietly, "I don't feel that's all that made you cry. If you want, you can tell me what's wrong. I'd like to help—if I can."

"My father died," she told him, and started crying again.

Charles watched helplessly while she wept.

"He died calling for me," she said, more to herself than Charles. "Oh, God, when I think of it . . . my daddy lying in some hospital, with pain, wanting me. Me! And I wasn't there. What did he think?" She cried harder, making it difficult for Charles to understand her. "He was alone and hurting, don't you see? Even a bum doesn't deserve that, and my father was a great man! I loved him so much, and he didn't know! I never got the chance to tell him. He died all by himself. He must have been so hurt. Damn Simon to hell!" she howled. She looked at Charles beseechingly. "I would have gone to my father the minute I knew he was sick. I would have! I wouldn't have let him die alone." She was crying too hard to continue.

Charles had the same feeling she had—that they'd known each other for a long time. So he wrapped his arms around her. "I'm so sorry, Meghann." He had an idea. "Would you like to go to church and pray for your father? My master believes the dead can hear us— you can tell your father that you're sorry."

The thought of church was like a balm to Meghann. She hadn't been in a church to pray since Simon, but that was exactly what she wanted. She felt the smallest spark of hope within her. Had God sent Charles to help her? She liked him already—liked the arm around her that offered friendship and respect. She wiped her face with the sleeve of her coat and said, "I'd love to go to church."

She and Charles walked out of the alley. "Why are you being nice to me?" she asked with her old bluntness.

"Because I suspect no one has been very nice to you in the last thirteen years."

"How do you know so much about me?" she asked suspiciously.

"A new vampire always sparks curiosity. . . . Simon Baldevar's consort, now that is front page news in our small world."

"I'm not his consort," she snapped. "Not anymore."

Charles studied her nervously. "Meghann, I won't tell you what to do, but please exercise caution with Lord Baldevar. I'd hate to lose a new friend." They stopped in front of a small church that was still open.

Inside, Meghann saw many winos and bums—the nuns were handing out blankets and fresh clothing.

"On cold nights like this," Charles told her, "they take them in so they won't freeze."

Meghann was touched—the way she would have been when she was mortal. She walked over to a statue of the Virgin—where she had always prayed when she was a child.

She knelt before Mary, made a small donation, and lit a candle. Just the ritual made her feel a little better. She wasn't really praying—she was letting all the good memories of her father come back to her. She saw him taking her to see Santa Claus at Macy's, sternly interrogating her dates, teaching her how to throw a knuckleball, making her take off a dress he thought was cut too low. *Daddy*, she prayed. *I would have come to see you if I'd known. I'm so sorry, but you have to believe I loved you so much. . . .*

Meghann felt someone pinch her cheek—the way her father used to. And she smelled his cigar smoke and the Lifebuoy soap he liked to use.

"Daddy?" she asked wonderingly, but the feeling was gone. Then she started crying again, but this time it was from joy. "You felt it too?" she questioned. "Charles, my father was here and he forgave me. . . . I know he did!" She was crying because she was so relieved. She felt like a huge weight had been lifted. For the first time in months, she didn't feel that gray cloud choking her. Everything looked fresh and new.

"You have great summoning power," Charles told her with some astonishment.

"What?"

"Has Simon taught you *anything?*" he asked with exasperation.

"I guess not." She looked at him intently. "Is it possible to drink blood without killing people?"

"Yes."

Meghann digested that information. All these years, all those deaths didn't have to happen. She didn't feel depressed anymore. If there was a way to be a vampire without murder, she wanted to learn it. And she wanted to try to atone for the things she had done.

"Can you wait here for a few minutes? I'll be right back." She was out the church door before Charles could object.

Bemused, Charles sat in a pew to wait for her. He had no doubt she was coming back. He felt vindicated. When he'd gotten back from Cuba, all the others had tried to convince Alcuin that he was wrong—that Simon's paramour had to be evil. Well, he could hardly wait to bring her to his master—they would see that he had judged her character well. At least, he *hoped* Alcuin got a chance to meet Meghann. How was she going to get away from Simon Baldevar?

Meghann came whirling back into the church. He could not believe the change in her. What had Simon done to her? At the party, he had seen a pretty but pallid young woman. Now he saw that when her spirit wasn't being crushed she had a dynamic presence. He watched her go up to the elderly priest and hand him something. The priest's eyes bulged. He tried to give it back to Meghann, but she was adamant. After a minute, the priest shook her hand and disappeared.

"What's going on?" Charles asked her.

"I wanted to buy a mass card for my father, and make a charitable donation."

"What kind of donation?"

"Five thousand dollars."

Charles gasped. "Where did you get that kind of money?"

"From Simon's safe," she replied nonchalantly.

The priest returned, and gave Meghann her mass card. She thanked him, and they left the church.

"How do you feed without killing?" was the first thing out of her mouth.

"You control the blood lust," Charles told her. "You learn the moment you've had enough to drink, and you use your will to stop. It takes some time to learn— and of course, you must have a master who teaches you."

"And your master taught you?"

Charles glanced at his watch: three o'clock. "Meghann, I'd like to escort you home."

She frowned. "What does that have to do with killing?"

"I'll tell you everything you want to know, but I think you've had a very difficult night. I'd much rather discuss this when you're more relaxed. Perhaps we could meet early tomorrow night?"

Meghann considered that. If she'd waited all this time, what was one more night? And Charles had a point. Did she really want more revelations tonight? It would dilute that moment she'd had with her father.

On the way back to the town house, they talked of general matters. A story in the newspapers, a good movie Meghann thought Charles might enjoy, poetry they both liked.

On the steps of the town house, Charles asked, "We're on for tomorrow night?"

She smiled sunnily. "You bet. Shall we say seven?"

"That's perfect. I'll pick you up. And, Meghann, please use caution if you should speak to Simon. Don't antagonize him." Charles kissed her on the cheek, then left.

Meghann examined the living room. Trevor had cleaned up admirably. All the broken glass was gone, everything back in its place. She decided to look through the box Frankie sent.

She found one of her favorite photographs—her, Johnny Devlin, Bridie McGovern, and George Lynch, Bridie's date. It was from July, 1942—to celebrate her seventeenth birthday and one last fling before Johnny went overseas.

She smiled at her sodden, dripping clothing and Johnny's. Would some stranger looking at the picture ever guess why they were soaking wet?

"Come on, Johnny," Maggie pleaded. "Take me on the Atom Smasher!"

"Didn't I take you on Hell-n-Back? And the fun house? What do you want from me—blood? You know I hate roller coasters!"

Maggie rolled her eyes at Bridie. "Can you believe this is what they're sending to Europe? A chicken that won't even go on a little roller coaster?"

"I don't think they're gonna be asking to go on too many roller coasters over there." Johnny tore off two Playland tickets, and handed them to Maggie. "Here, go yourself, Miss Bravery."

Maggie snatched the tickets. "Anyone else coming?"

"I will," Bridie volunteered.

George eyed the huge roller coaster with its steep inclines dubiously. "Maybe me and Johnny could get a beer while you two go on."

The girls laughed and made many clucking noises before heading over to the coaster.

"Hands off?" Bridie asked while the clown-faced cart made its slow crawl to the top of the first incline.

"No other way to do it," Maggie replied as they sank down. They laughed and screamed as they got tossed to one side and then the other while the roller coaster sped through the inclines. They waved to some of the people watching from their rooftops.

They stepped off the ride, slightly dizzy, and headed back to their boyfriends.

"Chicken," Maggie taunted Johnny.

"Maggie, I'm warning you. Don't call me chicken again if you know what's good for you."

"Or what?"

"Or you'll find out, Raggedy Ann."

Now that he'd waved the red flag in her face, this was war. "Chicken!" she screeched.

"Last warning," he said, lunging for her.

"Chicken!" she shouted, ducking behind Bridie for protection.

"Who's chicken now?" he asked, trying to grab her while a giggling Bridie did her best to protect her friend. "Get over here and say that."

"Nope," she answered, giggling. "Come and get me, chicken."

George grabbed Bridie. "Get her, Johnny. Show her who's boss."

Johnny pounced and threw Maggie over his shoulders. He could barely hold on to her because they were both laughing too hard.

When she saw what he was carrying her toward, Maggie gasped. "Oh, no! You wouldn't. Oh, come on Johnny!"

He dragged her to the Olympic-sized swimming pool in the center of the park, and threw her in the water.

She came up, spluttering and choking. She swam over to the side where Johnny was leering down in triumph. "It's freezing," she complained. "You bastard!"

Johnny tsk-tsked in mock reproach. "You curse like a sailor, Raggedy Ann. Are you sorry for calling me a chicken?"

"Nope!" She laughed riotously and grabbed his right leg, pulling him off balance. "You're a chicken—and a heartless brute for attacking a poor, defenseless girl." She yanked him into the pool with her, to the cheers of some amused onlookers.

"You're about as defenseless as a boa constrictor," Johnny countered, laughing and splashing water in her face. "I'd like to meet the guy who could attack you."

The water really was freezing. They both clung to each other to warm up.

"You know something, Maggie? I really love you."

"I love you too," she replied while they climbed out of the pool.

"What do you say we get hitched?"

"You mean it?"

"Why not? I have two more weeks before I have to report in. We'll do it quick and maybe have a big ceremony when I get home." Johnny got down on one knee, a large puddle forming around him. "What do you say, Maggie. Will you marry me?"

With a whoop of glee, she threw her arms around Johnny and kissed him. Then she yelled to Bridie, who was watching from a safe, dry distance, "Hey, guess what? We're getting married!"

Meghann studied the picture, charmed by the dazzling smiles on her and Johnny's faces. They were so innocent and carefree that day. They really thought nothing could go wrong for them. Even the war had seemed more like an exciting adventure than a dangerous situation.

I should be holding this picture right now, and telling my daughter this story. It's the kind of thing people pass down from generation to generation—Grandpa threw Grandma in the water and they got engaged.

She blinked back tears at her fiancé's strong, handsome face. This story was all wrong—the hero survived the war so that the heroine could kill him when a heartless monster transformed her into a vampire. Why couldn't Johnny have still been in Europe? Still, what would have happened then? Whose blood would Simon make her drink to smash her links with her family? Bridie's? Her father's?

The phone rang, making her jump. Meghann's heart started beating rapidly. She knew who it was. Should she pick up? She decided Simon would be suspicious if she never answered the phone. "Hello."

"Where were you, little one?"

This despicable snake had kept her from seeing her father and denied her the life she should have had with Johnny Devlin. Meghann felt a little reckless. After all, what could he do from far away? "Hello to you too. Can't I go out without being interrogated?"

The silence on the other end was ominous. Meghann regretted her hasty words. She couldn't tip her hand and let Simon know what was going on in New York.

More silence. Meghann said quickly, "I'm sorry, Master."

"Meghann," he said in a voice that made her break out in a cold sweat, "I shall deal with your new insolence when I return. For the moment, let's start again. Where were you?"

"Out walking," she quavered.

"For nearly four hours?"

"You know how much I like New York."

"Did you feed?"

"Yes."

"Then," he informed her, "you'll have no need to leave the house for the rest of the time I'm away, will you?"

Meghann wanted to scream. If vampires really did live forever, was this going to be the rest of her life? Never being allowed to do a damned thing without that vicious beast by her side?

"I want an answer, Meghann."

"I'll have no need to leave the house," she replied dully.

"Then I shall expect you to pick up the phone when I call tomorrow." The flat dial tone informed her he had hung up.

Meghann flung a vase at the wall. Goddamn him! She hated being stifled like this. Was she supposed to sit in this dungeon for five nights like some prisoner? Well, why not admit it? She was Simon's prisoner—nothing more. Sure, the cell was a little more glamorous than what they had in Sing Sing, but all the same she was as captive as the victims at his blood orgy.

Then she remembered her date with Charles Tarleton. Well, to hell with Simon Baldevar, she thought while she went downstairs to sleep. She was keeping that date—maybe she'd find a way to leave Simon for good.

EIGHT

Meghann came upstairs for a drink before she started dressing for her "date" with Charles Tarleton.

Trevor came hobbling over. Meghann examined his injuries. He had a bandage wrapped around his head, his ribs were bandaged, and he was walking with a limp. He deserves a hell of a lot more, she thought, for serving that prick.

Trevor shoved a large box into her hands, then limped away. She opened it, and a small card came out. The box was from Charles. The note asked her to forgive his forwardness, but would she please wear this outfit for their evening out?

Meghann pawed through the tissue covering the clothing. When she fished it out, she whooped in delight.

Charles had enclosed a black poodle skirt, along with two petticoats, one horsehair and one taffeta, to make the skirt full. There was also a green cashmere sweater, a green scarf, bobby sox, and shiny black patent leather shoes.

I'm going to look like a teenager, she thought with glee. She went upstairs and hurried into her new clothes. She had just wrapped the scarf around the ponytail she'd seen young girls wearing recently, when the door-bell rang.

Meghann hurried downstairs, shooing Trevor away from the door. Charles stood outside. He wore crisp black pants and a fraternity sweater. The outfit made her laugh.

"I only go with greasers," she informed him airily. "Would you like to come inside?"

Charles looked around uncomfortably. "Actually, I was hoping you'd be ready to leave. I can't relax in Simon's house."

Meghann could certainly understand that, so she went to the hall closet to get her warm black wool cloak. Before she left, she stuffed two thousand dollars into her purse. There would be hell to pay when Simon discovered she'd defied him and gone out—so why not disappear before he came home?

Meghann and Charles had not been gone for ten minutes before the phone rang. Trevor hobbled over eagerly. That bitch was going to pay for what she did to him. He'd tell the master everything—the way she tore the house apart, the money she took from the safe, and most important, that she'd just left the house with a young man.

The master will tear her limb from limb, Trevor thought as he picked up the phone.

"Having fun?" Charles asked.

"Wonderful," she panted, completely out of breath after three solid hours of dancing.

When they left the house, Charles informed her that he was taking her out for some fun—all "business" talk was suspended. She'd been happy to go along, and he took her to a sock hop sponsored by a local school.

"This is great," she enthused while thirstily gulping down a Coke. "You like rock and roll?"

"I love it," Charles answered.

She thought he must. He was fantastic on the dance floor. After she caught on to the new dances, they'd whirled to "Jailhouse Rock," "Whole Lotta Shakin' Goin' On," "Rock Around the Clock," "Hound Dog," and "Tutti Frutti". She loved the new music teenagers were dancing to. It had never been so much fun to dance.

She was humming "Earth Angel," and Charles grinned. "I take it you like rock and roll too?"

"It's fantastic," she replied, and made a face. "But of course *he* disapproves, so I have to buy albums on the sly and listen when the master goes out."

"Tell me about it," a young girl complained to her. "My dad's the same way. They never want to let you have any fun!"

Meghann laughed. The girl thought she was discussing her father. But in a way, that was what Simon was. Outside of bed, he usually addressed her the way a parent did an errant child.

"You guys were great out there," the girl complimented. Then her boyfriend came over and pulled her back onto the dance floor. She threw over her shoulder: "You're a real cute couple!"

Meghann considered that. At first, she'd been worried that maybe Charles would make a pass at her—not that she didn't like him, she was just tired of feeling like her looks were the only thing she had going for her. But Charles was treating her like a little sister. Even when they were dancing, she felt a certain impersonal quality in the way he held her.

"Hungry?" Charles inquired.

"Starving."

"Well, I have a room at the Algonquin. They still

have room service, and it would be a private place where we can talk. Would you like that?"

"Sure." In a way, she was a little disappointed to leave the dance. Pretending to be just another dance-crazy teenager was so much fun. But now it was back to the boring business of being a creature of the night—and figuring out what Vampira was going to do now that she'd spat on her master's orders.

Charles saw the corners of her mouth pull down and said, "Hey, this is just the beginning. You think I took you out so that I could dump you back in his clutches? I promise you, there's a lot more where tonight came from."

While they were walking to the hotel, Meghann decided to clear the air. "Charles? I just want to get things straight. You're not thinking I'm going to exchange you for Simon, are you?"

"Meghann, I swear you need not worry that I find you attractive."

Her mouth dropped and he said hastily, "I knew I wouldn't put that right! Meghann, it's not that you're ugly—far from it. I think you're one of the most beautiful girls I've ever seen. It's just that—I don't like girls."

Meghann was perplexed. "Well, if you don't like girls, who do you like?"

Charles stared at her calmly and then the answer came to her.

"Oh!" she cried in embarrassment. "I'm sorry . . . I shouldn't have said anything."

"No, Meghann, I'm glad we got it out of the way early. Do you mind?"

"Mind?" She giggled. "I think it's great!" At his quizzical look, she replied, "Not that you're homosexual. I don't mean that's great. That's just a fact. No, it's just that for years I've been with somebody who when he looks at me only seems to think of . . . well, you know.

I meant it's great to be talking to a guy—Simon doesn't really talk to me about anything important; he treats me like a little simpleton."

"Simon's a fool if he doesn't want to talk to you," Charles said in contempt. "You're quite intelligent, and I enjoy your company. In fact, I feel very close to you."

Meghann replied shyly, "I feel very close to you too—like I've known you for a long time."

Charles considered. "Maybe we knew each other in a past life. Or maybe it's because we're so close in age—I've only been a vampire for twenty-five more years than you. I think we're both among the youngest vampires in the world." He escorted her to his small room where they both ordered substantial meals from room service.

At first, they were both too hungry to talk. Meghann demolished a cheeseburger, fries, and a cheese omelette while Charles devoured two plain burgers, fried clams, and an ice-cream sundae. Vampires had incredible metabolisms—she never had to worry about gaining weight.

"Charles," she asked while sipping a chocolate malted, "how did you become a vampire?"

"It was 1918. I had recently finished medical school and was an intern. America had entered World War I, and I was drafted. I was put to work in an army hospital on the front lines. My father was a wealthy congressman—he could have easily arranged a safer post. But he had discovered my predilections. I guess he thought better a dead son than a homosexual one. So off I went to France.

"I arrived in September 1918, in time for the Battle of St. Mihiel, an important skirmish. The Allies won an important salient from the Germans. But there were heavy losses. All day, I was up to my knees in blood and gore. By noon, I no longer felt like a physician—I was an assembly-line worker, rushing to get one soldier sewed up so I could start in on the next."

Charles poured some coffee. "Around ten at night, I had enough. I had become used to the bombs and the planes. But I was tired of seeing so much suffering. I begged my supervisor to let me take a walk for a few minutes, get some fresh air.

"I walked for a bit when I heard a terrible keening, and the more awful sounds of someone crying from pain. I thought a soldier had been wounded, and no one had found him. So I decided to go see if I could offer some assistance. I found two young men—one appeared uninjured. He was cradling the other man."

Charles stared above Meghann. "I told him very gently to move away so I could help his friend. He told me, in French, that there was no way anyone could help him. I saw right away he was right. The young man had been gassed—he had those appalling mustard-colored blisters all over, and I saw that he was gasping for breath. It was a very painful way to die, Meghann. The gas ripped apart the mucous membrane and caused internal bleeding. This boy was like all the others I'd seen, panting and screaming for someone to let him die.

"The other man, he was weeping and told me I can't help him die—I can't. I completely misunderstood. I thought he meant he was powerless—which he was not. I should have guessed something odd was going on because he was holding the wounded man perfectly still—the pain from the gas was usually so terrible the soldiers had to be strapped down to their beds, nothing else could hold them."

Charles offered Meghann some coffee and a cigarette. She took it gladly; the habit was coming back.

"I took the Hippocratic oath, and I knew I should get help, bring the boy to the hospital. But I also knew that meant he would be kept alive for four agonizing weeks. So I did what I thought was right. I told the man I could help his friend if he'd let me. He moved away a bit, and I reached into my coat for some morphine injections I was supposed to give later on. I injected the boy, and he died minutes later.

"When he died, the other fellow grabbed me. He kissed me on the lips, thanking me for doing what he could not bring himself to do. He was quite handsome—with blond hair and green eyes a bit like yours. When he saw that I didn't object to the kiss, we started making love. For me, it was the classic reaction to seeing all that carnage—I needed to prove I was still alive. The man—I later found out his name was Paul—was still crying and thanking me for helping his lover. He was babbling about giving me a gift in return. I hardly paid attention. And then I felt two teeth rip into my neck."

Charles smiled at Meghann's wide eyes. He had a feeling it had as much to do with hearing about two men having relations as it did with hearing about him being bitten by a vampire. "Meghann, you know that in the moment of being bitten, there can be ecstasy, if the vampire wants you to feel it. I had never experienced such pleasure. But then Paul threw himself off me. He begged my pardon profusely and said he didn't know what had come over him—to repay a good deed with a curse. Then he vanished before my eyes."

"What did you do?" Meghann asked.

"Why, I pulled myself up and walked back to the hospital. When I was there, I made up a tale about someone attacking me and stealing my needles. Then I completed my tour of duty and returned to the States."

"But what about—"

"Being bitten? You know what happens—the first reaction in the face of such madness is denial. I told myself that my own experiences that day had unnerved me and I imagined the whole encounter. Of course, there were the marks, but I managed to ignore them. I went back home, and tried to forget the strange young man."

"So what happened?"

"In December 1919, he came to my home in Chicago. He reintroduced himself to me, and told me the whole story. Then he asked me if I would like to become his eternal lover." Charles smiled gently. "Paul always did have a tendency toward hyperbole."

"And you said yes?" Meghann questioned.

Charles sighed. "At the time, I was very tired of my constrained, predictable life. My father was pressing me to marry because I was becoming an oddity—a handsome young doctor who never showed any interest in the many pretty, presentable, young women in society. Of course, Father knew what I was, but appearances meant the world to him. If I was a deviant, that was unimportant. What was important was no one catching on that I was a deviant. So I thought Paul was a godsend. I would join him in this strange but wonderful life he promised me.

"I doubt our life together was the hell I imagine yours has been with Lord Baldevar. Paul was very gentle about my transformation. He brought me bowls of blood until I was strong enough to find victims. For that is what people are . . . we rob them of their blood. But from the start, Paul taught me to guard against the blood lust. So I never was initiated to the kind of world you've seen. Indeed, it was five years before Paul even told me about people like Simon."

"Where is Paul now?"

Charles smiled—a bit sadly. "Paul and I were a mismatch. That was apparent after the thrill of a new lover wore off a bit and we attempted to talk to each other.

But neither of us would admit it for fear of hurting the other. Finally, after ten years, we decided to go our separate ways. The split was quite amicable. But one thing terrified Paul—he had to tell Alcuin about transforming me. He had broken a very serious rule. He begged me to come with him when he stood before his master."

"Did Alcuin hurt him?" Meghann asked worriedly.

"Alcuin never hurts anyone," Charles told her gently. "I hope you learn soon that a master can be good for you—teach you and guide you, not terrorize you into blindly obeying his will. Paul was upset because he did not want to lose Alcuin's respect, because he knew how disappointed Alcuin would be. He was right. Alcuin reprimanded him for making a new vampire when the world can barely sustain those already in existence. He questioned Paul closely, and Paul discovered he was terrified of being alone. So Alcuin told him he must take twenty years in isolation to overcome this fear. As for me, Alcuin invited me to become his apprentice." Charles grinned and lit a new cigarette. "And that, Meghann, is my vampire history."

"Do you ever regret it?"

"Accepting Paul's offer? No, I really don't. I miss certain things of course—the sun above all. But I am a doctor, Meghann, and I have been blessed with something mortal doctors never have enough of—time. I hope one day, with my higher intelligence and unlimited time, to discover the cure to a deadly disease."

Meghann wrinkled her nose at him, and he laughed through the smoke. "You're quite right—what a pompous speech that was. Perhaps I should consider politics? What were you . . . before?"

Meghann was trying to relearn the art of blowing smoke rings. She managed one ragged one before answering Charles. "I was a college student about to be married. I wanted to be a psychoanalyst."

Charles's eyes lit up. "A colleague! And what do you miss most about mortality? I don't mean the weighty issues like family, friends, and the sun. I mean the little things. What do you most miss that you used to do as a human?"

Meghann thought about that. What would she most like to do again? "Baseball," she said after some consideration. "I'd give anything to pitch another game. But even more, I would love to be able to root for the Dodgers in July, with the sun beating down on my shoulders. Of course," she said with some bitterness, "I could't do that anyway since O'Malley had to move the team to L.A. Right now I don't have a favorite team to root for."

"Become a White Sox fan like me," Charles suggested happily. "Meghann, I knew we were going to be friends. Finally, a vampire who loves the game! Do you know I was at the 1918 Series?"

"You saw the Black Sox?" she asked in awe, referring to the infamous Series where the Chicago White Sox had eight team members blow the Series after being bribed by gamblers. "Did you know they threw the game?"

Charles frowned. "In retrospect, people like to say they could see the scam from a mile away. I don't think that's true. No, I didn't suspect. I was angry and disgusted with some of the players, but lots of fans were. We suspected them of being idiots, bunglers . . . not cheats." He inhaled and blew a few ostentatious rings at Meghann. "But I know how you feel. Do you know I missed Babe Ruth's entire career? I could kick myself for that. Oh, well, at least night games are gaining popularity."

"Or the 1955 World Series," Meghann mused. "To sit in the stands and see the Dodgers finally whip the Yankees. There's another thing to hate Simon for—taking baseball away from me."

Charles studied her gravely. "Tell me why he's given you reason to hate him."

Meghann poured another cup of coffee. "I guess you want my story now?"

"Take your time. I know it can't be easy. But please don't feel ashamed or embarrassed. I'm here to help, not admonish."

So Meghann told him about meeting Simon Baldevar at a friend's house, and what he later did to that friend. She laughed wryly when she told him that her first fear about Simon was that he would get her pregnant. She described that awful night when he made her drain Johnny Devlin.

"At first," Meghann said softly, head bent down, "I thought I loved him. He would give me anything I wanted. And I couldn't get enough of him in . . . well, I was very attracted to him. So a few years passed, and I was very happy. When Simon wants to, he makes me feel beautiful and adored. He can be so tender and loving. I can't tell you how many times he has brushed my hair, or held me close when I've awakened, screaming from a nightmare. To tell you the truth, my whole world revolved around him. I thought of him like a god. Every minute of the night, he was there. I was never lonely, and there was always something exciting to do. Or there were wonderful romantic nights together where he would hold me close all night and tell me stories. Not about himself . . . I know nothing of his history. But he would tell me about the Elizabethan court or life in France before the revolution and make me feel like I was there."

"Then why did you look so sad at that party?"

Meghann seemed absorbed in her coffee cup; she would not look up. "I'm scared of him," she said so quietly Charles almost didn't hear her.

He took her hand. "We're all scared of Simon Baldevar. Tell me what he did to make you frightened."

"He does bad things to me," she said in a child's voice.

Charles started rubbing her icy hands. "It might help to talk about it—get it off your chest."

When she started speaking, her eyes had a very distant look and her voice was barely above a whisper. "I told you of the good things. But sometimes, even when he's doing them . . . he hurts me. I never know what's going to provoke him. Usually, it's some foolish thing I say, or a certain tone. He gets this horrible look in his eyes. They just turn into hard, mean gold—like some rabid dog you just threw a rock at. And I . . . I hate myself for it, but that look makes me start begging him to forgive me. Sometimes I get on my knees. Usually that's all he wants. But other times . . . oh, God." She trembled and lit a cigarette. "He grabs me. I learned early on not to fight him because that only makes it worse. So he grabs me and drinks my blood until I can't even stand. I don't know if you know this, but if vampires lose blood, it weakens their natural defenses. Your body doesn't heal the way it's supposed to. So when he starts beating me, those bruises stick until I feed again. And when I'm lying on the floor, covered in bruises and so drained that I'm dizzy, he . . . Charles, he . . ."

"OK," he said soothingly. "You don't have to say it. It's all right—I know what you mean."

"No!" She threw her head up, and he wanted to cry at her desolate eyes. "That's not the worst part. The worst part comes after. When he's done and I'm bleeding with the scent of him all over me. Then I have to tell him how sorry I am. I have to beg and plead for him to forgive me. One time, I didn't. I just lay there and refused to speak. So he got a torch from the beach. He was going to burn me. . . . I didn't know if it would kill me or not. So I screamed. I screamed that I was sorry and I'd never be bad again. He let me scream and cry for mercy for six hours before forgiving me." Her eyes were glassy. "I never hesitated to apologize again."

Charles was looking at her with great pity. "It's not like that all the time. Usually, he loves me. The first few years, I could count the times he hurt me on one hand. But then—"

"After the party."

"Yes, after the party. Now not a month goes by that he doesn't beat me." Meghann looked at the floor. "I wasn't supposed to go out tonight—"

"Then it would be very dangerous for you to go back to his home."

"I thought of that," she replied. "I have some money . . . enough to get away."

"Meghann, money cannot help you. Simon is your master—he has an unbreakable link with you. There is nowhere in this world you can go that he will not find you. You need, particularly as a novice vampire, a protector."

Meghann looked at him steadily. "Are you offering me protection?"

Charles went to a trunk and pulled out a stiff piece of parchment. "Read this."

Meghann squinted at it. The writing was quite heavy, and a bit difficult to read with the elaborate, strangely shaped letters. It invited Meghann to accompany Charles to Ireland for the "Yuletide" holidays.

"This isn't a temporary respite," Charles told her. "We mean to offer you sanctuary from Lord Baldevar . . . if you want it."

Meghann was stunned. In two days, her life was changing. Who were these strange people who offered her an escape? She didn't care—she would have accepted a home with Lucifer if it meant a chance to get away. "I accept."

The phone rang in the sitting room. Charles excused himself.

He came back in a few minutes, obviously upset. "Meghann, we have a bit of a crisis on our hands."

"What?"

"I don't have time to explain everything, but our meeting was planned. My master lured Simon away. He intended to give us time to speak. But now Simon has injured Paul . . . found him in his lonely spot. I must go to him, help him."

"Of course."

"I want to take you with me, but I can't. It would be dangerous for you to be near Simon." Charles pulled out a huge black steamer trunk. "Meghann, under no circumstances are you to return to that town house. There could be a trap. In fact, you are not to stay in New York one more night. I want you to crawl into that trunk before sunrise. The hotel has instructions to ship it to my master's home in Ballnamore. Don't worry; there are airholes at the side. Promise me you'll be in that trunk."

"I swear," she told him, a bit dazed by all the turmoil.

Charles threw on his overcoat, and kissed her on the cheek. "I'll see you in Ballnamore."

"Charles?" she called before he left. "Would it be all right if I left the hotel tonight? I want to go to the cemetery and visit my father."

"You know where he's buried?"

"He and my mother have a plot together—I've been there a thousand times."

"I don't see the harm in it. Just make sure you're in that trunk by sunrise." He came back in, and hugged her fiercely. "Good luck."

NINE

Meghann entered Calvary Cemetery through one of the side streets, where all you had to do was climb over the rock facade to gain entrance.

She'd never been in a graveyard at night—although according to movies, it should be her home away from home since becoming a vampire. It was very peaceful and still. She thought it might be the only place in the city where you could get total peace and quiet. Vampires could see as well as cats in the dark—she admired the round photographs of the deceased carved into headstones, the fresh flowers and rosary beads some people put by the graves.

She walked with no hesitation. Her father had taken her to visit her mother's plot one Saturday a month. They would bring roses, and Jack would tell her stories about the mother she hardly remembered.

Meghann remembered that one time she admired the view of the skyline from her mother's plot. Her father had told her, "I wanted your mom and I to have a pretty place when we were gone. It would be boring to just stare at a tree or somebody's rooftop. Now we've got Manhattan to keep us entertained."

Meghann found the grave, and thought the view was even better at night. Two bare trees a few feet away from the grave encircled the twinkling lights of the sky-line. To the right, there were a few houses and on the left she could see the dome top to First Calvary Chapel.

She knelt down and ran her hand over the large oval stone with a stone cross carved on top and a trail of vines carved on the side. On the bottom of the tombstone, there was a small opening carved out of the stone. Protected by a small gate were a votive candle and a statue of the Virgin. Meghann opened the gate and lit the candle with the lighter Charles had given her.

She touched the two inscriptions, one already somewhat worn away and the other recently chiseled: MEGHANN FLYNN O'NEILL, 1893–1929, BELOVED MOTHER and JOHN PAUL O'NEILL, 1890–1957, BELOVED FATHER.

She smiled at the inscriptions. "You sure were beloved, Daddy." She wiped the tears away and said with a grin, "I didn't bring any flowers 'cause I knew you'd want something better." She reached into her purse and pulled out a fifth of Jameson Irish Whiskey.

While she poured it over the grave, she said, "I remember what you told us kids. You said we shouldn't let you get thirsty."

Meghann knelt down again at the foot of the grave, and stared into the candle flame. "I know I felt you last night, Daddy, and I'm glad for that. But I couldn't go away without telling you the whole story. I know you must have wondered why I never visited, why all you got from me was that one letter Simon made me write and some lousy Christmas cards.

"Do you want to know something, Daddy? It's not that he ever forbid me to see you; it was that I didn't think I could see you or talk to you. I didn't want you to see me with him. I guess I was always afraid if I looked at you, if you hugged me . . . I thought the whole thing would come pouring out. And I didn't want that because I was sure you'd hate me, be repulsed by me."

The cemetery was so quiet Meghann felt quite detached from the world—it was like she'd found one of the fairy knolls her father used to tell her stories about. The isolation allowed her to focus her thoughts. She continued talking to her father.

"You would be right to be repulsed. God knows I'm pretty repulsed by the thought of all I did. Do you know I can't even count the number of people I've killed so I could stay alive?" She didn't say aloud what she feared most—that her soul was condemned to eternal damnation for what she'd done. "And I never gave Johnny a second thought. I was a vampire, Daddy, plain and simple. I sucked people's blood and I didn't care one bit about them—their lives, the people who'd be hurt when they were gone. Nothing mattered except drinking blood . . . and Simon."

Just thinking of him enraged her. She glared at the headstone. "Someone just told me you don't have to kill people to drink their blood. Do you know what that means, Daddy? That bastard let me commit murder, had me thinking it was the only way I could survive." She laughed bitterly. "Oh, Daddy, I swear you wouldn't have recognized me if I did see you. Your little Maggie afraid to open her mouth, getting on her hands and knees before her master. Does that sound like me? I used to have a mouth and a temper . . . and I was never afraid to use them."

Meghann found some rocks by a neighboring grave. She started launching them at the tree, careful not to strike any of the graves. "Damn him!" she yelled. "I know it's awful, but do you want to know the truth? The dead people aren't what kills me. It's what he did to me! What he changed me into—a doll, a toy. That's all I'm supposed to be. Half the time I don't even pick out my own damn clothes. For thirteen years, I haven't been myself."

Throwing rocks was helping—so was that last thought. "Daddy? That's what's different these past two nights—I feel like myself again. Like I can say and do and think what I please. Well, to hell with Simon—I'm going to this Alcuin's tomorrow and I never have to be in his presence again."

The still quality in the cemetery changed abruptly. The quiet stopped being soothing and became ominous. Something else was in the cemetery with her— something malignant.

Meghann became absolutely still. She turned around very slowly, and saw Simon standing behind her.

How long had he been there? What had he heard? "You're back," she said unnecessarily. How had he known where to find her? Trevor, Meghann realized with a sinking heart. If Simon had called home and Trevor informed his master of Meghann's reaction to her father's death, Jack O'Neill's grave would be the first place Simon went to look for his missing consort.

"Will you come into my arms and welcome me? Or would you care to finish that treacherous soliloquy? Go on, child—spit on my gift to you and tell me it's a curse."

If you don't stand up to him now, you never will, she told herself. Falter and you'll be right back to being his timid little plaything. She grabbed Simon's face with both her hands.

He gazed down at her with amused speculation, and she kissed him firmly on the lips. "Master," she told him in a poisonously sweet tone, "that is the last kiss you get from me."

Simon yanked her hands off his face, and twisted them behind her back. It hurt, but she refused to give him the satisfaction of crying out. Then he kissed her so hard she could feel his blood teeth. She tried to twist away, lost her footing, and struggled to her knees.

"Now that," he told her smoothly, "is the position I want to see you in. If you beg me for forgiveness, I'll show you mercy."

"You should be begging me for forgiveness!" she yelled with her old temper. "How dare you keep my father's death from me! Who the hell do you think you are? Go away—we're through!" He released one of her hands, and backhanded her viciously across the face.

"Hit me all you want—you don't scare me!"

"I have not yet tried to scare you, little girl." Simon spoke in such a sinister whisper that her skin broke out in gooseflesh, but she refused to give up. She tried to use her free hand to punch him in the groin, but he grabbed her hand in a steel grip.

"Try that again," he told her in the same rancorous tone, "and I shall break every bone in your pretty little body. Then I will drain you of blood and leave you here to die when the sun rises."

He let go of her other hand, and she stood up shakily. She had no doubt he meant what he said, and that any attempt to harm him would be fruitless.

That didn't mean she wasn't going to try to gain her freedom. Defiantly she raised her head and gave him her most disdainful look. "You can break every bone in my body twice over, and you still won't get me to love you."

"Keep trying my patience, Meghann, and you'll find out all I can do to wipe that self-righteous look off your face."

"Why does the truth try your patience?" she asked boldly.

"Have you lost your mind to speak to me this way? Some cretinous boy-lover fills your head with sanctimonious notions and you forget all I have done for you?"

"How could I forget all you've done?" she asked venomously. "You took the sun away, along with my innocence, and turned me into a depraved bloodthirsty killer like you! And if that wasn't bad enough, you kept my father's illness from me."

"You ceased to be the daughter of some coarse Irish peasant when my blood started flowing through you. As your creator, I am all to you—you may put no one before me. I gave you everything when I made you my consort. Is this how you repay me, you ungrateful hellion?"

"Don't you call my father a peasant!" she yelled, shaken by his lunatic thoughts. "And I don't want anything from you, so go find some other girl to fuck you!"

"I will rip that viperous tongue from your mouth if you dare use language like that to me again." Lightning fast, he whipped his hand into her hair and lifted her off the ground. "I do not care what you want from me. I want so much more from you, pet. And we will start with what you promised me—love and obedience."

"You can't force someone to love you."

Simon laughed—a chilling sound that had no humanity or joy in it. It was like listening to a demon laugh. "Pretty child, I have spoiled you if you do not know that I can force anything I want from you. But the time has come to rectify that error."

In the dark, she could see his amber eyes glinting with fierce malevolence. *I'm so scared,* she thought as he leaned toward her. *Oh, God, I don't want to be here.*

And she found herself facedown in sand. Dazed, she pulled herself up and glanced around. When she saw the dark silhouette of the roller coaster, she knew exactly where she was. *Why, I'm on Rockaway Beach—this is the exact spot where my father always took me.* She had glanced at that roller coaster a thousand times from the water.

Wait a minute, she thought in growing amazement. *How did I get here? I traveled . . . by myself,* she thought with glee.

How had this happened? Of course—fight or flight! She'd learned about that in college. When you were threatened, your nervous system responded by either fighting or escaping. Her panic gave her the ability to travel the astral plane by herself. It hadn't been like those times she'd been with Simon—it had gone by too fast for her to remember anything.

Anyway, what does it matter, her practical side wanted to know. The important thing is you got here, safe from Simon. At least she hoped that was true. She looked around the deserted beach—she seemed to be alone.

Then she remembered what Simon had told her—you couldn't fly to a place you'd never been before. And she was fairly certain he'd never been to Rockaway.

She started dancing and shouting with joy. She was free, free, free! *I did it,* she thought with exultation, *I got away from the bastard! He can't follow my here—I'm free!*

Meghann walked up to the boardwalk. She consulted her watch: three o'clock. Well, there was no way to leave New York City tonight—it would take her at least an hour to get back to the city. She sat down on the boardwalk, enjoying the view of the moonlight on the water.

Meghann considered her situation. Sure, she'd mentioned Rockaway and the carefree summers she'd spent there to Simon in passing but it had been a long time ago—hopefully he'd forgotten. At any rate, it was unlikely he'd find her tonight or even tomorrow if she left Rockaway immediately after sunset. Therefore, it seemed logical to spend the day here, and leave New York the next evening. She thought she definitely shouldn't go back to the Algonquin—when Simon found her at Calvary, he knew about her meeting Charles. She might be walking into a trap if she attempted to get to that trunk. Well, all right. She still knew where Charles's master was—Ireland. And she had that money she'd taken from Simon. She would purchase her own trunk tomorrow and make the necessary arrangements.

The only thing that worried her was Charles telling her Simon could find her because they shared a link. Did that mean it wouldn't matter if she hid in Timbukto—Simon could always find her? No, there has to be some sort of limit . . . doesn't there? She decided since she couldn't do anything about it, she wouldn't worry.

So, she thought to herself, *what do I do now? It's awfully late.* She walked a few blocks and found a bar, The Black Bottom, that was still open. *Well, I escaped Satan's spawn tonight; I think I owe myself a drink.*

She walked in, and saw that the bar was empty except for a young bartender and an elderly man who was talking the ear off of the bored but tactful barkeep.

She sat on a stool by the elderly man.

"Does your father know you're out this late, lassie?" the elderly man demanded.

"What's the matter with you, Charlie?" the bartender spoke with an Irish lilt. "Anyone can tell plain as the nose on his face she's after leaving a jealous husband."

"How did you know that?" Meghann asked.

"Ah, well, when you've kept bar for a few years, you see everything. It's in your eyes, darlin'. . . . You look mad enough to spit and at the same time your eyes keep dartin' around like you're expectin' your man to storm in after you any second." The bartender grinned, and stuck out his hand to her. "I'm Roy Lynch, darlin', and don't ya be worryin'. . . . I'll throw the bum out of here if he tries to make you leave by force."

Meghann smiled back, and shook his hand. "I don't suppose you'd have malt whiskey back there?"

"Sure, and isn't this a good Irish bar? I have what you need—and I ain't discussin' the whiskey, mind." Roy gave her a lascivious smile, and poured a double shot.

Meghann appraised him—not especially good-looking with that sharp nose and thin lips, but nice enough with his curly black hair and blue eyes. Plus a wiry body with good, strong arms—he'd do very well. She returned his leer with one of her own, and raised her glass high. *"Erin go bragh."* She took the whiskey in one swallow, and placed it on the bar. "Hit me."

Charlie and Roy gaped at her. "And where did you learn to drink like that?" Charlie asked. "One gulp and not a gasp or choke from you."

"A performance like that rates a free drink," Roy said when he set the refilled glass in front of her.

"Let me buy you a drink instead," Meghann told him. "And one for you too," she told Charlie.

"Well, I'm not drinkin' with anyone whose name I don't know," Roy replied, bottle poised to pour.

"Meghann O'Neill."

"A good Irish name." Charlie approved heartily and thanked her for his drink.

Meghann and Roy chatted amiably until closing. "How mad are you at that husband, darlin'?" Roy asked around four A.M..

"He's just a boyfriend," Meghann said. "Why?"

"Well, darlin', what do you say to a drink at my apartment?"

A ridiculous thought struck her. In a way, she was still a virgin. She'd only slept with a vampire, never with a mortal man. Wasn't it about time to find out if there was a difference? And maybe she could find out if she was capable of drinking blood without killing her host.

At his apartment, Roy gave her a drink. After a few minutes, he started kissing her, and then they were in the bedroom. Roy mauled her breasts in a manner he seemed to think was designed to elicit pleasure for about thirty seconds, and then rammed himself into her. After a few thrusts, he screamed, "Holy Jesus Christ!" and collapsed on top of her.

Well, Meghann thought sourly, *I guess I have to give Simon his due—the bastard sure knows how to make love. Is this what most men are like? Wham, bam, thank you, ma'am.*

Roy rolled off her, and gave her a sleepy smile. "Want a cigarette, darlin'?"

"Sure."

They smoked silently, and then Roy yawned. "You wore me out, darlin'. Stay, if you want—I'll make you breakfast." Then he put his cigarette out and went to sleep.

That was it? Meghann thought incredulously. Simon liked to make love for hours, usually four or five times in a night. Well, vampires probably had more stamina. Still, that seemed awfully quick. And what did he have to be so tired about? He'd hardly done anything.

He started snoring—he was deeply asleep. Meghann decided that if he couldn't satisfy one desire, he could probably satisfy another. She pushed his thighs apart gently, and used her blood teeth to drink from the artery in his left thigh.

Roy sat up and screamed, "Hey!"

"Sleep," she told him and he dropped off without another word.

She felt the usual euphoria, and started drinking thirstily. Then she remembered her vow not to kill anybody. The blood lust told her to forget about it and keep drinking. No, she told herself. But how could she do this, she thought, her mouth filled with blood.

Maybe she could try counting—a minute's worth of blood should be enough.

She counted to sixty slowly, the act of counting pushing the blood lust back. After she got to sixty, she raised her head and looked at Roy. He seemed all right; he hadn't even woken up. His skin color looked good. She put her hand on the pulse in his wrist—it was strong and steady.

And how did she feel? Well, she wasn't glutted like she usually was, but there was a feeling of well-being. Charles was right. She could feed without killing. She leaned over and kissed Roy on the cheek. "Thanks for breakfast."

Breakfast! How could she have forgotten that she had to find a place to sleep before the sun rose? She looked at Roy's alarm clock—it was already five A.M. Where was she going to go? She needed a place that would allow in no sunlight and where she wouldn't be discovered. But where?

Wait a minute! What about Playland? The amusement park was closed for the season, so she should be safe there. She could hide in the fun house or the haunted house. Roy's apartment was on Beach 112th Street, and Playland was on Beach 97th. It shouldn't take more than twenty minutes to walk there.

Then again, why walk when you can fly? Meghann got out of bed and put on her clothes. Then she closed her eyes, took a deep breath, and thought Playland with all her will. Nothing happened. After five more minutes, she was still in Roy's bedroom.

Apparently, she still didn't have the hang of astral projection. Maybe she could only do it in emergency situations. Why had she landed in Rockaway? Because it was safe? Because she'd been thinking of her father and she associated the place with him? She left the apartment and began walking to Playland quickly, keeping a cautious eye on the brightening sky.

Three blocks from Playland, she started feeling very tired and weak. She had to force herself to climb the iron gates protecting the park. She managed to stagger to the door of the haunted house. It had a padlock and chain guarding the entrance; it took the last of her strength to break the lock.

Once inside the dark haunted house, she felt a little better. She took a tarp off one of the little gondolas people rode in through the house, and put it under the door to block any rays of sunlight. Then she used another tarp to make a bed of sorts on the hard, cold floor.

Before going to sleep, she took a glance around. She saw an ancient mummy and a papier-mâché Dracula leering in the darkness, awaiting summer when they would have people to scare again.

"Guess what, guys?" She yawned at them. "I used to come in here all the time—never thought I'd be a ghoul, though. Fit in pretty well with you monsters, don't I?"

Her words had a wry tone; she wasn't depressed or self-pitying anymore. For the first time since Simon had transformed her, she was content. Look at her accomplishments for the evening—she had escaped Simon and she'd taken blood without killing. If she had to live as a vampire, so be it. But from now on, it's going to be on her terms was her final thought before she fell asleep.

Meghann didn't rise in her usual, quick manner. She came to slowly, feeling very drowsy. *Feel like I was drugged,* she thought drowsily.

She dragged herself up off the floor, remembering

the previous evening. It was time to see about leaving for Europe. What time is it? Meghann peered at her watch, but the darkness was too thick for her to make out the time.

She opened the double doors to the haunted house and stepped outside. The first thing she noticed was how foggy it was. The mist was so thick she could barely see her hand in front of her face, even with the superior vision a vampire enjoyed.

She consulted her watch—twelve o'clock! How on earth had she slept until midnight? She never slept that late—the latest she ever woke up was a half hour after sunset. Then she remembered feeling drugged when she woke up, and her mouth went dry with fear.

Simon! Could he have commanded her to sleep this late? That was the only explanation that made any sense. But how had he found her? Oh, dear God—Roy! She had to make sure he was all right.

Meghann started running toward his apartment, the mist making her feel like she was in the middle of some horrible nightmare. This was the worst fog she had ever seen. There was no one on the street; she was completely alone. The streetlights were out on a few blocks. She ran, scared to death of what she might find. Please, God, she prayed, let Roy be OK.

At his apartment, she knocked on his door. The slight pressure made the door swing open—it had been unlocked. Heart in her throat, Meghann entered the living room. Too late, it occurred to her that if Simon had already been here, she was walking into a trap.

Now I'm really in a haunted house, she thought, feeling the psychic residue around her. Terror, great pain—they were all in this place. The air was thick with horror. The door to the bedroom was closed.

Whatever happened, it happened in that room. Meghann didn't want to see, but she found herself unable to stop walking over to the bedroom. *If there's a trap, I'm already caught.*

She threw open the door, and saw Roy's body immediately. It hung over the bed where he had been impaled to the wall by a wooden stake that was coming out of his chest. Her horror-struck eyes looked into his empty sockets—his eyes were gone. He had also been castrated—his penis was dangling limply out of his mouth.

Meghann screamed and the bedroom windows shattered. She felt an iron hand clamp over her mouth, and an equally strong arm circle her waist.

As she struggled wildly, a voice whispered, "Miss me, sweetheart?"

Simon! She struggled harder, squirming and thrashing. What was he going to do to her?

"You have disappointed me, Meghann." He buried his blood teeth in her neck, seeming intent on sucking the life out of her.

She bit his hand with her blood teeth. He cursed and pulled his hand away. She let out a howl of fright—putting cracks in the plaster. Before she knew what was happening, they were back in Simon's town house. Through flight, Meghann had not stopped screaming.

Simon paid no attention. He simply dragged her to the whirlpool he'd recently installed in the master bathroom and threw her in the steaming, bubbling water. "You still have the stink of that man on you."

"Yow!" How hot was this water if it was scalding her skin? Livid purple welts broke out all over her body and Meghann tried to jump out, but Simon grabbed her and forced her head under the water. She was going to be burned alive!

"The temperature is two hundred fifty degrees," he informed her calmly when he allowed her to resurface. "A mortal would already be severely disfigured, if not dead. Don't look so aghast. Do you think I have any desire to keep a deformed consort? Your body will recover from those burns, if I allow it to, so there's no need for histrionics. Now sit still and let me clean you." Simon picked up a vicious-looking brush and scrubbed her skin roughly, telling her he'd make her bleed from head to foot if she screamed.

Meghann forced herself not to move, and after an interminable length of time, Simon yanked her out of the water by the hair, using a coarse towel to dry her. She cried out when the towel opened up more cuts on her already bruised, aching skin. At her cry, Simon whacked her on the back of the head with the brush. "Be quiet." Then he attacked her hair, nearly pulling it out of her scalp with each vicious stroke.

When he was done, Simon put a white shift over her and left her whimpering on the bathroom floor. "There—at least now you're somewhat purified.

"What is the opposite of love, Meghann?" He kept his back to her while reaching into a large linen closet.

"Hate," she croaked, her voice gone from screaming and some of the boiling water that had gotten in her mouth. Meghann squirmed miserably on the floor, her only relief coming from the cold marble pressed against her flaming, burned skin.

"You don't ever want me to hate you. And let me warn you, I am very close to that." Simon turned around, a bullwhip coiled in his hands. He smiled when he saw her eyes bulge.

"Why did you do that?" she whispered through the pain in her throat. "You didn't just kill him. . . . You tortured him. Why? He didn't do anything wrong."

Simon cracked the whip, and it caught her arm. She yelped and curled up into a ball to protect herself from the lash. "He touched what is mine. However, if you wish to blame someone for his untimely passing, then blame yourself, trollop. It was you who broke your vow. And now you must be punished."

Simon cracked the whip again and she felt searing pain on her back. "You have a choice, Meghann. Get on your knees and beg me to forgive you for your betrayal. Do that, and I will give you a hundred lashes as punishment for your infidelity. In case you're thinking of further defiance, keep in mind that minor reprimand is mild compared to what I shall do if you anger me any further tonight."

She limped over to the whip and spat on it. Then she glared at Simon and used the last of her voice. "If I can't escape you, I don't want to live. Do your worst."

He smiled sadly. "Poor deluded child . . . I was hoping you would show some sense tonight. But I see you must learn the hard way. Meghann, you are no saint or martyr. But you have some romantic notion of yourself bravely facing death rather than living with me. However, when you are pushed, you always choose life, don't you? You did so when I offered to transform you, and let's not forget—you did kill your own fiancé so you could keep living. Your first instinct is for survival—a trait I admire greatly." Simon raised an eyebrow. "One more chance. Do you reject the gift of immortality I have given you?"

Meghann nodded. It was impossible to speak.

"If you don't want my gift, I'll take it back." Wave after wave of shock hit her as he drained her of blood. *He's going to kill me,* she thought dimly. *This is what it's like to die; what it felt like for all those people I bit.* It hurt, but the worst part was the feeling that the beast who was killing her was growing stronger as she grew weaker.

She thought she felt his teeth slide out of her neck. Is it over? Meghann couldn't see or hear. She couldn't move one finger; she didn't know if she was lying down.

Dimly she felt herself being dragged. Then she felt

cold air. The air revived her a bit. She heard a hammering noise, then felt a slight pain in both her hands. *I'm being crucified, she thought hazily.*

Simon lifted her head up. "I know you can hear me, Meghann. You are on my rooftop and you are so drained of blood you cannot move. However, should you get some strength, I have nailed your hands to the floor. When sunrise comes, you'll die. Isn't that what you want?"

Go to hell, she thought.

"We'll see if you're that brazen when the sun comes up. What I want you to understand, love, is that you can end this anytime you wish. All you have to do is beg my forgiveness. I'm rather interested to see what will happen. Will you nobly sacrifice your life to keep your pride intact, or will you yield to your master?" She felt his lips on hers. "The choice, which you insist I never gave you, is yours." She heard a door slam.

Meghann must have lost consciousness for a while, but she woke up when the sky became light. *I'm still on the rooftop—guess I'm gonna die. Poor butterfly,* she thought in delirium.

When the sky turned pink, an intense agony ripped through her. She tried to scream but couldn't. And she couldn't move one finger to save herself—she was trapped.

No, she thought grimly. *Won't do it—won't beg. I'll die.* At least she could see now—she wanted to see the sun.

It began to appear over the city, and Meghann felt like she was being stabbed with a thousand needles at once. *I'm in hell.* But still she didn't call out to Simon.

Then the first rays hit her, and she was blinded. Every where the sun hit, her skin burst into flames. She could smell her skin being burned.

No! Oh, God! The fire was killing her from within.

It was in her bones, eating through her heart, causing unbelievable agony.

Master, she screamed, unable to take the pain. *Oh, please forgive me!*

She heard a sickening tear of flesh as her hands were torn away from the nails. In seconds, she was safely inside the house.

But I'm deformed, she thought before she fainted. *Blind and burned all over . . . I'm a freak.*

TEN

Meghann woke up from a nightmare she couldn't remember. She looked around the bedroom in relief. What had scared her so?

Then she remembered the rooftop. That was no dream! She had burned, and the sun had taken her sight away.

But she could see now. She stretched her arms out— no scarred, blackened flesh. The skin was red with a slight purple tinge. It looked like that awful sunburn she'd gotten when she was twelve and fell asleep in the sun. Some of the cuts from the hell bath were still there, and she felt exhausted.

"You'll feel better after you feed."

A thin scream escaped her lips. Meghann looked up at Simon in complete terror. There was no thought of defiance now—she could not take that pain again.

She backed away, terrified of him.

"What's this? You have no reason to be scared—you were properly chastised for your behavior. Now prove you learned your lesson—on your knees."

Meghann knelt before him. When she looked up, he pushed her head down to his feet.

"Kiss your master's feet."

She complied without argument.

He yanked her up by the hair. "We still have a few minor matters to clear up." She started to rise, and he pushed her down. "Stay there. What do you have to say?"

"I'm sorry, Master," she said tonelessly, and felt a hand stroke her hair. Good doggie, Meghann thought bitterly, and looked up from her servile position when Simon laughed.

"You should make an effort to curb that self-pitying streak. Look at all the trouble it's gotten you into of late." He gave her cheek a hard pinch and then strolled toward the bed, stretching out while he kept his bright, hard eyes on her.

"Come here."

Meghann walked over to the bed apathetically and removed her white shift without comment when Simon ordered her to undress. She felt a dull flush of embarrassment at his appraising gaze; it occurred to her that standing naked before the fiend was even worse than kneeling before him to beg his forgiveness.

Meghann kept her eyes lowered, not wanting the bastard to see her defeated expression. She knew now Simon was right—she was no martyr or saint, able to withstand whatever torture he'd inflict before letting her die. How had all those people she'd read about as a child withstood persecution? How did you allow yourself to be subjected to the worst kind of agony, knowing all you had to do was renounce your beliefs or beg forgiveness and it would stop? *I'd give anything to be able to do it,* she thought, *but I'm just not strong enough.*

Simon moved over. "Sit down." She eyed him with growing suspicion. Did the martyrs have to do this? Still, like the cowardly thing she was, she perched on the edge of the bed, not allowing her body to touch his.

"The martyrs you unfavorably compare yourself to

were fools, sweet. And I would consider you a fool if you had allowed yourself to die."

"They weren't fools," she replied. "They went to their death with a belief in their ideals—and themselves." *What do I have,* she thought bitterly. She couldn't stand the thought of continuing to be Simon's slave.

She thought it would probably anger him, but she got up and sank to her knees by the bed, meeting Simon's eyes without anger or sadness, just a level stare. "Please let me go. Why are you forcing me to stay with you?"

Simon stretched his hand out, and she flinched. He laughed, and used his hand to pull her back up on the bed. Meghann thought briefly of resisting, remembered the agony he'd put her through the night before, and remained still as he placed her body between his legs with her back against his chest. "I'm not forcing you, Meghann. You had a choice to make last night."

"Why does the choice have to be life with you or death?"

"Because I can make it so. Last night, you had a small taste of the power I hold over you. I am in love with you. I refuse to live in this world without you. Since I have no desire to die, that means you live with me as my consort or you may greet the sunrise."

"Doesn't it bother you to live with someone who doesn't love you back?"

Simon moved the heavy length of her hair to one side and kissed the exposed nape of her neck. She tried to jump away, but he held her in place.

"Who doesn't love me back?" he murmured while one hand started moving up her leg.

God, no, Meghann prayed, knowing what Simon meant to do. It was what he always did after beating her—now harsh, cruel fists would turn into gentle, caressing hands that sought to make her respond to him while her body still bore the marks of his brutal treatment.

"Don't," she said, but her traitorous body relaxed; her cold, clammy, blood-starved skin sought out the warmth emanating from him.

"Poor little girl," Simon whispered, and Meghann heard the diabolical mockery underneath his seeming compassion. "You're so cold, so frightened. Why do you do this to yourself, Meghann? Why not simply behave and avoid punishment?"

"Leave me alone!" She moaned as one hand slyly insinuated itself between her legs while the other fondled her breasts. "Don't do this to me."

"Don't you like it?"

"No," Meghann said through tightly gritted teeth. "I . . . I hate it when you touch me."

Simon laughed nastily while his thumb flicked casually across her nipple, instantly making it tighten into a hard rosy peak. "Your body says otherwise. Was it like this with that mortal? Did you enjoy your adulterous encounter?"

"It was better than you!" Meghann cried recklessly. Maybe if she made him angry, he'd stop touching her like this, stop trying to make her respond to him. . . .

"Truly?" Simon said, and his nonchalant tone sounded as though he'd asked Meghann about nothing more important than the weather. "What did he do to give you pleasure? Did he do this?" Picking her up, Simon started moving her back and forth on his leg; the delicious friction of his hard, muscled thigh against her sensitive flesh made her whimper slightly. Jesus, it felt good!

Meghann tried to hold herself rigid, but Simon started kissing her neck, using his blood teeth to take little nips at her skin that made her shiver uncontrollably.

"Does it feel good?"

Meghann refused to answer and squeezed her eyes shut, feeling large, fat tears roll down her cheeks, tears of frustration and self-reproach. What was the matter with her? Why couldn't her body be cold and unresponsive when he touched her?

"Frigidity and self-denial are not in your nature, little vixen. Now, why not end this ridiculous farce and admit you desire me just as I want you?"

"No," she countered, and Simon shoved her beneath him, continuing to caress her.

"Say you love me, Meghann," Simon ordered, his clever fingers bringing her to the edge of climax and then withdrawing, leaving her aching and unfulfilled.

Meghann's lips trembled to keep from speaking, but after Simon began to toy with her again, she couldn't keep from sobbing out, "I love you!"

Simon made her see his vulpine grin and then he took her, slowly and lovingly. He made her scream in ecstasy, made her spread her legs and beg for more. The spell of lust and desire he weaved over her body pushed hate and fear to the most remote corners of her mind, and to Meghann's complete shame, there was no part of her not completely open to him and the pleasure he gave her.

When he was done, Meghann understood that he'd gotten her to sacrifice her last bit of pride. With dawning horror, she was beginning to understand his words of the night before—he could force love from her, or at least lust.

"Still feeling rebellious? What a challenge you are." Simon's words held no anger—he continued to pet and stroke her the way he always did after they made love.

"Much better than that riffraff you picked up, hmmm?"

What a vain, insufferable . . . It wasn't enough to make her want him—now she had to compliment him. "At least he wasn't after my soul."

"Then he was an imbecile." Simon gave her an emerald-colored dressing gown. "Come upstairs. I have a marvelous entertainment planned for this evening."

When they got to the living room, Trevor took in Meghann's injuries and smirked. She stopped dead, and Simon turned around. "What is it?"

"Maybe I am stuck here, but I'll be damned if I have to put up with that scum"—she pointed at Trevor—"leering at me."

"Apologize," Simon ordered Trevor.

"Master, I have done nothing wrong," Trevor said haughtily.

"You are forgetting your place," Simon told him in a cutting, whiplash tone that made the servant blanch. "You are also forgetting that you are eminently replaceable. Now, you have offended my consort. Beg her forgiveness."

Trevor started mumbling something, but at a sharp look from Simon, he dropped to his knees and said clearly, "I beg your pardon, Mistress."

Meghann wasn't interested—maybe Simon got some twisted pleasure from making people abase themselves, but she didn't. She glanced around the empty living room. "Where is your entertainment, Master?"

"Late. People are so unreliable." Simon gave her a pointed glance. "They make promises and then attempt to worm out of them."

Meghann ignored that, curling up into the sofa. She put her head on her knees—feeling the familiar depression take over.

The doorbell rang, and Meghann raised her head.

What did the archfiend have in mind for the evening? Some soul-crushing tragedy, no doubt.

Trevor admitted a woman, dragging along a small child.

It was impossible to determine the woman's age. She could have been thirty or fifty. She had badly peroxided blond hair, with dull black roots showing through. Her mascara stuck to her eyelids in thick clumps, her foundation was at least two inches thick, and her mouth was an imperfectly drawn scarlet slash. She wore a black dress too tight over an emaciated frame. Track marks marred the length of her arms—a junkie.

The boy seemed to be about five. Like the woman Meghann assumed was his mother, he was too thin. His face was dirty; his hair was an oily, unbrushed tangle. The cheap slacks and T-shirt he had on were badly wrinkled. He was very quiet, and Meghann knew why when she saw his enlarged pupils—he had been drugged.

The woman gave Simon a brief glance of acknowledgment, then took in the bruises on Meghann's arms. "If you want to slap me around, that's two hundred extra," she mumbled at Simon, swaying slightly.

Meghann got up, drawn to the pathetic little boy. She said, "Hi, sweetie," and extended her hand, but the woman snatched him away. Meghann thought it a protective gesture until the wicked bitch spoke.

"I told you," she snapped at Simon, "any action with the kid is five hundred—no less."

Meghann was sickened. "Action?" She looked at the whore's flat, expressionless eyes. "How can you sell your flesh and blood?" The depression fell; she was enraged at the thought of what this sweet child must have been through. She grabbed the prostitute and cracked her hard across the face. "You evil cunt! I hope you burn in hell! How can you let people—"

Simon laughed softly and pulled Meghann off the

apathetic woman. "Now, now, little one, you cannot hit our guest. I have not paid her yet." Meghann wrenched the little boy from his mother's greedy grasp. They retreated to the fireplace.

Simon removed ten $100 bills from his wallet and held them high above his head. The prostitute lost her apathetic expression; she was fixed on the money like a starving dog seeing a huge bone. She made a lunge for the cash, and Simon let it drop to the floor. Without any dignity, the woman scampered about, picking up the bills.

When she had the money secured in her garter belt, she asked Simon, "What's the deal? I do a show with your wife while you play with the kid?"

Meghann clutched the child to her. Simon could put her back on the roof—there was no way she was letting anything degrading happen to this boy again.

Simon saw the anxiety and fierce protectiveness on Meghann's face. "Now, little one," he chided, "when have you known me to seek out men or children for my pleasure?" He grabbed the whore and spun her around so she was facing Meghann.

"You had it wrong, harlot. You and I are the 'show'— for the edification of my young consort. She seems to believe I bear sole responsibility for all the evil in this world. Simply because I snuff out a few worthless lives." Simon grinned over the prostitute's head at Meghann. "Isn't that right, sweet? You have that sentimental, overly romantic view that mortals are good, that they don't deserve to be slain."

Meghann glared. What was he up to now? "I can't stand killing anymore. It's tearing me apart."

"Killing is doing nothing of the sort. It's your overactive Catholic conscience that is destroying what should be pure pleasure for you. As it is for me." Simon raked his short but sharp nails across the hooker's face. Instantly three bloody scratches appeared.

The woman yelped at the stinging pain and protested. "Not on the face, mister."

"But you have no need of an unmarked face where you're going."

The drug stupor drained from the prostitute's expression as she became aware of the danger she was in. She pleaded with Meghann. "Lady, you've gotta help me. I'm a mother."

Meghann rushed over and raked her own nails over Simon's light scratches. The woman screamed as Meghann clawed her. "You rotten, vile bitch! You would have let him violate that baby, and now you dare use your motherhood to get out of what you justly deserve!" She backhanded her. "I hope he makes you suffer."

Simon laughed that low, chilling laugh. "The pity of it is how sincere you are, Meghann. But we'll attend to that momentarily." He turned the hooker around so she had to stare at his piercing, evil eyes. "First I have a sentence to carry out." He tore into her neck, pulling back for a moment in distaste at the heavily drugged blood flow. Then he bent down again.

Meghann watched; at first, she was disgusted, but then blood lust started taking over. She needed blood so badly; she still hadn't fully recovered from the torture of the sun. Simon extended his hand, and she rushed over, past caring about right or wrong.

But Simon used his hand to keep her at arm's length while he finished the woman off. Meghann was fighting tooth and nail, desperate for blood. "Please," she begged, despising herself. "I need it. Please, Master!"

Simon raised his head from the corpse and easily caught the hand Meghann tried to slap him with. He pulled her close. "But I thought it was wrong to kill people."

Meghann was so starved her blood teeth were out. She even made a frenzied grab at Simon's wrist, but he held her back by her hair. "If you need blood, take him." He let go of her and indicated the boy.

The shock of his suggestion cut through the blood lust like a slap across the face. It was the worst thing he'd ever suggested.

"No," she gasped, horror-struck.

"Why not?"

"He's a little boy," she cried out, "a baby. He doesn't deserve—"

"Now, it's deserve, is it? Poor little girl. I'd bet all my possessions that you will not lose one moment's rest over this bit of trash." He kicked the dead prostitute. "But if I touch the child, you'll probably do your best to kill me. Who are you to decide which mortals 'deserve' death because they cannot live up to your exacting standards? Sweetheart, you glare at me like I'm some repulsive imp fresh from hell, but you don't even realize that you are breaking one of the seven deadly sins. Pride, Meghann." Simon traced her jaw with one finger. "What kind of vanity and arrogance does it take to decide that you alone are worthy of deciding who deserves death and who should be spared? Do you think of yourself as a god to pass judgment on the human race? If you do, I applaud you. But somehow, I doubt that. You seem to suffer from the misguided belief that most people are good. You're wrong, child. People are not good—they are low, stupid, petty creatures."

Simon gave her that vile, arching grin that made her flesh crawl. "Even your sainted father had some skeletons in his closet. What if I told you that the man you have on such a pedestal once had a union delegate beaten to death when the man tried to organize your father's construction company during the depression?"

"No!" Meghann shouted. "You're a liar."

"Now, Meghann, don't be angry with your father. Why should his workers get a decent wage when your father wanted to buy his little girl pretty dresses and expensive toys? Little one, your upbringing was paid for with blood money." Meghann was shaking her head furiously. "Or perhaps you'd like to know about the prostitute your father patronized once a month—after he took you to Calvary?"

"Why are you saying these terrible things?"

"I was curious. Do those sordid revelations make your father 'deserve' death?"

Now Meghann saw the point of all this. Well, Simon Baldevar could go to hell—he wasn't boxing her in that easily.

She raised her head high, and spoke in a clear, calm voice. "You're saying that people are flawed . . . inherently, hopelessly flawed. That even someone I revered, like my father, was capable of doing terrible things." She indicated the young boy. "So why shouldn't we kill young children, or anyone we wish? After all, they're tainted with original sin, right? Maybe that's true, Simon. But I have no desire to pollute my own soul any further by committing atrocities. I will not kill anyone." Simon's eyes darkened. He grabbed Meghann, but she continued. "Yes, I hated that woman. But I wouldn't kill her. She should be in jail. And that's where my father should have gone if what you say is true. I am not going to kill anyone ever again, Simon. So bring all the trash in the world through here. What you do is wrong and I want no part of it."

Simon searched her eyes, and she saw his orbs narrow in frustration. She felt a small bit of triumph; he hadn't been able to make her do or think what he wanted.

In disgust, he dropped her and went over to the child. Even through the murder of his mother, the child hadn't perked up. What the hell had that bitch given him to keep him so still?

Simon took the child in his arms, and the boy started crying. Meghann thought he probably did what he'd done to Johnny Devlin—heal the boy just enough to allow in pain.

The boy's crying cut through her like a knife. How could Simon just look down at the boy's face with no emotion other than blood lust?

"A child's blood is a rich, delicious banquet of innocence and fright. Since you choose to deny yourself the indulgence, I will take it for myself."

"No!" She could not allow such an abomination. As Simon bent his head toward the screaming, terrified boy, Meghann glanced around the room in a frenzy. Was there anything she could use as a weapon? Then her eyes fell on the two floor-to-ceiling windows. The glass would wound Simon if she could make it blow into the living room. . . .

In the same moment Meghann imagined the glass shattering, the windows exploded with such force she was thrown off her feet. Meghann fell against the fireplace as the glass flew into the living room—all toward Simon.

He had to drop the child to protect himself from the onslaught. Meghann grabbed the boy and shoved him behind her. Then she picked up the fireplace poker and held it out in front of her for protection.

Simon took his hands away from his face and Meghann cried out in terror. There were rivers of blood dripping down his bone-white face. His gold eyes stood out against the blood, glowing with insane hatred.

"What have you done to me?" he snarled at Megh-ann. He lunged toward her, but a shard of glass on the floor made him trip. He flew toward Meghann, and in a reflex action, she thrust the poker up . . . into his chest.

He screamed and collapsed on top of her. His body weight forced the poker deeper into his heart.

Meghann crawled out from under him. Simon was still and drained of color; the cuts on his face stood out in harsh relief from his pallor. Was he dead? She prodded him cautiously, jumping back when his eyes opened. They were full of pain—the only time she had ever seen him hurt.

Simon was panting and trying to raise his hands. He started saying something, but it was too low for her to understand. After watching him flounder like a dying fish for a few minutes, Meghann decided he was too wounded to hurt her. She pressed her ear to his lips.

"Get . . . it . . . out," he croaked.

"You can't take it out?" Then she remembered what he told her the night he made her kill Johnny Devlin: a stake through the heart would kill a vampire, but it took hours. Meghann wasn't going to sit around waiting for him to die. But how could she make sure he was dead? Burn him? She dismissed that idea. This was New York City—there was nowhere for her to light a funeral pyre without attracting notice. But she had a better idea—one Simon had given her.

She looked into her master's pain-racked but still arrogant gaze. She tried her best to match the malicious grin she'd seen on his face a thousand times. "Do you read the Bible, my dying worthless master? Are you familiar with 'An eye for an eye'?"

She turned her back on him and screeched, "Trevor!"

The servant entered the room, plainly not wanting to but unable to resist the command.

"Sweet Jesus," he intoned when he saw Simon on the floor, "you killed him!"

"Well, I'm trying to." She walked over to the man she loathed and forced herself to stroke his arm. "Trevor?" she purred. "I know we don't like each other, but can we make a deal?"

Trevor peeled his eyes away from his ailing master. "What kind of deal?"

"I'll double Lord Baldevar's retirement bonus to you if you help me get him on the rooftop. Two million dollars—payable tonight." Her businesslike demeanor couldn't mask the cold triumph in her eyes.

Trevor had no idea how she'd managed to gain the upper hand from Simon, but the master was obviously dying. He couldn't move and his eyes were becoming unfocused. "How do I know you'll pay me?"

"You don't," she said calmly, "but you're in no position to argue with me. Help me and I'll reward you. Argue, or try to help that bastard, and I'll put you on the roof next to Simon with your own hook through your chest. It takes hours to die from being impaled, Trevor. Agonizing, excruciating hours." She didn't know how much Trevor knew about vampires, or that she was drained of strength because of last night—she couldn't drag Simon up there by herself.

Her bluff worked because he went over to Simon and grabbed both arms. Trevor tried not to shake; he had never touched the master before. When he grabbed him, Simon focused his eyes long enough to make Trevor feel icy fingers grabbing his heart.

"Could you . . . er, grab his legs?"

Meghann worried briefly about leaving the child alone, but he seemed to have become numb again. He had stopped crying when the windows blew out. Now he was lying on the floor with his thumb in his mouth.

When she and Trevor got Simon to the center of the roof, Trevor dropped his burden. "When do I get my reward?"

"Why, I don't know." She yanked him close and bent toward his neck. "God will have to decide on your final reward after a lifetime of service to an evil scoundrel."

"No!" he yelled when he saw those sharp fangs descending. "You promised—"

"Never trust a vampire—particularly one who despises you." This was self-defense, Meghann told herself. She needed to regain her strength, and if she let Trevor live, she was sure he'd try to double-cross her.

The blood healed her. However, she got little pleasure from Trevor's sour taste. Her bruises faded and her strength returned. She should have felt more triumph at Simon's death, but she was still in shock at the dizzying turn of events.

A strong hand grasped her ankle, and the world went black. Through the void, she heard a voice order her, *Meghann, take it out.*

In a trance, she had her hands on the poker before she realized what she was doing. Then she backed away in terror. How much strength did Simon still have that he nearly got her to do something that would result in her own death?

She stumbled to the door of the roof. She had to get away from here, fight the voice that was trying to take over her consciousness again.

With much fumbling, she managed to throw on jeans and a flannel blouse. She yanked a suitcase from her dressing room and hastily threw in some underwear and clothing. She didn't want much, none of the jewels or furs. Just enough . . .

Take it out!

"Stop," she cried, and hastily closed the suitcase. No, wait—she threw in her father's mementos and flew down the staircase, nearly breaking her neck.

Help your master.

She threw open the safe with force of mind. Without thought, she grabbed a few stacks of money, not caring how much.

Help me, Meghann.

She had to hold on to the desk to keep from walking. *I won't,* she thought haltingly. *I won't.*

When she thought it was over, she grabbed the child and threw a coat on. She had the door open. . . .

Come to me.

Her feet were on the stairs when her eyes snapped open. By summoning every ounce of volition, she managed to rush through the front door with the little boy and the suitcase.

God must have been with her because a cab was going down the block and she hailed it. "Lady, are you OK? You look like you've seen a ghost."

It seemed to be a little better now that she was out of the house, but there was still something there—like a hand on her shoulder. "Where to, hon?"

What was she going to do with the child? His mother, pitiful excuse for one that she was, had been killed. Then she remembered the church she'd gone to with Charles. She gave the driver the address.

Outside the church, she knelt down and patted the boy's head. "What's your name, sweetie?"

"Mike," he said in a rusty voice—like he didn't speak that often.

Meghann wanted to do something for this child, help him somehow. She reached into his mind and inspected his harsh, traumatic memories. His mother had put him through hell, allowing all sorts of perverts to have their way with him. Meghann decided to make him a child once more—give him back his innocence.

She put her hands on his head; then she concentrated on obliterating his memory. She didn't know exactly how one went about this; she tried envisioning a blank slate and making the boy share the image. After a few minutes, she questioned him again.

"What is your name?"

The little boy looked at the pretty lady he thought he'd never seen before. "I don't know."

Thank God, Meghann thought. Now she was almost happy to be a vampire—Simon was as good as dead and she'd been able to help the boy.

She smiled and smoothed down the unwashed hair. "Your name is Mike. You don't remember your mommy's name or where you live. You're going to go into that nice church and tell the priest your name. But you're not going to mention me. Just your name, OK?"

The child nodded and kissed Meghann's cheek before he scampered into the church. She thought he'd be all right. Under the dirt, he seemed to be a handsome boy, and now he had no memory of the depravity his mother had forced him to take part in. Maybe the church would find good adoptive parents or a well-run orphanage.

Now she had personal business to do before she left New York.

Meghann walked along 58th Street and Roosevelt Avenue, picking out familiar childhood landmarks. The neighborhood had not changed much at all; most of the row houses still looked the same. Some had new coats of paint or different siding.

There it was—her father's handsome two-story brick

house. It would be Frankie's house now. This close to Christmas, she thought, there was a good chance the whole family would be there for the return of the prodigal sister. She thought back to the old days—getting together, picking out a tree, and fighting over the decorations. Goddamn Simon Baldevar to hell for taking that away. Well, hopefully, he was on his way there this minute. Meghann couldn't feel that oppressive hand anymore.

Meghann stood on the steps of the doorway, unable to summon the nerve to ring the doorbell. What if they wouldn't listen? What if they hated her? *Then I deserve it,* she told herself angrily.

While Meghann stood in a quandary, the heavy oak door swung open. Her brother Brian stood there in a black wool coat, with a priest's collar peeking through. He gasped at the sight of his long-lost sister. "Maggie!"

"You became a priest," she said in shock.

Brian didn't say anything else; he just grabbed her fiercely and plucked her off the ground. "I knew you'd come; I prayed to the Savior," he said through tears.

"Hey, Brian? What the hell is going on out there? I thought you had to head back. . . ." Her brother Frankie came to the door, wearing a sweater and pants. He stopped dead. "Maggie?" he whispered.

She looked up from Brian's protective embrace. Before she could say anything, Brian spoke up. "Now, Frankie, don't you yell at her. She's here; that's what counts."

"She should have been here for Daddy." Frankie didn't sound angry; he was too surprised.

Meghann started crying, loud and full of grief. "I didn't know!" she burst out. "He didn't tell me. I never got any of the calls or letters. . . ."

Frankie was startled. He placed a clumsy hand on his sister's hair. "For God's sake, you can't carry on like this in the street." His own voice was rough with with-held tears. "Theresa!" he shouted into the house while he grabbed the suitcase. "Maggie's here! Get her a brandy or something; she's upset." He headed inside, with Brian pulling Meghann along.

Brian deposited her on the familiar plush green sofa. Theresa was as shocked as the rest of them. She handed Meghann the drink and said, "I'm gonna get her a cold cloth for her eyes."

"Good," Frankie told her. "And call the rest of them. Tell our brothers their sister is finally home." He took Meghann's hands. "Jesus, you feel like ice. What the hell happened to you?"

"Frankie," Brian said warningly, "maybe we should give her a chance to relax—"

"No," Meghann said. "I want to tell you. I'm so sorry. I didn't know about Daddy or I would have come home."

"Aw, Maggie—you think I don't know that?" Frankie asked her. "I know what I wrote, but Brian told me I was wrong. We know you loved Daddy, but I was so . . . I didn't understand why you never came home. . . ."

Brian came to her other side while Theresa put the cloth on her forehead. Meghann wanted to cry again—from happiness. She had missed them all so much, missed the attention and simple love that asked nothing in return.

Theresa took one look at her sister-in-law's woebe-gone face and knew the answer to the whole mystery. "It was what I've told you all along, Frankie. That man, the husband—he probably kept it from Maggie."

"He's not my husband!" Meghann shouted. Every-one looked stunned, and she reminded herself of her upbringing. "I meant we're getting divorced. I hate him!"

Brian looked uncomfortable. "Honey, divorce is a mortal sin."

"Easy there, priest," Frankie cautioned. "Let's hear her side first. Why do you want a divorce?"

Meghann told them a tale that bore some resemblance to truth. She began with the letter she'd written her father. She told them that Simon Baldevar swept her off her feet with his charm and wealth (partially true). But after a while, he did terrible things. He beat her all the time (true). She left out the bondage and sadistic sex; it would shock them. Of course she told them nothing of him being a vampire (or her being one). What she did tell them was that she was not allowed any opinions or interests he did not approve of, that he controlled and dominated her life, beating her whenever she protested. She pointed to his wealth and influence as the reason she had a hard time leaving him. She finished by telling them she had only found out by accident about their father's death. Plus he beat her to within an inch of her life when she went to his grave.

"Were you married in the church?" Brian asked.

"I don't care if she was married by the goddamned pope," Frankie snarled. "She's not spending another night with the prick!"

"Frankie!" Theresa admonished.

"I'm sorry, but no one slaps my little sister around and then doesn't even have the common decency to tell her when her father's dying." Frankie tossed back his whiskey. "Asshole probably knew Daddy and the rest of us would tear him apart if we heard about how he treated her." Frankie threw his arms around Meghann. "You're home now, kid. You'll get your divorce and stay here till you meet someone else."

Meghann smiled. "Thanks for the offer, but I can't stay." She cut off his protests with more half-truths. "He's got more power than you can imagine. . . . I wouldn't be safe here. But I have friends . . . in Ireland. They can help me."

Frankie looked doubtful. "Frankie, please. I can't go from being his little wife to your little sister. I need to do this on my own. I left him on my own, didn't I? I promise, I'll be safe with my friends." Anyway, it wouldn't take too long for her family to figure out something was wrong. Should she ask her brother if she could sleep in the basement so the sun wouldn't kill her?

Frankie thought about it. "I guess you know best. But you better write. No more being such a stranger."

"Deal." She grinned at him.

"Still, can't we do anything for you?"

"Do we still have that trunk Mom and Daddy traveled over with?"

"The big steamer? Sure, it's in the attic."

"Let me have it. And, Frankie, do you think you could deliver it to Idlewild Airport tomorrow, around eight A.M.? It's going to my new home, but I don't have time to get it over there. It'll be in my hotel room."

"Hotel?" Frankie was aghast. "You'll stay here."

Meghann shook her head. "Can't—I have too much to do."

Frankie and the others looked downcast, but Meghann used a slight touch of persuasion. "You'll at least stay to see the others?"

"I wouldn't miss it for the world."

Her brothers came over, and Frankie cornered each in the hall, telling them Meghann's version of life with Simon. One by one, they trooped into the living room, vowing revenge and hugging the sister they thought they'd never see again.

Once death threats against Simon were done, the evening became very festive. Except for Meghann, they all got drunk, and before long, photo albums were out; the record player spun out loud, lively music. The neighbors didn't dare complain—Frankie was a precinct captain.

They expressed mild consternation that their baby sister had no children, then decided maybe that was for the best considering what a bastard her husband was. They all ordered her to find a better man in Ireland—the whole trouble was that Simon was British, they agreed.

Meghann danced with her brothers until they were all on the floor, gasping for breath. Around 4:00 A.M., Frankie finally gave her a ride into the city with their parents' trunk.

At the hotel, Frankie insisted on lugging the trunk up to the small room she'd reserved before going into Woodside to visit her family. Meghann had also called the airport to book a flight to Ireland for the next day, and had gone to Idlewild to pay for the cost of shipping herself over.

Frankie gave her a tight hug. "Keep in touch?"

"Of course."

He kissed her lightly on the forehead. "Forget what I wrote in that stupid letter. I always knew it wasn't your fault; there had to be an explanation. I love you, kid."

"I love you too," she told him.

Frankie left before he started crying. Meghann watched him leave, thankful that she'd had a chance to make amends with her family.

She packed her few belongings into the trunk, and swiped the hotel quilt. She had to at least try and make the damn thing comfortable. Meghann waited until the very last second before sunrise to climb inside. She pulled the lid down, then used her telekinetic ability to lock it.

I did it, she thought with wonder. *I escaped; Simon is dead. Wonder what's going to happen next,* she thought before going to sleep.

ELEVEN

December 18, 1957

Charles Tarleton took the trunk past a door saying NO ADMITTANCE. When he was satisfied that no one else was around, he opened it. "Meghann!"

She tried to leap up and hug him, but her legs were too stiff. He helped her up. "I know—it's uncomfortable."

"There's got to be a better way to do this," she grouched. She felt like a pretzel, and the light was hurting her eyes after the darkness of the trunk. Travel hadn't been a problem for her since Simon brought a private plane a few years ago. Still, it could be worse—she could have used a coffin.

Charles withdrew a small silver flask from his tweed coat and handed it to Meghann.

"What is it?"

"Blood—it will make you feel better."

Meghann grabbed the flask and gulped thirstily. What a terrific idea—you couldn't get caught up in the blood lust and kill people with a bottle. After she drained the flask, she was able to walk on her own. But first she threw her arms around Charles.

"Thank you for helping me with Simon."

"But I've done nothing," Charles protested. "When I came here and found my trunk empty, I was scared to death. But then I called the Algonquin and they told me your message—that a new trunk would be arriving in two days. How did you do it, Meghann? How did you escape Simon?"

Meghann sighed. "It's not something I want to think about. Would you mind terribly if I waited to meet Alcuin to tell you what happened? I don't want to have to go around telling this story over and over, like the Ancient Mariner."

"I understand." It could not have been easy—even with fresh blood, Meghann was too pale and had circles under her eyes. But those bright green pools also seemed more serene. Charles could barely wait to hear how she escaped Simon.

Charles led her to his Aston-Martin; he threw her scant belongings in the backseat.

Meghann looked at the Irish countryside. She finally got to see Ireland, but it was night. Why didn't she get to see the full beauty of the Emerald Isle?

They drove along in silence for a while, Meghann deriving some pleasure from the cottages and castle ruins she saw. At last, Charles pulled up to an immense structure that Meghann gaped at in awe.

"What do you think?"

Meghann looked in amazement at the tremendous brick structure with its clusters of chimneys, balustrades, and hipped roof. This wasn't a house—it was a small kingdom. She'd heard people talk about the stars in the sky making them feel insignificant—that was how she felt when she looked at the colossal manse in front of her.

"Georgian," Charles informed her, "built in the late eighteenth century."

"Do you ever get lost?" Meghann asked him.

Charles snickered. "I had the same thought when I first saw this place."

"Do people from that village we drove through work here?"

"Of course."

"But," she questioned, "don't they suspect that we're . . ."

"They know we're odd creatures," Charles answered. "But they don't care—their gratitude to Alcuin more than overcomes any concern over our eccentricities."

"Why are they grateful to Alcuin?" she asked curiously.

"That's an involved tale." He smiled. "Shall I tell you now, or do you want to go inside?"

"I'm not ready to cross the threshold to that monolith just yet," Meghann replied. "Tell me the story first."

Charles lit a cigarette and extended the pack to Meghann. Then they took a seat on a wrought-iron bench situated to view the Big House.

"What do you know of landlords in Ireland before the Easter Rising, Meghann?"

Meghann remembered some of her father's stories concerning the Anglo-Irish and their Big Houses. "That these houses were built at great expense by people who didn't give a damn about the poverty of their tenants," she replied with some bitterness. "How did Alcuin come to own this place?"

"He bought it from the owner." Charles took a dramatic pause. "Simon Baldevar."

Meghann gaped at him. "Simon Baldevar owned this house? When?"

"He wasn't using the name Baldevar; it was still too close to his mortal lifetime to risk it. Interestingly enough, you encountered him at the only time since mortal life he has used his real name. Lord Robert

Ashton, Earl of Wexford, built this Big House in 1795. Lord Ashton was a drunkard and a gambler who managed to lose the house in a wager to Simon, going by the name of Sir Edward Pembroke, in 1826." Charles studied her profile. "Do you know what 1847 was, Meghann?"

"Black '47," she answered promptly. "The worst year of the Irish Potato Famine."

"A dark time here—although most of the landlords weren't affected at all. No, they had their palatial homes; their extravagant lifestyles didn't abate one bit while their tenants starved. At a house like this, there would be a fete with lavish refreshments that guests gorged themselves on while in the village at least ten people would die—from starvation or fever brought on by their weakened state."

Meghann shivered, imagining the heartless bastards enjoying themselves while people like her great-grandmother ate the grass to survive.

"The Irish could not understand why God had turned His face and allowed this horrible suffering to go on. But the people in Ballnamore were convinced that God hadn't merely allowed the Hunger to plague them—he had sent a daemon to torture them too."

"Simon," she guessed.

Charles nodded grimly. "Indeed. Lord Baldevar wasn't content to ignore the pain like most of the Anglos. Oh, no—he thrived on it. He would have a starving family brought to him. Then he would dangle food before their pleading eyes. Only after the father had thrown himself on the floor, having completely debased himself in front of the guests, would Simon give them one loaf of bread for the whole family. Then he had the added entertainment of watching the family either give the food to the children, or attack each other for the largest portion."

Charles spat on the ground before he continued. "But our Simon is a pragmatic man. Although he has always enjoyed torment, he decided to sell his interests in Ireland in 1847. He knew the country would never completely recover from famine, and he would lose money if he stayed. Besides, even Virgins for Food was starting to bore him."

"Virgins for Food?" Meghann asked cautiously.

"Every full moon, Simon would have his steward go into the village to collect ten virgin girls between the ages of twelve to twenty. The girls were told they would be given enough food to last them and their families for a fortnight if they would agree to entertain Sir Pembroke for the evening."

"You mean he slept with those poor young—"

"Meghann!" Charles rebuked sarcastically. "That's hardly subtle. Oh, no. Lord Baldevar had a very different definition of 'entertain.' Sometimes he made them perform homosexual acts with each other—imagine what a shock that would be to a simple peasant girl. Or they would be gang-raped by his guests. Or simply tortured until the sun rose—whatever struck his perverted fancy that particular evening. Some, of course, were discovered by their grief-stricken parents in the morning . . . bled white.

"But like I said, Simon had had his fun and was ready to sell. Not that many people wanted to buy land in Ireland during the famine years. But he eventually found an earl who wanted to use the land to raise sheep—or so he told Simon. Actually, the earl owed Alcuin a favor, so he bought the land in name only. Once the papers were signed, the place was immediately deeded to Alcuin."

"How did this earl trick Simon?" she asked.

"The entire transaction was done through letters and factors. Not at all unusual for the time. Simon was furious when he discovered that the land had gone to his enemy, but there was nothing he could do about it."

"Why didn't he harm the earl?"

"He was already in Australia when he discovered the ruse. Simon wasn't going to travel all that way for an essentially minor inconvenience."

Charles smiled. "But the people of Ballnamore rejoiced when the sale went through. They figured, rightfully so, that no one could be worse than Simon. Imagine their joy when Alcuin called them up here for a night meeting."

Charles gestured to the long, curving driveway and the wide expanse of land. "Imagine all this space taken up by wooden tables. And imagine each table sagging under the weight of food—eggs, meat, ale, and bread. The townspeople were stunned—particularly when Alcuin informed them that for the people of Ballnamore the Potato Famine was over. There was enough to feed each family and they were to start eating. Then he showed them wagons stuffed with supplies. He said there would never again be hunger in the village—until this famine ended, he would provide each family with food. They never had to repay him either. Alcuin said that there would never be an eviction in Ballnamore again because the town had suffered enough under Simon."

Meghann clapped her hands together. "That's wonderful—I've never heard anything so grand!"

"Yes, Alcuin is quite proud of his work here. It's one of the few times he's been able to completely destroy Simon's intentions."

Meghann began to see why the people of Ballnamore didn't mind the vampire colony. "And since no one ever goes hungry or loses their house—"

"Or isn't given the finest medical care," Charles finished, "they have never revealed to an outsider the secret of the people who occupy the house but never leave it in the daytime. Or the fact that said people never age."

"The finest medical care?" Meghann asked.

"We have a small hospital on the premises," Charles explained. "Equipped with the most up-to-date equipment. We care for the town folk, of course, but we also conduct extensive research and leak our findings to selected mortal doctors." He grinned, and extended his arm to her. "Time to meet Alcuin. Don't be shy, Meghann. He's looking forward to meeting you."

Outside the parlor, Charles hesitated. "Meghann, there's something I didn't tell you." He smiled and pecked her on the cheek. "I don't want to scare you, but you're about to meet some people who may be a little cold. It has nothing to do with you—it's Simon they're leery of. But don't worry—whatever they say or do, remember I'm here for you."

Meghann smiled back. "Well, as long as I have one friend."

Charles opened the double doors to the parlor. It wasn't very well lit—Meghann could barely make out the hooded man on a thronelike chair in the center of the room. He was surrounded by four guards, all of whom were male and were holding swords.

"Is this Baldevar's whore?" one of them growled at Charles.

Meghann started to reply, but Charles grabbed her hand tightly. "This is Meghann O'Neill, who was invited here by our master."

"She's still that bastard's wench," another guard snapped. Coming over to Meghann, he used his substantial height to loom over her. "I don't know what kind of tricks that swine taught you," he hissed at her, "but you try anything to hurt my master and you'll answer to me, harlot."

Meghann raised her head, refusing to be intimidated. "I lived with Simon Baldevar for thirteen years," she told him in the whispery voice she'd learned from Simon. "Do you honestly think your boasts frighten me?"

The hooded man laughed. "Well put, *banrion.*" She could not place his accent at all—it was very queer. What had he called her? It sounded like *banreen.* He saw her quizzical look and explained. "That's Gaelic for a queen, or a regal, strong woman—which you most certainly are. My speech sounds odd? When I became a vampire, we still spoke Old English—which I doubt you would even recognize as English." He got up and walked over to Meghann and Charles. He took Meghann's hand and shook it firmly. "I am Alcuin, formerly the bishop of Kent. Welcome to my home, child."

"Thank you," she said shyly.

Alcuin asked one of the guards to fetch seats for Meghann and Charles. "I would like the rest of you to leave. Surely, you don't think this lass means to harm me?"

The guard who had snapped at Meghann and Charles came over and bowed his head. "I beg your pardon, miss. But you must understand that your presence threatens our master. Who knows what Lord Baldevar will do when he finds out that we harbor his consort?"

"But I killed Simon," she informed him.

Immediately the entire room went still, and they all gaped at Meghann.

"You have brought us his head?" one of the guards asked eagerly.

Meghann felt the first pangs of apprehension. "Why would I do that?" she asked uneasily.

Alcuin held up his hand to silence the room. He guided Meghann to the seat one of the guards had placed in front of his. "Why don't you tell me what happened?" he asked her gently.

Meghann told him the whole story, from Simon finding her in Rockaway to her leaving him on the roof. "Wouldn't daylight kill him?" she asked.

"Master," one of the guards said in disbelief, "how could he have not told her about the beheading and the heart rituals?"

"Guy," Alcuin said with patience, "use your head. Simon Baldevar has probably not told her anything that would not benefit him in some way. And I am sure that when he transformed her, he saw the possibility that one day she would wish to leave him. Why would he hand her the secret of how to do it?"

Alcuin grasped Meghann's hand. "*Banrion,* don't be anxious. In all likelihood, from what you tell me, Simon is dead. But my 'guards' are worried because the only ways to be sure a vampire is dead, aside from witnessing daylight killing him, are to cut off the head or cut out the heart and drink its blood."

"You mean he could still be alive?" she cried out, alarmed.

"Don't be upset," Alcuin soothed. "Granted, it sounds like you had more luck than skill that night. But has anyone here had even that much when they dealt with Simon Baldevar?" He glanced around the room, and all were silent. "I believe he is dead. And if he is not, you need not worry. He cannot set foot upon this property—it is protected land."

Meghann looked up at Alcuin, intending to thank him. Instead, she burst into tears.

Alcuin immediately handed her a white cotton handkerchief. "Except for Charles, I would appreciate it if everyone left. This child's grief is private, and I ask you to respect it."

The four guards left, muttering to themselves in discomfort. Alcuin whispered something to Charles, then took Meghann's trembling hands in his warm ones.

"Why do you weep, child?" he asked in a soothing, gentle tone, like she had never heard before.

"It's just you've accepted me and I—" She broke off, sobbing. "I don't deserve it. Sir, you do not know the horrible things I've done!"

"I am not *Sir,*" he said in that same gentle way. "I am Alcuin. You are Catholic, *banrion?*"

"Yes." She sniffled.

"I am a priest. Would you care to take the sacrament of penance?"

Meghann wanted nothing more than a chance to tell someone all that had happened since meeting Simon. She began as she had been taught: "Bless me, Father, for I have sinned. This is my first confession in thirteen years."

As she confessed her sins, the debaucheries, all the innocents killed so she could live, and killing Johnny Devlin, Alcuin never interrupted. Nor did he show any disgust or anger when Meghann described the horrible things she had done.

When she was finally silent, Charles came up to her and handed her a glass of green liquid. Meghann sipped it and started choking from the strong, vile drink.

"Absinthe," Charles told her, "favored drink of Rimbaud, the French poet, and the only alcohol capable of intoxicating a vampire."

"Simon never told me about it," she rasped.

"Lord Baldevar does not care for simple pleasures like alcohol—not when there's a world full of debauchery and evil awaiting his attention."

Alcuin gave her a sugar cube. "Suck on that while you drink," he suggested. He and Charles also drank the absinthe. "If we are going to discuss Simon," Alcuin said to Meghann, "I think we deserve a drink."

"Why are you being so nice to me?" she asked him. "I don't deserve soothing."

"Of course you do—anyone who spent so much time with Simon Baldevar deserves soothing."

"But I chose him," Meghann protested.

Alcuin put his drink down with a large thump. "I cannot believe the way that swine has manipulated you. If I never loathed him before, I most certainly would after hearing your tale. I will not allow you to blame yourself for a situation that was never your fault, Meghann."

When she started to reply, Alcuin grasped her hands again and continued before she could interrupt. "Think back. When did Simon offer to transform you—when you were strong and healthy, or when he'd already bled you to the brink of death?"

"I could have chosen death," she said softly.

"At eighteen? At that age, most children believe they're immortal—death is something they cannot imagine. No, *banrion*, don't blame yourself. You were frightened and sick." He paused. "Besides, what makes you think it would matter if you had begged Simon to kill you?"

"You think he would have made me a vampire anyway?"

"I am certain of it. Simon has never been swayed by consideration for others when taking what he wants."

"But still"—she looked down at the floor—"what about Johnny?"

Alcuin tilted her chin up—something Simon had done a thousand times, but this time was different. There was nothing possessive in the gesture. "How despicable he is. No one, and I mean no one, can control the blood lust when they first transform. The wonder of it is that you were able to resist for so long—most new vampires would have attacked anyone, even their own mothers, the second they walked through the door."

Alcuin took her hands in a hard grip. "You asked me to hear you as a priest. As a priest, and your mentor if you decide to accept me, here is your penance. It is the same penance I give to all who join my circle. Simon Baldevar made you a vampire. He gave you a need for blood that you had no way of controlling or understanding. Therefore, you are not accountable for anything in the past; you didn't know any better. Now, though, you will devote yourself to understanding your power. With my help, you will learn to control the darkness in your soul and you will never again take a human life to further your own. Furthermore, here is your Act of Contrition. You may never attempt to commit suicide. First, it's a mortal sin. Second, it is a vampire's responsibility to give back what we take from mortals by doing all we can to help them. We must stay alive as long as we can so we can help the most people. Do you accept?"

"What do you mean?" she said in confusion. "Of course I accept. Why wouldn't I?"

Alcuin nodded to Charles. At his nod, Charles flipped on the bright overhead light. When the light came on, Alcuin threw off his hood and Meghann gasped in shock.

Alcuin was horribly deformed. He had no hair or eyebrows, and his skin was completely translucent. Meghann could see all his veins, his gums, and even his skull. His blood teeth were rotted, vicious-looking things that curved past his jawbone.

"I see Simon neglected to mention the different

bloodlines," he said dryly. "Do you still wish me to be your mentor?"

At first, his appearance sickened her. But then she looked at his eyes and discovered they were Simon's eyes; they both had the same amber eyes. But where Simon had always reminded her of a hawk, this man had the eyes of a dove. They were filled with things she never saw when she looked at Simon—kindness, a gentle spirit, and a soul completely at peace.

Meghann did not have the words to convey to this man how much his acceptance meant to her, that his appearance meant nothing to her. So she leaned over and kissed his grotesque cheek.

Alcuin put his hand on her forehead and made the sign of the cross. *"Banrion,* Simon has not left any mark upon your soul."

"Why do you have his eyes?" she asked.

"Very perceptive. It is because I am his uncle."

Meghann gasped. "You're related? But how are you both vampires . . . Did you make him a vampire?"

"Thankfully, I do not have that grave sin on my soul. No, I was transformed two hundred years before Simon—during the Black Death. The fact that we are both vampires is merely coincidence."

"What was the Black Death like?" she asked with great curiosity.

"It is almost impossible to describe—especially to someone who lives in our modern, relatively disease-free world. Oh, there is still and always will be illness, but I have never seen anything like that plague in all my years upon this earth."

Alcuin gazed into the depths of his glass. "The term Dark Ages is in no way an exaggeration of that time. No knowledge, less than five percent of the population literate, abominable living conditions. My God, Meghann, I believe you or Charles would faint from the odors alone if you could be transported back to that time. If you bathed twice a year, that was considered a great deal. If you could have seen the people—dirt-encrusted, running sores all over their bodies, black rotten teeth by the age of ten. It was a hard, brutal life. Most people were employed in backbreaking physical toil. You lived on a manor that most people, even the nobles, did not stray more than five miles from in their whole life. Or you lived in a town that was wall-to-wall filth. Which is of course where Black Death came from—the vermin."

Alcuin shivered, and wrapped his cloak around his body tightly. Both Meghann and Charles were completely caught up in the tale—it was almost like they were there. "Now into this comes a fierce disease that wipes out whole towns and villages in a matter of days. I hope to God I never see anything like it again. Can you two children who have known penicillin and modern medical care even begin to imagine? Try to picture this. You're both living in a town and suddenly people are stricken ill by a terrible sickness that kills after days of fever and unimaginable agony. I believe even transformation is mild compared to what those afflicted with Black Death suffered. Now you see people die in excruciating torment over and over. Your mother, sister, husband, friend—everyone is sick. You wait in terror. Are you next? Will that awful curse strike you? Let's say it doesn't—still, the world has come to an end. Everyone you know is dead or dying. You flee the town or manor—go to a new place. And discover the Black Death has beaten you there. Everywhere you go there are hideous, black, swollen bodies. There is nowhere to run—chaos and fear rule the earth."

Alcuin took a large drink; Meghann and Charles followed suit. Charles held her hand for reassurance—she squeezed it hard while Alcuin continued. "As a bishop, people looked to me for answers—which I did not have. All I could do was what the other clergy did—the last rites. Sometimes I administered extreme unction to as many as thirty people a day. After a while, I simply said it over whole villages or a heap of bodies about to be burned. Within a year, I was in the same shell-shocked state as everyone around me. I did my duty blindly—I no longer even had the strength to question God for allowing this to happen. I didn't even wonder why I wasn't stricken—like many, I wished I would be so I could leave the hell on earth I found myself in."

He broke off, and held his deformed hand up—studying it. "You must understand, everyone was driven insane by the madness we had to live through—and that included vampires. Vampires have superhuman intelligence, but they are limited to the knowledge that exists in the mortal world. For example, a vampire can learn the entire French language in three hours, but first there must be a language for him to learn. So vampires had no idea what was causing the plague—and they were just as paranoid and superstitious as any mortal. Many vampires died during the Black Death because it meant there were precious little mortals left to feed off. They would not dare attack the sick for fear they would be stricken. And so one day, one attacked me. You see my deformities; the kind that attacked me usually kept to itself. But the plague terrorized it. So rather than kill me, in its demented mind, it figured that perhaps God would bless a vampire that was also a priest. Therefore, I would end the whole mess. Or so the poor thing rationalized."

Meghann found her voice again. "I don't understand. Are you saying that besides physical deformities, you also become deranged in your bloodline?"

"Oh, no, *banrion*. My mind remained sound—the creature that transformed me was insane because of the plague. When I had no more answers as a vampire than a mortal about the plague, it despaired. It begged me to greet the sun with it, but I could not do that. Although I was heartsore and horrified by my new grotesqueries, suicide remained a mortal sin. So I kept living—and I saw the end of the Black Death. I adapted. I learned to never let anyone see my face—that used to be far easier before Mr. Edison. I found other vampires—miserable creatures who despised the blood lust. I have done my best to help them, and I shall continue to do so. I believe God wanted me to be transformed so I could guide vampires. Perhaps that sounds arrogant, but I truly believe that is my purpose."

Meghann and Charles exchanged glances of awe. Charles had never heard Alcuin's entire tale. He looked into his new friend's leaf-green eyes and saw a mirror of his thoughts. They were quite comely, he and Meghann. Would either of them have accepted becoming grossly deformed with such equanimity? Or would it have driven them to the coward's way of suicide?

Meghann spoke their thoughts aloud. "You are not arrogant, Alcuin. I . . . I do not know what to say. All this time I looked at immortality and what it did to me. Me and my problems are all I ever thought about. You make me ashamed because I never once thought of others. But I will now. You're right. . . . We have a responsibility." Charles nodded in agreement.

"There's no need to feel shame, *banrion*. To have lived with Lord Baldevar all this time, and still be capable of feeling duty toward mortals, to want to change, makes me hold you in very high esteem. You do honor to my house . . . as do you, Charles. You risked a great deal to reach out to Meghann. I compliment you . . . once for seeing what a fine young lady she is and once for braving Simon's wrath."

"Alcuin," she began, "how well do you know Simon?"

"About as well as anyone can know that blackguard. Why?"

"Is it true that he never had a . . . consort before me?"

Alcuin nodded. "He transformed many people . . . to gain their wealth, for slaves under his dominion. But you are the only one he made for a companion."

"But why?" she asked. "Why me?"

Alcuin sighed, and finished his drink. "Two reasons. First, you remind him of his second wife."

"Wife!" Meghann exclaimed. "When was he married? Why do I remind Simon of her? Why was he married twice?"

"You know nothing of Lord Baldevar?" Charles asked in shock.

"He never told me anything." She turned to Alcuin, who was pouring a second hefty glass of absinthe. "Will you tell me about Simon? I think I have a right to know."

"Of course you do. But I am warning you—it's not a pleasant story."

"Knowing what I do of Simon, I would expect no less."

Alcuin nodded. "I'll start at the beginning, *banrion*. Simon Baldevar was born on a small estate near York in 1560. He had two older brothers, Roger and Michael. Roger was the eldest and destined to succeed their father, Payton, as baron."

"Baron?" Meghann questioned. "Simon is an earl."

"A title given to him by Queen Elizabeth I," Alcuin replied. "To put it mildly, Simon was frustrated at being born the youngest son in a declining family. The Baldevars were a minor noble family, and they fit into a typical Elizabethan pattern. Venerable lineage, some land but no real wealth. What little there was would of course go to Roger. Simon was enraged by the thought of living the life of a third son—marriage to some landless woman of no account, his home some minor keep his brother would dower him."

"So what did he do?"

"In 1578, a young explorer came to Baron Payton with a proposition. He wanted to mount a voyage to the Middle East and he needed to sail under the protection of a noble name. If Payton would finance the trip, and provide protection that he could obtain from the queen, the explorer would give him seventy-five percent of the profit. Alas, the baron was a cautious man. He was not willing to risk his crumbling estate on what seemed to him a risky venture."

Alcuin paused to take a drink. "Simon was furious with his father. He called him a fool, an idiot. Simon insisted that the family rebuild their wealth, as other noble families were doing—through investment in trade, backing merchants, shipping. Simon was quite right about the chance for success, but Payton unfortunately couldn't see that. He ordered his youngest son to leave his sight."

"What happened next?"

"The next morning, a maid discovered the baron's body in his bed."

"Did Simon kill him?" Meghann was fascinated.

"It was never proven. There were no signs of a struggle or poison. But many people—retainers, the explorer, serving girls—had heard Simon argue with his father the night before. The rumors began to fly that Simon had killed his father through sorcery—rumors that Simon did his best to encourage."

"Wasn't he worried about being burned at the stake?" Meghann asked.

"Not at all—and to some extent, the gossip was true.

From a very young age, Simon dabbled in the black arts. A fact his brother Roger, now the baron, was well aware of. Roger was a deeply superstitious man and was terrified that Simon would use his black magic on him too. It took very little to persuade him to mount the expedition. His only stipulation was that his younger brother must accompany the explorer to the Levant."

"Probably hoping the journey would kill him," Charles put in.

"No one should underestimate Simon," Alcuin said. "He didn't die—that first exploration was a smashing success. Simon, without consulting Roger, purchased more ships—bound for the New World, India, and Algiers. In a few years, he tripled the Baldevar fortunes. He remained in Constantinople for ten years—I understand the Ottoman was quite fond of him."

"Why come back?" Meghann asked. "If the Sultan favored him, then he could have made his own fortune in Turkey."

"He didn't desire a Turkish fortune—he wanted what he thought was his. To his way of thinking, Roger was a stupid leech, who by a simple accident of birth was enjoying the profits of Simon's hard work. As far as he was concerned, he wanted everything he thought should be his—all the wealth, his brother's title, and marriage into a good family."

"So he had to come back and kill Roger to gain all of that," Meghann concluded.

"Correct," Alcuin answered.

"Had Simon married while he was in Turkey?" Meghann asked. "You said he married twice, and he would have been twenty-eight when he returned to England. I thought people married young in the Renaissance."

"They did—Simon was married for the first time when he was seventeen to Alice Joyes, eldest daughter of a prosperous merchant. He left her behind when he went to Turkey, and she contracted 'white throat' a few years after he left. He had nothing to do with her death, but I'm sure he regarded it as good luck. Now he was free to pursue a high-born woman for a better match."

"Did Simon kill Roger when he came back?" Meghann wanted to know. "And why didn't he kill the other brother too—Michael?"

"Michael died in the same epidemic that killed Alice—more good luck for Simon." Alcuin gave Meghann a sad smile. "Now we come to the part of the tale that pertains to you, *banrion.*"

"Me? Oh, you mean Simon's second wife."

Alcuin sighed heavily. "Indeed, Simon's second wife—and his brother Roger's first wife, Baroness Isabelle Baldevar."

"He married his brother's wife?" Meghann asked incredulously. "But why? Why did she marry him? Did they love each other? Did he kill his brother for her? And why do I remind Simon of her?"

Alcuin stood and offered his arm to Meghann. "Come with me and you'll understand. Charles, would you like to join us?"

Alcuin took her into the library where he guided her to a portrait over the fireplace. Meghann looked up at it and gasped.

"There is an uncanny physical resemblance between you and Isabelle," Alcuin told her. "The only substantial difference is in your eyes."

The painting stunned Meghann. It was like looking at a portrait of herself from another time—except the woman in the painting had violet eyes while Meghann's were light green.

Charles spoke up. "Isabelle's features are a bit more delicate than Meghann's."

"Isabelle was French," Alcuin replied, "but the likeness is eerie—same color hair, even the shape of your eyes is similar."

Meghann couldn't stop gaping at the painting. *You could be my sister,* she thought as she stared at the woman above her, *or you could be . . . me.* Isabelle's hair was gathered into fiery red coils that rested on a lavender neck whisk. She was wearing a violet gown that matched her eyes. Meghann stared at the gown in wonder; she had never seen anything like it. The gown had a square-cut neckline with huge puffed sleeves that were slashed to reveal a light violet material. They tapered at her elbows. The gown had amethyst and diamond chips sprinkled all over the bodice and overskirt. There was an underskirt that matched the material in the sleeves. Isabelle was wearing a diamond and amethyst necklace. Pearl and diamond bob earrings dangled from her ears. Meghann frowned, trying to remember what that gown reminded her of. Her eyes widened when she realized that the violet gown was the same color as the dress she wore the night she met Simon Baldevar. That thought made her extremely uncomfortable. Had Simon looked at her and seen a woman he'd been married to nearly four hundred years before?

Meghann reached up and touched the painting. "She's beautiful. I wish I had eyes like that."

"Are you sure?" Alcuin questioned. "Take another look at her eyes—tell me what you see."

Meghann studied the painting more closely. At first, she had thought the woman's expression was tranquil, but now she saw that Isabelle's lips were tightly compressed. There seemed to be some tension in her face—like she was trying not to cry.

She turned to Alcuin. "Her eyes are stunning—I've never seen that shade before. But they seem filled with sadness—it's like her heart is breaking."

"That portrait was painted on the day she married Simon Baldevar," Alcuin informed her.

Meghann pulled her hand away as though she'd been scalded. "But she looks like she's dying!"

"I'm sure she regarded marriage to Simon as a living death," Charles said softly.

"What did he do to her?" Meghann demanded. The hair stood up on the back of her neck. "He didn't make her a vampire too?"

"Simon wasn't a vampire when he married Isabelle. . . . No, he never transformed her. In a way, what he did to her was far worse. Are you sure you're ready to hear this?"

Meghann and Charles nodded their heads. Charles only knew a little of Isabelle Baldevar's tragic tale.

"Isabelle married Roger when she was fifteen years old—two years before Simon returned. The marriage was arranged to join land the two families owned in France, but over time it became a love match—rather rare for the time. One year before Simon came home, Isabelle gave birth to a son, named Michael for his deceased uncle."

Meghann, veteran of a thousand radio soap operas, picked up the thread of the story. "Then Simon came back and shattered their domestic bliss."

Alcuin nodded. "Your choice of words is quite accurate. Naturally, Simon always had it in mind to murder Roger, but that desire intensified when he became infatuated with Isabelle."

"Did she return his feelings?" Charles asked.

"Not at all. Isabelle was devoted to Roger, and she had a strong sense of honor. She would never betray her wedding vows. Now, Simon is a very good-looking man and can be quite charming when he wishes. He was not used to being turned down. Isabelle's refusal drove him wild."

"What did he do?" Meghann whispered.

"He never left the poor girl alone. She didn't know what to do; she was scared Roger might blame her. Matters came to a head one night when Roger came back from a hunt early and found Simon attempting to rape his young wife."

"And Roger—"

"Roger attacked him. They fought and Simon killed his brother before Isabelle's horrified eyes."

Alcuin paused and studied the painting. Meghann started in on her third glass of absinthe. She was starting to feel a bit intoxicated.

"With his brother slain, Simon had everything he wanted within his grasp. The only problem was Isabelle—she was the sole witness to the murder. Simon told her precisely what they were going to do. They would go to court where Isabelle would tell the queen that one of her husband's men had attacked her. Roger bravely fought him, but he was killed. At this point, Simon entered the room and killed the rogue. After Isabelle explained the situation to Elizabeth, Simon would petition the queen to name him Michael's guardian to rule as baron until the young boy reached his majority and assign him Isabelle's hand in marriage."

Meghann looked at the sorrowful woman. "Is that what happened?"

Alcuin gave a half smile. "Not exactly. Isabelle was a bit like you, Meghann—a determined young lady. She was more resourceful than Simon gave her credit for. While Simon thought she was sleeping, Isabelle fled the estate. Her plan was to beat Simon to the court and tell the queen the true story of her husband's murder. She rode at a furious pace, taking only two of Roger's most trusted retainers for protection."

Good for you, Meghann told the picture silently.

Then she frowned. "But what about her child, Michael? Wasn't she scared to leave him alone with Simon?"

"She didn't. Isabelle gave the infant to the captain of Roger's guard. Her plan was for the guard to take Michael to her father in Nice—along with a letter detailing what Simon had done to Roger."

Meghann felt like cheering for Isabelle, but then the tortured eyes caught her attention again. "What went wrong?"

"Four days later, Isabelle appeared before Queen Elizabeth and told her that she'd been widowed when a brigand guard murdered her husband. Only the quick action of her brother-in-law saved her life."

Meghann was crestfallen. "Why did she do it?"

When Alcuin spoke again, his voice was calm, but his lips were as tightly compressed as the painting of Isabelle. "Because when Isabelle arrived at court, Simon was already there. He escorted her to the suite of rooms the queen had given them. Once they were there, he produced her infant son, Michael. He put a knife to the infant's throat and assured her that he would murder the child if Isabelle did not back his story."

Charles spoke up before Meghann. "But how did he find the baby?"

"When Simon discovered Isabelle's disappearance, he had Alma, her tiring woman, brought before him. She refused to tell him anything, until he removed her fingernails with a hot pincer. Once he knew Isabelle's plan, it was easy to capture the captain of the guard who had to ride at a slow pace because of the baby. As for Isabelle, she was from France, and Roger's retainers had never been more than fifteen miles from the estate. None of them knew the most direct route to London, or which castle Elizabeth was holding court in—Simon did."

"Well," Meghann said practically, "why not agree to Simon's terms and then tell the queen the truth anyway?"

"He put a full-time guard on the child—his guard. The man had specific instructions to slaughter the child the second Simon was arrested."

Alcuin gave Meghann a twisted smile. "What do you know of Elizabeth?"

Meghann searched her brain for all she'd learned in history classes. "She was the Virgin Queen, and she made England a powerful empire."

"She may well have been 'virgin,' but she had an eye for handsome men. Appearing at court was the best thing that could have happened to Simon. The elderly queen became infatuated with his looks and charm. But what really enthralled her was his financial wizardry. Simon truly was an alchemist—everything he touched turned to gold. By 1588, the Crown was heavily in debt. By following Simon's advice, Elizabeth was able to recoup some of her losses. She made Simon a member of the court. Within a few months, she created him Lord Simon Baldevar, Earl of Lecarrow. Simon could do no wrong in the queen's eyes—even when he began beating Isabelle."

"Why did he beat her?"

Alcuin avoided Meghann's eyes. "Isabelle was a simple, Catholic noblewoman. You see, in Constantinople, Simon developed very . . . sophisticated tastes, and Isabelle was incapable of . . . pleasing him."

Meghann blushed scarlet. She knew what tastes Alcuin was referring to. That guard was right. . . . She was Baldevar's harlot.

"No, *banrion*." Alcuin looked at her again. "You mustn't be ashamed of being a healthy, passionate young woman. Simon is attractive and . . . responding to him was a perfectly normal reaction. Indeed, Isabelle's life would have been far easier if she could have pleased him. But she found sex distasteful . . . particularly the way Simon wanted it. On their wedding night, he beat her black and blue in disgust. After a while, he entertained himself with the ladies of the court . . . sleeping with Isabelle only for the purpose of procreation."

"Procreation? Simon wanted children?" It had never occurred to Meghann that Simon could have had mortal children. "Did he have children?"

"No, at least none that I know of."

"Was Isabelle scared to give him a son—for fear he would murder her child with Roger?"

"Quite the opposite. She was terrified of what he would do to Michael if she didn't produce an heir. You see if Simon had a son, that child would be in line to succeed him as earl. Roger was the former baron—the earldom started with Simon. So if she could give him a son, Michael would be quite safe from his stepfather's wrath. Indeed, Simon told Isabelle that once she gave birth to a healthy male heir, she could live out the rest of her life in France with her firstborn. Simon would even give the boy the land in France. So she wanted a second son almost as much as Simon did."

"But you said he never had children."

Alcuin bowed his head. "Oh, Isabelle—centuries have passed and your story still hurts me. After three months of marriage, she discovered she was pregnant. At first, Simon was so thrilled he was nearly cordial to her. He no longer forced her to his bed, and the beatings stopped—he would not harm his heir." Alcuin stopped and looked at Charles. "My young physician, what do you think medical care was like in the sixteenth century?"

Charles considered the question. "Horrible, Master. Did something go wrong with the delivery?"

"No, in her sixth month, she had a miscarriage. I believe she had what we now diagnose as toxemia. Anyway, she lost the baby—which was a boy."

Alcuin shuddered. "Simon was enraged. She told me how . . . he came to her bed and started throttling her. Before the midwife managed to get someone to pull him off, he screamed, 'You rotten, lazy, stupid wench! How dare you bleed my heir away! What the hell is wrong with you? You disgust me!' But that wrath was nothing compared to what he displayed when the court physician informed him that the miscarriage had so damaged Isabelle that she would never again be able to conceive a child."

Meghann and Charles exchanged sickened glances. Charles asked the question Meghann could not bring herself to say aloud. "What happened next?"

"As far as Simon was concerned, Isabelle was worthless now . . . and that is the way he treated her. He punished her morning, noon, and night. There were horrific beatings, and he made her participate in orgies. He knew her feelings . . . and it gave him no end of pleasure to see her cry and beg for deliverance from the sick acts he made her perform. The first night, he expected to see her copulate with two other women . . . and a dog." Meghann choked on her drink, and Alcuin waited until she regained her composure to continue. "With her last show of spirit, Isabelle said no. And then she told me, he gave her the most venomous look she had ever seen and told her that if she did not participate . . . her child would take her place."

Meghann was shaking all over with revulsion. "But why didn't she tell the queen?"

"Do you think she would believe that of one of her favorites? No, Isabelle had no allies at court, and Simon read any letters she wrote to her family first. And the depravity was only the beginning of his revenge. Isabelle was extremely suspicious when Simon took a sudden interest in Michael.

"Naturally, everyone at court thought it was wonderful . . . said what an excellent stepfather Lord Baldevar was. He took the boy riding, taught him how to read. . . . In short, he made the child adore him. This went on for four years. Simon simultaneously drained Isabelle of all her dignity while he made her son love him."

"Why did he want Michael to love him?" Charles asked.

Meghann answered the query lifelessly. "So it would hurt more when he killed him."

"Excellent, *banrion*. When the boy looked upon Simon as a god on earth, he made his move. Oh, he was clever. What he did was 'accidentally' leave the boy alone in the stables. He knew Michael was enthralled with his stallion, Sulieman. A five-year-old could not control the horse, but the little boy's desire to ride overcame common sense—as Simon knew it would if the child got the opportunity. So Michael climbed on Sulieman. The stallion took off. . . . Michael had no way of controlling the wild horse. Soon Michael was thrown off. It took a few days for him to die of his broken bones and internal bleeding. Two hours before he died, Simon visited the little boy, who joyfully cried out 'Papa' when he saw him. When Simon left the room, the child was sobbing as though his heart had broken. Within an hour after the visit, Michael died in his mother's arms."

"Poor Isabelle," Meghann said softly, "now she had nothing."

"Her mind broke. She appeared before Elizabeth, screaming wildly and incoherently of all Simon had done: Roger, Michael, the sick acts. Elizabeth declared the woman mad and had Simon flog her for uttering such filth in the queen's presence. Once Isabelle was able to rise from bed after the whipping, she hurled herself out the window of her bedroom and fell two stories."

"Did she die?" Meghann asked.

"It would be better if she had. No, the fall merely crippled her. She would never walk again. Simon arranged for her to be sent to their estate. Isabelle was utterly mad with grief, and most of the time, she was kept quiet with sleeping herbs. The servants cared for her as well as they could . . . eager for the day God would end her suffering. So most of the time she was kept calm . . . except when Simon came to visit. He would order her medication halted. . . . He wanted her lucid when he tormented her with memories of her dead child. Then she began raving that Simon was a daemon. For she said he would hover over her bed in the air and display long, vicious fangs that he used to suck the blood from her."

"Couldn't she be checked for bite marks?" Meghann asked.

"Who around Isabelle cared enough to? Around the time Isabelle made those accusations, Simon fired the entire staff that had loved their lady and moved in new workers whose loyalty was to him alone. Their 'care' consisted of never changing Isabelle's linen and leaving her to lie in her own filth—per Lord Baldevar's orders. They never washed her either. She was not fed regularly—when I first saw Isabelle, I promise you she was unrecognizable as the woman in that portrait. What greeted me was an emaciated bag of bones. She was also covered in the same running sores I had not seen since the plague, when people did not bathe regularly, and she was losing her hair due to starvation. But the worst was her eyes—they sank into her skull."

Alcuin stopped. Meghann and Charles both looked

away; they knew that he was wiping away tears. Meghann wondered if Alcuin might have fallen in love with Simon's wife. When he spoke again, his voice was ragged with barely concealed sobs. "But I'm jumping ahead. First I should tell you of Simon's transformation."

"Of course, Isabelle's tale of a bloodsucking creature was true," Meghann said.

"Oh, yes. After she was banished from court, Simon was free to pursue even more women, and how the women of the court flocked to him. They fell in love with his looks and his wealth. Of course his reputation as a smooth, accomplished, virile lover spread like wildfire."

Alcuin smiled with grim satisfaction. "But his reputation wasn't the only thing spreading through the court. After a few months, Simon became violently ill. In confidence, the court physician told him that he had the pox—or what we would today call syphilis. In a few months, he would go mad. After a few years, he'd be dead."

Charles angrily muttered, "To die of venereal disease would have been a perfect end for Lord Baldevar."

"Indeed," Alcuin replied. "Unfortunately, it wasn't to be. If anything would make me believe that Simon has sold his soul to Satan, it would be the many times he has managed to defeat death. For around the same time Simon received his death sentence, a new member of the court arrived—Nicholas Aermville."

"A vampire?" Meghann asked.

"Oh, yes," Charles informed her. "A homosexual vampire who was desperately lonely and completely infatuated with Simon."

Meghann was perplexed. "But Simon's not—"

"Why would that stand in his way?" Alcuin pointed out. *"Banrion,* Simon was a dangerous man. The rumors of sorcery were not idle gossip. He was heavily involved in the occult. Have you ever heard of Dr. John Dee, Elizabeth's astrologist?"

Meghann shook her head.

"A brilliant scientist and mathematician. He is best known for his interest in the occult, though. He left the court in 1583 in the company of Edward Kelly to tour the Prague Hradeany. Their alchemical experiments brought them the patronage of a Polish nobleman, Albert Laski. But he quickly became disillusioned with the pair and their empty promises. Eventually, Dee saw through his charlatan companion and returned to England in 1589, disgraced and impoverished. But he soon found a wealthy patron at Queen Elizabeth's court."

"Lord Baldevar?" she guessed.

"Indeed. Simon was never foolish. He knew that a pact with the Devil and drinking the blood of goats was for simple, backward people. But he saw the power in alchemy, Rosicrucianism, Enochian magic, the cabala. John Dee became one of his best friends at court . . . and the only person besides the physician who knew Simon was dying. And Simon confided that he had found a way to outwit death."

"But," Meghann puzzled aloud, "I don't care if he studied the cabala backward and forward. . . . He was still mortal. A vampire should have been able to see his thoughts."

"Meghann, if his interest in sorcery did nothing else, it sharpened his power of mind through the constant meditation and lengthy rituals. And frankly, there are supernatural forces in the world. Aren't we proof of that? Who knows? Perhaps Simon did manage to conjure up a spirit or two through the Enochian Aires to help him. At any rate, you can see how dangerous Simon is—if even as a mortal he could fool a vampire into believing he was in love with him. Nicholas offered

Simon a bargain—transformation in exchange for Simon becoming his lover."

"So Simon slept with this man?" Meghann asked.

Charles snorted. "Oh, no. The bargain was transformation first, sex second. First Simon claimed he could not possibly sleep with anyone when he was ill. Then, to further manipulate Nicholas, Simon told him that he wanted their lovemaking to be done when they were equals . . . not vampire and subordinate mortal. Nicholas agreed—"

Alcuin interrupted. "Perhaps I should mention Nicholas was a novice vampire when he met Lord Baldevar. He had only been transformed two hundred years before—perhaps that's why he was no match for Simon and his friend Dr. Dee. All Nicholas did was bleed Simon and provide him with vampire's blood. Dr. Dee and Lord Baldevar worked out transformation all by themselves. How these two mortals managed the process I'll never know. But through some of John Dee's writings, I've pieced together that the transformation took fifteen days, with lengthy rituals and fasting. At the end, Simon was on the brink of death and John Dee was no better. That caught the court's interest—particularly when Simon was no longer seen by anyone during the day. John Dee had planned for Simon to transform him after he became a vampire, but watching the process of transformation changed his mind. He was far older than Simon, and he thought the experience would kill him."

"What happened to Nicholas?"

"Once he became a vampire, Simon slaughtered Nicholas," Alcuin said in completion. "It was at this point that I became involved with Simon Baldevar for the first time. Nicholas had been a vampire I tried to help. His immortality and his sexuality confused him.

I begged him to accompany me to the New World in 1580, but he preferred to stay in Europe."

"Why were you in the New World?" Meghann asked.

"The Spanish were brutalizing the Indians. I set up a mission in Mexico. If the Indians were going to be forcibly converted, I wanted at least a few of them to receive some comfort from the church. One of my apprentices wrote to me describing Nicholas's murder and this horrifying new vampire who was shocking my circle with his heinous acts. When I saw the name Baldevar, it occurred to me that my sister, Mary, had married a John Baldevar in 1390. When I came back to England to deal with Simon, I did some research. It turned out Simon was my nephew, several generations removed. So I had a special interest in him—one, because he had killed my friend; two, because this evil spawn was of my own mortal bloodline. I felt it was my duty to rid the world of him."

Alcuin poured the rest of the absinthe into his glass, Charles's, and Meghann's. "When I returned home, the first rumors I heard concerned Isabelle. I decided to go see the poor girl—see if I could help her." Alcuin paused and eyed the two young vampires. "Did it strike either of you as curious that Isabelle's care so utterly deteriorated?"

Charles and Meghann exchanged blank looks.

"Well, Master," Charles said haltingly, "I thought it was more punishment—"

"To a degree, it was. And I also made the great mistake of assuming that. But no—another reason for Isabelle's neglect was that there was no one to look after her during the day." He let his words sink in.

"No!" Meghann gasped. "You mean Simon's servants were all—"

"Vampires. An entire estate—some one hundred people. That land was a vampire stronghold. Simon had gathered up as many small, evil people as he could find. Cutthroats, highwaymen, whores, the criminally insane—he transformed them. When I went to the estate, I could feel the evil ten miles away."

Alcuin shuddered. "It took months to kill them all, but we had to. Such an abominable group could not live. They had practically bled the countryside dry—it would only be a matter of time before they inspired a true witch-hunt by the terrorized population. And in that battle, I lost many friends. I came close to losing my own life on a few occasions."

"Where was Simon?" Meghann asked. "Didn't he defend his vampire haven?"

"Simon wanted to see what the opposition could do. At first, I thought he was merely a coward. That was another mistake. At any rate, with the guard down, we were finally able to rescue Isabelle. Of course, her care had further deteriorated when the fiends became more concerned with saving themselves. She was dying, but we tried to give her some dignity. We bathed her . . . trying not to hurt her, for she was merely bones covered with abscesses when we found her. I told her I was a priest, and she begged me for extreme unction, which I performed. I also had to listen to her terrible confession, everything I have just told you. At that moment, I wanted to kill Simon . . . for completely destroying this young woman far before her time. I made a vow the moment she died . . . that he would die by my hand. For four hundred years, I have been trying to honor it. And at the moment I completed the rites, Simon appeared."

Alcuin hurled his glass into the fireplace. "I will never forget the arrogance I saw on his face. He stared me down, asked why I dared to trespass on his property. When I explained our relationship to him, he didn't even express surprise. Simon truly had no fear of me;

he laughed in my face. Told me I was as pious as his deceased wife and it was time for me to die."

"What happened?"

"For the first time in his young life, Simon met someone he could not overcome. Not that he didn't try. It took hours for me to subdue him, and I don't know that I could have if he'd had the remotest conception of my power. But finally some friends and I restrained him. We chained him up outside so the sunrise would kill him. We were going to behead him, but it was too near the dawn and we were battle-weakened. We had to flee into the darkness. And before the sun could end Simon's miserable existence, a human companion hiding in the village threw him into a closed carriage and sped away."

"Who was the companion?" Charles asked.

"Dr. Dee—the only person I believe Simon has ever respected. But our encounter frightened Simon. He retreated from Europe the next night. That did wreak havoc—my apprentices were able to seize all his property. Simon was a penniless outcast—in fear for his life. It took him nearly a century to recover his wealth."

"Why didn't you track him down and kill him?"

Alcuin sighed. *"Banrion,* I don't want to misrepresent myself to you. I am strong and have dealt with many adversaries over the years, but I cannot allow you to think I have some wonderful ability to murder Simon whenever I wish. He is the most powerful vampire I have ever encountered. Over the centuries, our situation has developed into a cold war—much like the one between the Soviet Union and America. We despise each other, but we do not attempt any acts of aggression because the cost would be too dear on both sides. Rather, I have spent several hundred years attempting to undo his evil deeds and waiting for an opportunity to slay him that would not cost an inordinate amount of bloodshed. So far, it has not happened. The only way to destroy him would have put far too many mortals and vampires I have promised my protection to at risk."

"Do you think I killed him?"

"I sincerely hope you did—that with one lucky accident, you managed what I have not been able to accomplish. But if you did not—then I have committed an act of open warfare. I have offered my protection to his consort—the chosen mother of his children."

Meghann yelped. "What?"

Alcuin smiled gently. "Did you forget I said Simon had two reasons for transforming you? Meghann, he still wants a son."

"But . . . but . . . ," she choked out, "I can't!"

"Why not?" Alcuin paused delicately. "You do still—"

"Huh? Oh! Oh, er . . . yes, I do," Meghann replied with the same strained delicacy. She remembered how surprised she had been that her menstrual cycle did not stop when she became a vampire. But it had undergone a radical change—it only occurred once or twice a year.

Alcuin saw the shock on her face. "It's quite rare, Meghann. And extremely dangerous—for the mother."

"So Simon took a chance that I'd be hurt?"

"He did that when he transformed you," Alcuin informed her. "He did not put those manacles on because of his fear that you'd harm yourself—he had a far more pressing fear that you'd harm him. Transformation is quite dangerous, Meghann. Most people either die or go insane."

"And then he took a chance that I'd become pregnant."

"A remote chance," Charles chimed in. "Meghann, in almost two thousand years, we only have a handful of proven instances of vampire pregnancy."

"What happened?" She wanted to know.

Charles stared into the fire. "None of the mothers survived—all died from hemorrhaging. But who knows? Perhaps now that could be fixed. The last known pregnancy was in 1110."

"And the children?" she asked.

"Almost all of them were stillborn. Those that survived were terrible monstrosities, like the one who transformed me," Alcuin told her.

"Then why does Simon want a vampire child? Why not have a child with a mortal woman?"

"Mortals and vampires cannot reproduce. As for his desire for a child . . . Have you ever heard of the philosophers' stone?"

Meghann shook her head.

"Alchemists believed that there was a spirit that linked everything in the universe together. By subjecting raw materials to lengthy chemical processes, the alchemists believed they could reproduce the spirit of the universe into the philosophers' stone, or elixir of life. The philosophers' stone would grant its possessor eternal youth, freedom from death and sickness, knowledge, power—the gifts a vampire enjoys. So Simon, alchemist that he was, decided the philosophers' stone was a metaphor for vampirism."

"What does all this have to do with having a child?" Meghann asked.

"Vampires are nearly invincible, Meghann, but for one flaw. They are powerless and vulnerable to attack during the day. Lord Baldevar and John Dee puzzled over this problem and decided that the elixir of life was diluted when it came into contact with mortal blood, producing a miraculous but flawed substance that led to a disease that made sunlight poisonous to vampires. Lord Baldevar decided the true power of the philosophers' stone could only be realized through the mingling of the blood of two vampires—when they created a child together."

"So Simon thought the offspring of two vampires wouldn't be vulnerable to daylight?"

Alcuin nodded. "But he also thought, at least according to John Dee's writings, that he could walk in daylight if he drank his child's blood."

Meghann was aghast. "You mean he'd kill his own child?"

"Oh, no, *banrion*. Lord Baldevar is far too much of an egoist to harm his own descendant. No, he thought a small portion of the blood—the same amount you need for transformation—would be enough to make him immune to the sun's power."

Meghann stared into the fire before speaking. "Am I to understand that the reasons I'm a vampire are that I resemble a long-dead spouse, and I'm expected to give birth to the Antichrist?"

"Antichrist is a strong term," Alcuin replied, "but in my opinion—yes. That is why Simon transformed you."

Please, Meghann prayed to anyone who might be listening, let Simon be dead. Her eyes wandered back to the painting and she paled when she examined Isabelle's left hand. Meghann lifted her trembling hand up to the painting—to put the two signet rings together. "This was Isabelle's ring?" she asked Alcuin.

He nodded. "I had buried Isabelle, but Simon had her corpse exhumed by some of his minions so he could get the ring. The exhumation took place on April 22, 1944."

Meghann shuddered at the thought of vampiric ghouls desecrating Isabelle's grave so Simon could put a ring he'd given to a woman he'd beaten and brutalized on her hand. *What was he trying to do with me? Re-*

create his marriage with Isabelle? Get the son he thought he deserved?

Meghann pulled her attention away from the garish fantasies, and asked Alcuin, "Why have you invited me here? Simon waited nearly four hundred years to find someone to replace Isabelle with, and conceive his imp. Why endanger yourself by taking me in?"

Charles answered. "At first, we were merely curious. Simon has always had women around him—but they were mortal and he usually killed them when he became bored. What made you so special that he transformed you and never left your side? When our spies informed us that Simon was throwing that evil fete, Alcuin chose me to go to the party. We knew Simon would observe the uneasy truce, and let me leave in peace."

Alcuin picked up the story. "And then Charles came back—quite upset. First he told me you could be Isabelle reborn. Then he looked up at that portrait and told me, 'Master, I have finally seen sadness to rival that which I observe in Isabelle's eyes.' He told how you left the room the second the debauchery started. He begged me to invite you here . . . not that he needed to. I made up my mind the second I heard you resembled Isabelle. At first, I thought you were Simon's consort because he had finally found a woman to match his own malfeasance. But when I heard Charles's description of you, I made up my mind that this time Simon wasn't going to destroy another young woman. If you were unhappy, you would be given a chance at a different way of life."

"Teach me to be strong," Meghann said urgently. "I never want anyone to be able to hurt me or dominate me the way Simon did."

Alcuin reached into his cloak and withdrew a small Celtic cross on a long chain and handed it to Meghann. "Merry Christmas, *banrion*. I will be honored for you to become my apprentice. I think you should understand you broke Simon's hold over you by yourself. . . . You're already quite strong. But I will help you develop your abilities. It won't be an easy path." His warning was accompanied by a small grin.

Meghann smiled back and attached the cross to her waist. Charles showed her his own cross around his neck.

Alcuin observed the brightening sky. "We've talked the night away. Charles, please show Meghann her quarters. Tomorrow we'll begin your training." Alcuin gave Meghann a lighthearted smirk. "Get your rest. . . . You'll need it. Starting tomorrow, you will be engaged in rigorous physical, mental, and mystical instruction. Charles once accused me of rivaling the Spartans for pure physical torture, but it's necessary. You cannot hope to achieve your full potential in a soft, spoiled body."

Meghann didn't care if he ran her ragged—just so long as she never looked like that painting. *Isabelle,* she told the portrait silently, *no one will ever get the best of me again. And if Simon is still alive, I'm going to learn all I can so that next time I kill him—for you and me.*

TWELVE

March 17, 1998

Jimmy Delacroix examined the music selection in Maggie's living room. He thought some music might take his mind off what was going on, and he couldn't use liquor to relax. Maggie hadn't said anything, but he knew he couldn't drink now. What help would he be to her if he was drunk all the time?

Not that he was much help now anyway. He guessed Alcuin was the one who could help her get rid of Simon Baldevar—unless of course they found out where he slept during the day.

Max, the five-year-old Irish setter they had liberated from the ASPCA, came padding into the living room. Although Maggie had a grim BEWARE OF DOG sign outside, Max was no threat to anyone. Still, his bark and growl did scare strangers away. Maggie said that was all he had to do—if someone entered the house during the day, she just wanted them to flee; she didn't need some merciless attack dog that would tear them limb from limb.

"Hey, boy." Jimmy called the dog over and started petting him. "Maggie's downstairs, doing God only knows what with that . . . whatever he is. I guess they're doing some kind of magic—she says I can't go down there because it would be dangerous."

Jimmy sighed, and threw a rubber bone for Max to retrieve. He felt left out. Most of the time, he could forget Maggie was a vampire. He'd grown accustomed to never seeing her during the day—there were plenty of couples where someone worked at night and slept during the day. He never saw her drink blood or anything.

Max brought his bone back, and Jimmy threw the toy again. He was worried about the future. Not just Simon Baldevar, but what was going to happen between him and Maggie. They'd been together for six years. He was thirty-one now and she hadn't aged. What was going to happen? Would she nurse him through his old age and then find some other guy when he was in the ground? That's why he'd thought she should transform him—that way, they could be together. But she wouldn't even listen.

The basement door opened, and Maggie came into the living room. "Oh, good—some music." She started sifting through the albums and CDs with him. Max came over, eager for attention. Jimmy thought that was as sure a sign as any that Maggie wasn't some evil creature. The dog had never growled at her; he loved her. Or maybe Max was just a lousy judge of character.

"Did dogs like Simon?" Jimmy asked her curiously.

She laughed while Max licked her face. "Down, boy. I can't really answer that, Jimmy. In thirteen years, I never saw an animal around him. No, wait—he took me horseback riding in France. The horse didn't seem to have a problem with him. But dogs—who knows?"

"What were you doing downstairs?" he asked.

"Making the house safe," she explained. "You can't feel it, but we've just put up . . . kind of a shield around this house. No one can enter unless they're invited."

"Like in the movies—the vampire has to ask permission to come in."

"Something like that. But there's only one vampire I want to keep out—and he is not getting an invitation."

Jimmy handed her a CD. "Remember this?"

Her face lit up. "Of course—Johnny Thunders! You played it the first night we met." Meghann was relieved to be off the whole dreadful subject of Simon. She just wanted to relax for a few minutes. As much as she could relax knowing that fiend was alive.

She put the CD on. Jimmy flirtatiously asked, "What was the first thing you thought when you met me?"

Meghann put her tongue out at him. "I never saw such a shambling wreck of a man in all my life."

"And I never saw such an out-and-out slut in mine! Hanging around sleazy bars—picking up trash for one-night stands . . ."

"And look what I wound up with!"

They reminisced about the night they met—anything to forget the threat hanging over their heads.

February 20, 1992

Meghann and Dr. Harlowe entered Mona's, a place in the East Village that gave new meaning to the word dive. Since it was a Tuesday night, and freezing out, the place was rather quiet—not at all its usual rowdy self.

Dr. Harlowe sat down reluctantly, seeming to expect the scarred wood seat to bite him. "Meghann, please let me take you somewhere else. Maybe something a little more upscale?"

"I like it here," she said firmly. Actually, after Simon anything with ambience or class tended to remind her of him. Anyway, better bars tended to have mirrors all over the place.

The renowned psychiatrist resigned himself to his sleazy surroundings and ordered two double-whiskeys. At first, he tried to order a martini, but the glazed, simple stare of the bartender informed him that such things were beyond the talents of this place.

Meghann watched the suffering doctor with some amusement. It wasn't nice to make people uncomfortable, but damn it the man wouldn't leave her alone! She knew she had no business sleeping with one of her teachers, but it was only once. Now he was pestering her constantly, unable to understand her aloof behavior. She hoped that a place like this would convince him once and for all that their lifestyles were too different to pursue a relationship. Maybe then he'd go back to his wife.

"Your thesis is coming along beautifully," he told her—making a vain attempt at conversation. The compliment was sincere for Meghann was one of the brightest students he'd ever had. Harlowe had no doubt she'd already be a practicing psychologist if not for the debilitating photophobia she'd developed after suffering through meningitis as a child. Now, as she'd explained at her admissions interview, Meghann's eyes were so sensitive to sunlight she could not leave her home during the day so she only took classes at night.

"Thank you." She eyed a tall biker type playing pool. Maybe later . . .

"You describe abusive behavior so well. Meghann, I was wondering . . . Was anyone in your family ever involved in an abusive relationship? Your insights seem like something you could only have through personal experience."

Meghann swallowed the cheap, watered-down whiskey and considered the question. Should she tell him she was the one who left an abusive relationship nearly forty years ago? "No family skeletons." She smiled. "I just find the abusive partner interesting." She thought, as she often did, of Simon Baldevar's psychological profile. Had he been a sociopath? Certainly, he lacked a conscience and an empathy toward humans. But she imagined he'd excuse that by pointing out he wasn't human. Still, look at his relationship with Isabelle—a pure sadist with no capacity to love.

Her thoughts were diverted by a commotion at the bar. The bartender was snarling. "I told you—you ain't welcome here! What do you think this is—a charitable institution? Tabs went out years ago, pal. Now get out!"

Meghann observed the object of the bartender's insults. In profile, she saw a young man with long, shaggy, dark brown hair and a black leather jacket. Their eyes made contact, and she felt a despair she'd almost forgotten existed emanating from him. The poor man, he had that same horrible, suicidal desperation she'd had the night Charles found her. . . .

He was turning to leave, and Meghann yelled across the bar, "Hey, wait up! I'll buy you a drink."

"Meghann!" hissed the scandalized doctor.

"Don't you like to make new friends?" she asked facetiously. She had to know more about that man. What kind of pain was he in that it pierced through all her shields?

The young man put on an arrogant air and swaggered past the disgusted bartender. He threw himself down next to the aggrieved doctor, and smiled cockily at Meghann.

"Thanks, sweetheart. Hey, barkeep!" he yelled. "Make it J&B with soda . . . two of them!"

The bartender thudded down the drinks, and gave Meghann a look reserved for the hopelessly insane.

Meghann inspected her new find. He was scruffy, with a shaggy beard and bloodshot eyes. He was too thin, and indifferently dressed in ancient jeans and a ragged Ramones T-shirt. But the eyes were an engaging blue-gray shade, and beneath the arrogance and inebriation, she sensed a sharp intelligence. So she smiled and raised her glass.

"What's your name, honey?" the young man questioned, completely ignoring Dr. Harlowe.

"Meghann Cameron," she replied. She probably could have continued to use her real name—she was not likely to encounter anyone she used to know. But Meghann had decided she wanted a fresh start, a new identity.

Her drinking buddy made a face, and swallowed his second drink rapidly. The unhappy bartender was summoned for a new order. "Bring three this time, and whatever she's having," he told the bartender magnanimously, as though he was paying. Then he turned his attention back to her. "Meghann . . . that's a mouthful. You don't have a nickname?"

Meghann's heart started beating a little faster. "Well," she said cautiously, "people used to call me Maggie . . . but that was a long time ago."

The young man downed his third drink, and snorted. "What the hell is a long time to you, honey? When you were twelve? Don't get me wrong—I'm thankful for the drinks, but there's no way you're any older than twenty."

Meghann was startled. Sometimes she forgot that to mortals she looked young. . . . She certainly didn't feel like a teenager anymore. And what business did this drunk have being so perceptive anyway? "I'm twenty-five," she informed him.

He howled. "Sure, babe—save it for the bartender." Seeing her brow crease, he hastily added, "Not that it's any of my business. But I like Maggie. . . . You definitely look more like a Maggie. Meghann's too serious and boring."

"And what is your name?" This conversation was like a reverse of the one she'd had with Simon all those years ago—when he decided he didn't like Maggie. What was it with her anyway that made people want to give her some sort of tag?

The man stuck out his hand, managing to knock over Dr. Harlowe's barely touched drink. He seemed unconcerned. "Jimmy Delacroix."

The doctor jumped up. "You idiot! Look what you've done."

Jimmy bristled. "It was an accident."

The doctor fussily tried his best to wipe the stain out of his pants with a napkin. "It's time we were going, Meghann."

She knew he didn't mean to, but that presumptuous tone reminded her of Simon. And after him, no man told her what to do. Besides, that name . . . Delacroix. Where had she heard it before? She wanted to get to know Jimmy, find out what was eating him. "No one's stopping you," she said coolly.

Dr. Harlowe gave her an incredulous glare, and stormed out of the bar. She hoped he was mature enough to not let this interfere with being her thesis adviser.

"Who was the old guy?" Jimmy asked.

"My psychology professor."

Jimmy's whole demeanor changed. He sat up ramrod straight and gave Meghann a freezing glare. "So you're studying to be a goddamned witch doctor? And I guess you saw me shamble in and thought you could do a little psychobabble on me—find out why the poor soul is a boozehound? Screw you, sister."

Meghann sensed that his anger must have come from some other encounter with a psychiatrist. He stood up, ready to leave, and she grabbed his hand.

"Sit down, and stop making an ass of yourself," she

hissed, careful to keep any command out of her thoughts. "Yeah, I want to be a psychologist, but that's not why I invited you over." She took the sting out of her words with a slow, arching smile she'd stolen from Simon. "I just want to get laid."

Jimmy was stunned at the words that came out of this dainty-looking (but damned attractive) girl's mouth. He sat down, saying with a half laugh, "Why didn't you say so in the first place?" He tipped an imaginary hat at her and leered. "Happy to oblige you, ma'am."

Meghann lit a cigarette, not bothering to ask if it offended him. He responded by removing his own pack.

"You always go around making offers like that?" he asked.

"Most of the time. Why wait around for the guy to make the first move?"

"Look," he said uncomfortably, "I don't want to pry, but if you, er, go out a lot—"

"Don't worry," she told him flatly. "I don't have AIDS." She remembered the first time she and Charles became aware such a thing existed. They'd been at Studio 54 in late 1980 and he called her over from her dancing partner. He asked her to meet a young man, and tell him if she sensed anything. So she shook the young boy's hand, and was overwhelmed by the putrid, foul odor in his blood. It was death lying there dormant, waiting for an opportunity to ruin the promising life. After a while, she'd smelled it on a lot more people, and then the doctors put a name to the disease. She doubted a vampire could catch the disease by drinking infected blood, but that didn't matter. You couldn't force yourself near somebody with that stench; it repulsed vampires the way garlic was supposed to.

She knew Jimmy was clean even before he told her;

she had known from the moment he sat down. The rank odor could be spotted the minute you shook someone's hand or stood close to them.

Jimmy was speaking, interrupting her dark thoughts. "So what's a pretty little thing like you doing in a place like this?"

"I could ask you the same thing." She smiled.

He laughed. "Girl's got a mouth." He nodded approvingly. "I like that. I hate little demure chicks who don't have two words to say for themselves. But I've gotta tell you, Maggie, you can't go around propositioning guys in a place like this. I mean there's a lot of crazy people in the world."

"Are you one of them?" Meghann thought the advice was sincere, and quite sound if you didn't know her power. A few times, one of her transient partners had attempted to hurt her and then found out the hard way what they were dealing with. Of course, she hadn't killed them—however much she wanted. Alcuin had instilled in her that it was not her place to play judge and jury and pass judgment on the mortal world. So she simply kicked the living shit out of them and then called the cops to have them hauled away where they couldn't hurt anyone else.

"Shucks, ma'am, I ain't no psycho killer—just a lonely drunk." Jimmy's face darkened, and he polished off the drinks on the table.

Meghann got up to put some quarters in the jukebox and order fresh drinks.

They stayed in the bar for a few more hours. Jimmy was drinking like prohibition would come back tomorrow and Meghann matched him. They didn't talk much, just listened to the jukebox.

The last song Meghann put on was "House of the Rising Sun." Maybe Jimmy's melancholy was rubbing off on her—she found herself nearly crying at the words. They reminded her that the rising sun was something she was never going to see again.

Jimmy noticed her change in mood. He thought maybe it was a bad memory—her song with some other guy. But even though he hardly knew her, he didn't like to see her sad. Getting unsteadily to his feet, he asked, "Wanna dance?"

Meghann was touched. There were few people in the bar, so they swayed to the poignant song.

"What are we hanging around this dive for?" Jimmy asked her when the song was over.

They went into the bleak, freezing night. Meghann hoped the air might revive Jimmy a bit. He was cute, and it would be awful if he were too drunk to . . .

Jimmy was cursing the cold. "I hate winter!" he complained.

"I like it." Summer used to be her favorite season, but it was terrible for a vampire. There was barely any time awake before the damned sun was out. So now she loved winter, all the time it gave her, the wonderful darkness.

Meghann had been fortunate enough to find a parking space only a few blocks away from the bar for her nearly block-long 1958 Cadillac convertible. Jimmy was going to compliment the car, but they were both taken in by the two teenagers trying to gain access.

"Get away from my car," she ordered before Jimmy could stop her.

The boy by the hood came around to leer at her. He was at least six feet tall, and although he couldn't have been more than fifteen, already had the flat, menacing eyes of a much-convicted felon.

"Who's gonna make me, white bitch?" The boy slammed Meghann against the car while the other goon held Jimmy back with a switchblade.

Meghann looked up at him with no fear, merely contempt. "I'm going to make you," she said clearly. "I'm afraid you and your little buddy are now going to have to find another car to vandalize to support your crack habit."

Who the fuck did this stupid bitch think she was talking to? The thug was about to carve up that pale face when the world went blank. The street disappeared, and he was back in the detention center. He was only thirteen, and those guys got him down on the floor, peeled his pants down, raped him repeatedly, and then said they'd jam their knives in if he didn't start sucking. . . .

The image faded, and he was back on the cold street. He looked down, and the redhead smiled cruelly. "What I have in mind will make that look like your mother's kiss, Juan," she whispered so that only he could hear.

He backed away, terrified of her shining emerald eyes that dared him to touch her. How the hell did she know his name? How could she know what he never even told his brother about?

"Bruja," he croaked at her. His friend, holding back Jimmy Delacroix, looked uncertain when he saw Juan back down and run away. Jimmy took advantage of his indecision and slammed his elbow in the boy's solar plexus. He fell to the floor with a grunt.

The kid tried to get up, then thought better of it when Jimmy produced a .357 Magnum. Before Meghann or the would-be-thief could react, Jimmy smashed the punk's nose with the butt of his gun. "Now get the hell out of here," Jimmy growled and the boy, clutching his broken nose, ran off into the night, no doubt to find his friend so they could prey on some more docile victims before the night was over. *And to think I'm the one they call vampire,* Meghann thought bitterly.

Meghann thought of calling the police to find the thieves, but she didn't want to get Jimmy in trouble—somehow, she doubted he had a carry permit for that hand cannon. The best thing to do now was get out of here and take Jimmy with her.

"What the hell is wrong with you?" Jimmy demanded when they got in the car.

"What do you mean?"

Jimmy looked at her in complete disbelief. "What do I mean? They could have killed us! You're damned lucky I have a gun—and that I got the opportunity to take it out. What the hell happened between you and that kid?"

"Maybe he saw the light." Meghann didn't know if Alcuin would have approved, but she thought scum like that needed a lesson. Why, if she and Jimmy were a normal couple, she'd have been raped and they'd both be dead by now. Well, maybe not—Jimmy had that hand cannon. Obviously, Jimmy Delacroix was used to trouble. Why else would he be toting around a gun like that?

Jimmy snorted. "And here I thought I was the one with the death wish. Is that what they teach you in psychology class—to go around taunting dangerous scum who could kill you? Pull over," he snapped abruptly.

Meghann pulled over, and he stalked into a liquor store. He came back, took a long swallow of Wild Turkey, and said belligerently, "The last person I need any lectures from is you."

"Agreed. Where do you live, Jimmy?"

"Williamsburg." He gave her the address, and asked, "Where do you live, wild child?"

"Rockaway."

"Why so far?"

"I like it out there."

They drove over the Williamsburg Bridge, and

Jimmy's mood seemed to improve as the level of liquor in the bottle plunged alarmingly. Something bad had happened to him—Meghann was certain of that now. Even when that little punk had the switchblade to his throat, Jimmy hadn't seemed upset. He had the same look she had—that once the worst happened, nothing else really bothered you.

They arrived in front of the seedy apartment complex on Havemeyer Street that Jimmy called home, and he'd killed half the bottle of Wild Turkey. Still, he only staggered a bit. What was this man's drinking capacity?

They climbed the stairs to a fifth-floor walk-up. Meghann took in her surroundings. Well, if dives and sordid areas were what she was after . . . The place had little furniture except for an incredibly tacky baby-blue plush sofa that had probably been in the apartment since 1930 and a circular coffee table struggling under the burden of numerous empty bottles and cans.

"Why do you lug a .357 around?" she asked him.

Jimmy staggered over to his CD player and put on "So Alone" by Johnny Thunders—one of Meghann's favorite songs. "Night's not safe," he told her cryptically.

Of course—the Delacroix murders! Now Meghann knew what had happened to this young man. Not that she was going to bring it up. If he wanted to, he'd confide in her. Poor thing, she thought to herself, no wonder you drink and live like this. She was surprised he wasn't in an institution after all he'd been through.

Jimmy seemed a little uncomfortable, his bravado temporarily abandoning him. She smiled up at him. "Why so quiet?"

"Were you joking in the bar?"

"About what?" she asked softly.

His arrogance came back. "Getting laid."

Meghann slowly pulled off her tight leopard-print blouse and jeans. When she stood before him in merely a bra and panties, she said huskily, "Do I look like I was joking?"

Without another word, Jimmy came over and carried her into the bedroom.

Three hours later, Meghann felt utterly sated. She hadn't had that good a time in bed since . . . well, since Simon. But he and Jimmy were as different as night and day. Simon had been utterly smooth and accomplished, knew every trick in the book. Whereas Jimmy . . . What he lacked in style he made up for with enthusiasm. She'd never met anyone who approached sex (and her body) with such simple joy and excitement. It was enough to make her wonder what he would be like when he was sober. If after a night of heavy drinking, he could still perform four times . . .

Jimmy reached over to kiss her deeply. "You're awfully young to know that much." He yawned, then put an ashtray between them for the all-important after-sex cigarettes.

"Like to shake the hand of the guy who taught you some of your tricks." Jimmy looked a bit alarmed. "Promise me you're not jailbait, Maggie."

Meghann threw a pillow at him. "I told you I'm twenty-five."

"And I told you to save it for someone who might believe it." Jimmy suddenly looked a little green, and hastily stubbed out his cigarette. "Shit, I guess the booze is catching up to me after all. Think I'm just gonna rest my eyes . . ." In seconds, he was out cold.

Meghann got dressed, and kissed Jimmy on the cheek. It was time for her to head home—beat the sun.

"When did you know you were falling in love, *banrion?*" Alcuin asked. He had come up from the cellar, and was fascinated with the tale of Meghann meeting her young lover. She had never told him the whole story before.

Jimmy had become far more relaxed around Alcuin. The man made you feel safe. Besides, Max liked him. "She never has said she's in love with me—or that she plain old loves me."

Alcuin looked at the shadows in his young apprentice's eyes. Even though the boy was mortal, it would have been wonderful for Meghann to heal to the point that she could fall in love. Were the memories of Simon still so bitter and painful that she could not allow herself to trust somebody enough to make herself vulnerable by loving them?

Meghann interrupted. "What I knew was that Jimmy was . . . special." She gave him such a sweet smile he nearly forgot how much it upset him that she never said she loved him.

Alcuin was consumed with curiosity. "And when did you tell him you were a vampire?"

Meghann cut her eyes to Jimmy, and he said, "I think I should take over from here."

February 21, 1992

At around three, Jimmy Delacroix woke up with his usual excruciating hangover. Well, how the hell else was he supposed to get through the night?

He noticed the strewn sheets and remembered. Maggie! Jesus, she was crazy, and gorgeous, and great in bed. No way that kid was twenty-five. So why lie about her age?

He thought about her, feeling happiness and curiosity push away the usual bitter mix of emotion he woke up to. She was damned pretty—with that flaming hair and green eyes—but there was something strange about her. Jimmy laughed aloud. Something? Try a few things. Especially that scene with those car thieves. Didn't she know she could be killed? Then again— maybe she couldn't be killed. She sure scared the hell out of that kid. The kid had called her *"bruja."* Jimmy knew enough Spanish to understand that was the word for witch. Could the kid have been right?

Don't be an idiot, he told himself, and got out of bed. He staggered into the bathroom, where he over-dosed on Excedrin. Then he dragged himself into the kitchen to make some coffee. Maybe that would make him start to feel human. But what's the point, Jimmy? a voice asked him. You know you're just going to go out and drink again tonight.

Jimmy saw a note on the kitchen table. He examined the contents, and grinned. Maggie had nice handwrit-ing—but it was a little old-fashioned, like the way his grandmother wrote.

> Jimmy,
>   Want an encore? Why don't you meet me at my house tonight around seven? Can't make it any earlier—have to work on my thesis. We can have dinner, or something.
>
>   Maggie

She'd written down her address, but no phone num-ber. Jimmy grunted in amusement—be there or be square, huh? Well, he would definitely be there. And what's more, he was going to show her he was some-thing more than a low-life drunk.

While the coffee was brewing, Jimmy picked up the phone. "Darlene?"

"What do you want, Jimmy?" his twin asked in res-ignation.

Jimmy felt the familiar resentment and anger. Why

did she treat him like this anyway? Who had committed whom?

"Just a few bucks on the credit card," he said, hating to have to beg.

Darlene sighed heavily, and Jimmy steeled himself for a lecture. "Honey, when in the hell are you gonna get your life back together? The doctors say I ain't helping you by giving you money to drink. Someday you're going to have to put Amy and little Jay behind you—"

"Don't mention Jay's name," Jimmy said through tightly clenched teeth. "And I don't want the money for drink."

"Is it for a job interview?" Darlene brightened.

"No . . . a girl."

"One of them whores you've been hanging around with?"

"She's not a whore," Jimmy snapped, feeling protective of a girl he barely knew. "She's a nice girl, and I want to take her out to a good restaurant."

"What's the girl's name?" Darlene asked suspiciously. A few times before, Jimmy had made up wild tales to get his hands on drinking money.

"Maggie," he told her sullenly. "And she's got the prettiest red hair I've ever seen and she's going to school to become a psychologist. Are you satisfied that she's not a figment of my imagination?"

"A psychologist—and she's in college? Oh, Jimmy, maybe she could help you go back—"

Jimmy interrupted Darlene's fantasies. "Let's not rush to the altar or anything. I think if I want to keep her around, at the very least I should take her to a place a little classier than McDonald's."

"Okay, Jimmy, I'll put three hundred on the card, but I want to meet this girl. . . . You bring her up here for Sunday dinner this weekend, OK?"

"Assuming she's still speaking to me, I promise."

* * *

Jimmy eyed the large Victorian house. Was this her parents' place? Well, at least he didn't look like some beggar. He had on his good black overcoat (Christmas present from Darlene), a crisp navy blazer, and black slacks. His hair was in a neat ponytail, and he was sporting his diamond stud earring. So he rang the doorbell, sure he could pass any parent-meeting with flying colors.

Maggie answered the door; she was wearing a forest-green velvet dress that came down to her knees. She had her hair up in a French braid with dark green ribbon interspersed throughout the braid. He nearly sucked his breath in with appreciation. "You look great! How did you know I wanted to go someplace nice tonight?"

"Just a hunch . . . and you're looking very nice tonight too." She gestured inside. "Please come in."

He came inside, appreciating the decor of wood furniture, built-in bookshelves, and some Tiffany lampshades. He thought it was perfect for the mood of the house. "Who else lives here?"

"I live alone."

"How?" he asked, perplexed. "Graduate students can't afford a place like this. Assuming, of course, that you're telling the truth and your parents aren't on vacation."

"My parents passed away; they left me this house." Maggie grabbed her black cloak.

Jimmy noticed a painting over the fireplace. At first, he thought it was Maggie; then he saw the purple eyes. "Relative?"

Maggie looked up. "Ancestor, actually. That portrait was painted during the Renaissance."

Jimmy whistled appreciatively, noting the excellent

condition the painting was in. "Must be worth a pretty penny. Is your family wealthy?" Her face darkened, and he put in hastily, "Not that I'm a gigolo or anything."

"It wasn't that." Maggie sighed, and looked at the painting with the strangest expression—almost like pity. "Wealth is something my family has not had since 1957."

Jimmy nodded. "You ready to go?"

They decided on a small seafood restaurant within walking distance. As Maggie promised, the food was great. Jimmy remained on good behavior and only ordered soda. Maybe Maggie didn't want to spoil the mood because she stuck to soda too.

The conversation was light, getting-to-know-you chit-chat. They discovered an affinity for punk rock, *Goodfellas,* and the writings of Charles Bukowski.

"So why are you living like Charles Bukowski?" Maggie asked over dinner.

"Maybe I want to be another boozed-up poet. Think about it. There's him, Dylan Thomas, Rimbaud. . . . A lot of the greats were drunks."

Maggie held his eyes. "Is that your reason for drinking so much?"

Jimmy put down his fork and took her hand. "I like you a lot, Maggie. And someday I think I'd like to tell you why I . . . what went wrong. But not tonight." Please just let me enjoy myself, he pleaded silently.

Maggie nodded and went back to her scrod. She didn't seem offended at all. "So why do you want to be a headshrinker?"

"Because I think I can help people." Maggie sighed and took a sip of soda. "Same deal as you—someday I'll tell you more. For now, let's just say I knew someone who . . . who was involved in a very bad relationship. So I know how people, women in particular, can feel trapped—like there's no way out. And after a while, they start to think they're as worthless as the guys are always telling them they are. I'd like to help people like that, make them realize that there is another way, like someone helped, uh, . . . I mean, my friend realize."

Friend, my ass, it was you. Still, she had respected his privacy, so Jimmy wasn't going to start hammering her. So that explained the sadness, and the need for no one to see her as some doormat.

They changed the conversation back to lighter subjects, and things were going very well until a young couple walked in with a small blond-haired boy who looked about two years old.

Jay, Jimmy's heart screamed. Oh, Jay . . .

Shit, he couldn't deal with this. And look at that goddamned pitch blackness out there. "Hey, waiter!" Jimmy's entire demeanor changed—he was the arrogant drunk of the night before.

Maggie said nothing, but she kept her cool green eyes on him as he poured scotch after scotch down his throat. What an asshole he was—thinking some girl he didn't know would care. No one cared anymore. . . .

He became belligerent. Other diners were staring when he started cursing the waiter because he refused to bring him a seventh drink. Then Maggie put her hand over his.

"Jimmy, it is time to leave." He was about to shrug her hand off and scream louder when he felt . . . How could he describe it? It was like her hand weighed a ton, and some new voice spoke up in his brain—*Jimmy, don't disobey her.*

So he sat docilely while Maggie settled the check. Then he stood up obediently when she told him they were leaving.

As they walked to her home, he was weaving. Goddamn, why had he ruined everything because of a little boy who resembled Jay? His little guy, his slugger . . .

Jimmy staggered to his car, and Maggie grabbed his arm. "Not so fast."

"Why do you want anything to do with me?"

"Even if I hated you, I wouldn't let you get behind the wheel in the state you're in. You're going to come inside and sleep it off on my couch. Then you'll wake up and I'll make some coffee. After that, we're going to have a long talk."

Jimmy thought of arguing, but if she was still willing to talk to him . . . He stumbled on the stairs leading to her porch, but her arm held him up. How strong was she?

He collapsed on the luxurious, soft sofa and a few minutes later felt a light blanket placed over him and a pillow behind his head. He drifted into an uneasy sleep, seeing Jay. Jay and Amy, he thought drowsily. . . .

"Jay!" he yelled, caught up in the nightmare again.

He felt somebody shaking him. "Jimmy, wake up!"

He opened his eyes and saw Maggie leaning over him. He put his trembling hands in his hair and tried to catch his breath. "Jay," he cried helplessly. He grabbed Maggie and started sobbing.

She didn't try to shush him or tell him everything was OK, the way Darlene did when she comforted him after the dream. She just held him close and stroked his hair, like he was a small child.

When the worst of the crying abated, he forced himself to look at her. Maggie didn't seem upset or uncomfortable with his outburst. She just looked concerned.

"I'm sorry," he muttered.

"Don't apologize."

Jimmy waited for her to ask who Jay was, or what the nightmare was about, but she didn't. She left the room, returning with a cold washcloth and a glass of ice water.

While she was putting the cloth on his forehead, he pulled her close and kissed her. On impulse, he said,

"I'm falling in love with you." Idiot! he berated himself. First he cried like a baby and now he was telling her he was in love after knowing her for one day. She was going to think he was a mental case.

At least she wasn't running for the phone. She seemed touched by what he said, but there was a very distant look in her eyes. "That's very sweet, Jimmy."

"Look, I know it sounds nuts. But I feel good when I'm around you, and let me tell you, it's been a hell of a long time since I felt good about anything. Why do you think I drink like a fish? I want to be with you, Maggie. And I don't mean as some guy you have a few drinks with and lay."

Maggie started to say something, but he pressed on. "Don't worry—you don't have to give me any 'let's just be friends' routine." He took a deep breath. To hell with it—he was going to tell her everything. "But I can't get serious about any girl without telling her the truth about me. Believe me, once you're done listening to my story, you'll have a great excuse to get rid of me. You'll think I'm crazy."

"I doubt that," Maggie responded. "I've seen lots of crazy things in my life. And I don't want to get rid of you. But, Jimmy, I don't get 'serious' with any guys. I have some reasons why I can't let anyone close."

"I know. You act like you have some deep, dark secret; maybe that's why I feel I can trust you. But let me tell you my secret first, OK? Then, if you still want anything to do with me, you can tell me anything you want."

Maggie nodded, and sat next to him on the couch. She took a pack of cigarettes out of a crystal bowl on the table and lit two, passing one to Jimmy.

"What did you want to tell me?" Maggie asked.

Jimmy looked away from her, out the window. "I used to be married," he said in a tight voice, trying not to cry again. "And I had a son. His name was James, after me. We called him Jay. He was three when he died."

Maggie offered him her hand, and he squeezed tightly.

"I got married when I was seventeen. Amy, my wife, was sixteen. Same old story—sex in the backseat and the next thing you know, she's pregnant. Amy was very religious, didn't believe in abortion. So we both dropped out of high school, her to take care of the baby and me to work in a factory where my sister was a supervisor. I wasn't happy. I liked school and I wanted to go to college. And Amy—well, she was sweet but really dumb. I could never talk to her about books or music or the news or anything." Jimmy sighed. "I figured I'd make the best of it. I had a good job with benefits, and our parents chipped in to buy us a small house. Then Jay was born."

Jimmy ground out the cigarette and started crying again—harsh, rasping sobs. He grabbed Maggie. "I loved him so much." He sobbed against her breasts. "Maggie, the first time I saw him, I couldn't believe he was mine. He was beautiful; I loved him. I promised that I'd be a great dad to him. I'd go back to school so I could get a better job and he'd have everything he needed. I wanted him to be proud of me."

Jimmy took a shaky breath. "So I got my GED and I went to community college at night. And I wound up killing Jay by doing that." He liked that Maggie wasn't interrupting him with a bunch of questions. She'd probably make a good therapist. "I told you our parents bought us a house. What I didn't tell you was that it was really isolated. Our nearest neighbors were a mile away. So there was no one there to help Amy when . . . when . . ." He started hyperventilating.

Maggie put his head between his knees and placed her hand on the back of his neck. "Calm down, honey."

He could swear he felt some warmth from her hand spread throughout his body and calm him down. In a few minutes, he was able to start talking again.

"I came home around midnight. My last class ended at ten, and it took me an hour and a half to get home. I noticed that our front door was hanging off its hinges, like there had just been a storm or someone tore it off. The first thing I thought was burglars. But why would they bother with a cheap little house like mine? Then I got really scared. I thought of serial killers, psychotics. I had a gun in the glove box. I got it out and went into the house."

Jimmy stopped again. "Could I have a drink? I know you probably think I have a problem. Maybe I do, but I can't get through this without one."

Maggie brought over a bottle of whiskey and two glasses. Jimmy took two double shots before resuming his story. "The light in the living room was off. I was scared to turn it on, thought then they would know I was in the house. Then I heard . . . I don't know how to describe it, a tearing noise. Like someone eating. It came from Jay's room. So I ran there really quick and threw on the light."

Jimmy shuddered violently. "Maggie, there's no way I can describe what I saw. Jay was on the floor, white as a fucking ghost with two gashes on his neck. I knew he was dead the second I saw him; his eyes were wide open. And there was this . . . thing in the room."

Maggie's reaction so far was not what he expected. She seemed very resigned and bitter. "Aren't you going to ask me about the thing?"

"Just tell me what you saw," she said in a flat tone.

Jimmy was perplexed—even the doctors hadn't been that detached when he told them the story. "It was a vampire." Her expression didn't change, so he elaborated. "I've never seen anything like it.

Two huge, hooked fangs were sticking out of its mouth; it was monstrous-looking. If you think vampires are like those good-looking guys in all the movies, think again. This thing was hideous. It had ugly veins all over it, and its eyes were pink, like an albino's. Not that I had a lot of time to stare at it. It was holding Amy." Jimmy's lips trembled, and he banged his fist down on the table. "And that's another thing . . . It wasn't like she was in some cute nightie with two little pinpricks on her neck. Maggie, this thing mauled her. Her head was barely attached to her shoulders, and her wrists were slashed up to her elbows. That wasn't it either. Her breasts were ripped off, and there were slashes on her thighs. When it saw me, it dropped Amy and ran at me. I didn't have any time to think; I just started shooting. I got it four times, I think, in the chest and it went down."

Maggie frowned. "You shot it with the Magnum?"

"Yeah."

That seemed to satisfy her. "I went to Amy and Jay. They were dead. So I ran out of the house and went to get the cops."

"And when you came back, the vampire was gone."

"How the hell did you know that?" Maggie didn't answer, so he continued. "They locked me up— thought I must have done it. But then the coroner's report proved that Jay died at least sixty minutes before I could have gotten home; lots of people saw me at school that night."

"So they let you go?" Maggie asked.

Jimmy laughed harshly. "Hell, no. I insisted on telling the truth. So I told them a vampire ripped my family apart, and before you can say committed, I was in an institution. The doctors convinced Darlene, my twin sister, to sign the papers."

"How long were you there?"

"Two years. But aside from my story, there was nothing else wrong with me. And there were a lot of people crazier than me in the world, with too few beds in the madhouse. It wasn't like my family could afford private care, so they released me. The doctors convinced my family that the whole problem was that I had seen something very traumatic, maybe the real murderer raping Amy, so I blocked it all out with this delusion of a vampire. They all expect that one day I'm going to wake up and tell them who the real killer is."

"You know who the real killer is," Maggie said softly.

Jimmy looked at her; there was no denial or shock in her expression. "So you believe me?"

She nodded.

"Why? Why don't you seem surprised or upset? No one believes in vampires. If I tell you Santa comes down my chimney every Christmas, will you believe that too?"

Maggie got up, and touched the portrait of her dead ancestor. She turned around and smiled crookedly. "Shall I tell you my birthday?"

He was dumbfounded.

She laughed, almost a mirror of the harsh sound he had made a few minutes ago. "Don't worry, Jimmy. It's not that I believe you because I'm crazy and I don't know any better." She stared into his eyes, and told him quite matter-of-factly, "I was born on July 3, 1925."

For a minute, he didn't understand what she was telling him. Then it hit and he screamed, "No! You're fucking nuts!"

Maggie raised one red-gold eyebrow. "I accepted what you told me. Why can't you do the same?"

"You are not a vampire," he said through clenched teeth. "Are you forgetting I saw one? You look nothing like that. The story grabbed some headlines, you know. I got a bunch of letters from crackpots like you . . . stupid kids who think vampires are gothic, exciting

things. I know your type." Jimmy took his glass and
shattered it on the wood coffee table. He used one of
the shards to slash his forearm. A thin trickle of blood
soon appeared.

He held it out to Maggie. "You're a vampire? Come
on, let's see your fangs—suck it down!"

She looked repulsed—and concerned for his state
of mind. "I don't want your blood!"

Jimmy moved closer. "Sure you do—if you're a
bloodsucker. Why aren't you leaping on my arm—sali-
vating at the sight of fresh blood?"

Maggie laughed. "Jimmy, I do have a bit more restraint than that. But if you want proof, I can provide
it without injuring you."

Maggie moved quickly and grabbed his arm. She
dragged him upstairs, with him yelling, "OK, so you're
strong—big deal! That doesn't make you . . ."

She stopped in front of the medicine cabinet mirror.
He saw his own reflection, but Maggie . . . He could
not believe it. He could feel her iron hold on his arm,
was looking right at her, but there was only a very hazy
outline of her in the mirror.

She let go and he sank to the floor. "Now do you
believe me?"

"It's a trick mirror," he said weakly.

She glanced at it, and it cracked. "Is that a trick?"

"Probably." He refused to accept this.

She grabbed him again and took him outside to his
car. He tried to get away, but she had a firm hold on
him. They stopped in front of the driver's-side mirror
on his car. She leaned down in front of it, forcing him
to see the same evil image he'd seen upstairs.

She let him go and started walking back toward the
house. "Wait!" he yelled.

Maggie turned around, expressionless. "Yes?"

"You can't just walk away!" Anger was overpowering

fear and common sense. He took out his gun, the Magnum he was never without at night. "I'll make you pay. . . . You're just like that thing that killed my son!"

Maggie eyed the gun and laughed bitterly. "Put it away, Jimmy. You can't kill a vampire at night."

"We'll see what I can do—" He choked off when Maggie reached over and yanked the gun from him. He tried to wrap his hands around her neck, but she pushed him away like an annoying fly. He flew into the street, and she was standing over him in a split second.

He tried to shrink away, but all she did was pull him up. Then she sat on the front steps of her house. "Mortals are powerless against vampires at night, Jimmy. Calm down, I'm not going to hurt you. Just get in your car and forget about me."

"Just like that?" he said incredulously. "Just pick up and forget I've met"—he made a disgusted face—"and screwed a vampire!"

"You forgot about the other one," she pointed out.

"No, I didn't!" he screamed. "Why do you think I drink? I can't stand the dark anymore . . . knowing evil things like you are outside! The only way I get through the night is by getting so drunk I can barely think." He stopped and glared at her . . . at her beauty. "But I thought you were deformed! Why are you so goddamned pretty?"

"There are different types of vampires."

Jimmy rolled his eyes to the heavens. "Well, isn't that just great! I don't just have to be on the lookout for that monstrosity that killed Jay. Oh, no! Now anyone I meet at night could be one of you."

"You don't have to worry about your son's killer."

"How the hell do you know?"

"Because I killed it . . . about a month after it attacked your family."

Jimmy inched closer to her. "You killed your own kind?"

"That thing was not my own kind!" Her eyes flared in anger. "It was a lunatic, deranged . . . That happens sometimes. Transformation doesn't always work, and you wind up out of your mind, with no thought but getting blood."

"How did you find it?"

"You said it yourself . . . Your case received media interest. I read the papers and I monitor police files for cases that could have to do with vampires. I'm not the only one; other vampires also abhor reckless slaughter of human beings. So when we find something like . . . that thing, we put it down like a rabid dog."

He glared into her green eyes, and she stared back calmly. He didn't know why, but he believed her. Still, maybe she was making him believe her.

He glowered suspiciously. "I guess you can read my mind?"

"I can, but I won't. I've had it done to me, and I think it's a shocking invasion of privacy."

Jimmy couldn't accept that she was a vampire—no matter what she showed him. She was still the same pretty, strange girl who picked him up in a seedy bar. Where were the fangs and that hideous appearance? "Are you going to hurt me?"

Maggie smiled sadly. "I don't hurt people, Jimmy. I like you; I don't want to violate you."

"I like you too," he blurted out.

There—she finally looked surprised. "How can you? I'm a vampire."

"You're not like that thing that killed Jay." He asked her the question that was needling him. "Have you ever killed anyone?"

Maggie looked down at her shoes and sighed. "Jimmy, when I first became a vampire, I was transformed by a

very evil man. And he taught me to kill people; I won't
lie to you. A lot of people died before I was fortunate
enough to meet my mentor, Alcuin. He taught me that
I didn't have to kill people to survive. And since the
night I met him, I haven't killed anyone."

Maggie got up and kissed him on the cheek. "I do
like you, but I'm sure now you understand why we can't
be involved. Godspeed, Jimmy Delacroix." She turned
around, heading back into the house.

Jimmy didn't question what he was doing; he just
thought he didn't want to stop seeing Maggie. "Hey,
Cinderella!"

She turned around.

He grinned. "What time do you turn into a pump-
kin, Vampirella?"

She grinned back, a bit uncertainly. "Around six-
thirty. Why?"

"What do you say we take a ride upstate? I want you
to meet my sister, Darlene." He smiled wider at Maggie's
astonishment. "She'll be thrilled that I have a girlfriend."

"Girlfriend?" Maggie questioned.

"I said I thought I was falling in love with you. Why
can't we see where this goes? Come on, take a ride with
me."

Jimmy Delacroix never knew how close she came to
walking over and forcibly wiping his memory clear of
any thoughts of her. But then she thought it wasn't like
she'd told him about vampires. He already knew they
existed, and had had his family destroyed by them. And
she was so damn tired of having no real attachments.
She hadn't seen Alcuin in years, and she only saw
Charles a few times a year. Why shouldn't she have a
friend?

Maggie grinned, and his throat closed up. Jimmy
thought she was so much prettier when she smiled and

that mourning expression left her eyes. What had she seen to make her look so sad and wistful most of the time? *I'll make you smile all the time if you let me,* he thought to himself.

She eyed his beat-up Dodge in distaste. "Perhaps we could take my car?"

Jimmy's eyes lit up. "The Caddie? Please let me drive," he begged, and she laughed. "Besides, the house is hard to find. I should drive."

Maggie went into the house and came back with her car keys. "You don't have to beg, Jimmy. I've seen you coveting my car."

They got in, and Jimmy was in heaven. He loved classic cars; he used to have a model of the 1958 Cadillac convertible. Too bad it was February; he'd love to put the top down.

They drove in silence for a while, and then he decided to find out more about her. "You said you don't read people because someone did it to you, right?"

"The man who made me a vampire," she replied. "He reached into my mind whenever he felt like it. You don't want to know what it's like to feel that your innermost thoughts are on display. I think I hated him for that as much as anything else. . . . He didn't even have the common decency to leave my mind alone."

"What was his name?"

She grimaced and replied in a cold, tight voice, "Simon Baldevar."

"Shit!" Jimmy exclaimed. "What the hell did this guy do to you? You sound like you're choking just by saying his name."

"I don't like to think of him," she told Jimmy, and lit a cigarette. "So please—ask your questions and then I'm never discussing him or my early days as a vampire again. Understand?"

"Uh, sure," he replied, disconcerted by her harsh

tone and shaking hands. "Where is . . . uh, Simon? Where is he now?"

"Dead. Thank God."

"Who killed him?"

Maggie smiled—it was a bitter, vengeful smile. "Me." She nodded at Jimmy's astonished look. "I told you that I met someone who helped me. Well, Simon didn't want me to leave. . . . So I killed him."

"Don't worry, Maggie. You tell me we're through and I won't give you a hard time."

Maggie laughed—it sounded more like amusement than that harsh, cynical sound before. "It was a little more complicated than that. You see, I told him we were through and he threw me in a tub of scalding water, bled me, and left me on a rooftop exposed to the sun until I begged his forgiveness."

"Jesus Christ," Jimmy whispered.

"Oh, that wasn't even the half of it. Let's just say he wasn't a very nice guy. Anyway, the only way for me to leave him and the evil insanity he forced me to participate in was to kill him. I got in one hell of a lucky shot and put a stake through his heart. Then I left him on the same rooftop where he put me. End of story."

"When did you meet him?"

"1944—at a friend's house."

"I guess he's like you?"

"Like me? Oh, I see what you mean. Yes, you wouldn't know to look at him that he was a vampire." Jimmy noticed Maggie couldn't even bring herself to say the guy's name. There was a lot more that she wasn't telling. But that was fine—he wasn't going to try to force it out. Let her tell him when she was ready. "Very handsome man, actually. So the movies weren't completely wrong—the tall, dark, handsome vampire exists along with the grotesque ghouls."

"Why did he make you a vampire? Did he have a lot of vampire girls?"

"No, he wasn't running a harem. It wasn't a Hammer Films production—beautiful, bosomy women in lingerie serving his every need. Remember that picture in my living room?"

Jimmy nodded.

"Well, that was his wife. She died back when he was a mortal, and I look like her."

"Then he couldn't have been all bad," Jimmy told her. "I mean, if he loved his wife so much—"

Maggie laughed, and choked on cigarette smoke. "Jimmy, he did not love Isabelle. He made her life hell, and he did the same to me. I don't want to talk about him anymore," she said abruptly.

"So what happened after you killed him?"

"I went to Ireland, and Alcuin became my mentor."

"When was that?"

"1957—when I said my family lost money that year . . . Well, Simon," she said, scowling, "was wealthy. But when I left, I didn't take anything. Just clothes and some things my father left me."

"But you had enough to buy that house."

"That was a gift from Alcuin. He gave me and my friend Charles enough money to put us on our feet. He said that both of us, since we'd been transformed really young, never had much chance to live in the mortal world. And he knew we were both going stir-crazy, so he told us to pursue lives and careers on our own— the ones we might have had if we hadn't become vampires. Of course, we had both needled him for years about going out into the world, but at first he said it wasn't safe. But when he was finally convinced Lord Baldevar was dead, he gave us his blessing." Meghann sighed. "But that wasn't the only reason he had for encouraging us to leave his home."

"What else? Didn't he like you?"

"He liked us fine—that was the whole problem. You see, part of what Alcuin trained me in was magic, the occult—using my psychic ability. If I say so myself, I'm pretty good at it. But Charles and I—well, we work together extremely well as priest and priestess. And Alcuin started letting us conduct all the High Holidays—Samhain, Imbolc, Beltane. Now, there were other vampires—centuries old—who got jealous about all the attention Alcuin lavished on us . . . particularly me. They thought I didn't deserve it."

"Why?"

"Because I was Simon's consort—or whore as more than a few of them referred to me. As far as they're concerned, I can never be fully trusted—because Simon was my first master—so they really loathed the idea that Alcuin gave me an exalted position. And then some simply objected because Charles and I are, for vampires, quite young. What had we ever done to deserve being at Alcuin's side?" Maggie laughed harshly. "I guess putting a stake through Simon's heart—something *nobody* else ever did—wasn't enough for them. So Alcuin simply gave us his blessing to live on our own for a while—let everything smooth over."

"How long have you been on your own?"

"About seven years."

"That's it? I thought you said you met this guy in 1957."

"I did, and the basic apprenticeship took twenty years—the same amount of time it used to take for someone to become a Druid."

"Are you a Druid?"

"In a way. I study a lot of different religions, Jimmy."

"So what did you learn in those twenty years?"

"For the first five, it was my body that was developed—not my mind. Have you ever engaged in any kind of backbreaking physical labor?"

"I worked on a farm when I was a teenager."

"Then you might know what happens when you're constantly exerting yourself—it clears your mind completely. Which was what Alcuin wanted. When I think back—the Spartan exercises, the constant practice with a broadsword and jousting like some medieval knight, the huge stones I had to lift—ick, I feel my muscles tightening again. But it worked—all the anguish and frustration I brought to him started dropping away. And when he felt that I had achieved some tranquility in mind, the meditation began. From there—magic."

"What kind of magic?"

"Some relatively simple things—for a vampire. Things Simon should have taught me, but had never bothered. Levitation, telekinesis, hypnosis—basically, using the power of the mind to alter reality. Learning to concentrate, focus thoughts. As for the more mystical side—I'll tell you some other time."

"So, Alcuin taught you how to control those punks from last night."

Maggie looked uncomfortable. "No. Alcuin would not have done that—he would have very gently 'suggested' that they leave."

"And Simon?"

Maggie laughed, a bit shrilly. "If he found someone attempting to steal from him? At the very least . . . hang them from the streetlight by their own entrails. So I guess you could put my reaction somewhere in the middle. Didn't kill them—but I damn sure hurt them. And I liked it. That's always been the biggest problem—and where I need Alcuin's guidance the most."

"What do you mean?"

Maggie sighed. "I've never tried to explain this to a human." She thought a minute. "OK. Let's say some-

one cut you off in traffic—caused a fender bender to
this gorgeous machinery. And then they were a real
asshole about it—refused to fess up. Think you could
get so mad you'd want to kill them?"

"Yup."

"And what if you could do it and get away with it?"

Jimmy began to see what she meant.

She saw his understanding and nodded. "Jimmy,
what I have inside me makes your dependency on alcohol look like a joke. It's knowing that the power is
there, knowing I can do whatever I want and knowing
how damn good it feels. Everyday things—small annoy-
ances are a damned trial for me. When I saw that kid
quake, I can't tell you how badly I wanted his blood.
How good I knew it would taste with the fear and sub-
servience I could put in him. Every night I want to do
something like that, and every night I have to fight. If
I hadn't met Alcuin, I don't think I could do it. He
gave me the ability to control the darkness inside me—
darkness Simon put there for good. As long as I live,
it will be there."

"And you'll have to fight it—so that you're not like
the thing that killed Jay."

"Yes."

Jimmy examined her profile, her hand resting on
the dashboard. He saw the emerald ring that had in-
trigued him before, its gems reflecting the overhead
lights. "Did Alcuin give you that?"

"No, he gave me the cross you saw around my waist—
I like to wear it close to me. This was a gift from Simon."

"So why not take it off?"

Maggie shook her head. "Jimmy, that's one thing
about the modern world I can't stand. People seem to
think they can forget, or worse still, rewrite the past.
Every time I look at this ring, it forces me to remember
what I did—what I enjoyed doing for a time. And that

at one time I truly was Simon Baldevar's consort. I'm not going to forget that I was infatuated with him, or that I admired him. It would be dangerous to try and deny it, pretend he never existed. No, this ring is my hair shirt. I want to see it and remember what I was. What I could be if I ever let my guard down."

"Did Alcuin teach you to kill vampires?"

Meghann nodded. "Please don't get the idea that I do it all the time. There aren't that many vampires in the world . . . and very few like that thing you encountered. Of course, there are those who enjoy killing. But they're intelligent, cunning. It's very difficult to track them down."

"You kill them at night?"

"No, at twelve noon!" she said sarcastically. "Of course I kill them at night."

"Don't fly off the handle. I was just thinking . . . Why don't you teach me?"

"Teach you what?"

"How to kill vampires."

Alcuin glanced at his watch. *"Banrion,* I think you should go pick up Charles now. His flight is due in at one-fifteen."

Jimmy frowned. "You're going out—alone? What about Simon? Why don't I go?"

Alcuin answered him. "We do not feel Simon's presence—I think it's safe enough for Meghann to pick up Charles."

"But not safe enough for me to go with her, right? So you don't know for sure that he isn't out there."

"There are no guarantees anymore, Jimmy," Meghann told him. "But I will not skulk and hide from him. Now I'm going to the airport—alone. Stop that protesting! The car is in the driveway—that's protected land.

From there, all I have to do is pick up Charles. We'll be fine. You stay here and finish our story for Alcuin." Jimmy probably could have come with her, but she simply wanted some time alone to absorb all that had happened tonight. And she wanted to talk to Charles alone—something Alcuin was aware of.

Jimmy swallowed back his protests and watched her leave. Was this what it was going to be like until Simon showed up? Would he be scared to death that every time she was gone she might be killed? Would he sit in the house, locked up for the night, quaking at any sound?

Alcuin put a comforting hand on his shoulder. Jimmy was starting to see what Maggie had told him: "If you look in his eyes and see the gentle tranquility and love, you'll forget all about his appearance."

"Meghann will be fine. Don't underestimate her strength."

Jimmy nodded. "She's one tough lady—after that night, both she and Darlene went to work on me."

Alcuin smiled, happy to distract the mortal from his worry. "Yes, what did happen when she met your sister?"

"At first, Darlene wasn't too thrilled about us showing up on her doorstep at midnight. But then she took one look at Maggie and told me that for the first time in three years, I'd done something right. She doesn't know about . . . well, what Maggie is. She just thinks I found a girl who got me on the straight and narrow." Jimmy chuckled. "Darlene has no idea Maggie turned me into Dr. Van Helsing."

"How did Meghann train you?" She had not discussed Jimmy Delacroix with Alcuin—training the young man was her project alone.

"First I had to give up drinking for one year; then I had to go back to school. Next she taught me self-defense. Says I can thank you for all the nights I went to bed barely able to walk—the U.S. Marines had nothing on Maggie."

"A sound program."

"I know, but she had a slightly different concept of vampire-hunter than what I had in mind. She didn't mean going around dank castles ripping up coffins. No, no, no. I'm a *computer* vampire-hunter. At school, I learned a lot about computers and then I met some hackers. My job is to monitor all the police, federal agencies, newspapers, magazines, and TV shows in the tristate area for any stories that could be vampire related—what she did herself before I came along. Ninety-nine percent of the time, it doesn't pan out; it turns out to be satanic cults or serial killers. In six years, we've found five instances of vampires. Twice she took care of them herself—but she let me handle the others."

Alcuin kept silent. He knew about those slayings. Meghann only let Jimmy do it because she was absolutely sure nothing could go wrong. She wanted to protect Jimmy, but now it had backfired. There was no way he had a prayer if Simon Baldevar found him and he, Meghann, and Charles weren't around to protect him. And even if they were there . . .

Still, Alcuin thought he had found a way to get Jimmy's mind off Meghann. "You say you can break into protected files with a computer?"

"Sure."

Alcuin guided him into Meghann's study. "Then let's find Simon. Can we search investment companies?"

"No problem." Jimmy handed him a yellow legal pad. "Write down every alias he's ever used that you know about. The names of his friends, people he admired, family—everything. When people choose false names, they want it to be something they'll remember—most of the time. I'm going to start with anything

I can find on him from 1957. If you all thought he was dead, someone must have taken over his holdings. Or maybe he kept administering them himself with a phony name. And Maggie told me about that lady whose daughter he killed. He was using the name Simon Baldevar to make business deals, right? And that was nearly fifty years ago. So he must have killed off that identity. . . ."

Alcuin smiled over the legal pad. The young man had nearly forgotten he was there; he was completely absorbed in his task. Now he wasn't feeling sorry for himself or unincluded. He was participating, helping with the battle against Simon. And who knew? Perhaps he would find some useful information.

THIRTEEN

Meghann spotted Charles leaving the plane and ran over to him. "Charles!"

He caught her in a fierce hug, and inspected her black equestrienne jacket, skintight blue jeans, and cruel black boots a dominatrix would envy. "Young consort," he thundered in his dead-on imitation of Simon, "how dare you appear before your lord and master in those rags."

He was relieved to see the tension drain from her face slightly—she always laughed when he mimicked Simon Baldevar. Meghann widened her eyes to comic proportions. "Oh, Master," she cried piteously, "I was sure you would like my beautiful boots planted up your—"

Charles laughed. "I'm glad to see you can still joke about him."

"What else should I do—cry and crawl into a corner? Fuck him!" Beneath her defiant words, Charles saw the glimmer of tears on her eyelids and heard the slight tremor in her voice.

He picked up his tote bag, and they hurried through the crowd to the airport parking lot. Then Charles hugged her again and told her, "Let it out, Meghann."

She started crying. These tears were the reason she

hadn't allowed Jimmy to come with her—she wanted a chance to pour all her fear out where he couldn't see her. "I'm so frightened," she sobbed against her best friend's chest.

"Of course you are, Meghann, only a lunatic or an imbecile wouldn't be frightened of Lord Baldevar. I'm scared to death." He handed her a handkerchief, and she wiped her eyes.

Meghann pulled herself up on the hood of the car and stretched out against the windshield. Charles followed suit, handing her a cigarette, and they glanced up at the planes overhead for a few minutes, smoking silently.

Then Meghann turned to her friend. "You're only in danger because you helped me—that's why Simon hates you. Are you sorry that you went out of your way to help me leave him?"

"Sorry that I made the best friend of my life? Sorry for enjoying the past forty years of that friendship? Simon would have already won if he could make me regret all that. Meghann, I love you—and I will never regret helping you."

"Will you regret it when you greet the sunrise with a stake in your heart?"

Charles paled. "I can only hope Simon would show that much mercy. But I think if he did manage to corner either of us, it would not be a quick death. My God, Meghann—we, particularly you, humiliated him. The great Lord Baldevar spurned by his consort when she met a vampire who offered her a new path. And he couldn't stop you from leaving. Everyone knows the story—the dark master of the underworld defeated by a mere slip of a girl when he tripped on a piece of glass. And then his age-old enemy offers her sanctuary. Meghann, his flock will not obey him—or fear him—

the way he desires if he does not make an example of us."

Meghann didn't reply; Charles had just put her deepest fears into words. Long ago, Simon had warned her that she would never want him to hate her. What would he do to her now that he despised her? *Please, God,* she prayed, *if he finds us and we can't defeat him, let it be quick. Don't let him subject any of us to a death that will leave us no pride or dignity.*

Charles saw her lips whiten and said briskly, "No more brooding! We will not give Simon the satisfaction of making us sit and tremble in anticipation of him. We shall proceed as always—now put that damned top down and take me to your home!"

The night was chilly, but the cold didn't bother Meghann or Charles. While she maneuvered the huge car out of the busy airport, Charles reached into his tote bag and popped a CD into the player Jimmy Delacroix had recently installed in her classic car.

ABBA filled the air, and Meghann grinned. The sappy pop music was precisely what she needed. When "SOS" came on, Charles commented, "This could be Simon's song to you . . . pining away after his faithless lover abandoned him. . . ."

Since traffic on the Van Wyck Expressway was its usual bumper-to-bumper self, Meghann was able to take her eyes off the road long enough to whack Charles on the head with the CD cover. "Swine!"

In a lisping falsetto, Charles warbled the lyrics to "SOS."

Meghann howled with laughter and Charles joined her, happy to see his foolish joke banish her fears and anxieties for a few minutes.

Finally Meghann wiped tears out of her eyes and gasped, "For your information, love was never nice or good between us."

"Was anything good between you in those thirteen years?"

She considered and finally said, "Sex . . . I'll give the bastard that much. That was the bond between us . . . lust, nothing more."

Charles was curious about the relationship Meghann rarely discussed. "Did you ever think you were in love with him?"

She sighed and lit another cigarette. "Maybe . . . at first. But it wasn't love . . . It was infatuation. I'd never met anyone like him, anyone so utterly self-assured or charming . . . or mesmerizing. I guess I was in awe of him. But love was never there . . . on either side. I was overwhelmed by him, and he . . . Simon was enchanted, or perhaps infuriated, by my resemblance to Isabelle."

"What about Jimmy? Are you in love with him?"

"How can I be? He's mortal."

Charles stared at her. "Meghann, this goes no further than the two of us—you know that. Now, don't tell me what you should feel—tell me what you do feel."

"I wish to God I knew. At first, I thought I could help him. He'd had his life destroyed, his son slain by a vampire. So I thought, I'll make him want to live again. He'll learn from me how to defend himself. And after enough time passes, he'll heal. He'll want a normal life again . . . maybe remarry. But I didn't count on how close we'd become. Now I don't want him to leave me . . . but what can I do? Do you know he asked me to transform him?"

"What?"

"That was my reaction. How can this man, who saw what vampires are capable of, possibly want that life? How can he watch me arise night after night, never seeing the sun, and think it's a good thing? To which he replied, that makes no difference—we're in love. So what happens if Jimmy and I end up like you and Paul? Will he still want to be stuck with immortality if we break up? Tell me, Charles. Did you ever regret being a vampire when you knew you and Paul would not stay together?"

It was Charles's turn to sigh. "I was frightened by the thought of being alone for the rest of my life. I know what you're saying—Jimmy wants to be a vampire because he wants to be with you. Would he still want it if you two separated? Would he be able to handle the constant temptation on his own? And then there's the other matter."

Meghann nodded. She and Charles had discussed this before. "Should I transform anyone knowing I'll pass Simon Baldevar's blood to them? How much of my tendencies are inherited from him, like a disease?" She told Charles briefly about what had happened earlier that evening at the hospital.

"That isn't like you, Meghann. That's what intrigues me about the bloodline. Simon, yes, he would enjoy something like that greatly. But that is foreign to your personality and inclinations. Would you fight the same demons if Alcuin or I had transformed you? Perhaps it is an inherited trait. If Alcuin could inherit his master's deformities, why couldn't Simon's depraved tendencies be passed along to you?"

"And then passed along to Jimmy," Meghann said thoughtfully. "So even if I thought Jimmy should become a vampire, which I don't, I'd want someone else to give him blood." She eyed Charles meaningfully before turning onto the Belt Parkway, where traffic was moving at a quicker pace.

He shifted uncomfortably in the passenger seat. "I would have to have a long talk with Jimmy before I would even consider—Jesus Christ!" A Jaguar abruptly cut in front of them. Meghann had to slam down on the brake, and if there had been any cars right behind her, they would have crashed.

"What an asshole," she gasped, nearly going through the window. "You OK?" Charles nodded.

The Jaguar was a few cars ahead in the left lane. Meghann checked to see if any cars were blocking the right lane, then she cut in and maneuvered around the cars in front of her in the center lane.

"Meghann, what are you doing?"

"What do you think? I'm gonna ask that creep if he got his license out of the Cracker Jack box." The Caddie easily caught up with the Jaguar, and Meghann screeched, "You fucking dimwit! You could have killed us. . . ."

The words choked off when she found herself staring into a pair of amber eyes that had haunted her dreams for fifty years. Simon Baldevar—sitting in the passenger seat, staring right at her—nearly able to reach out and touch her. Dimly Meghann had an impression of a woman driving the car, but her entire attention was taken by his evil eyes radiating fury and cold hate.

Then she became aware that the road was far too quiet. She took her eyes off Simon long enough to register that every car on either side of the road was still, all passengers sitting in utter silence. *My God, he's stopped the fucking traffic on the Belt Parkway!*

A minor parlor trick, the invasive voice that she'd never forgotten told her. Her attention was drawn back to Simon. He stretched his hand out and ran one finger over her jaw. *There's such terror in your gaze, little one. It makes me want to throw you to the ground and ravish you. Who knows? Perhaps I shall—before I make you beg for death.* She felt something land in her lap.

A honking horn brought her back to her senses. Meghann looked around—the spell was broken; traffic was up and moving again. The whole encounter could not have lasted more than ten seconds. Dimly she heard humans in all the surrounding cars muttering angrily about the sudden traffic jam. Why was there such a slowdown when there was no accident?

She looked around for the Jaguar—it was long gone. While she waited for the traffic to thin, she repeated to herself, like a mantra, *I will drive this car and not think about anything until I get home; I will drive this car and not think about anything until I get home. . . .*

She and Charles drove to Rockaway in silence, both shaken by the encounter. When she reached the house, she cut the engine, and started shaking. Her teeth were even clattering. A glance at Charles told her he was no better—she had never seen him that white.

When she could speak again, she said, "He wanted to scare us."

"Yes."

"Let us know we can't go anywhere or do anything without him watching."

Charles nodded and got out of the car.

Meghann was about to get out when she noticed a flat jeweler's box—it must have been the thing she felt land in the car. She shuddered, and picked it up. Then she got out of the car and handed it to Charles. "Please open it—I can't."

Charles didn't want to open it either, but he did. He gave out a high-pitched cry.

Meghann flew to his side and picked up the box he'd flung to the ground. In the center was a severed index finger with a plain gold ring.

She looked down at Charles, weeping like she'd never seen him cry before. She put her arms around him and he clung to her in a bone-crushing grip. His keening had attracted Alcuin and Jimmy, who came running out the front door. Meghann held up her hand to ask them to stay back.

"Mark!" Charles finally sobbed out.

Meghann understood. "Charles, I'm so sorry." Mark was a mortal Charles had dated off and on for almost ten years.

Jimmy misunderstood the ring. "You guys were married or something?"

Even through his tears, Charles looked embarrassed. "He was married . . . to a woman. We had an understanding."

Charles slammed his fist into the cement sidewalk, making a sizable hole. "I'm so stupid! How could it not occur to me that Simon would kill him?"

Alcuin came over. "This is not your fault."

"It is!" Charles yelled. "I could have warned him . . . protected him. But I never thought . . . It never occurred to me that he knew about Mark. I thought he would just focus on Meghann's life."

Alcuin sighed and pulled his apprentice up from the sidewalk. "You have only known Simon is alive for two nights." He touched the finger. "Your lover has been dead for at least two weeks."

Charles looked up. "He was going to a conference in Jerusalem. A sudden invitation came a few weeks ago. . . . Damn him! Damn! How long has he been planning his revenge?"

"Since Meghann left him on that rooftop."

"I want that bastard to die!" Charles screamed. "Why don't we just find out where he rests and kill him?"

"Do you think it will be that easy to seek him out? Jimmy has been diligently searching for him for hours. . . . We've found nothing."

"I can find him," Meghann spoke up.

The two vampires turned to look at her and she said, "Let me look in the scrying dish. I can use the link of him being my master to find him."

Alcuin eyed Meghann. "Do you think you can handle the duties of seer tonight?"

She nodded, and headed into the house, the other three following her. For Jimmy's benefit, Charles told Alcuin out loud about their encounter with Simon.

"Meghann was correct—it was a scare tactic, nothing more." At the front door, Charles found himself unable to enter, and nodded. "At least we're safe here."

Alcuin stepped over the threshold, and then extended his hand to Charles.

They found Meghann sitting on the ottoman, eating a plate of cold bacon.

"Hungry?" Jimmy asked her in bewilderment.

"The Druids believed that one could acquire visions by consuming pig flesh, or the flesh of dogs and cats. Of course, they took that to mean you should grab some live animal and start munching. But times have changed. . . ." She indicated her bacon. Max came sniffing around, and she gave him a few pieces.

"So you're eating that for visions?"

"Meghann is my seer," Alcuin explained. "She possesses *Himbas Forosmai.*"

"Huh?"

"The gift of prophecy," Meghann explained while she ate.

"A gift that must be used with extreme caution," Alcuin told her. "Meghann, you do remember what I taught you about the astral plane?"

Meghann nodded, and explained for Jimmy's benefit. "The astral plane is divided into two realms. The Higher Astral—where beings you would think of as angels exist—and the Lower Astral—where one encounters demons. When we fly, we choose one of those two paths to guide our travels, or to seek out beings to help us. Needless to say, Simon spends most of his time on the Lower Astral. Certainly, when he flies, that's the path he travels."

"So any attempt to see into his future could lead you there," Alcuin warned.

Meghann paled. "But Charles is here . . . and so are you. One of you should be able to bring me back if I run into any . . . trouble."

Alcuin turned to Charles. "Are you capable of putting your grief aside and serving as Meghann's priest? If you feel at all unsure, tell us now—don't risk her safety."

"I would never put Meghann in a precarious situation. I'll meditate quietly, and find my equilibrium." He went out the back door. He needed to be on the beach for a while.

"Why did Alcuin make you seer?" Jimmy asked Meghann curiously.

"Fifteen years ago, I looked in his scrying bowl and I saw a vampire he trusted attempt to kill him. It turned out this man, his name was Ignatius, had been one of Simon's spawn. The boy took it upon himself to strike Alcuin in the name of his dead master." Meghann looked up thoughtfully. "Alcuin, how many vampires have known Simon Baldevar was alive all this time?"

"My guess is very few—even within his circle. He wanted the world to believe he was dead so he could develop his strength in total isolation. Meghann, do you remember how I told you Simon fled Europe after our first encounter?"

"Of course—and I asked you why you didn't track him down and slay him." Meghann stopped and looked up at her mentor. "And you didn't tell me the whole truth. That was the first time he vanished and then reappeared with more power decades later . . . right?"

Alcuin nodded. He hadn't wanted Meghann to think Simon could be alive when he met her. He'd wanted her to develop her ability without looking over her shoulder.

Meghann finished her pork, then dug into an exquisitely carved ivory box on the mantelpiece. She fished out the pendant Simon had given her. He had handled it recently so it would have some psychic residue from him.

She turned to Alcuin. "I'm going downstairs to meditate. I'll be ready to start in one hour."

Meghann stripped off her clothing and donned a plain white shift. She let her hair down and removed all her jewelry—except the signet ring. Simon had not been joking when he said she'd have to break her finger to get it off. And it simply wasn't worth it to crush her finger every time she wanted to take the ring off.

She stretched out on the cold cement floor of the cellar and tried to center her thoughts. She found herself thinking about magic—all she'd learned from Alcuin.

Alcuin helped her find her true potential as a vampire. When she thought of all those years with Simon, all that ability going to waste . . . She laughed at herself. Why would Simon teach her, mold her? The more she learned, the stronger she would become—well, that would have increased her independence, and thus the chance she might walk out on him.

So Alcuin developed her ability. She discovered her amazing knack for clairvoyance, and what Charles had noticed when they prayed for her father—the ability to summon. That was why Alcuin allowed her, a not even century-old vampire, to lead the High Holidays as priestess. She could draw power into her and bring it to the ceremonies.

Of course, she wasn't omnipotent. She still had little

ability to travel the astral plane. Any vampire could learn to use the astral plane to fly short distances. But when you wanted to use the plane for magical purposes, you had to leave your body behind and travel with only your soul. Alcuin had taught her how, but it was not something she did easily—and she could not fly at all if she was unwell or blood starved.

Alcuin and Charles came downstairs. There were no lights—none of the three had any need of them. Alcuin had never been here before, but Charles had worked in this room with her previously.

Alcuin took a stone bottle from his cloak. He poured water into a bronze bowl with fine sand on the bottom. The water came from Llyn Cerrig Bach—a lake in Britain that had been a Druidic sanctuary.

Meghann and Charles (her priest and guide when she looked into the future) clasped hands over the bowl.

"Fedelma," Meghann intoned, invoking a Celtic goddess of war and prophecy, "allow me to see he who gave me this." She let the pendant break the surface of the water, and then she leaned down to look into the clear surface.

"What do you see?" Charles whispered.

Meghann did not answer at first. Charles had to ask again—something that rarely happened. Usually he maintained a bond with her throughout.

"The circle has been broken . . . ," she finally whispered.

Where was she? The bowl and the room were gone. Damn— she'd lost touch with the physical world. Now her soul was wandering aimlessly. Why wasn't Charles pulling her back?

Calm down, she told herself. She was surrounded by total darkness. Images swirled abruptly and then disappeared into the pitch blackness. She saw a sharp-nosed woman call out,

"Master." Meghann reached out and forced the image to remain with her.

There he was—Simon Baldevar. Who was the woman? Did he sense Meghann's presence? They were bent over some crumbling, ancient parchment with arcane script on it.

"The Language of the Birds," Meghann whispered. *Suddenly, the Sight descended on her and she found herself screaming, "Don't! Don't!"*

Charles slashed his wrist—they needed to make a sacrifice to bring Meghann back. He allowed a few drops of blood to fall in the water. "Don't what, Meghann?"

She thought she heard a whisper in the darkness, but then it was gone. Now she felt icy hands grab her. Dear God, she was trapped in the dark, terrible world of the Lower Astral. When she flew the plane with Simon, she always felt the clutching hands of daemons—now she was in their realm as an unwelcome visitor.

Why was she here? Meghann felt the Shadow-beings. They put their dank, icy presence on her soul—invading it, desperate to possess her. She closed her eyes. I don't want to see them; I'll go crazy if I do. "Help me!" she shouted, and it only came out a hoarse whisper.

"Come to me, child—I can guarantee safe passage from this world."

"Simon, what have you done?" she screamed, caught in some confusing mix of the Otherworld and the future. *"The circle is broken—make them go away, make them go away!"* Then the evil entered her, and she was fighting for her soul.

Charles grabbed her away from the scrying dish, and the cursed visions it was giving her. "Listen to me, Meghann! I am your priest—come back!"

She did not hear him—she was fighting with the force of someone in the grip of a terrifying menace. *"It's Azazeal, it's Azazeal—get it out of me!"* Unseeing, unhearing, she broke Charles's hold and he was flung across the room.

Alcuin came forward. He needed all his strength to pin Meghann to the ground. Yanking the simple wooden cross from his neck, he pressed it to her forehead. He had worn it since he was mortal—it was the only thing in the room with enough power to banish the evil inside his apprentice. She thrashed and screamed, trying desperately to leave the hell she was trapped in.

Alcuin looked up from his struggles with Meghann. "You are her priest—bring her back," he ordered Charles.

Charles placed his hands over his master's and pressed the cross down on her forehead, making a harsh imprint on her pallid skin. "Listen to me, Meghann. You can fight this awful thing. Listen to my voice, and feel the cross. Let it help you come back." He felt Meghann start to relax slightly, and he started praying over her, along with Alcuin.

It was nearly dawn when Meghann finally returned to them. She glanced around the room in shock. With the last touch of Sight, she told Alcuin tiredly, *"He'll set them free to keep me."*

"Who will he set free?"

The spell was broken—Meghann could hardly remember anything of that strange, evil place except the utter terror when the icy, grasping fingers touched her. "I don't know." She tried to stand, but her legs were weak.

"We were fortunate to bring you back," Alcuin told her. "I was worried you might only respond to Simon."

Instantly she was on her feet—disbelief and hurt plain on her face. "How dare you say that to me! Have those others poisoned your mind—made you think I am his whore? I'll never respond to him."

"No, Meghann—I did not want to hurt you with this

knowledge, but now you must know. What do you remember of your transformation?"

"The pain."

Alcuin held her eyes, hypnotizing her slightly. "I am here, *banrion*. The pain cannot touch you."

"No," she responded in a haze. "You cannot hold back the pain—only my master can." The trance broke when she said those words, and she looked at Alcuin in complete anguish. "No, I can't still think of him as my master—no!"

"Meghann, my first lesson to you was that you must always be honest. Simon transformed you—and he used your suffering to create an unbreakable bond between you. His is the voice you will always hear—be aware of that. What took us hours tonight would have taken him minutes to do. There will always be a link between you."

"What does that mean—that I'm powerless to resist his commands? That I'm his zombie?"

Alcuin was uncomfortable. He took her hands in his. "Meghann, for forty years you have been my pride and joy—the daughter I never had, a woman with dazzling gifts. But you are, for a vampire, very young. And Simon . . . No novice vampire, especially one with a blood link to him, can hope to handle him. I do not believe he could turn you into a zombie, but I do think you would have a very difficult time resisting him. I don't want to see you in a position where you have to resist him."

"Then what's going to happen?"

"You will attract him—and that is all you will do. You are not to be alone with him. Let him come to you, and then I shall deal with him. Once he is dead, this link will be behind you forever."

"Master, how will I be involved?"

"Charles, the only reason you are here is because

Simon presents a threat to you. Neither of you should attempt to deal with him on your own. If worst comes to worst, you two can assist me—that is all. You are not strong enough to destroy him on your own."

Reluctantly they both swore to leave Simon to Alcuin's more experienced hands. They also promised to stay together at night and not stray too far from Alcuin (should they need his help).

Meghann frowned. "Alcuin, what did I see? Was that the future or some terrible visitation he sent to frighten me?"

"I am not sure, Meghann. Tomorrow night, after you have rested, I will put you in a light trance and see if we cannot clarify your vision. What worries me is that last thing you said. . . . What will he set free?"

Meghann thought of the infernal presence she'd felt and shivered. What indeed?

FOURTEEN

April 30, 1998

"Carlo wants to come here, Dr. Cameron—for one of my sessions. Don't you think that's progress?"

Diana looked expectantly at her psychologist, but the woman didn't respond. "Dr. Cameron?"

"What? I'm sorry, Diana. Could you repeat what you just said?" Alcuin was right; she was doing her patients a disservice by continuing to see them.

At first, Meghann had been firm about continuing her practice—Simon or no Simon. She was not going to disrupt her life any more than she had to. But then Alcuin convinced her that she could not be a responsible therapist if she knew that at any moment she might have to stop seeing her patients to deal with her own crisis. So she referred her small caseload of ten patients willing to see a therapist who only had night hours to other psychologists, gently weaning her worst patients. The patient she was seeing tonight was having her last session with her; after tonight, she had arranged for a leave of absence.

It wasn't just the fact that she might not be available to her patients—in her current state, she wasn't doing them much good. It was so hard to concentrate, she thought as she forced herself to listen to Diana's tale of woe concerning the louse she had married. Lately Meghann's thoughts always drifted to Simon. Where was he? When was he going to attack? It had been over a month. A month of constant, unceasing tension as she looked over her shoulder at any unexplainable noise. A month of nightmares that woke her, leaving her drenched in sweat and screaming. Jimmy had managed to find not one but several possible identities for Simon. He found financial information—basically stock portfolios—no personal information, no addresses, nothing. And Alcuin had not been able to clarify her vision—every time she attempted to remember, those evil beings reached out for her again. After three attempts, Alcuin had given up, saying it was far too dangerous to try to gain information.

Now Meghann took a deep breath. "Why do you think Carlo wants to come here, Diana?"

The woman looked puzzled. "So that he can explain his side to you . . . help you understand."

"What am I supposed to understand?"

"Why he does those things."

Meghann fixed her patient with a steely stare. "What things are those?"

Diana dropped her eyes. "When he . . . hits me sometimes."

"And what will he tell me that will make me understand why one person has a right to hit another?"

"I didn't say he had a right to hit me," the patient answered uncomfortably. "It's just that he's under so much pressure with that new job, and I don't always keep the house clean, even though I'm home all day. . . ."

Meghann forced herself not to roll her eyes. How many times had she heard this? *Oh, it's not his fault I have a broken arm—the carpet wasn't vacuumed; my mom bothers him; the Yankee game got rain delayed. . . .* Meghann did not always understand her patients—she would have had Johnny's balls if he hit her. All that stuff about how domestic abuse was more acceptable in the old days was crap in her estimation. Her dad never lifted his hand to her mom; Frankie didn't abuse Theresa. Sure, they'd known about people who roughed up their wives . . . but they were known as degenerates. All that had really improved in Meghann's estimation was that in those days people tended to blame it on booze and assumed once you were married, it was for good. At least now there were places for women to go . . . if they would just leave as Meghann was trying to encourage her patient to do.

"Diana, let me see if I understand you. Carlo is going to come to your session, on your time, and tell me that your black eye wouldn't have happened if only his boss didn't give him a hard time?"

"I know how it sounds!" The woman sobbed loudly. "But I really believe it's just the pressure he's under. Once he gets the job under control, he'll be fine."

Meghann went to a small wooden cabinet and took out a tape labeled ELTON, DIANA, 10-19-95. Diana watched with some apprehension as Meghann placed it in her tape deck. Soon Diana's sobbing voice filled the room.

"But he doesn't mean it—it's all the pressure of living at home with his mother. As soon as we're married, it will all work out. . . ." Meghann shut the tape off, and stared at her patient. "What has changed in the past two-and-a-half years, Diana?"

The woman flushed. "Are you saying I make excuses for him?"

"Answer my question."

Now the patient was angry—a good sign. If only the woman could channel her anger to the right source— the bastard who used her for a punching bag.

"Fine—nothing's changed!" Diana bellowed. "Is that what you want to hear?"

"That wouldn't be true," Meghann told her softly. "When you first started seeing me, Carlo hadn't abused you physically—it was all mental."

The patient fell silent.

"Diana, your relationship has gotten worse—not better." Traditional psychology demanded that therapists not make judgments or even clarifications for their patients. But domestic abuse counselors were abandoning the soft, impersonal role in favor of getting women away from potentially dangerous situations. But it was a fine line—Meghann had no desire to shame her patient, or castigate her to the point that she abandoned therapy.

Diana sighed. "Maybe you're right, but I love him!"

To hell with it, Meghann thought. This was the last night she'd see Diana, and she wanted to make some sort of progress. "And what about your children? Do you love them too?"

"Of course I do!"

"Then why punish them with the torture of a miserable marriage like the kind you witnessed between your parents?"

"My marriage is not miserable!"

"You don't mind when your husband calls you a fat pig at your office Christmas party, or gives you a concussion because you forgot he likes his steak medium rare?"

"Of course I do . . . but . . . but . . ."

Meghann came over to the woman's chair and squatted in front of her. Then she took her patient's hands, and looked her in the eyes. "Diana, I won't tell you what to do. But this is our last session, and I'd like you to think about something for me, something you might want to work on with your new therapist. You are a mother now, Diana. Are you going to be like your mother—treated like a doormat by your husband and making your kids grow up forced to sit through that? You told me how much it hurt every time your dad would come home and beat her. How do you think your children are going to feel when they're old enough to understand? You think it won't hurt to see their mother cry because of some horrible thing their father said? Are you going to force them to choose sides as your parents did? Or when Carlo attacks them, are you going to continue to excuse his behavior?"

Diana looked down. "I'm frightened to leave him."

"Have you thought about the list we worked on? All the resources you might have—how you could drain the checking account while he's at work? Anyone you could stay with?"

"My sister said I could move in with her."

Meghann told her gently, "Maybe you should consider it. And I'll be happy to put you in touch with a safe house if you need one."

Diana sat silently until her time was up. Then she wrote Meghann a check. At the door to the study, she turned around. "Dr. Cameron?"

"Yes?"

"I know psychologists aren't supposed to answer questions like this, but . . . I want to know. Supposing it were you trapped in a bad relationship?" *I'd get my stake out,* Meghann thought to herself, fighting a ridiculous urge to laugh. "Could you force yourself to give up a man you really love?"

Meghann considered the question. Had she ever been in love? Johnny Devlin—well, that was puppy love. Who could say if their marriage would have worked out? And you could not call what happened between her and Simon love—more like lust mixed with domination. Jimmy—oh, Jimmy.

Meghann looked at her patient. "I could give a man up—if he was costing me other things. My pride, my dignity . . . I need those too much to give them up in the name of love. It isn't love if it costs you your self-worth, Diana. Love is supposed to give you a reason for living—not take it away. There are plenty of good men in this world . . . and no reason you can't have one."

The woman smiled shyly at her psychologist's candid answer and bid her a good night.

Meghann went upstairs to wash off her sophisticated makeup job Jimmy had applied and to change out of the stuffy gray suit that she always wore seeing patients. She got out a Mets jersey and her baggiest jeans. Ah, that was much more comfortable. Now she took her hair out of its schoolmarm bun and put it into pigtails.

"You look about sixteen." Charles smiled at her when she came into the living room.

"And I feel about five hundred." She groaned and collapsed on the sofa. "When is Alcuin coming back?"

"Soon, I imagine. He wasn't going far—he merely wished to be alone to perform the Beltane magic."

Jimmy came into the living room. "I'd like to talk to you, Maggie."

"So talk." Meghann regretted her harsh tone, but she was so restless and angry. Angry that Simon had managed to trap her once again, angry that they couldn't seem to find out where he slept. Jimmy had scoured every apartment, house, estate, and condominium purchased within the tristate area in the past six months. He'd also tracked down any Baldevar property from the 1940s and 1950s—nothing. A tedious, time-consuming task that had been a waste of time.

Jimmy glared at Charles. "Alone."

Charles picked up his coffee mug. "I do believe I'll finish this on the porch."

Meghann sat up in dread. For over a month, she'd

used every pretext to avoid being alone with Jimmy. Now, apparently, he wanted to finish the argument they'd had before Alcuin showed up.

He gave her a small gray jeweler's box.

She knew what it would contain before she opened it—a ring with a small diamond in a yellow-gold setting. *Jimmy, why are you forcing this on me now?* "It's very pretty."

"It belonged to my mother. I had Darlene send it to me a few days ago."

Meghann closed the box, and said the words she had always known she'd eventually have to say to Jimmy Delacroix. "I can't accept this."

Jimmy didn't yell, but she saw his fists clench. "Why not?" Before she could answer, he flicked the signet ring on her left hand contemptuously. "Is it because you're still carrying a torch for your master?"

Meghann managed to hold on to her temper. "That has nothing to do with it. But how can you bring this up now, with Simon—"

"No!" Jimmy roared. He glared down at her. "You stop using him as an excuse to push me away, Maggie. This has nothing to do with him—it's between me and you."

She got up, and glared right back at him. "Jimmy, I explained this once before. There can never be a you *and* me. And I do not use Simon as an excuse for anything."

"Bullshit! You're afraid, Maggie. Afraid to say you love me—even though I know damned well you do. But you don't want anyone to get close, so you use him as your excuse, your reason you can't get involved."

"Do you think you're Oprah?" she questioned sarcastically. "Jimmy, have you forgotten the minor matter of my being a vampire? I would say that's a pretty good fucking reason for why we can't get married."

"So make me one too."

"Oh? Just like that?" She snapped her fingers. "I told you before—I will never transform anybody. It's a curse, Jimmy!"

"But we'd be together—"

"In hell! How will you feel when Darlene dies, huh? Or better yet—how will you react when you can never see her again because it's starting to get damned weird that you never age? Will you enjoy seeing your world, the one you were meant to live in, drift away and change while you remain the same? People were meant to die, Jimmy—to go on to a better place at the end of a good life. Immortality is a curse."

"Screw you. You're not cursed."

"I'm not cursed?" she asked incredulously. "Some lunatic wants to destroy me and I'm not cursed. After all I had to live through—"

"Well, I wouldn't know about that since you never talk about your life with your lover boy. What are you hiding, honey—how good a lay he was?"

Meghann went white with fury. "No, I'm hiding what it is to live with blood lust, to have depraved impulses you cannot control—"

"I could learn."

Meghann laughed harshly. "You couldn't learn shit. You hide in a bottle every time something goes wrong."

Jimmy sank to the ottoman, and buried his face in his hands.

"Jimmy, I'm sorry. . . ."

He shrugged her hands off. "I don't want your apologies, you bitch! And I know why you won't transform me . . . won't marry me. You don't want a relationship with an equal. . . . You want some little helpless mortal you can push around, a boy toy!"

Outraged, without thinking, Meghann cracked him across the face. "How dare you talk to me like that!

Why should I marry some pathetic drunk I fished out of the gutter?"

Shakily, Jimmy pulled himself to his feet and Meghann felt remorse stab her when she saw the vicious red handprint standing in stark relief against his white skin.

Jimmy, clutching his cheek and backing far away from her, screamed out, "I'd rather be a pathetic drunk than a vicious cunt! You're just like Simon Baldevar!"

The black rage that came over her at Jimmy's words made Meghann fear he was right, that anything good or noble in her had died the night Simon transformed her.

Afraid of what she might do if she stayed, Meghann turned on her heel and stalked out the front door. Jimmy heard Charles yelling, "Meghann, wait!"

Charles rushed into the living room, where Jimmy was applying ice from the bar to his wounded cheek. "What happened?"

"Fuck you, bloodsucker!"

Charles glanced worriedly at the dark—he couldn't let Meghann wander around by herself. He grabbed his coat, and admonished the human. "I don't care if you and Meghann quarreled. You are to remain in this house; it's the only place where we can guarantee your safety. Do not leave."

Then he rushed out the door after his friend.

Jimmy picked up his wallet and leather jacket. Fuck them all—he was getting out of this madhouse! He'd come back during the day for his things—while the bloodsuckers were asleep. And maybe he'd drive a nice, juicy stake through that bitch's black heart. . . .

He stormed toward the bus stop at Beach 116th Street. He knew he shouldn't have ditched the Dodge, and relied only on the Caddie. But maybe it was for the best. The long walk would help clear his head, give him a chance to think, make some plans. He'd get a little hotel room for now, then figure out what he wanted to do. He stalked by a bar—goddamn Maggie! He did not live in a bottle. Like she was any better than him . . .

He smashed one fist into the other. That was the whole problem, wasn't it? Maggie (at night anyway) was better than him, and she wanted it to stay that way. Sure, she had it great now. Her pet human to do her bidding and screw her whenever she felt like it . . .

Jimmy choked back tears. He wasn't sad, he told himself. Why should he be? Because she didn't love him back? Who wanted her love anyway? Who wanted that beautiful, stubborn, brave . . .

Bitch! I meant nothing to her, nothing at all. And now all I am is some burden; something she has to protect. Well, the hell with her and her precious fag friend and that other . . . they could all rot in hell. Jimmy hoped he did run into Simon Baldevar now that he'd left the patronizing protection of Maggie's house. He'd tell the guy: *Well, man, I don't know what you want with her, but here's the address. We have no argument—she's all yours, buddy.*

Jimmy arrived at the bus stop. He saw a bus pull away—damn! Now he'd have to wait at least a half hour. He lit a cigarette.

"May I have a light?"

He glanced over at the girl sitting on the bench. He hadn't seen her sitting there before. No, that was no girl—this was a woman in her late twenties. Apparently, someone forgot to tell her Halloween was over—she had on a black cape with silver boots. Maggie always laughed at the "Wanna be Undead," as she called them. And this woman wasn't nearly as pretty as Maggie—she had a very sharp nose, badly cut black hair, and was pale as a ghost. Maggie wasn't even that pasty-looking. Still, he behaved like a gentleman and gave her a light.

"Thank you."

Jimmy retreated to his corner, brooding on Maggie.

"You seem sad."

Jesus Christ, the last thing he needed was some gothic trash coming on to him. "What's it to you?"

The woman flushed angrily—the blush sticking out like makeup applied to a corpse's face. "Just trying to be friendly."

"Don't—I'm not in the mood."

"Is it a girl?" the woman persisted.

Did this idiot not know how to take a hint? Oh, well, the bus wouldn't be showing up anytime soon. Might as well pass the time. "My girlfriend"—the closest description of his relationship with Maggie—"doesn't want to get married."

"Why not?"

"She won't admit it, but I think she's hung up on this other guy and won't make a commitment to me."

The woman seemed genuinely interested. "Well, what does the other guy have that you don't?"

"Nothing! I mean, she hates him. It's not that she's still in love with him, but he didn't treat her well. So I don't know if she trusts me."

"What did this man do?"

"Beat her—wouldn't let her live her own life." That was about all Maggie told him about Simon. Other than that, all he knew was that she'd gotten away from him when she put that stake in his heart.

The woman came closer, and he saw she had pretty eyes—dark blue. "Maybe your girlfriend is lying about her fellow."

"Maggie doesn't lie!" he snapped. Well, so much for thinking he didn't care anymore—he'd tear some stranger's head off for saying one bad word about her.

The woman shrugged. "Didn't mean to offend, honey. It's just that you're handsome and I'm lonely." She gave him what he imagined she thought was a seductive smile. "What do you say we go down to the beach?"

"Are you insane?" he asked. This one was a beast; he wouldn't fuck her with a rented dick.

The woman's eyes flashed. That didn't look like hurt to Jimmy; it was more like rage. Was Rockaway crawling with crazy people? Great, now he was probably going to have this psycho screaming at him until the bus arrived.

The woman tried to shrug her anger away, and rearrange her face into come-hither lines. "I thought it would take your mind off your problems."

Jimmy was about to say no, and then he reconsidered. Why not? It would make Maggie good and jealous.

As they headed for the boardwalk, he told the lady, "Sorry if I hurt your feelings back there. You just surprised me."

"It's quite all right." This woman wasn't so bad after all. Why not go with her?

"What's your name?"

"Renee." The woman tried to purr. Something was wrong in all of this. Jimmy felt like the woman had no real interest in him or sex. It was more like he was an assignment. . . .

"Holy Shit!" he exclaimed. "Are you a hooker?"

"No, not at all. Let's walk a bit farther."

Jimmy thought of declining, and then that strange impulse came over him again to go along.

They were walking an awfully long way. They were no longer by the apartment houses; the beach was starting to look isolated. Well, maybe she was being prudent. You wouldn't exactly want to have sex in full view of a neighborhood, would you?

Renee put her leather satchel down and threw off her cape, revealing a torn black lace dress with a dog chain used as a belt wrapped around her waist. She lay down on her cape, holding her arms out to Jimmy invitingly. He backed away—disgusted with her, with himself. What the hell was he doing here with this strange lady he didn't even like? He decided to head back and find Maggie—maybe now that they'd both had time to cool off, they could talk.

"What's the matter, Jimmy?" she called after him.

Shit! Jimmy very slowly reached into his jacket pocket for the Magnum. It wouldn't kill this thing, but it would stun her long enough for him to run away. He wanted to keep his back turned, but it would be fatal to take his eyes off the thing.

He turned around, and Renee was right in front of him. If he hadn't turned around . . .

"What's the matter, babe?" Jimmy taunted. "Can't get laid unless you use that power?" The thing's lips twisted, and Jimmy knew he was on the right track in provoking her. He kept insulting her so she wouldn't catch on to his gun. "Now I thought you got prettier when you became a vampire. . . . What kind of pig were you before?"

With an inarticulate cry of rage, Renee threw herself on him and he yanked the gun out of his pocket. But he had no time to shoot because the pistol was torn from his hand and Renee was flung away from him.

Jimmy turned around, intending to thank his rescuer—it must be Maggie or one of her friends. But then he saw the impassive yellow eyes looking down on him. *No, God, don't let me be with* . . .

Renee tried to attack him again, and the other vampire held her off with one hand. "Master," she screeched, "this mortal dared to insult me; give him to me!"

"Renee," the evil thing said her name slowly, pronouncing each syllable separately. There was no inflection in the quiet whisper, but Renee turned paler by several shades and became still.

Jimmy hadn't been this scared when he saw that thing feeding on Amy and Jay. Even that monster hadn't emanated evil and cold, deadly menace the way this man did by simply staring at him. *Don't look at me,* Jimmy wanted to scream, but he couldn't speak. If it didn't stop looking at him, he'd lose his mind. *Maggie, how the hell did you escape this thing? How strong are you? Now I know why you didn't want to talk about him—why you just wanted to forget he existed.*

"Meghann can never forget me." Jimmy longed to hurt this bastard—hearing him speak her name in that evil monotone was an abomination. "Tell me of your relationship with her."

"No," Jimmy whispered, "you can't make me tell you."

"I can disembowel you and make you thank me for it." The man didn't raise his voice when he issued the monstrous threat. "And you will betray Meghann."

And then the saffron eyes fixed on his, and Jimmy heard himself telling Simon everything he wanted to know. How he and Maggie met, what little she said about Simon, Alcuin's plans for killing him, even the argument they'd had tonight. A part of him was crying and screaming, desperate to keep quiet. Jimmy didn't understand how, but he intuited that Simon wanted him to be aware of his pain, wanted him to feel himself resisting the monster's questions but answering anyway. Jimmy knew vampires could read minds—Simon could have easily reached into his head for the thoughts he wanted. But no, Jimmy had to hate himself while he answered the interrogation.

Finally the vampire seemed satisfied and he took his

evil gaze off Jimmy to address Renee. "She will know his pain." He dropped Jimmy on the sand. "Feed on this worthless specimen and deal with my wayward consort when she arrives. That is my reward for your good work this evening."

Then the fiend was gone as suddenly as he had arrived. Jimmy tried to get up, but Renee leaped on him and began drinking his blood.

At first, Jimmy was too shaken from his encounter with Simon to even register what was happening to him. Then the pain hit and he thought he heard himself screaming. The ache wasn't just in his neck; it was all over his body as he was drained of blood. The skin became numb when his circulation was cut off, and then he heard drums beating. No, that must be his heart.

I'm dying, he thought hazily. *Maggie, I've got to tell her . . . Maggie!* Jimmy cried out from the bottom of his soul. *Maggie I love you!*

FIFTEEN

Charles caught up to Meghann—she had walked into a schoolyard. She looked up and tossed a baseball at him. "Some kid must have left it here. Throw it back."

Charles wanted to protest that this was hardly the time for a game of catch, but he thought he should go along with anything to calm that feverish glint in her eyes. So he lobbed it back at her.

She assumed a pitcher's stance and drilled the ball at him—screwball pitch, he thought, and felt a sting in his hand when he caught it. He thought it might have gone through the brick wall of the school if he hadn't caught it.

"If I do say so myself, I used to be a goddamn good pitcher." *Whack*—the fastball nearly broke Charles's hand. He decided to hold on to the ball for a few minutes. "I was taught by the best—my brothers. And they never went easy on me for being a girl—if I was missing the plate, believe me I heard about it that night at dinner. They would've been real proud if they saw the last game I ever threw—it was a shutout. And I thought that's all I was going to do all summer after I got married—pitch games for my team while Johnny cheered me on, go to Playland . . . all sorts of fun stuff."

Meghann glared, and Charles threw her the ball. "And you want to know something? It never occurred to me even once to be grateful for what I had. I had no knowledge, none whatsoever, of what kind of evil there was in the world. Maybe if I did know, I would have treasured the last game I ever pitched, the last time I ever stood on a mound in blazing sunlight and screamed at the umpire for a miscall. But I had no idea April 21, 1944, was going to be the last truly good day of my life—that a mere three days later I would drink my fiancé's blood. Did I ever tell you Jimmy doesn't know about that?"

"What does he know about, Meghann?"

"That once upon a time there was a guy named Simon Baldevar and this cute little girl called Maggie. Same old story: guy bites girl; girl turns into a vampire, falls out of love with guy; guy leaves her on a rooftop to die; girl turns the tables on him." Meghann gave him a cynical glance. "Now, you don't think I left any details out, do you?"

"Maybe you could tell him—"

"I could tell him lots of things. His hair would turn white when I finished. But that's going to happen anyway—the hair turning white, that is. Because I will not transform him, or any other person." Meghann smashed the ball into Charles's palm, and he cried out. "Sorry, Charles. You know, Jimmy hates me because I won't talk about Simon and I won't transform him. He can't understand why."

"Make him understand."

"No can do—no one understands, not even you. What I can't talk about isn't what Simon made me do. No, my problem is what I became—nothing. For thirteen years, I didn't exist. You see, I was Maggie before Simon stole that away. But that girl died the night I became a vampire. She was innocent—and believe me, that stopped the moment Simon brought Johnny through the door. So what was left of me? Nada—all I could be was anything Simon wanted. His whore, his partner in blood lust, but not a person. Just a shell—an evil, amoral shell."

"That's not true."

"Yes, it is!" she screamed. "I was evil! And I did evil things that I will never forget. They haunt me . . . but what haunts me more is that the potential to do them isn't gone; it's just dormant. Sleeping, if you will. Eagerly awaiting me to lose my temper or self-control long enough to let the blood lust have its way. That is my life, Charles—a constant, unceasing battle to fight the thing Simon put in me. And that is what Jimmy wants—and what he cursed me for denying him."

Charles grabbed her. "Stop it, Meghann! Stop torturing yourself."

Meghann collapsed. It was like someone shot her. "Meghann!"

She sat up, dazed. *Maggie, I love you!* The thought had hit her hard. Jimmy was hurt. She had to go to him.

"Jimmy," she whispered to Charles, and then she disappeared.

"Meghann!" he screamed at the air. Where was she? What trap had she wandered into? He flew back to the house. He had to summon Alcuin.

Meghann allowed her soul to follow Jimmy's anguished call and found herself on the beach.

NO! Some horrible thing was sucking her Jimmy's blood. He was bled nearly white. . . .

"Get off him," she ordered in a cold voice.

The thing whipped around. Meghann saw that it was the woman who drove the car the night she encountered Simon. It dropped Jimmy, and he fell to the sand helplessly.

The bitch didn't even bother wiping Jimmy's blood off her face. She just smiled through it. "Hello, Meghann."

When she got no response, she queried further. "No tears, no weeping at your lover's plight?"

"He's alive," Meghann said coolly, "which is more than you'll be able to say in a few minutes." She spied a piece of driftwood and made it fly into her hands. She held it out in front of her for protection—and attack.

Renee was unsettled. Simon told her the girl was weak, and the mere sight of her lover hurt would make her unable to fight.

"Don't believe everything Lord Baldevar tells you."

"Don't speak his name, bitch!" Renee hissed at her. "You betrayed my master." She kicked at Meghann, who easily held her off with the driftwood. They spun around, Renee striking out with her arms and legs, unable to knock the driftwood out of Meghann's hands.

Meghann didn't dare glance at Jimmy, but she couldn't fight this thing too long. She needed to get her out of the way so she could help Jimmy. How much blood had he lost?

Meghann deflected another blow—good, Renee was getting angry. Now, hopefully, she'd become careless.

"He promised I could slaughter you," she whined, and made a vicious kick at Meghann's face.

"Simon shouldn't make promises he can't keep." Meghann laughed, further infuriating the other vampire. "How stupid are you, anyway? I nearly killed him; do you honestly believe he'll give anyone but himself the luxury of killing me? I have no idea why, but apparently he's decided to make you a sacrificial lamb."

"No!" the thing roared at her. Meghann was curious—why on earth had Simon chosen this as his new consort? This girl was stark raving mad—as well as ugly. Simon was a connoisseur of beauty.

"I'm not his consort." Renee grabbed the driftwood and Meghann shoved her off. The woman landed on the sand and was up quickly. "He values my intelligence. You were merely his concubine—I shall be his partner when we rule the world."

"Simon does not take partners, you stupid bitch."

"You know nothing!" Renee spied the signet ring; she hissed. "How dare you wear the master's ring after what you did to him! That should be mine!"

"You want it? Come and get it." Renee delivered a sharp kick to the driftwood and broke it in half, then she managed to kick her opponent hard in the jaw. Meghann went down. The vampire tried to leap on top of her, but Meghann took the jagged end of the driftwood and rammed it into Renee's chest. The vampire crumpled on the sand.

Meghann ran over to Jimmy. "Honey, can you hear me?"

He looked up at her with glazed eyes. "I'm sorry. . . ."

"Shhh. Nothing to be sorry about." Jimmy's eyes filled with fear, and Meghann turned around. Renee had managed to yank out the stake, and she attacked again.

They struggled on the ground. Renee was filled with fury—and fear of what Simon would do to her if she failed to subdue his consort. Meghann did her best to deflect the blows, but Renee did manage to claw her face and pull one of her pigtails right out of her scalp. Meghann got a hold on Renee's wrists, sickened by the sight of her skin and a large chunk of her bright red hair dripping from the vampire's long nails, and shoved her down to the ground. Like a hellish jack-in-the-box, the bitch launched herself at Meghann again. Meghann flew a few feet away, and reappeared by the shore. Renee, so incensed she was not thinking clearly, chose to run at her rather than fly. When Renee was a few inches from her, Meghann delivered a vicious kick to the bitch's chest. Her foot smashed through the vampire's breastplate. Meghann broke her ankle on impact, and Renee's chest collapsed.

They both fell to the sand. Meghann raised herself up, wincing at the pain in her foot. She looked at the broken, concave thing on the floor. Was the injury fatal? For a mortal—even though it was nearly impossible to shatter someone's breastplate—it would be. But a vampire?

Incredibly, Renee glared up, and started chanting in a low monotone. The language wasn't familiar until Meghann caught the phrase *"Unchi om ors"* and felt that cold emanation from the night she looked into the scrying bowl.

"No!" Meghann screamed, and spun around clockwise. Jimmy saw a circle of white-blue light appear. Immediately Renee's curses were powerless when she was trapped in Meghann's circle.

She kicked Renee. "You fool," Meghann spat. "You would conjure demons with your broken body?" Meghann did not understand what force was giving this shattered thing the ability to speak through what must be unimaginable pain. Could a vampire heal from an injury like that? Meghann's ankle already felt better; her scalp was tingling with hair growing back once more. How long until Renee's bones knitted together?

The thing didn't answer her but hissed, "Master!"

Meghann felt her skin crawl. "Why are you calling Simon?"

Renee gave her a smug smile.

"He was here, Maggie," Jimmy whispered.

"Simon was here?" That meant he was nearby. So

why couldn't she feel his presence? Knowing it was useless, she again asked, "Where is he?"

Renee laughed—until Meghann kicked her and broke her jawbone.

Meghann turned her back and yelled at the sky. "Where the hell are you, Simon? You cowardly, vile bastard! Come out and show yourself!" She felt a hand on her ankle and looked down at the gloating in Renee's eyes—at her inability to do anything against Simon Baldevar. That smug sureness made Meghann want to kill her, smash her—wipe it off her face for eternity.

She knelt down and gave Renee a diabolical grin. "So you would curse me with darkness, wretch?" She saw the uncertainty on the evil thing's face, and her grin widened. "Oh, yes, I understood your little chant just fine. Now I believe a fitting punishment would be for the Dark to enter you, and take what you so clearly have no use for."

Meghann stood up and focused her eyes on the moon. She had never done this before. Alcuin had shown her the ritual, but she did not know if she could perform the only magic capable of destroying a vampire.

Jimmy became aware of a change in the air. The wind picked up, and the dark seemed to grow denser; he could barely see. All he could make out was that sphere of light and Maggie's pale hands extended toward the moon.

"Taranis, Esus, Teuta." She called upon the darkest gods of the Druids—the ones who demanded human sacrifice. Her voice had nothing in it—no tone, no pitch, no inflection.

Lightning flashed in the sky, and thunder erupted. Jimmy thought he must be delirious. It seemed like the moonlight was pouring into her hands. But when it hit her hands, it lost its silvery luminescence and turned into a dark shadow. Meghann, her eyes blank, turned back to Renee.

She placed her hands, with that dark shadow, on Renee's concave chest. It seemed like the darkness absorbed the area around her heart and Meghann's hands. Jimmy pulled himself up—what had happened to her hands? Then she pulled her hands away from Renee's body—clutching the vampire's heart.

Meghann held the heart to the moon for a moment—an offering to Andraste, the goddess who could only be appeased by impaled female victims.

Meghann sank her blood teeth into the beating heart. The other vampire yowled and shrieked as Meghann drank the heart's blood. Renee's body shriveled, started smoking, and disappeared. When she vanished, the heart burst into flames in Meghann's hands.

Meghann fell to her knees on the sand, and the circle of light surrounding her disappeared. The heart's blood of Simon's protégée had merely given a small fraction of the strength she'd lost by performing the ritual to remove her heart from her body.

With every ounce of strength, Jimmy crawled over. "Maggie, are you okay?" His words were barely audible.

Meghann put her head in her hands—her head was pounding. "I feel so sick."

Jimmy put his hand on her shoulder. "What would make you feel better?" He shrank back in terror when she looked up at him.

Her green eyes were clear as glass; they seemed to shimmer with urgency and craving. He was scared but couldn't move away—those eyes were bewitching him.

Meghann put her hand on the back of his head and started drawing him closer to her. But then those alien eyes he was staring into changed. The inhuman quality disappeared as despair and anger colored her eyes. She shoved him away from her roughly.

"Goddamn it!" she screamed, kicking and beating the sand furiously. She yelled, howled, and kicked like a wild thing until the worst of the need left her. Then she pulled herself up off the ground and glared at Jimmy. "This is what you want?" she yelled, and then laughed shrilly. "You stupid fool, did you think of this when you asked me to transform you? Did it occur to you that being a vampire means, above all else, a constant, unbearable need for blood? Blood is your master; in many ways, you're no better than a drug addict. Look at me, Jimmy. Look at what just happened! I nearly killed you! And I love you! I love you . . . but, God help me, in a choice between love and blood, love is a poor second." Meghann laughed again, bitterly.

Jimmy looked at her in wonder; he didn't even hurt anymore. "You said you love me." He ignored her protests. "You finally said you love me."

"Of course I love you. And I refused to admit it so I could spare you all this." She indicated the spot where Renee had been sacrificed. "You didn't understand. But that's all right—I never let you understand. Jimmy, if we get through this, I swear I'll tell you everything you want to know. For now, understand this. The curse of being a vampire is knowledge. Knowledge of the evil that you're capable of. Can you truly deal with that night after night? The unending temptation to gorge on people's pain and misery? Once you become a vampire, there's no turning back, Jimmy. Unless you greet the sunrise. And there's a risk that you won't survive transformation. You can die . . . or lose your mind."

"Why are you offering it now? Is it because you love me?"

Meghann had to be truthful. "Partly . . . and Renee has infected you. I felt it when I put my hand on your neck. I don't know how long she drank from you, but she took enough to start transformation. You're going to be very ill soon. I don't know if you can recover and keep living as a mortal. I'll have to ask Alcuin. But if it's a choice between death and transformation . . . which do you want?"

Jimmy put his hands on Meghann's face, and kissed her. "I saw a lot tonight before you got here. I had to tell you I was wrong . . . you're nothing like him. What he and that bitch wanted . . . Maggie, they loved my fear. I could see them both almost licking their lips with it, lapping it up. Don't you ever try and tell me you're like that." Jimmy pulled himself up on one knee. "Let me try again. Maggie, I love you. And if there's something evil in you because of what that asshole turned you into, then let me fight it off with you. We'll be strong . . . together."

After seeing her nearly kill him for blood, Jimmy Delacroix still loved her enough to want to transform. She no longer thought it was her place to make that decision for him—not after what he experienced tonight. She might never get another chance like this. To finally be happy with a man she loved, who made her laugh, who could see the worst she had in her and still love her.

She looked down into her lover's face, intending to tell him what she'd decided. Then she saw a shadow behind her in the corner of her eye. She didn't need to turn around to know what it was—Jimmy's ashen face and shaking body told her.

Run, she mouthed at him. He was uncomprehending, on the verge of shock. The shadow was moving closer. "Run!" she screamed at Jimmy at the same moment she was flung away from him. She got to her feet, and Simon Baldevar already had Jimmy in a chokehold.

It wasn't simply his appearance that made Meghann feel panic. It was the unholy, nearly invincible strength emanating from him. He had an air of danger and ruthlessness that Meghann had never felt before.

He had trapped her so neatly. Renee found Jimmy, and Simon knew she'd come after him. But he hadn't stopped there—he knew she'd have no choice but to fight Renee. Now Meghann's energy was depleted. And even if she was at the peak of her strength, she knew it would not equal one-tenth of what she felt in him.

Simon gave her a moment to adjust, and then he gave her a truly malicious smile. " 'An eye for an eye,' my love? You murdered my apprentice; so I shall dispose of your plaything in the same manner." He put one hand over Jimmy's heart.

"Fuck you!" Jimmy yelled at him, coming out of his daze.

Meghann spied a large rock behind Simon. She made it whirl in the air and whack him in the back of the head. He winced slightly and told her, "Another trick like that and I'll snap his neck before your eyes. And tell your consort to mind his manners."

Meghann knew she could not separate them. "If you kill him, you'll have no hold over me, Simon Baldevar."

Simon raised an eyebrow. "Why should I kill him, Meghann? Unless you have lost your taste for the blood of your lovers?"

Simon saw the way she blanched, and smiled that nasty, cruel grin that had plagued her dreams for decades. "Surely, you have not forgotten your first feeding?" He inquired of Jimmy, "Does Meghann never speak of Johnny Devlin? Her fiancé? Come, child, tell your paramour how that romance ended."

I will not cry in front of this bastard, she thought grimly, hating him for his re-creation of one of her worst memories. Seeing Jimmy in his grip—Simon knew exactly what that brought to mind.

When Meghann didn't respond, Simon continued.

"Meghann needed blood . . . so she drained her young man until he lay dead at her feet."

Jimmy snarled at his tormentor, "Shut your mouth! Anything Maggie did was because you made her do it. I love you, Maggie—no matter what!"

"How very touching," Simon told him in a chilling whisper. "And you, Meghann? Are you capable of such poignancy? Tell me, what is this mortal's life worth to you?"

Meghann looked at Jimmy struggling to break out of Simon's grip—if only she could pry him loose. "My own," she answered simply.

"If I release him, will you give me your word you won't try to escape?"

Release him? Meghann frowned—why on earth would Simon let Jimmy go? He had to know she'd send Jimmy right back to the house for Charles and Alcuin.

Which was exactly what Simon wanted her to do. Meghann grasped his strategy—Jimmy had been the bait to lure her here, now she was a pawn in trapping Alcuin.

Meghann thought of saying no to save her friends but her refusal would ensure Jimmy's death. Maybe Charles and Alcuin, with her help, could destroy Simon when they arrived.

Meghann started to nod but Jimmy howled, "No! Don't you do it, Maggie! Let this asshole—ow! kill me, but don't you give him anything. . . . Get away from here!"

"What a heroic speech," Simon said softly. "But I hardly need Meghann's permission to kill you." Simon put one hand on Jimmy's neck and started twisting Jimmy's head.

"No!" Meghann screamed. "I'll accept your terms— let Jimmy go!"

Simon dropped Jimmy on the sand, and Meghann

went to him. She put her hand over his mouth to keep him from speaking, and glared up at Simon. "I want to say good-bye to him—alone." She knew Simon would hear every word she said but Meghann wanted Jimmy to have some illusion their parting was private.

To her surprise, Simon walked a few yards away without comment.

Meghann was focusing all her energy on not shaking. She had not recovered from fighting Renee, and with the shock of seeing Simon again, she started swaying slightly.

Jimmy put his arms out to keep her from falling. "Jesus Christ, Maggie, I'm not leaving you alone with him! You can't even stay on your feet."

Meghann took a few deep breaths, then turned her will on her own body—the way Alcuin had taught her. In a few minutes, she was still tired but able to stand. "Jimmy, you have to go back to my house. Charles is there—he can summon Alcuin."

"No . . . he's going to kill you."

"Think," Meghann told Jimmy. "If Simon wanted to kill the two of us, he could have done it before we were aware of his presence. Simon is up to something—I don't know what he's got in mind, but he's not going to kill me right away. Now, leave—get to the house as fast as you can!"

"Do you hear yourself, Maggie? You're admitting you can't take him on. He can tear you in half anytime he wants. What kind of man would I be if I left you alone with him?"

Maggie saw Simon glaring at them impatiently. She knew he wasn't going to give her much more time with Jimmy. "Listen to me, Jimmy—you know if I want to I can reach into your mind and make you leave. Don't force me to do that. You're not a coward because you leave. Please go home."

Jimmy searched Meghann's face. "I'll do it—on one condition."

"What?"

"You promise to transform me if we get through this."

Jimmy didn't know that she had already made that choice. Meghann put her hand over her heart. "I swear I'll transform you if . . . when we get through this. Now, go!"

Jimmy turned to go, but Meghann called him back. "Jimmy?"

He turned around hopefully. "Yeah?"

"I love you." Meghann was very conscious of the fact those might be the last words she ever said to him.

Jimmy did not care what Simon Baldevar might do. He reached over and kissed Meghann. "I love you too, Maggie."

She kissed him back before she pushed him away. "We shouldn't try to provoke him. Who knows what that monster might decide to do? Go before he changes his mind."

Maggie watched Jimmy walk until she couldn't see him anymore. She'd managed to keep herself from crying while he could see her, but now the tears fell down her face. She was scared to be alone with Simon; for all her bravado, she was near panicking. Meghann refused to turn around—let Simon make the opening move.

"Dry your eyes, little one." Simon offered her a handkerchief.

Meghann glared at him suspiciously. Why was he being nice? He'd just threatened to tear her lover apart in front of her eyes. Ignoring his handkerchief, Meghann used the back of her hand to wipe away the tears and managed to smear Renee's blood over her face.

Simon started to use the handkerchief to wipe Meghann's face clean, but she slapped his hand away and took the handkerchief. After she was done, she flung it into the sea.

Amused by her actions, he offered his arm to her. "Shall we walk along the water, Meghann?"

Meghann didn't move. Simon raised his eyebrows slightly. "Did you think I would ravish you the minute your lover disappeared?"

"Why wait?"

"Foolish girl, all these years, and yet how little you know of me. I'm not planning to kill you—merely humble you." Simon extended his arm again, and Meghann accepted. She had to stall him, until Alcuin arrived.

Before they started walking, Simon plucked up the leather satchel by Renee's cape. "What's in there?"

"Your discovery of the contents of this bag depends upon how . . . cooperative you are this evening."

They wandered on to land that belonged to Riis Park before Simon broke the uneasy silence between them.

"Allow me to offer my sincere congratulations on your new gifts, and the delightful way you employed them on my apprentice." Simon caressed her cheek. That familiar gesture was more unnerving than anything else he'd done so far. He saw her discomfort and grinned sharply. She felt Renee's scratches fade off her face when he touched her. She put her hand to her head—all her scalped hair had grown back.

"Congratulations? Lord Baldevar, I hardly expected praise for killing your protégée."

"You have developed new talents, child—abilities I will be happy to nurture properly. And you have saved me a distasteful chore by disposing of Renee."

Meghann glared at him in disgust. "Why kill such an obvious soul mate, Simon? She was obviously the perfect lover for you . . . depraved, bloodthirsty, completely without a soul or the ability to love."

"She was not my lover—not all women are as attracted to me as you are. And I do have the ability to love. I love you, and you broke my heart."

"Love is not sexual bondage and mental domination, my lord. Stick with women like that harpy who tried to harm my—"

Before she could go on, Simon lunged for her. The move took her by surprise, and he pinned her to the ground with her arms above her head. His amber eyes had darkened to copper with anger. "Meghann, never speak to me of any other man."

"Why not?" she taunted. "I had lovers, Simon—lots of them! Haven't you heard of the sexual revolution? What the hell are you going to do about it?"

Simon gave her an amused glance. "Why are you trying to provoke me, little one? And let me assure you, this is far from the first time in history people have indulged in sexual freedoms. We used to be a bit more discreet." With one hand keeping her down, he used the other to stroke her hair.

"Discreet? I'm not the one who caught syphilis!" she screamed.

Simon laughed—it was honest amusement, none of the threat he usually had. "So your new spineless allies fill your ears with tales of my bygone youth? From what I know of your behavior, your escapades could have caused you to pick up all sorts of nasty illnesses if you were not a vampire. But I shall forgive your infidelity— you were laboring under the delusion I was dead. And I'm sure it never felt as good as this." He kissed her neck, on the spot where he always bit her.

She struggled to move away, and he grinned smugly. "Why are you frightened when I touch you? Do you find yourself enjoying it?"

"I'm not frightened!" she shouted. "I'm repulsed!"

"I don't believe you," he said smoothly. "And I have every intention of proving to you just how wrong you are." He bent to kiss her, and she took advantage of his lust by kicking him hard in the groin. It probably didn't hurt that much, but it did cause him to loosen his grip. Meghann stood over him, uncertain what his next move would be.

Simon made no attempt to recapture her; he merely smoothed his ruffled hair. "Meghann, if you're wise, you won't make me hurt you tonight."

"Is that a threat, Lord Baldevar? Should I tremble and throw myself into your arms, pleading for forgiveness? Go to hell! You sound just like every other wife-beater . . . telling a woman she should sit still and take abuse she did nothing to deserve!"

To her surprise, Simon started laughing. "I had forgotten your love of that twisted science you call psychology. But, my love, you cannot compare us to those dreary women and their loathsome partners that you counsel. I am your master, and you will give me all you owe me before the night is over."

"I will die before I call you 'Master' . . . so kill me if you can," she said flatly.

"Never."

That gave Meghann pause. Seeing her confusion, Simon told her in that soft, menace-laced purr, "My love, did you think I went to all this trouble to simply slay you? Do you think I will gift you with a martyr's death . . . allow you to die with your arrogance and pride intact?" He tilted her head up. "Child, I promise you that I'll see you precisely as I want you . . . prostrated before me, accepting me as your master."

She wanted more than anything to spit in his face, but she simply didn't have the nerve. There was an aura of danger and menace to him that she could al-

most see. She had never felt that kind of power in another living being before—not even Alcuin.

Simon saw her fear; he smiled cruelly. "Good girl,
you have some prudence after all." He dropped her
chin, and she had to force herself not to sigh in relief.

Where the hell was Alcuin? Meghann had to keep
Simon talking before he decided to do other things.
"You never answered my question. Why did you want
Renee to die?"

"As you correctly diagnosed, the girl was insane.
And, my love, she had in her head the deranged notion
that she would rule the world with me." Simon laughed
heartily. "As if I have any interest in involving myself
with all the headaches attendant to governing mortals.
Do you know she sought me out?" Meghann found her
interest rising despite herself. "Oh, yes. The woman
was obsessed with becoming a vampire. For twelve years,
she researched every recorded mention of a vampire.
Apparently, a member of Queen Elizabeth's court left
behind a diary discussing Lord Baldevar—the evil nec-
romancer who was never seen in daylight. And then
she found the writings of my good friend, John. So
Renee, full of macabre and precious notions concerning vampires, made it her business to find me. And
when she did, she begged me to transform her—give
her 'eternal darkness and power' is the way she put it."
Simon took Meghann's hands. "What Renee failed to
understand is what you were well aware of—I do not
take partners, as I have never found anyone I considered my equal. However, I do have a consort—and no
interest in replacing her with some small-minded fool."

Meghann tried to yank her hands away, and Simon
tightened his grip. "Be gone. I have no desire to return
to merely being your pretty puppet. I have a mind, Simon, and a career, and no desire to spend eternity as
your little playmate."

"Do you recall my asking your preference? Way back at the beginning, I told you what I wanted—body and soul. You agreed."

"I was eighteen," she countered. "As I recall, I thought it was your idea of a game. And you damn sure hadn't told me you were a vampire when you extracted that promise. Nor did you tell me that you'd make me kill my fiancé, beat me if I looked at you the wrong way . . . damn you! You treated Trevor with more respect than you treated me."

The intensity in Simon's eyes seemed to pierce through her. "If you wish to discuss the past, I'm going to insist that you be truthful."

"I'm always honest!"

"Then tell me what happened after I bled Pauline to death before your eyes."

Startled, she said, "Nothing . . . I mean, you transformed me; that's all."

Simon used her hands to yank her closer. Then he tilted her head up so she was looking into his sardonic gaze. "Perhaps you can convince your priest of that. Have you forgotten that I gave you one final chance to choose death? And what did you do, Meghann? I can still remember, even if you choose to forget. You chose me, Meghann. The choice for you had nothing to do with life or death—you put your sweet hand on my face and I will never forget what you thought: *'I want him, nothing else matters.'*" Simon gave her his Cheshire cat grin. "After seeing me for what I truly was, you still wanted to be with me. What a rare and perfect gift you gave me that night. You did not want power, as all the others did, or even immortality—you wanted me. And that is why I transformed you, because you gave yourself to me wholeheartedly—or I would never have done it."

"No!" she cried, embarrassed by returning memories. "You . . . you manipulated me. How could I possibly think straight when you had nearly bled me to death? Maybe, maybe I did want you for that one moment, but I never would have if I had known what you were going to make me do . . . killing people and wallowing in darkness."

Simon still had a firm hold on her, and he pulled her very close. "What I made you do? Was I at the hospital the night you made that addict kneel before you?"

Seeing how completely he caught her off guard, Simon smiled unkindly at her shock. "Oh, yes, I know all about it. You sank your pretty little teeth right into him, and savored his pain. He died, by the way."

She bit her lip. "I'm sorry," she whispered—unsure whom she was addressing. Alcuin? Her victim? Herself?

"Meghann, why are you engaging in this useless struggle? You are my consort. It is *my* blood that flows in your veins—not the simpering cleric's. You will never be free of the desires I bestowed upon you." Simon's eyes glowed. "Have you forgotten how good it felt, sweet? How you rejoiced in the taste of your own fiancé's blood—"

"You stop throwing that in my face, you bastard!" she howled. "How dare you make it sound like I sought him out. You brought him to me, you vicious—"

"I brought him to teach you that there is no connection between vampires and mortals outside of a need to feed, a lesson you continue to disdain. Why do you think I never taught you anything, kept you cloistered and sheltered? Every time I showed you the smallest bit of power, you shrank from it. The blood feast in Cuba, do you know how much power I derived from the pain in that room? Then I gave you the chance to partake in the sweetest of all pleasures, the blood of a child . . . But no, you foolishly cling to a code of ethics that forever bar you from realizing the true power of a vampire."

"That is not power," she hissed. "It's madness and depravity, the indulgences of beasts like yourself who have no decency inside their rotting souls. You're right, Simon. I want no part of that . . . or you."

"I've had enough of this foolish quarreling, Meghann. It is time for you to assume your rightful place . . . by my side."

"No!" She twisted and screamed when he tried to kiss her. Then she felt a change in the atmosphere— something peaceful.

Simon felt it too; he let her go. "I see my beloved uncle has come to join us."

Alcuin stood silently—comparing Simon's calm, un-ruffled visage to the anxiety and fear on Meghann's face.

I want to go home, she told him silently.

Alcuin stretched his hand out, and she ran to it gladly. "I'll take you home, *banrion.* You need not stay here."

"Meghann isn't going anywhere," Simon said softly. "Leave her to me, and I'll spare your worthless life. I'll even overlook the insult you dealt by taking my consort from me."

"I would not leave a dog in your care," Alcuin replied. "Meghann left you, nephew, and I offered her sanctuary; I would do it again. I will certainly help her leave your vile presence."

"She will never leave my side again. And I'll even give her a final chance to make that decision herself. Tell him, Meghann—say you choose to remain by your master's side."

Meghann was dismayed by the capacity for malevo-lence she saw in those tawny eyes; still, she raised her head high. "I choose to live a free life—away from you."

Two things happened at once. Alcuin tried to grab her so they could leave and she felt herself fly backward into Simon's grip. He pushed her hair back. Before Alcuin could stop him, Simon pushed his fangs deep into Meghann's neck.

Simon didn't merely bite her; he ripped her neck open. Blood spouted everywhere. Meghann had forgotten the terrible, invasive pain of being bitten, but it was nothing compared to the agony she felt when he started sucking on the wound.

She could not say how long he drank from her before Alcuin managed to pull him off. Alcuin grabbed Meghann by the hair and flung her from Simon. She landed knee-deep in the ocean.

Vaguely she heard Alcuin say, "Leave here at once and let me save Meghann. I'll call off the hunt for you."

"No, Uncle—it is time for us to end our conflict."

Meghann heard the sounds of fighting, but she couldn't concentrate anymore. She was being assaulted by waves of nausea. She started retching. Oh, God— Renee's heart's blood was coming up. Meghann had never tasted anything so awful in her life, and she kept vomiting. She thought her ribs were going to crack from the force of it. When it finally ended, Meghann started drinking the salt water of the ocean. She had to get that taste out of her mouth. A huge wave crashed over Meghann and she was dragged farther from the shore.

Am I going to drown or bleed to death? Meghann wondered. She forced herself to swim, and thought for once about how fortunate it was that she was a vampire. If she were human, she'd be dead now—Simon had nearly decapitated her. She could feel the skin trying to come back together. Meghann put her hand to her neck—she was still bleeding, but not as much.

When she got to the shore, she managed to stay upright in a kneeling position. Meghann used her senses to try to find Alcuin and Simon—they'd both disappeared.

She jumped when she felt a hand on the gash on her neck.

"Don't worry, *banrion*—it's me."

Meghann turned to look at Alcuin. His cloak was gone and his left arm was broken. But the worst wound was a ragged hole in his chest three inches above his heart. *Simon must have used the driftwood I used on Renee,* Meghann thought.

"Simon put a stake through you?"

"He tried," Alcuin replied. "Fortunately for me, his aim was off. But I am unimportant. . . . You must leave here at once. Simon truly loves you, *banrion.* And your rejection is driving him to the brink of madness. Get away from him at once! Can you fly, Meghann?"

Meghann tried. She was able to disappear for a split second before she reappeared—sweating and panting. "I can't," she gasped.

Alcuin sighed heavily. "I was afraid of that. Meghann, I'm going to die tonight."

"No," she cried.

"Banrion, I've known it since Jimmy staggered back to your house. Simon cannot be killed—not tonight, and not by me. That is why I would not allow Charles to come here with me. I only came here tonight in the hopes of saving you."

"Then you shouldn't have come." She wept deeply. "I don't understand. Why—"

"God only knows what he has been up to these past forty years—but he now has a power that is unholy. I know you felt it too. As if that were not enough, Simon is possessed by two ferocious forces—the desire to have you, and an unimaginable hatred of me. They are giving him a strength I cannot cope with." Alcuin put his wrist to her mouth. "Drink, *banrion*. Take what little strength I have and use it to fly away from this cursed spot before he attacks again." Alcuin overrode her protests. "I am ordering you as your mentor to do this! I'm going to die and I will not let that fiend have your life too." Alcuin hugged her close—she knew the gesture meant farewell. "You and Charles must continue to battle Simon after I am gone. Do what I was unable to accomplish, Meghann . . . slay that bastard and end his obscene existence."

Meghann's blood teeth hadn't even come out fully when Simon reappeared. Unlike Alcuin, he was barely injured. He grabbed Alcuin before she could drink, and they spun away from Meghann, struggling.

Simon kicked Alcuin, and he sprawled on the ground. Simon withdrew a small but vicious ax from Renee's satchel.

I don't care what Alcuin told me; maybe I can help him. I won't stand here helplessly and watch him die.

Meghann aimed several rocks at Simon. Her aim was on target—one hit him on the wrist and he dropped the ax. Meghann tried to make the ax fly to her, and it did start to go toward her, but then it halted in midair. Simon grabbed it.

Still, Alcuin's arm had enough time to heal and he lunged at Simon, trying to wrestle the ax away from him. He managed to grab the ax, and when he moved his hand, Simon fell to the ground. He brandished the ax in the air, poised to cut off Simon's head.

Simon glanced at Meghann and she felt an evil presence enter her. There was no other way to describe it—she felt like something malevolent was inside her. Blood started pouring out of her nose and ears. At the same time, she felt something warmer try to enter her and the hemorrhaging stopped. Then it started again—

Meghann was caught in a tug-of-war between the two master vampires.

"Malus Ultor!" She heard Alcuin curse Simon through the haze taking her over. "Let her live."

"Perhaps I shall." She heard Alcuin cry out in pain. "But you should really keep your mind on your own troubles. Come, Uncle, at least try to fight. Otherwise, I won't be able to enjoy my victory. . . . Who wants a worthless opponent?" More screams.

I'm sorry, Alcuin, she tried to say. *I'm sorry I couldn't help you.*

When Meghann woke up again, the sky was lighter. Were Simon and Alcuin still fighting? Then Meghann smelled smoke and the unmistakable odor of burning flesh. She turned slightly and saw a body burning on the rocks. Who was it?

"You should be grateful it isn't you."

Oh, God—Simon had won. Over the smell of searing flesh, Meghann detected something fresher—her own blood. Meghann pulled her hands close to her face— both wrists had been cut open, and her neck was in agony. Simon must have fed from that hideous gash in her neck.

Meghann knew she should be upset, terrified—but all she felt was a curious sense of peace. *Maybe that means I'm dying,* she thought.

Her vision was blurry. It wasn't until Simon was standing right in front of her that Meghann was able to make out his features. What was he shoving before her eyes? No, no—it was Alcuin's severed head. Meghann didn't even know she was crying until she tasted the salty tears on her lips.

"The ancient Celts had a tradition of nailing the heads of their enemies to their doors," Simon told her. "While I consider that a bit much, I do think I should find a special place for this treasure. Perhaps my mantelpiece?"

Meghann couldn't respond. Simon went on chatting while he drank blood from a vein in her left thigh after his blood teeth punctured the denim fabric of her jeans.

"I remember the first time I drank blood from you, my love. I'd never tasted blood like yours—fresh, sweet, bursting with life and vitality. If I hadn't already been in love with you, the taste of your blood would have done the trick.

"You're on the brink of death—but I'm merciful. I won't leave you here, exposed to the sunrise—which is only about an hour away. I'll let you share the fate of your good friend," Simon told her cheerfully. She heard him pick up the ax.

Meghann was too sick to feel any fear. The ax was poised above her, and she thought incoherently, *Look how pretty the blade looks with the moonlight shining on it.*

Meghann came back to life at the fresh agony she felt from the wound in her neck when Simon started strangling her.

"Damn you, Meghann!" Simon yelled as he choked her. "In four hundred years, I've never had difficulty killing anyone—except you! Why won't you admit you love me? Why?"

Meghann thought he was doing a fairly good job of killing her since she couldn't breathe and his voice was ringing in her ears. But then he let her go. Before she could react, he put his hand in her hair and brought her mouth to his neck.

Meghann was so starved for blood she started drinking the second her lips touched his flesh. She had never needed blood so badly. *I don't want to die,* Meghann thought—the same way she had all those years before when Simon had transformed her. The blood was healing her—her vision was clearing and she was becoming more lucid. But drinking Simon's blood was sharpening the link between them—Meghann tried to fight the closeness she was feeling toward him.

Abruptly Simon pushed her away.

For long moments, they simply stared at each other. *He can't kill me,* Meghann thought in wonder. *Certainly, he should have.* From his point of view, it was a perfect victory—killing her after he made her witness the death of her chosen mentor. But he had not been able to behead her. That did not make Meghann feel any less anxious. Even if he couldn't kill her, he didn't seem to have any problem with hurting her. So what would he do if she continued to defy him?

He reached out to caress her face, and she backed away. Ruthlessly he grabbed her by the shoulders and started shaking her.

"Stop struggling!" Simon roared. Meghann thought her eardrums would have burst if she'd been human. She had never seen Simon like this—no matter if he was angry or engaged in blood lust, he was never out of control. Alcuin had been right about how dangerous love could make Simon.

"Why are you resisting me?" He was yelling.

A plan to defeat Simon flashed through her mind. Meghann knew a direct assault would have no chance, but she thought she might be able to trick Simon. The only trouble was going to be in becoming involved with him again—Simon might not wind up being the one who got fooled.

"Stop . . . stop shaking me! Why shouldn't I re-resist you?"

Before she could continue, Simon let go of her. Meghann nearly crashed into Alcuin's burning corpse.

"Why shouldn't you resist me?" he repeated incredulously. "I gave you life!"

"You took my life!" she caterwauled, keeping a wary eye on the brightening sky. "You're not God, you egomaniac! You didn't give me life—you *stole* my life and condemned me to a living hell!" Meghann was threading a very fine line. If she gave in too quickly, Simon would never believe her. On the other hand, if she pushed him too far, there was no telling what he might do.

Simon circled around her and viciously prodded Alcuin's body with a long stick. Sparks flew all around. "This simpering cleric has warped your view of immortality. How can you call the gift I gave you 'hell'? You'll live forever—and you have eternal youth."

Meghann yanked the stick from him. "You've already murdered a saint," she hissed. "Do you have to compound your crime by desecrating his body? Now back away—I am going to pray for him." She glared at Simon, silently daring him to stop her, but he stood back and watched.

Meghann bowed her head and prayed for the soul of her deceased mentor. She said the prayer for the deceased she had been taught as a child by the nuns—Alcuin had been a bishop; she thought he would appreciate a Catholic prayer.

"Almighty Father," she began, "eternal God, hear my prayers for your son, Alcuin, whom you have called from this life to yourself. Grant him light, happiness, and peace. Let him pass in safety through the gates of death, and live forever with all your saints in the light you promised to Abraham and to all his descendants in faith. Guard him from all harm, and on that great day of resurrection and reward, raise him up with all your saints. Pardon his sins and give him eternal life in your kingdom. We ask this through Christ our Lord—Amen."

She removed the Celtic cross from her waist, kissed it, and threw it on the pyre. "Rest in peace, my friend."

Meghann cried out—she felt more pain. It was in her bones—almost like a deep itch that would turn into agony later on.

"It's the sunrise," Simon told her. "Better finish the last rites—unless you want them performed over your own body." She had never been outside with Simon this close to dawn. Some of his magic was gone—he was entirely too pale, almost ghoulish-looking. *Where is my handsome lover?* she thought mockingly. Not that she looked any better. *Our time is done. What is a vampire? Invincible at night, and then the sun renders us powerless. Now people can rise, live, and love while we scurry from the sun.*

"For God's sake, child. Why lament the sun anyway? Or do you want all that goes with it—senility, a broken wreck of a body, perhaps a miserable end in a nursing home?"

The sky turned rose, and Meghann screamed. Simon staggered over to Meghann—the coming of the dawn was crippling him too.

Without a word, he grabbed her and she felt the wind pick up as it always had when she traveled with him. The sun started to appear above the horizon at the same moment they disappeared.

SIXTEEN

May 1, 1998—Beltane

Meghann watched the sun set over the ocean—it was beautiful; the dying light on the water, and the sky turning dark rose and then purple.

"I'm sorry I'm late." Meghann turned around and thought she was staring at her mirror image—until she saw the violet eyes.

"Isabelle?" she whispered. It had to be Isabelle, and she looked absolutely radiant. The sadness was gone from her eyes—in its place was a shining peace and happiness. Her beautiful hair had gold ribbons and pearls braided through it, and she was wearing a stunning gold lace gown. Without being told, Meghann knew it was the dress she wore when she married Roger.

"I'm so sorry I'm late, Meghann. I've wanted to help you for so long. You call me if you ever need me." Isabelle faded away as Meghann shouted, "No, wait! Please don't leave. I have so much to ask—"

"Another time, banrion." Meghann saw a man wearing the black robes of a priest at her side now. He was very plain, with thinning brown hair, but his eyes . . .

"Alcuin!" She smiled. "You look wonderful!" Then she sobered. "I'm sorry Simon killed you."

"That does not matter. Meghann, there's very little time, so listen carefully and don't interrupt. Don't fight Simon with his own weapons—use the only thing you have on your side."

"What's that?" she asked.

"Love. But promise me you'll be careful."

"Be careful?"

Alcuin looked up sharply—the beach was becoming obscured by a gray mist. *"Fly, Meghann!"* he ordered, fear in his voice. *"Your soul is free right now. . . . Go to Charles."*

Meghann concentrated, then found herself in the peaceful world of the Higher Astral. She could see the pinkish silver cord that bound her soul to her body. Now all she had to do was visualize her home and her dear friend . . . call him to her.

With sickening abruptness, she felt herself plummeting. *"No!"* she screamed into the terrifying mist. Desperately she fought to get herself away from this evil place where she had no power. . . .

The thing was in the mist, closing in on her. She sensed the icy hands reaching out for her, wanting to possess her. I can't let it touch me. If it touches me, it will take over. The malevolent presence was all around her, honing in on its prey. Meghann kept still, scared to even move her hands enough to cast a circle for a protection. She found herself holding her breath but maybe it would hear the violent chattering of her teeth . . .

"Aufuge a ea," a voice ordered curtly, and she felt the daemon reluctantly back away.

"Let me help you," the same voice told her, and pulled her close.

"Don't let it get me," she cried, her eyes still closed.

"Shhh—I'll never let anything hurt you."

Meghann's eyes flew open. It was Simon Baldevar holding her, comforting her the way he had after a thousand bad dreams.

"Don't you touch me!" she yelled. "I hate you!" She

tried to push him away, but he held her tighter and she felt his lips on her hair.

Meghann was too tired and heartsore to struggle much. She was still shaking from the nightmare, plus she had plenty to fear in this world. What was this monster going to do to her now that she was alone with him, with no chance to summon help or escape? Certainly, she couldn't fight him—look what he'd done to Alcuin, the one vampire who should have been able to hurt him. She had a better chance of surviving sunlight than hurting her former master.

"Present master, child." His voice had no hint of reprimand in it. What was he up to now? Why was he comforting her? "Stop that fretting and accept what I give you."

Why was he able to do this to her? Why did the trembling cease and then get replaced by a feeling of well-being simply because he stroked her hair and held her close? Alcuin had warned her not to be alone with him, but she would never have believed he had this much power over her. To think that she could witness all his atrocities, be the recipient of more than a few of them, and then feel so secure when he wanted her to. Well, why not let him hold her? Simon would cuddle or torture her as he damn well pleased—she could gain nothing by pulling away and demanding agony.

"Don't tell me you are finally learning common sense." The words were teasing, but his voice was still pleasant.

"Tell me something." She put her hand against his chest and pressed herself closer to him—remembering her plan from last night.

"What do you wish to know?"

"Are you going to kill me?"

Simon laughed softly. "Are my actions those of someone bent on slaughter, Meghann? While you do tempt me—particularly when you promise devotion to a mortal weakling or weep for that sanctimonious cleric at the same moment you pray for my death—I think you would do well to remember what I told you last night. All I'm going to do is humble you, little one. With vanity such as yours, I consider that adequate repayment for all the unpleasantness between us."

"If that's all you want to do, then why did you nearly behead me last night?"

"As I said, the prospect of killing you is tempting from time to time." Simon tilted her chin up, giving her a sinister grin. "But not nearly as tempting as seeing you accept me as your master once more."

Meghann paled and he laughed again. "No, little one—no pain this time. I've learned physical agony only makes you more stubborn. I can think of better ways to make you mine once more."

Simon dug his hands into her scalp and massaged her hair. If she had been a cat, she would have purred—it felt so relaxing. "You have a strange way of playing the pining suitor, Lord Baldevar. Most men don't attempt to woo women by nearly decapitating them and causing hemorrhaging."

"The injuries you sustained last night were necessary."

She glanced up at him. "Necessary?"

He smiled wickedly. "One, you need to understand who your master is—a lesson you've always had difficulty absorbing. And then there was the matter of your smarmy cleric. It never pays to underestimate one's opponent. He was a worthy foe, but I knew his goodness would be his undoing. He could not concentrate his complete energy on defeating me when he was worried about your fate. He might even have severed my head if he had not been distracted when you started to bleed."

"So you would have let me die to save your own precious skin."

"Of course not—you were in no danger of dying. I knew he'd come to your aid, and then I had my opportunity to strike."

Meghann knew Alcuin did not blame her in any way for his death—otherwise, he would not have come to her, offered a final bit of advice. But what had he meant when he said love was her weapon against Simon? Did he mean what she had thought last night on the beach? She had seen Simon lose control for the only time in their relationship—obviously, she meant something to him. Should she press her advantage and try to regain his trust?

"To regain my trust, you would have to accept me completely." Simon gave her a wry grin—letting her know her thoughts were as clear to him as ever. "And if you did that, you would have no desire to help my enemies or leave me, would you?" He gave her hair a playful tug.

She would have been happier if he raged at her for her thoughts. That soft amusement meant he considered her no threat. Well, if he could read her anyway . . .

She glared up into his amber eyes—so damn beautiful in spite of the evil soul behind them. "Lord Baldevar, I'll never accept you or your continued cursed existence. I mean to see you dead—as you should have been forty years ago."

He kissed her lips very softly, then placed her head back near his heart. "I wish every menace I ever dealt with were so pretty and spoke in such a honeyed tone."

Damn him! Simon was right about her voice—what was wrong with her? She was practically flirting with him. *We'll see if love for me doesn't destroy you,* she thought to herself. *I'll put a stake in your heart the second you lie vulnerable to me.* But she was beginning to wonder whether love (or lust, maybe) would be her ruination.

She was disgusted with herself. She'd like to believe what she was up to was merely clever playacting, but she liked his hands on her. How could she want him to caress her . . . when those same hands murdered a saint?

"One action has nothing to do with the other. And you may thank your exalted mentor for your fright this evening."

Meghann turned around and glared at him. "My nightmares are not Alcuin's fault."

"That was no nightmare, and you know it. Tell me how often that presence has tried to invade you since my foolish uncle allowed you to peer into my future."

She shivered, remembering the nameless, awful monster that always seemed to plague her dreams now, that made her frightened to travel the astral plane. Even last night, when she went to Jimmy, she felt those icy, grasping hands reach out for her.

Simon pulled her close again. "Don't be afraid, little one. It will obey me; it won't try to hurt you again. You accuse me of all manner of treachery, but it was not I who risked your life and sanity by having you come in contact with beings you have no way of controlling."

"Stop twisting the truth!" she cried. "Alcuin didn't risk anything. . . . He was always there if anything went wrong. Maybe he simply had faith in my abilities, my ability to take care of myself."

Simon gave her a mocking glance. "So you can take care of yourself, pretty little consort? Tell me who just rescued you from the clutches of something you should never have been near."

Unwilling to concede he was right, she exploded. "I wouldn't need protection if you had ever taught me anything. At least Alcuin taught me to develop my gifts, something you couldn't be bothered to do. I don't want to be rescued like some helpless maiden in a romance novel. You tell me Renee meant nothing to you, but you gave her more than you gave me. You taught her; why not me? Why didn't you ever teach me, give me power like her?"

"Precious child, Renee had no real power—although she certainly thought she did. She was very fortunate you killed her—for I would have destroyed her for daring to invoke what she could not control. Anything I ever taught her carried an inherent risk of being torn apart." Simon stroked her cheek. "Do you think I would be able to gamble with your safety that way? I love you too much to expose you to the beings I have dominion over. Yes, sweet, you do have gifts—and I will help you develop them. But stay away from the Lemegeton—it is not for you."

"I have no desire to go near it," she told him. "We were just trying to find you."

Simon lifted her chin. Then he whispered, "And why did you wish to find me?"

"To destroy you," she told him bluntly.

Simon laughed, twirling her long red hair around his wrist. Then he used her hair to yank her close to him with a vicious turn of his wrist. Meghann refused to cry out.

"You cannot destroy me, Meghann. The pontiff should have known better than to think he had any prayer against me. And he certainly should not have exposed you, novice vampire and novice sorceress, to that world in a pathetic attempt to slay me."

Meghann hated having to ask this fiend anything, but he was the only one with the answer to her question. "Tell me about that . . . that daemon. Is it part of my future?"

"Our future, pet." Simon gave her an amused

glance, then saw the fear in her eyes. "I won't tease you, sweet. Come along—I shall prove to you my little imps cannot bother you anymore." He got off the bed and wrapped himself in the black silk robe she remembered so well. Then he handed her the exquisite ivory gown she'd worn the night he transformed her.

She ran her hand over the satin and lace, remembering that night. *Alcuin says it wouldn't matter if I told Simon I wanted to die that night—that he would have transformed me anyway. But I think he was wrong about that. Simon made me a vampire because . . .*

Because we were in love. She looked up when Simon finished that thought.

"No," she told him out loud, her voice thin and weak. "You never loved me, never loved anyone. . . ."

"Meghann." He spoke her name very softly, and knelt in front of her. She was entranced by the way his golden eyes had softened.

Do you believe my eyes ever soften for anyone but you, sweetheart?

Please don't be nice to me, Meghann thought to herself. *Don't look at me like that; don't remind me that there were good times between us, times when I truly thought I was in love with you. . . .*

Simon put his hands on her face, drawing her close to him.

Completely ignoring the voice that screamed at her to pull away, Meghann closed her eyes and allowed him to kiss her.

It was sweet, she thought, when he kissed her very gently but very thoroughly. She had forgotten how he could kiss her so lightly she almost didn't feel his touch while still making her feel completely possessed by him. . . .

For one moment, she nearly forgot her bitter feelings toward this creature and entwined her hands in his hair, pulling him closer.

Simon broke off their kiss and told her softly, "Not yet, sweet." He slid the gown over her head and pulled her off the bed. "Come along."

He escorted her out of the room. Eager to forget what she had just done with this devil, Meghann glanced around the dark house. It was elegantly furnished, as Simon's homes always were, but there was a strong feeling of desolation to the place. "Who else is here?"

"No one, pet. No servants, no one but you and me. I did not want anyone to interrupt my time with you."

He escorted her through a large, airy living room and opened a set of French doors that led to a brick veranda. She examined the densely wooded area. "Where are we? Where are we going?"

Simon put a finger to her lips, and gave her his arm. They walked through the woods, the full moon lighting the path. Meghann wrapped the gown around her arm to keep it from getting soiled.

She found her thoughts drifting, fantasizing about what it would be like for him to kiss her again, in this beautiful lonely spot. Jesus Christ! She shook her head to clear away the unwanted daydream. Why did she want the archfiend to embrace her? Why did she have to force herself to remember Jimmy? Why were the past forty years starting to feel like some distant, barely remembered dream? Just how strong was this thing's hold over her? Why, after all this time and all she'd seen, was Simon Baldevar the most alluring man she'd ever known? If Simon caught the drift of her thoughts, then he was behaving with restraint for he said nothing but merely continued walking.

They came upon a small clearing with a stone kiosk. Inside, Meghann saw that the dome roof was glass, allowing the moonlight to illuminate the small pavilion.

But this was no ordinary pavilion—she could feel great power in this place. "This is your temple," she whispered, taking in the grimoires that lined one wall of the circular room, the sigils depicting various Seals of Solomon plastered all about, and the cedarwood table in the center of the room that had a red cloth draped over it.

She touched one of the sigils, or seals. It was circular, carved in wood. Meghann remembered reading somewhere that John Dee advocated the use of "sweet wood" in Enochian magic. This seal had the Star of David on top, with a cloaked hand carved in the center. The hand pointed to a phrase in Hebrew. She was able to decipher enough to understand that it promised protection from all evil. The sigil was marvelously drawn—with great care and diligence.

"Thank you, sweetheart."

She put her hand on the one that attracted her, and felt her fingertip tingle. She licked the finger cautiously. Of course—Simon had glazed it in human blood. She recognized many of the Seals—Alcuin had used them, and shown her their benefit. But some of the sigils—they made her shiver when she looked upon them.

Simon noticed her apprehension and told her, "Some of those sigils do conjure beings you should avoid." Simon picked her up and placed her on the altar. "You were instinctively drawn to the sign I wished to show you. Now focus upon that sigil and listen to my voice."

She concentrated on the outstretched hand, and found her soul drifting from her body. She wasn't worried—she could still feel Simon grounding her, keeping her from wandering away.

Now she was on the Lower Astral. When she tensed up, she heard Simon tell her, "Easy, little one. They won't touch you—just tell me what you see."

Meghann saw a very dark room, and—Jimmy! He needed her help; she ran to embrace him. . . .

She found herself right back in Simon's temple. He glared down at her. "You have nothing to worry about, sweet. My minions shall attack your lover . . . not you."

"Leave him alone!" she cried.

"Leave untouched a man you promised love and transformation to?"

"It's none of your business what I promised Jimmy. . . . I love him."

She expected him to hit her, to rage at her for saying that, but instead he gave her a sour grin. "You pity him, child, and you enjoy being with a man you can dominate. Did he not accuse you of that same tendency?"

Meghann went white at the insult. "He was upset because he couldn't understand why I wouldn't transform him. But you ought to know that later he said he loved me, and I told him I loved him! I love him . . . not you!" Simon's lips twisted, but before he could reply, she attacked. "And why the hell do you care if I love you? You never loved me!"

"What nonsense are you talking now? I loved you enough to transform you."

"Only because I reminded you of Isabelle!"

For a second, she saw complete surprise on his face. Then he gave her a clipped smile. "Perhaps you are growing up, little one. I cannot read your thoughts as well as I used to. All this time I thought it was Renee. . . . I had no idea it was my deceased wife you envied."

Rage choked her so hard she could only splutter for a few seconds, then she collected her thoughts. "I am not jealous of her. . . . I'm sad for her, all the vile things you did to that poor woman. And I'm angry because you put me through the hell of becoming a vampire just because I resemble someone who died four hundred years ago! You loved Isabelle and despised her for spurning you—so you thought you could re-create that twisted relationship with me!"

"How on earth have you convinced yourself that you're not in love with me? Meghann, if you don't love me, then why does it hurt you so to think that I don't love you . . . that I merely see my dead wife in you?"

That threw her. *This vile monster can't be right,* she thought. *I'm upset because of what happened to Isabelle, not because it turned out I never really mattered to him. But damn him! It has hurt ever since Alcuin first told me. It hurt to think I wasn't so special after all. Do I want him to love me, to see me?* She couldn't believe it when she felt tears running down her face.

Simon sat down on the altar and took her into his lap. She fought harder than she ever had, screaming and biting. All he did was hold her tighter.

"It's not true, no, no, no . . ." She sobbed brokenly.

"Yes, Meghann . . . my sweet child. Go ahead, scream and cry. Why do you think I couldn't kill you? We love each other."

She shook her head furiously. "No, I don't love you," she contradicted, all thoughts of deluding him forgotten. "I won't love such an evil man . . . I won't. And you don't love me; I'm nothing to you, nothing but a mirror image of a long-dead woman who hated you. . . ." She couldn't continue; she hadn't been this hysterical since she found out her father had died. *This is why he won't kill me. . . . No physical pain could strike such a blow as realizing I'm still in love with him. What is wrong with me? Please,* she prayed to anyone who might be listening, *don't let it be true. . . . Don't let me love this loathsome monster. Physical attraction—that's understandable. But love? It can't be so.*

Simon kissed her hard, cutting off her sobs. No, she thought, desperately fighting what she knew was true. They were in love. . . . They were both clinging to each other and trembling. *Why am I so cursed?* she thought wretchedly. *How can I love a creature that is pure evil?*

Simon pulled away from her. "Damn you, Meghann O'Neill. Do you think I ever wanted this?" He laughed, a shaky, desperate sound. "An evil, depraved fiend has no heart. That first night—when I drank your blood, I meant to kill you. I thought you would be one of my many conquests. You screamed when I bit you. Certainly, you were not the first to cry out and beg me not to hurt you. But when I looked up at your sweet, innocent face, it touched my heart in a way no woman ever has. I was in love with you . . . and I transformed you because I wanted you with me forever."

"No!" Meghann vehemently denied what she heard. "That's not true. You never loved me! How could you when there was a chance I'd die through transformation—"

Simon grabbed her close. "You were in no danger that night, sweet. Did the sham priest forget to tell you I am the expert on transformation? In that moment, when you gave yourself to me . . . I have never loved you more. And I used that love to hold you close all through that terrible night. There was never any chance that I would lose you. I know it hurt; I know it frightened you. But the pain could have been far more than it was, Meghann. I shared it with you; I made it my own so you wouldn't suffer. I've never done that for anyone else . . . only you."

"Only because I look like Isabelle, not because you loved me—"

"Stop!" he screamed, and kissed her again, nearly suffocating her. "I never knew my self-righteous, holier-than-thou uncle to be a gossip. What did he tell you? That I only transformed you because you were a doppelgänger for my dead wife?" Simon laughed bitterly. "Use some common sense, girl. Do you think in four hundred years I never met another redhead who reminded me of Isabelle? I met hundreds of them, sweetheart . . . and I murdered every last one of them." Simon stopped, and held her so hard she thought he'd break her bones, but she didn't object. To her eternal shame, she clung to him just as tightly. "Tell me what that wretch told you of my second marriage."

That helped Meghann remember all the reasons she had to loathe him. In a calm voice, she recited the litany of his atrocities that she knew by heart. "You ruined her life, Simon. You murdered Roger because you were jealous. And he died when he tried to stop you from raping her. She only married you to save the life of her child, which you later ended anyway. And when you were married, you beat her and tortured her. You broke her soul when she miscarried and made her life a living hell after she was crippled. You rotten, vicious, unpardonable bastard! How could you do that to someone? I don't love you, and if you think I'll stand by and let you treat me that way, well, think again! I'll find a way to kill you, Simon Baldevar! You vile beast . . . How could you? What did she ever do to you? And the little boy . . . and every other thing I heard or saw you do! You sicken me and I won't live that way! I won't!" She was panting with rage, wild-eyed and gasping for breath.

Simon didn't appear at all angry—instead, he looked at her with something akin to admiration. "Do you have any idea how beautiful you are right now . . . with your hair flying and your eyes blazing? Believe me, child, you do not remind me of Isabelle at all. All that makes me love you was missing in that cold, overly pious, stupid girl." He smiled. "If only Isabelle had your fire, my marriage might have been tolerable."

"Why should Isabelle have had any fire? You did your best to destroy it, to crush any spirit she might have had. And I might add, you've done the same to me."

Simon pulled her into his lap again. "Sweet, you accuse me of all manner of evil, but you and your sanctimonious friends have managed to miss the entire point of my marriage."

Meghann glared. "You married her because you were infatuated with what you couldn't have . . . and you had that pathological jealousy of your brother Roger."

Simon rolled his eyes. "Oh, yes, I had lived in Turkey all that time and never found any better woman than my brother's cold, foolish bride? Yes, Isabelle was pretty. And I did make overtures toward her. Certainly, it would have been far easier to dispose of my idiot brother if I could have enlisted her aid. But no, Isabelle wouldn't listen to reason."

Meghann stared down her nose at him. "Pardon me, Lord Baldevar, but rape is not reason."

Simon raised an eyebrow. "Rape? Oh, you're talking of Roger finding us that night. . . . No, precious, I was referring to when I first came home. I did my best to seduce that cold piece, and informed her that any wealth in the family—her new jewels, her pretty gowns—was the result of my labors. But Isabelle . . . She quivered, and quoted the Bible at me, that foolishness about Cain. So I knew she was a lost cause, but still, I had no choice but to marry her. I wasn't about to have her take *my* wealth and lands to some new husband."

Meghann continued to glare suspiciously. "Even assuming I believe your tale of the marriage merely being one of convenience, which I don't, why did you try to rape her?"

"First, if I wanted to have her, there would have been no 'try' about it." Simon laughed mirthlessly. "Dear girl, you are still so naive. The rape was planned . . . as was Roger coming home earlier than expected." Meghann's eyes widened, and Simon grinned. "Oh, yes, one of his guards was in my employ. I had the man arrange for him to come home that night. Think, Meghann. Would my brother be able to fight me with his senses reeling in shock from seeing me on top of Isabelle? Roger was rash with his sword . . . and I was calm, eagerly awaiting my opportunity. The bumbling dolt gave it to me, and I severed his head from his shoulders." Simon got up and paced his lair while he continued to tell Meghann his twisted story. "So I married Isabelle, and, yes, I beat her. My God, I had to have some diversion. Do you know the silly wench actually prayed while I attempted to make love to her? And what a chore that was . . . done only in the hopes of an heir, which she managed to bleed away."

"So you made her life hell."

"Of course. . . . She had displeased me and I was stuck with the damn albatross and no chance for legitimate issue." Simon shrugged. "She ruined my chances of children . . . so I saw no reason why she should be allowed to keep her son. Do you think I spent my entire life earning money, dealing with the danger of travel, and then wooing an elderly, vain, difficult queen so I could see it all go to Roger's son? Perhaps if I were already a vampire, I might have allowed the child to live."

Listen, Meghann O'Neill. That is what you are in love with . . . this abomination, this evil man who feels no shame for what he has done. "And Nicholas? He gave you your greatest gift . . . immortality . . . and you murdered him."

"Meghann, how can you say I don't love you? Do you think I've ever allowed anyone else to sit in judgment of me? Yes, my dear, I am an evil man. My love for you does not change that."

"I can't love an evil man."

Simon's lips compressed into a grim line. "But you do love me, sweetheart. Look at how you cling to me and weep when you think another woman might have meant more to me than you do. What you mean to say is you cannot admit to loving me."

"That's semantics. I'll never admit it and I'll never accept it, either. Do you think I could ever find solace in the arms of a man who tortured me?"

"You found quite a bit of solace tonight, I would say. Or will you deny feeling safe and sheltered when I held you? Precious child, if I ever wanted to torture you, you would know it. I chastised you when you misbehaved. But you see, I couldn't bring myself to damage you permanently."

For a minute, she simply gaped at him. "Never damaged me . . . you lying fiend! You would have let the sun destroy me if I didn't beg you—"

"After all this time, has it ever struck you as odd that Trevor appeared at the same moment you cried out? Sweetheart, I sent him up there for you before you reached out to me. I couldn't let you die . . . not then and not now."

Simon left the table and filled a silver chalice with blood, pressing it to Meghann's lips. She tried to twist away, but he forced her to drink it, and she nearly choked. "That tastes terrible. What the hell is in it?"

"Belladonna . . . among other things," he told her.

"Are you trying to poison me?"

Simon took her face in his hands. "Merely strip away your ability to lie about your feelings. Tell me you don't love me, and I'll let you walk away forever, Meghann."

She tried to avoid his searching gaze, but she couldn't. "I don't," she tried to say, "I don't. . . . Damn it!" she cried in confusion. "All right . . . I love you, Simon! God help me. I love you so much! Damn you." She cried against his chest. "I don't want to love you. . . . I don't."

She wanted to beat her fists on the stone walls. Why did she love Simon Baldevar? What twisted, venal part of her soul responded to him? Was the link between them so strong it could make her ignore good and evil? She wished again that she had died rather than allow this monster to transform her. *God forgive me,* she thought bitterly, *because I'll never forgive myself for this.*

Meghann started giggling and crying at the same time. "You know what happened last night?" she asked the fiend rhetorically. "I had this patient whose husband beats her. Nothing like you, of course—no boiling water, crucifixions, or dead partners. And I had the nerve to advise her!" Meghann screamed shrilly at the top of her lungs, tears still pouring down her face. "The unmitigated gall to tell her that if it were me, I would certainly never love anybody who hurt me or snatched my dignity." She cackled, completely hysterical. "I said it's not love if it makes you miserable . . . and that's all you do, Simon Baldevar! My life has been nothing but one miserable episode after another since I met you. That is not love!" Now she was crying again. "But if it's not, why do I want you so much? Why can't I say I don't love you and mean it? What the hell is wrong with me? How can I love some sociopath with no conscience? What does that say about me?"

Simon laughed, swinging her around in a circle. "I knew you were my fit consort! It's not your scruples or your conscience that is bothering you—it's your pride, that same delicious pride I always loved in you." He kissed the tip of her nose, her lips, and her forehead. "What an adorable creature you are. If you were Isabelle, what I do to others would disturb you. But that is not what bothers my precious girl—you are bothered by your vanity, the blow to your ego in realizing you can't resist me."

"Stop that! Put me down! And I am bothered by what you do to people—I want no part of it!"

Simon did put her back on the table, but he was still

grinning that annoying, self-satisfied smirk that made her want to claw him. "Perhaps it does upset you, but you cried for yourself first, not my victims. I've told you before what you've always resisted—you are no saint, sweetheart. Stop trying to live up to sanctimonious ideals and become what you were meant to be—my consort."

Simon saw the uncertainty in her eyes, and pounced. "Let me feed that vanity, little one. Let me tell you why you love me in spite of that conscience you should learn to ignore. You're a very privileged girl, Meghann. No other vampire spends the day in my arms. I do not hold other women close, soothing their fears away, or take them for moonlit walks. You love a side of me no one else is allowed to see. Do you think I care if any other woman's eyes light up when I touch her? I want to see you happy, Meghann. Let me take all that misery from you and give you joy in its place." He was mesmerizing her—it seemed like those golden eyes and the soft voice filled the entire world.

Suddenly her body felt heavy, languid. Meghann wasn't as upset. . . . Instead, she felt dreamy, soft, and feminine. Very feminine, she thought hazily . . . and never had such lust consumed her. It was like she was on fire . . . like there was something inside her. But it didn't scare her; it felt so good. Fight it, she thought dizzily. Can't give in . . . no. But she felt so peaceful and languid. What was in her?

"You feel the presence of the goddess entering your body. I knew the belladonna would bring her to you—that and your gift for summoning." Simon helped her lie down on the table. "It's Beltane tonight. Will you be my priestess?"

The potion was making her mind swirl. She tried to fight down the passion she felt, but she found herself holding her arms out to Simon. She knew what he wanted—even though she'd never attempted this before. He gave her that potion to invoke—but that wasn't his only reason. Without it, she could have refused to acknowledge those repressed feelings she had for him.

Vaguely she felt Simon peel the gown off her; she yelped when she felt a sting. "I need your blood for this rite, Meghann . . . and mine." She opened her eyes and saw him slash the vein in his left wrist . . . the same spot where he cut her. Then he mixed their blood together along with some oil and started drawing some seals on her body with a silver dagger. The cold touch of steel made her moan with desire. Everything—her knowledge of Simon, heartbreak, anxiety, hurt—was leaving her. Even her own ego, her awareness of herself, was fading. She was merely a vessel for the goddess now.

She had read about this ritual—wondered what it would be like to have a deity use her body. She felt very removed from what was happening. She also felt a wonderful warm presence inside . . . and it seemed she could almost hear it thank her.

And she felt something else in Simon, some other presence touching her. When she looked into his eyes, she saw a force even more powerful than he was.

Abruptly awareness came flooding back. It was just the two of them once more. Why lie? If she missed anything about Simon, it was his slow, careful attention, the way he seemed to worship her flesh. No one else made her feel so adored—he did know how to use pride and lust to bind her to him. Alcuin had been wrong. Even love was Simon's weapon—he had smashed every defense she had and made her accept him again. Why couldn't she die rather than cry out for him?

"Your pride again, my love. Is death truly preferable to the pleasure you feel now?"

She moved beneath him, finding the same wonderful rhythm they always shared together. One thing was different—he had never been this tender before.

"I told you I want you to be happy. Meghann, forget everything else for one moment. Hate me tomorrow if you must—but let me give you pleasure for one sweet moment."

She heard herself whisper, "You are giving me pleasure." She ran her hand over his chest, stopping short at the small, star-shaped scar a few inches over his heart.

He took her hand and whispered, "That's right, Meghann—the mark of the stake is one scar a vampire bears for eternity."

"I did that," she said, entranced by the mark she put on him.

His hand tightened over hers. "Don't give yourself too much credit, child. I still cannot believe I was so clumsy that night. It won't happen again."

No, she thought, such luck would not strike twice. She could not take her eyes or hand away from the scar—it mesmerized her. Without thinking about it, she put her lips to the mark and kissed it.

Shivering, Simon grabbed her close. "I forgive you, sweetheart."

A small part of her longed to spit on the mark and tell him she didn't want his damn forgiveness. But she was also overwhelmed by the need to give herself to him, to call him her master once more. What a fool she was to think she could play mind games with him and win.

Give yourself to him, some cursed treacherous voice told her. Let him possess you. Meghann arched her neck and heard herself cry out, "Bite me!"

Ecstasy and triumph lit his amber eyes at her words. He kissed her neck, then plunged his blood teeth into her. She screamed with the pain and pleasure no mortal man had ever been able to give her.

She heard Simon cry, "Now, Meghann! Tell me you're mine. . . . Be mine!"

In that moment, she would have cut out her tongue if she could. But she could not stop herself from screaming, "I love you. . . . I belong to you, Master!" She felt her soul reach out to touch his and forge an indestructible link between them.

Charles paced the living room of Meghann's home restlessly. His nerves were stretched to the breaking point with grief and fear. He had discovered Alcuin's charred body a few hours ago. Where was Meghann? *God,* he prayed, *please don't make me lose my best friend as well as my mentor.* But why hadn't Simon killed her? Was it to torture her at his leisure? *Be all right, Meghann, please be all right.*

Jimmy Delacroix staggered into the room. He had the classic look of a human transforming—the pasty, colorless skin and hideous purple circles. *What am I supposed to do?* Charles wondered. Last night, when Jimmy came staggering back to warn them of Simon's arrival, he hadn't looked this awful. Charles had put him to bed, and that's where he had remained until now. But it was plain to see the infection was advancing steadily. The man had at most three more days before it killed him. *Should I transform him? But how can I watch over the transformation when Meghann may need my help any minute? On the other hand, what will she think if she discovers that I let him die?*

Jimmy went to the bar. He didn't bother pouring a drink—he started swigging from a gin bottle.

"That will weaken you," Charles warned.

Jimmy glared, then flung the bottle at him. It missed, shattering against the wall.

"You should know all about weak, you sonofabitch," Jimmy snarled at him. "Sitting here last night like the chickenshit faggot you are—while Maggie was stuck with that bastard. Why weren't you there? Why didn't you help her?"

With difficulty, Charles restrained himself from slapping Jimmy and telling him everything was his fault. They'd all warned Jimmy: don't leave the house at night. And what did he do? Stormed out of the house in a childish rage. He played right into Simon Baldevar's hands. Alcuin would still be alive and Meghann would be safe if it hadn't been for Jimmy Delacroix.

But Jimmy wasn't the only one at fault—*I never should have listened to Alcuin last night,* he thought for the thousandth time. *This man is right; I should have been there.* But he had felt Simon's power just as his master had. Would his presence have mattered, or would his own headless corpse be on the beach right now?

Jimmy had collapsed by the bar. Charles picked him up, and took him to the couch. "Save your strength. You'll need it to help Meghann."

"How do you know if she's even alive?" Jimmy asked bitterly before lapsing into semiconsciousness.

Charles thought transfusions might help Jimmy—at least keep him alive until they found out what had happened to Meghann. He went to the refrigerator, to get some pints for the mortal, and then cursed his own stupidity. He was so used to simply drinking any blood that he almost killed his patient with carelessness.

Charles shook Jimmy awake. "Jimmy, what is your blood type?"

The man squinted at him. "Huh?"

"Your blood type . . . A transfusion will make you feel better."

"O negative."

"You're sure?"

"Uh-huh." Jimmy rolled over and drifted back to his half dream, half memory. Fortunately, Maggie and

Charles were too scrupulous to read minds. Charles
had no idea what had happened that afternoon. . . .

*Jimmy had pulled a pillow over his head in a vain effort
to shut out the noise, but the pounding on the front door just
wouldn't stop. So finally he staggered out of bed, down the
stairs, and over to the door.*

*"Who is it?" Jimmy asked while Max barked and snarled
behind him.*

*"Jones." Andrew Jones was a private investigator Meghann
had hired to try and find any information on Simon's whereabouts.*

*Jimmy opened the door and stepped out on the porch. The
sun was irritating the hell out of him. . . . He covered his eyes
with one hand. "You got anything?"*

*The ferret-faced man tried to peer around the open door.
"Where's Dr. Cameron?"*

*"She's not around. What news have you got? You know
she said you could leave any information with me."*

*"I didn't want to see her. . . . This information is for you."
The ugly little man smirked. "For a price."*

*Just the thought of smashing this asshole was making Jimmy
feel better. He grabbed the sleazy dick by the collar. "Tell me
whatever the fuck you know and I won't kick your ass. . . .
There's your price."*

*Jones squawked, but reconsidered fighting when Jimmy
raised his fist and Max growled. "OK, already. I just thought
you'd like to know your girlfriend hasn't been completely honest
with you."*

"What the hell are you talking about?"

*"Well, she sends my agency on this wild-goose chase for
property. And she never bothers to mention that she owns her
own multimillion-dollar estate."*

*"What the fuck are you babbling about? The only house
Maggie owns is this one."*

*"Not according to this." Jones reached into his briefcase
and handed Jimmy a deed of property.*

While Jimmy skimmed it, the annoying PI kept talking. "I got curious, so I put her name through the computer. And sure enough, Meghann Cameron inherited that mansion ten years ago from her father, Jack O'Neill. He paid the gift tax, and all the property taxes since. Is your girlfriend married? I thought Cameron was her maiden name."

Jimmy put a hand on the porch railing to steady himself. Of all the . . . When he'd been looking for any alias Simon Baldevar might have been using, it never occurred to him that the bastard might be using Maggie's name. Jimmy studied the deed. This was for some house in Manhasset. This had to be Simon's resting place!

Jimmy felt a hand shaking him. "What is it?" he mumbled.

"It's time for your transfusion. Come on, I've set up a small surgery upstairs." Charles prayed the transfusion would work—Meghann would never forgive him if he did nothing and allowed her lover to die.

Jimmy leaned on Charles, and mulled over his plan. He knew Charles wouldn't approve of what he had in mind. But his head spun with the possibility that he'd finally have a chance to help Maggie.

Tomorrow, while Charles slept, Jimmy would investigate the place. It was worth a shot. Finding Simon there, Jimmy would stick a stake in his heart and end the whole thing. Now he was relieved that Maggie hadn't transformed him. It wouldn't be a vampire helping her with Simon—it would be a mortal, during the day.

SEVENTEEN

Jimmy consulted his map and drove along Shelter Rock Road, trying desperately to stay awake. He'd already had one near accident this morning when he nodded off behind the wheel, and had to pull into an abandoned storefront parking lot for two hours to nap. He was losing time—it was already ten o'clock in the morning.

He examined the tree-lined road; it was an isolated area. Jimmy was thankful Lord Baldevar hadn't decided to live in some gated, heavily protected neighborhood. *Excuse me, sir, why do you want to enter the town? Well, you see one of your residents is a wicked vampire, and he's got my girl.* Yeah, right, Jimmy would find himself back in the nuthouse.

The dirt road led him to a brick whitewashed wall with an elaborate iron gate in the center. Jimmy stopped the car, and took his rifle from the front seat. He removed the safety, then held it out in front of him. Hard to explain to passersby, but better than being shot by some damned familiar of Lord Baldevar's. Then he grabbed a burlap sack from the backseat, got out of the car, slammed the door, and inspected the entrance. From the gate, he could see nothing but trees and grass—the house must be situated farther back.

There could be no question of hopping the wall—its elegant facade was completely ruined by the barbwire running along the top. A vampire's main goal was to discourage daytime visitors. Any professional thief would take in the wire, the alarms attached to the iron gate, the video surveillance, and decide it would be too risky to break in.

Jimmy heard a small, almost imperceptible click. He whipped around and saw a small swatch of black in the tree directly above him. Reacting on pure reflex, he aimed the rifle at the black and squeezed off three shots.

A man fell out of the tree and thudded to the ground, screaming in pain; his rifle fell a few feet from him. Jimmy ran over and kicked it away before the guy could reach for it. "Jones!"

The PI glared up at him, moaning and screaming. Jimmy inspected the damage—he'd gotten the guy through the shoulder and one shot took him in his right thigh. Not life-threatening but certainly painful—and the private eye wasn't in much condition to bother Jimmy anymore.

Jimmy glanced at Jones's rifle—he had heard the man removing the safety. How the hell had he heard that? Jimmy's sense had improved dramatically since that thing bit him. Did that mean he was a vampire, or becoming one? Well, he'd been able to see himself just fine in a mirror this morning—and the thought of drinking blood made him ill. But on the other hand, those transfusions were like magic—migraine and fatigue aside, at least he was up and around. So how close was he to becoming a bloodsucker?

Jimmy put the barrel of his rifle to Jones's head. "Start talking."

"Fuck you!"

Jimmy wrapped his finger around the trigger. "Do

you see anyone around, asshole? I could kill you and stuff you in the trunk, nobody's gonna know. Or I can shoot you in the stomach and leave you here with no medical attention."

Jones was clutching his wounded leg. "What do you wanna know?"

Jimmy was cautious. He didn't know what Jones knew. What would happen if he started babbling about Simon being a vampire? "Why are you working for him?"

Jones didn't need to ask who he meant. "Look, it's nothing personal. But out of nowhere, this rich asshole shows up. I don't know how, but the guy knows everything about me. He knows who I owe—who's about to break my fucking legs because I've got fifty thousand in gambling debts. And poof—he pays off everybody! And all I have to do is—"

"Kill me, right?" Jimmy grinned humorlessly. "What did that asshole tell you about Maggie?"

"Nothing," Jones said sullenly.

Jimmy whacked the butt of his rifle against the wound in Jones's thigh.

"I mean it!" he squawked, gasping with pain. "That guy didn't talk to me about anything. . . . All he did was hand me that damned deed."

"When?"

"He gave me the deed a week ago. Then, two nights ago, he calls me up and tells me to give it to you . . . only you. He was real specific about that. I had to give it to you during the day; I couldn't bring it by at night. Then I was supposed to watch the house today until you arrived and then kill you. Jesus, what did you do to the guy anyway?"

Jimmy considered what he had just learned. Baldevar must have called the PI after Renee caught him, and before the asshole trapped Maggie. How did he know everything would go his way? Jimmy sighed—did that matter? He'd disabled Jones, and now he was going into that house to kill Simon.

He hauled Jones to his feet, ignoring the agonized protests. "You're not hurt that bad." He dragged him over to the alarm and camera. "Who else is here?"

"Nobody."

Jimmy pistol-whipped him across the face.

"I mean it!" Jones yelled, clutching his bleeding nose. "That fucking camera is a trick. I don't get it— guy's got stuff in there worth millions and his alarm ain't even hooked up to a security firm or the cops. It doesn't make sense."

It made sense to Jimmy—and convinced him Jones had no idea what Simon Baldevar was. You wouldn't hook your home up to a surveillance team if you never wanted anyone around during the day. No telling what they might see . . .

Jimmy dragged his hostage to the alarm. "Punch in the combination."

Without argument, Jones put in the code and the iron gates swung open.

"Any dogs?" Jimmy asked him.

"Five."

"You know how to make them heel?"

"Uh-huh."

When they were about twenty feet on the property, the Dobermans came running over, snarling at the pair. Jones screamed, *"Obsequor!"* and they became still.

Jimmy wondered idly what *obsequor* meant . . . some weird demon thing, or maybe Latin? He hoped he got a chance to ask Maggie. He made Jones show him where the kennel was, and they locked the guard dogs up.

Jimmy took a look at the estate—a rose-brick manor house with two wings flanking the center structure.

Nice-looking, but so desolate. Jimmy couldn't shake the weird feeling that he was at the ends of the earth. It was stupid—there were other mansions around, a town a few miles away. But once he set foot on Simon's property, he felt completely alone.

Jimmy tried to shake off his unease, and made Jones open the front door. In a way, Jimmy was glad he'd found the guy—no need to break in the house, waste time trying to disable locks. Because without Jones, the front door would be about the only way to gain entry. Although the beautiful manor house had elegant French doors and deep, wide windows to allow in sunlight, every single one of them was protected by steel interior locking rolling shutters. You could not break through those shutters; Jimmy had encountered them before and had convinced Maggie to buy them for her house. He had no doubt now that Simon (and that must mean Maggie too) was in this house. The place was a goddamned fortress, and who but vampires would need to make sure that not even the smallest ray of sunlight could enter the house during the day?

With Jones's aid, the operation was going almost too smoothly. No need for his breaking-in tools, his glass cutter; his extensive knowledge of alarms wouldn't be called upon today. Goddamned asshole of a vampire might as well have put out a welcome mat. Something about that thought made the skin at the back of Jimmy's neck tighten, but he couldn't figure out what was making him uneasy.

When they entered the foyer, the dark, oppressive atmosphere made Jimmy feel like he was inside a crypt.

Jones turned around. "So what now?"

Jimmy ordered him to lie on the floor facedown with his hands behind his head. "I'm gonna tie you up."

Jones started shaking. "Come on, man, I did everything you asked me to—"

Jimmy ordered Jones to open the bag and get some rope. Biting his lip, the PI did as he was told, gave Jimmy the rope, and lay facedown on the floor.

Jimmy put the barrel of the rifle to the back of his head and fired. Jones's body convulsed once, and then he was still. Jimmy fired again to make sure he was dead.

Then he collapsed on the floor, not caring about the blood rapidly flowing out of Jones's head. He had just killed a man in cold blood. Ordering him to lie down like that—did he think he was Gary Gilmore? Well, maybe that guy did it that way for the same reason Jimmy did—he didn't want to see the person's face when he killed him.

Jimmy had killed before when he went vampire-hunting, but that had been different. Some guy and girl came at him with guns, and he shot them first. But Jones—the guy had been wounded, and he just killed him anyway. Jimmy was beginning to understand why Maggie was so sad—how the hell did she deal with killing people to stay alive?

Then again, Maggie didn't kill people anymore—said she hadn't done that since she left Simon. But how did she deal with the memories of all the people she had slaughtered? Maybe it was different when you were a vampire—maybe your conscience didn't hurt as much. No, Maggie was disturbed. Anyway, what choice had he had? If he just tied the guy up or even knocked him out, he'd have to spend the whole time he was searching for Simon worrying about Jones waking up. And that prick hadn't been some innocent bystander—Jones would have killed him if given the chance.

Jimmy pulled himself up, looking down in distaste at his blood-soaked clothing. If he were a vampire now, would it fascinate him? Would he lick every drop off himself? There was a disgusting thought. Jimmy was starting to have second thoughts about being a vampire. What would it be like to drink blood, to never see the sun again?

For God's sake, Delacroix! Why don't I try imagining what it's going to be like to never see Maggie again? Now stop this stupid moping and find the goddamned vampire!

OK, Jimmy thought to himself. What's the most logical place for a vampire to hide during the day? He started hunting for a door leading to a cellar or basement, trying to ignore the sudden dizzy feeling he had.

In the kitchen, he found a wooden door with a dead bolt barring entry—Jimmy simply blasted the lock with his shotgun. He glanced down into the thick darkness leading below. It made the funereal atmosphere of the house seem like blazing sunlight. Jimmy got his flashlight and started walking down the rickety staircase cautiously.

He could not see anything except what the small circle of light from his flashlight illuminated. Jimmy hated to admit it, but the pitch blackness was frightening him. His heart was in his throat—any second he expected something to reach out and grab him.

"Fuck!" There was a wet patch on the stairs and Jimmy went flying. He lost the flashlight, and his sack, laden with heavy vampire-slaying implements, landed smack on top of him.

Fortunately for Jimmy, the cellar floor was dirt. If he'd taken a header onto a cement floor, he'd very likely have a concussion. Then he could just lie here unconscious until the vampire woke up and found the tasty mortal snack waiting for him.

Jimmy pulled himself to his knees, groping in the dark. He hadn't fallen very far; he could still see the light (what little there was) from the kitchen and he started crawling toward it, dragging his bag along with him.

His hand connected with a soft lump and then Jimmy

felt something slither across his hand. A bug of some kind—no, wait a minute. He kept his hand in place, becoming aware of the bone beneath the rotting flesh, the putrid odor, and the unbearable sound of maggots hatching from a dead body. . . .

My hand is on some goddamned corpse was Jimmy's last rational thought. Then instinct took over, the need to be out of this dank hole with a feeling of evil all around him. Screaming like a banshee, Jimmy turned and ran as fast as he could to the promise of sanity coming from the dim light of the kitchen.

Jimmy took the stairs two at a time, only breathing normally when he stepped back into the kitchen. He staggered back into the living room, trying to ignore the still bleeding corpse on the floor. *I can't go back down there,* he thought. *Not even for Maggie can I face that fucking place. I don't know what the hell is down there, and I'm sure as hell not facing it with no light. For all I know, he's got it booby-trapped. . . . I could step into shards of glass, have battery acid pour down off the ceiling. . . .*

Why did he suddenly feel so tired? Was it the scare he'd just had? He thought that transfusion had patched him up, but now he felt awful. He was nauseous and his head was throbbing—he was having trouble focusing. All he wanted to do was rest. Jimmy forced himself to walk to the curving staircase leading upstairs, and then he collapsed on the fourth step. *Just a little rest,* he thought tiredly, *just gonna rest my eyes for a few minutes. . . .*

Jimmy snapped awake. Jesus Christ, how the hell had he fallen asleep? He consulted his watch with the glowing dial: 5:20 in the evening. Shit! Shit! Shit! Sunset might not be until 7:04 P.M., but Maggie told him vampires could rise as early as one hour before sunset. God-damn it—that only gave him about forty minutes.

Fear propelled him up the staircase. There were about ten rooms on this floor—all locked. Jimmy cursed—now the asshole decided to be cautious. Jimmy used a credit card to jam the old-fashioned locks.

Five rooms, and he had gotten nowhere. Jimmy might want to rescue Maggie, but he was running out of time. It was already 5:40. Jimmy promised himself he would only search this floor. If he didn't find the vampires—better luck next time. Maggie wouldn't want him to die at Simon's hands.

At the end of the corridor, he struck pay dirt. He slipped his card in between the lock and door. There they were on the bed—Maggie and Simon Baldevar. Jimmy flipped the light on and consulted his watch—5:50.

Jimmy's heart was in his throat—they could wake up any second. Then what? Could Maggie help him out—and what if Simon woke up before her? What if she lay there, completely oblivious to the fact that he was being slaughtered?

Stop wasting time, he told himself. Pray Simon is a late riser. Jimmy got his stake and ropes out of the bag. First thing Maggie taught him was restrain the vampire's feet and wrists—they'll be surprised if they wake up and you can use those precious seconds to drive the stake in. So he'd tie the bastard up, then shove the stake in his heart, and chop off his head.

Jimmy wished to God vampires did sleep in coffins—then he wouldn't have to deal with seeing Maggie sprawled on top of that thing, her body intertwined with his. Of course, he probably raped her, but why wasn't she huddled away from him? Why was her head on his shoulder, one hand carelessly thrown across him, her bright red hair covering their nudity?

Jimmy was close to hyperventilating. He hadn't been this frightened the other times he killed vampires. But he had been healthy and done by noon—now he was trapped with vampires that could wake up at any second. He couldn't resist a morbid stare—resting vampires was a sight you could never get used to or fully describe to someone else. They didn't look real. In the light, they were like waxen figures in a museum—stunningly lifelike but no animation whatsoever. He found it hard to believe that the doll-like figure on the bed was Maggie.

Jimmy put out an arm to gently tug Maggie away from Simon, but she was like deadweight. He had to yank her hard to move her away, but she didn't stir.

He reached for Simon's hands, and his own hands were shaking so badly it took over ten minutes to tie the vampire's hands to the brass headboard. Touching Simon made Jimmy feel ill; every minute he expected him to suddenly yank his hands away and wrap them around Jimmy's neck.

There was no time to restrain his feet: 6:04. Jimmy took the iron stake (Maggie said why use wood when metal was so much heavier) and placed it in the center of Simon's chest. Jimmy raised the hammer, intending to drive the stake through his heart. But it was Jimmy's heart that stopped and his breath went out in a soundless gasp when those yellow eyes flew open.

The vampire easily snapped the ropes binding his wrists. Jimmy's hammer fell harmlessly to the floor, landing softly on the carpeted floor. Now one hand wrapped around Jimmy's throat.

Simon glanced down at the stake, and casually threw it across the room with his other hand. Then his mouth stretched in an evil smirk; Jimmy almost lost control of his bladder in his terror.

"Many stronger, smarter, more resourceful men than

you have tried to end my life. You arrive rather late in the day to dispose of a vampire, boy. Could it be you are laboring under the illness my apprentice inflicted upon you?"

Maggie hadn't moved. Come on, Jimmy prayed, wake up and help me.

Simon laughed. "You came here to rescue the damsel in distress, and now you invoke her aid. It shall be my pleasure to feast upon your agony when you observe Meghann's love for me."

"She doesn't want you!" Jimmy tried to scream over the hand blocking his windpipe.

Simon held his eyes, and Jimmy felt the rage vanish beside the paralyzing fear that set in. The vampire didn't need to raise one hand against him; those evil eyes had entered his mind and Jimmy was hysterical. Before he passed out, he heard the monster say softly, "Meghann wants me as she has never wanted anything else. But I will not prove that to you—she will."

"Charles."

He looked up from the deed he'd found on the living room table. "Meghann, thank God!" He hugged her close, unable to convince himself she was real. She was wearing an ivory gown, but his attention wasn't drawn by the dress—he was shocked by the red punctures on her neck that were a ghastly contrast to her chalk skin.

Charles pushed her hair away, running one hand gingerly over the wounds. "Simon *bit* you?" What else did he do, Charles thought to himself. She looked like a wraith with her pallor, wild hair, and anxiety-filled green eyes. Charles also thought he saw deep humiliation and shame.

"That's not important," she said shrilly, and started

speaking frenziedly. "We have to get back there; he's got Jimmy. When I woke up, I knew Jimmy was there; I felt him. Simon took him somewhere, probably thought he'd make me do what I did to Johnny 'cause he thought after last night—" Meghann broke off, and blushed to her hairline. Then she started rambling again in the same high-pitched, hysterical tone. "But I tricked him this time. He thought I was too weak, but he didn't know that ritual gave me power too. He thought it was all for him, but I was able to fly here and get you. I need your help; God knows what he's doing to Jimmy, but I knew I couldn't stop him by myself any more than I could stop him from killing Alcuin. . . . Oh, Charles, he's dead. Did you know that? But maybe we can help Jimmy . . . damn it! Why did you send Jimmy to Simon's lair? He was in no condition to slay a vampire. It was a trap. Why couldn't you see that? How did you find his resting place?"

Charles grabbed her shoulders firmly. "Meghann!" He had to cut through her hysteria; she wasn't making sense. He settled her on the couch and handed her the pint of blood he'd started to drink when she appeared. "Feed, Meghann. You're starved for blood and hysterical." He overrode her protests. "You can't help Jimmy like this—now take that blood."

Meghann tore into the plastic bag with her blood teeth and drank greedily. Charles watched the pallor fade from her face as she demolished the entire pint. The shaking stopped, and she looked up at him with a much calmer expression.

"I didn't mean it," she said to herself. There was no mistaking the relief in her eyes.

Charles took her hand. "What didn't you mean?"

Meghann leaned over and kissed his cheek. "Thank you for making me feed. You were right—I wasn't thinking clearly. He didn't let me feed."

"Of course he didn't. Now, what didn't you mean?"

"Last night, he gave me this potion. Blood mixed with other things. He likened it to a truth serum—said I wouldn't be able to lie about my feelings for him." Meghann laughed bitterly. "And I was foolish enough to take his words at face value, to assume Simon Baldevar would tell me the truth about anything. It was no truth serum—more like the date-rape drug. Anyway, after he made me drink it, we performed this . . . ritual."

Charles did not want to press her for details about the ritual—the dull flush on her face was enough for him to guess what was involved. He took her hands and told her, "Meghann, the past two nights have been sheer hell for me—not knowing if you were still alive. I do not care what you had to do or say to save your life."

Meghann gave him a slight smile. "You're right, Charles—all that matters is that I'm here—able to fight that bastard to save Jimmy. I wasn't able to see that until you made me feed." She felt so relieved—Charles thought *he'd* been in hell? What about the torture she'd gone through since she told that despicable bastard she loved him? The whole thing seemed unreal now—she could almost pretend she'd imagined it. And what did it matter if she did say she loved him? She only said it because of the damned potion.

"Meghann."

She looked up from her reverie.

"Did you say Simon has Jimmy?"

She scowled at him. "Of course he does. You sent him there during the day, didn't you? Why did you do it? How could Jimmy possibly attack Simon in his weakened condition? What were you thinking?"

"Meghann, no! I didn't send Jimmy. . . . Look at this, though." He handed her the deed.

She read it quickly, frowning. "Where did this come from?"

"It must have come yesterday . . . during the day, when I slept. It's from that agency you hired."

"No, it's too much of a coincidence . . . Jimmy finding Simon's resting place. This came from Simon . . . somehow."

"There's more involved. Jimmy shouldn't have been able to keep that information from me. . . . He had help."

"Oh, God." Meghann sighed tiredly. "Simon must have used his power to shield Jimmy's thoughts from you. Why couldn't Jimmy see it was a trap?"

"He was worried for you . . . sick, not thinking clearly."

Meghann started to nod in agreement and then she let out a chilling howl that made Charles's bones tighten with fear. "He's torturing him!" she howled. "Oh, my God, no, don't—"

Charles shook her hard to bring her back to her senses.

Meghann got to her feet, and yanked Charles up. "Come on, we have to go now!"

"Meghann, how can I fly there? I've never been there."

"Yes, you have," she corrected. "Simon took me walking last night. . . . It's the Gold Coast! Do you remember that huge mansion we saw in Hempstead? Simon's estate is only a few miles from there. . . . If we fly and then walk, we can be there in ten minutes! Come on!"

Charles spoke softly, knowing how upset she was. "Meghann, you just asked me how Jimmy couldn't see that he was walking into a trap. Well, he's mortal, but you're a vampire and even you can't think clearly right now with all your fear for him. Simon wants us to just blunder onto his property."

Meghann knew her friend was right. But how could they help Jimmy?

"Tell me everything that happened since you encountered Simon on the beach," Charles told her.

Rapidly Meghann told him of Alcuin's death, the dream she'd had the night before, her own failed plan to bring Simon to his knees with the love he claimed to have for her.

Charles's eyes lit up. "You were right!" He smiled at her.

His sudden cheer surprised her. "What do you mean?"

Charles grasped her hand again. "Meghann, Simon's love for you does make him vulnerable . . . and that is the one advantage we have right now." He pulled her up. "We have to make you more presentable for your lover."

"What?" she questioned while he pulled her up the stairs. "What are you up to? I told you, trying to use his feelings toward me didn't work last night—"

"But that's because you were alone, Meghann. Of course you couldn't handle him on your own, but now we'll defeat him together. Alcuin was right—love will be your weapon." Charles explained the rudiments of his plan while they hurried up the stairs.

Meghann thought his plot had a small chance of working, but her own eyes lit up when she thought of a way to refine it.

"Yes!" she said excitedly while Charles hastily filled a bag with items they would need to rescue Jimmy and destroy Simon. "This can work, but I have a better idea. Something Lord Baldevar will never suspect. I'll explain to you while we walk to the estate."

Jimmy Delacroix regained consciousness when he felt an icy hand on his throat and heard a steely voice command, "Awaken."

He tried to jerk away from the cold touch, but he couldn't move. His arms and feet were tied down. No, not just tied down—the ropes were cutting into his skin, stretching his limbs to the breaking point.

"Your limbs ache? You are lying upon a rack—one I have owned since the sixteenth century," the same steely whisper told him.

Simon Baldevar! Jimmy's eyes snapped open. Everything came flooding back: Jones, seeing Maggie sprawled on top of the vampire, and his failed attack. Where was he? Jimmy felt a cold block beneath his head, propping him up. He raised his head as much as he could to get a better look at his surroundings.

What he saw made him think he had traveled back in time to the Spanish Inquisition. The dark, dank room was a torture chamber, lit only by a few candles attached to iron holders in the stone walls. In the center of the room, Jimmy saw a large wheel-like structure hanging ten feet off the ground, an iron casket, chains attached to the walls with iron spikes in the necks, and a long stone table littered with a variety of torture implements. There were thumbscrews, needles, pincers, daggers, and some other medieval-looking objects that Jimmy couldn't identify.

Simon followed his glance, and picked up one curious object that looked like a clumsy scissors. "You don't know what some of my little toys are, do you? Don't fret. Before the sun rises, you shall know the name of every object on this table and its use—intimately."

"What are you going to do to me?" Jimmy croaked.

"Whatever does my consort see in you? She certainly did not select you for your intelligence or resourceful nature." The vampire applied a bit more pressure to Jimmy's throat and the mortal gagged. "And I made it so easy for you, young man. Threw open the walls of my estate to see if you could damage me. Removed every barrier to finding my resting place. Of course, you failed miserably."

Jimmy cursed—he should have known the whole thing was a trap. But he'd wanted to help Maggie so badly, get her away from this monster. And where the hell was she? Hadn't she woken up yet? What had the monster done to her?

"I have not done anything to Meghann. She chose to leave my estate."

Maggie was gone? Why? She wouldn't just leave him here and save her own neck, would she?

Simon made the thumbscrews fly off the stone table and into his outstretched hand. While he attached the device to Jimmy's right hand, he spoke to him in a light, almost casual tone. "Although it would give me no end of pleasure to watch you wallow in the notion that Meghann cravenly deserted you in your hour of need, I far prefer to point out that you know remarkably little about a woman you claim undying love for." The screws were tightening; Jimmy felt a sickening wave of nausea and unbearable pain in his right hand. He screamed out and the vampire kept chatting in that same lighthearted tone, like they were having tea together. "That sweet child is not yet capable of turning her back on you. Poor girl . . . What she must suffer through because she is too stubborn to listen to her master." *Snap*—the screws went through Jimmy's bones and his right hand was broken.

The agony was worse than anything Jimmy had ever felt—it seemed like the pain shot waves of torment through his body. Hating himself, Jimmy screamed, "Stop! Please!"

Creak, creak, creak . . . Jimmy heard something behind him creaking. How was it moving? Simon was standing in front of him. The pain slammed into Jimmy as his limbs were stretched farther and farther apart.

He was drenched in sweat, moaning incoherently. *God,* he prayed desperately, *let me faint.* But he didn't pass out and his agony grew with each insidious creak of that damned machine behind him.

"You will not find any escape in oblivion, young man. For even if you did faint, I would revive you. I would not remove your pain. . . . I would increase your awareness of it. What a sight you will make for my Meghann."

"Stop it!" Jimmy yelled through the pain. "Don't you say her name. . . . Don't you call her yours!"

Simon raised his left eyebrow, and the rope around Jimmy's right ankle tightened again. It kept tightening until his kneecap popped. Jimmy vomited from the excruciating pain. He hoped he might choke on the vomit, but he couldn't with his head propped up.

"But she is mine," the fiend told him quietly. "She pledged herself to me for eternity before you were even born, worthless cur." Simon knelt by Jimmy's side and sadistically whispered in his ear. "Perhaps I did not need the rack at all. Which would hurt you more? Shall I introduce you to the pincers, or tell you everything I did with my inamorata last night?"

"Don't . . . you . . . call her . . . that," Jimmy hissed. "She . . . loves . . . me."

"In the same manner she would love a wounded animal she found on the street. Meghann has an unfortunate tendency to pity and empathize with mortals . . . one she will outgrow in time, under my tutelage. But I see by your bulging eyes and heaving chest that revelation will cause you more agony. So I shall tell you that last night I had her just as I desired . . . with her beautiful legs spread wide—"

"No!"

"To receive her master," Simon whispered smoothly, ignoring the interruption, "swearing love, telling me she belonged to me . . . but you need not take my word for it. You may see for yourself when Meghann arrives. That will be your last image of her, wrapped in my arms, Mr. Delacroix, calling me her master. And after that, if I feel merciful, I will end your worthless life."

Jimmy took a deep but shaky breath and forced himself to look right into the deranged yellow eyes. "You've got it wrong, motherfucker," he said without any break in his voice. "The last thing you're gonna see before we put you in the ground is Maggie telling me she loves me and telling you to go fuck yourself."

"I grow weary of your noise, wretch." Simon strolled over to the table and plucked a peculiar object from it. When Simon got closer to him, Jimmy saw that the thing looked like a dog collar with a double-pronged fork sticking out of the center. Simon attached it to Jimmy's neck, and the prisoner found he could barely breathe.

"This is called the 'heretic's fork.' Notice how one end keeps your chin rigidly in place and the other attacks your sternum. Speech is nearly impossible, but I am sure you will try to scream in a few minutes."

Simon raised his hand, and a pincer slowly drifted off a coal brazier and spun in the air for a few minutes. Then it leisurely made its way over to Simon's left hand. He took the cool end in hand and attached the warm end to the thumbnail on Jimmy's ruined hand.

"Nngh, mmph," he tried to scream when the searing hot pincer ripped his fingernail out down to the cuticle. Jimmy was literally choking on his pain because he couldn't scream and he couldn't stop trying to scream.

When he thought there could be no worse torment, the vampire leaned down and started drinking from his neck . . . reopening Renee's wound. It wanted his pain; it was growing strong on the agony.

"By my estimation, my consort should arrive in about ten minutes," the hateful fiend whispered in his ear while he attached the pincer to his left hand. "I promise you, Mr. Delacroix, that shall be an eternity of misery for you. But it will be a pale shadow compared to what you feel when you see Meghann accept me as her master . . . and lover."

As they neared Simon's estate, Meghann's euphoria gave way to rising tension and doubt. "Are you sure this will work?" Meghann questioned worriedly. "Simon's not a fool."

"Meghann, what other choice do we have? Shall we pit our combined strength against him in a face-to-face duel for your lover's life? It should take all of five minutes for him to crush us both. If he could defeat Alcuin, what prayer do we have? And you're right . . . Simon is not a fool. But he is in love. He'll believe you, Meghann, because he'll want to believe you." Charles saw her skeptical expression and sighed. "I wish I could reassure you . . . and myself. There are no guarantees anymore, Meghann. We may very well be walking to our deaths."

"Your death," she told him quietly. "Simon won't kill me. He'll make me sit and watch while he slaughters you and Jimmy, but he won't murder me. He has better ways of making me suffer."

Charles gave her his hand, and she nearly crushed it. They were like two frightened children, holding hands to protect themselves from the evil things in the dark. "We're approaching the estate. . . . Let's not give ourselves away by discussing this any further."

Meghann's Cadillac was still parked by the elaborate iron gate. Once Meghann had thoroughly engaged Simon, Charles would simply leap over the barbwired wall and follow his senses to his friend's whereabouts.

Charles handed her several items from the bag, and

she slipped them on. He hugged her close, and then she flew into the manor house. Meghann found herself by the French doors Simon had opened the night before.

She did not feel Simon's presence—but that meant nothing. Whatever he'd been up to for forty years had left him with an impenetrable camouflage. Meghann focused her senses on Jimmy. He was no longer conscious—all she could feel was pain, a severely injured person with no more awareness of their surroundings than a hurt animal.

Meghann walked toward the kitchen, but stopped in the foyer. There was dried blood on the polished oak floor, as well as on a lovely Persian rug by the staircase. She knelt down and touched the bloodstain. Poor Jimmy! Damn, why didn't she see through that little worm Jones? Maybe Simon hadn't made a deal with the man the last time she spoke with him. If she found Jimmy in one piece and got him out of this hellhole, she'd tell him he had no choice about murdering Jones—and that he'd never have to kill anyone if he still wanted to be a vampire.

Meghann wrapped her arms around her body and walked toward the kitchen, where the entryway to the cellar was located. She could already feel terror emanating from it. . . . What had he done to Jimmy? She had that same leaden, frightened feeling she had the night she ran through fog to find poor Roy. And again she was walking on when every instinct screamed at her to turn away. It was like she was irresistibly drawn to something she knew was going to harm her, but she couldn't help herself. Well, that neatly summed up her relationship with Simon Baldevar, didn't it?

She walked the long, unlit length of the cellar, gasping in disgust at the corpses lining the walls. This wasn't like Simon; in fact, she received little impression of him. This place was the domain of that awful hag; she hung the bodies so she could continue to take pleasure in their deaths. The emanations Meghann received from their desecrated bodies made her wince. . . . She saw a woman sliced in half, a man flogged to death, men and women starved for days in a small cell with vermin and water bugs crawling all over them, and a young girl having molten lead poured down her throat. Of course, the dominant image was that rotten bitch drinking the blood of her victims—savoring their agony while they were drained of life. How many people had been grateful to be bitten, thankful the pain was over? *I should have made her suffer more before I killed her.*

Now Meghann stopped before a massive steel door; she could feel her master's presence. . . . He'd been here quite recently. She waved her hand, causing the steel door to swing open. Meghann took in the dungeon—for there was no other way to describe the hellish room.

Meghann saw the ropes dangling from the rack, the pincers lying by it, but she did not see Jimmy. He was not on the wheel, not hanging from the chains attached to the wall; then her eyes fell on the iron maiden.

She swung the heavy iron lid open, and gasped. "No!" she cried loud enough to make the torture implements on the table tremble.

Meghann lifted Jimmy out of the hellish contraption. "Jimmy," she choked out, weeping when she saw what he had gone through. When she touched him, all his torment was clear to her. She saw the session on the rack, how he howled when the monster ripped out his fingernails and toenails; then he fainted and was brutally revived. She saw Simon dragging him over to the iron maiden and throwing him in. Meghann almost felt she was Jimmy, felt the fear and terrified anticipation when he saw the lethal iron spikes on the door coming toward him as Simon slowly shut the door. Then the spikes descended, lightly pinching his flesh at first, but then sinking in farther, stabbing him with a dozen sharp points at once, simultaneously attacking the heart, lungs, liver, spleen . . . maiming and mutilating, but not killing. Just wishing he would die as those vicious spikes drove into him, rooted in his vital organs, tore him apart. . . .

Meghann took a shaky breath. Jimmy was dying—she could not dare transform him now. In his shocked condition, he would not live through the process. She said a brief prayer, hoping Charles had been right about what Alcuin meant. She remembered what Charles had told her: "just pray, friend—like you did on the night we first talked."

Meghann thought back to that first night, and began saying the Hail Mary, her favorite prayer from childhood. Gradually her voice became calm and sweet. And she thought, not of the horror of the room she found herself in or her lover's hideous circumstances, but of all the good times they'd had together. This was what Alcuin had tried to tell her. Her weapon was love—not the dark, twisted thing that bound her to Simon but the love she shared with Jimmy, her friendship with Charles. And she could use it to heal Jimmy.

A warm glow appeared over Jimmy while she prayed. As the glow brightened the entire room, Jimmy's bones healed. The gaping, monstrous holes in his body refilled and the bleeding stopped. "What?" he muttered in a haze. "Maggie, what's going on?"

"Jimmy!" she squealed, and hugged him so tight he yelped. "Oh, Jimmy, you're alive! Alcuin . . . Charles, thank you. . . . Thank you for showing me this wondrous gift!" The glow had died when she stopped concentrating. Jimmy was nowhere near healthy. . . . He was too weak to walk, in pain from head to toe, and his fingers and toes were horribly disfigured. He was still suffering from the infection Renee had put in his veins, but he was no longer on the brink of death.

She barely had time to give him one small kiss before she felt her master's presence. Meghann turned around—prepared to try and make this insane scheme work.

She saw Simon's eyes light up in appreciation at her appearance. After Charles explained his plan, she had selected a violet gown cut in a medieval style—a tunic dress with a deep u-neckline and a fine silver chain around her slender waist. With her hair tumbling down in soft waves to her waist, and her cheeks flushed from the blood, she knew she looked beautiful. Would it be enough?

"Will what be enough, little one?" Simon glanced behind her at Jimmy's improved condition, then gave her a twisted grin.

Meghann didn't answer—she just gave him a seductive smile and walked over to him. Her high heels put her at eye level when she put out her hand to caress his face. Simon caught her hand and held it tightly while his golden glance burned through her.

"Don't you want me to touch you?" she whispered.

He kept that same wry expression on his face while Jimmy's face showed confusion and disbelief. Maggie had come here and saved his life, but now she was behaving like some courtesan with that monster. What was she up to?

"Your paramour wishes to know your intentions," Simon whispered to her, not letting up one bit on the pressure on her hand. "And I must admit, I am rather curious myself. Are you trying to seduce me, sweetheart?"

She widened her eyes—the same flirtatious but properly deferential gesture she'd always used to try to get around him in the past. "Is it working?"

Simon smiled down at her. "You make a pretty coquette, Meghann. Tell me why you healed that wretch."

Meghann pressed her body against Simon's and told him in a low, clear tone that carried throughout the entire room, "I healed him because I care for him—live with it." She gave him a wry smile of her own and put her hand in his thick chestnut hair. "Jimmy tried his best today to give me help he thought I needed. . . . I mean to repay him for that."

Simon didn't stop her from running her hand through his hair; he wrapped his other hand around her waist and pulled her close to him. Then he gave Jimmy a derisive grin over the top of Meghann's head—and ignored the obscenities pouring out of Jimmy's mouth. When Simon glanced down at Meghann again, his eyes had darkened noticeably. His voice sounded a bit thicker than usual when he asked, "How do you plan to repay your lover, Meghann?"

"By getting you to let him go," she said softly.

Simon raised an eyebrow, and gestured to Jimmy's injuries.

"Oh, I know you had your fun," Meghann purred at him. "And I won't lie to you and pretend what you did doesn't sicken me. But I should think that was enough to settle whatever quarrel you have with Jimmy Delacroix. You've broken him, Simon. Do you honestly believe he will ever brave your wrath again?"

"Sweetheart, you puzzle me. If my actions toward your paramour disturb you, why are you doing your level best to entice me? If you care for him enough to heal him, why on earth would I allow him to live?"

Meghann dropped the seductive look and told him earnestly, "Because you have me. Isn't that all you said you wanted? Jimmy is here because he doesn't realize what happened between us last night—he doesn't know that I love you. I wish I didn't, but I do. If he knows that, Jimmy won't want me. Please let him go—I don't want another death on my conscience."

Before Simon could reply, Jimmy yelled out, "What the hell is wrong with you, Maggie? You can't love him, you can't!"

"Say it again, Meghann," Simon told her in a husky voice. Meghann thought she heard the smallest plea in his tone.

"I love you, Simon Baldevar. I may not love your actions, and I certainly don't understand why I care for you, but I do. And I can't be with another man knowing what I feel for you." Meghann's eyes searched his. Did he believe her? "So let Jimmy go—I have no desire to live with him anymore. I'll stay at your side forever if you do this one small favor for me."

Simon let go of her hand and wrapped his hand in her hair—pulling tightly. She didn't flinch or try to move away. "Pretty speech, little one. But if you have come to accept your love for me, why flee my home to enlist the aid of your catamite friend?"

Meghann shook her head as much as she was able to with his grip on her scalp. "Not to ask for help . . . I wanted to say good-bye and tell him I would remain with you of my own free will. Please, will you let Jimmy leave here?"

"Stop giving me charity, you whore!" Jimmy screamed in a jealous fit. "I don't want your god-damned pity!"

"It would appear, Mr. Delacroix, that is all you shall ever receive from my consort. Did I not promise you the evening would end with you seeing Meghann in my arms . . . of her own volition?" Simon let go of her hair and wrapped his arms around her.

Simon was immersed in her—so immersed he did

not seem to hear Charles sneaking up behind him with a stake in his hand. Jimmy saw the whole thing, and allowed himself to pray that maybe everything Maggie had just said was a trick . . .

And felt that small hope shatter when she screamed "No!" and put her hands on the stake before it could go through Simon's back.

Charles backed away, disbelief and shock plain on his face. "Meghann," he choked out.

Simon let go of her and whipped around to grab Charles and his stake while Meghann sank to the floor, sobbing and howling.

"I'm so sorry," she apologized, weeping. "I told you I couldn't do it, couldn't kill him no matter how much he deserves it." Jimmy thought he was beyond surprise, but then one of the pincers on the floor rattled and flew into Maggie's hands. She prepared to shove the thing into her chest. . . .

Simon kicked her wrist hard, and she dropped the pincer. He used Charles's momentary lapse of concentration to drive the stake into his unprotected chest.

"Charles!" she screamed, and reached out to remove it from his heart.

Easily Simon caught her by the hair and dragged her away from her friend. Without letting go of her, he reached one hand out, causing Jimmy's head to crash into the stone wall behind him—knocking him out.

"I shall attend to him later, but now I wish to speak to you privately." He leaned down and bit her—taking away all the strength she'd gained from feeding that evening.

Simon attached her to a set of chains on the wall. They had spikes inside the neck and wrists. He chained her up and she moaned when the spikes invaded the punctures in her neck. "Now you won't cause any further mischief. Stop rattling those chains—they have magical qualities, so you won't be able to break the restraints in your weakened state. You'll have no choice but to watch me torment your pathetic allies." He looked down at her, lust lighting up his eyes. "How beautiful you look in your pain and helplessness." Simon stroked her cheek and kissed her.

When he kissed her, she bit him, and he slapped her hard. "Stop resisting, child. How many times have your tried to soothe your mind with the false notion that you would spurn me if you had a second chance?" Simon laughed and gestured to Jimmy and Charles. "Now you know the truth—you are mine, and you always will choose me. Did you or that fool honestly think such a transparent scheme could work? You cannot deceive me, Meghann. I knew you were playing a role—or rather that you flattered yourself with the idea you were playing a role. I also knew you could not allow anyone to hurt me; your loyalties still lie with me. Now your lover is barely alive, and that wretched sodomite who lured you from me will not see another night on this earth."

"No, I don't want them to die. . . ." she sobbed.

"Your wants do not concern me."

"I saved your life," she hissed. "Isn't that enough? Can't you let them go?"

"Don't be silly. At any moment, I could have taken the stake from that wretched cur. I simply preferred to make you do it. Let them go? Sweet, I've so looked forward to this moment . . . when you realize that I am all you have in this world. Meghann, even if I did not have strong reason to savor their pain, I could not allow them to live."

"Please," she begged, "don't make me watch everyone I love die!"

Simon drank from her again, from a vein in her breast through the flimsy material of her gown. She howled in pain . . . and some slight feeling of desire. He saw that and smiled cruelly. "It is your love for them that is their downfall. I know you, Meghann. You continue to deny your love for me because they give you false courage. If they are dead, if you have nothing to cling to, I shall have you eating from my hand."

Meghann spat on him. "If they die, I'll end my own life rather than be at your side!"

"Sweetheart, I am trying very hard to control my temper. But I won't be so nice if you continue to defy me. Now beg my pardon."

"Go to hell, you vicious beast!"

"You received psychic impressions when you wandered the halls, right, Meghann?"

She glared—unsure where this was going.

"Sweetheart, I have a large cauldron burning over a fireplace in the next room. Reach out with your senses—you'll detect the odor and know I do not lie."

Meghann sniffed hard, and choked at the foul smell.

"It is melting copper—a phrase you have used to describe my eyes in your sweeter, more poetic moments. Shall I pour it down your lover's throat? You may have some small skill in healing him, but I do believe he would die long before you could help him."

Her eyes widened, and he grinned at her shock. "Will you show your master the proper deference?"

All she could do was nod.

"Very good—but first we need an audience." Ignoring the unconscious vampire on the floor, Simon picked Jimmy up and attached him to a set of chains across the room from Meghann—where he had a very clear view of her. Simon put his hand on the mortal; he woke up again.

Jimmy no longer felt human—he was a damned puppet in the hands of these vampires. They could awaken him, knock him out, heal him, hurt him—until this moment, he had not realized how truly different Maggie was from him.

"You will realize a great deal before the moment comes when I smash your limbs upon the wheel and carefully interweave your bones into the spokes, leaving you to die slowly and horribly tomorrow while my consort and I rest. Meghann and I have come to an understanding while you were . . . indisposed." Simon walked back to Meghann, running one hand over the length of her body. "She's absolutely beautiful, isn't she?"

"Please," she whimpered.

"Are you defying me, little one?"

"No, Master," she answered lifelessly.

"Of course not." Simon took a straight-edge razor out of his pocket and used it to slice through her dress, also cutting her skin. He admired the straight crimson slash on her torso, and put his mouth to the wound.

Jimmy turned his head away in disgust.

"Our activities do not meet with your mortal paramour's approval, little one. Perhaps he'd like to see another game. . . . Confession, maybe?"

"What shall I confess, Master?" Meghann inquired in the same dull tone.

"What you said to me last night."

"I love you."

"No, no—you already said that. Tell me, why did the boy-lover tell you to take that tact?"

"He said you would believe me because you wanted to believe me."

"I want very much to believe you will accept me, embrace my ways. But I understand you spent far too many years absorbing the pontiff's sanctimonious creed to do that easily. Surely, there was another reason I was supposed to accept your sweet words?"

Meghann shrugged. "Because on some level they were true."

"On every level," the fiend corrected her. "You do love me. Someday when these pathetic worms are no more, that admission won't cost you so much. But in the meantime, I can savor your pain almost as much I will savor the moment when you truly give yourself to me. Now tell this wretch what else you said."

"I don't know what you want me to say."

Simon stroked her wounded breast—his grin widened when Jimmy Delacroix started to howl in helpless rage. "Allow me to refresh your memory, my love. You were on my altar, writhing beneath me while I drank your blood . . ."

Her lips curled, and Jimmy thought he saw tears glistening in her eyes. Or maybe it was the candlelight. But she said quietly, "I said I belong to you."

"Louder."

"I said I belong to you!" she shrieked. "Now, please, let them go! Torture me all you want, but let them go!"

"I have no desire to torture you, little one. Your friends are another matter. But for now . . . you belong to me, and I intend to prove that to your little boy toy before he dies." Simon leaned down and started kissing her. "You'll scream for me, Meghann," he murmured. "You'll forget your worthless allies and yearn for me as you always have."

Jimmy thought he'd almost rather go back on the rack—anything but watch that devil paw Maggie. And why didn't she turn away? Didn't she have any pride? What had happened to the woman he loved? Had Simon managed to destroy her completely? Jimmy took one last sickened look at the couple—Simon was kissing her breasts. But then Maggie held his eyes . . . and he could not believe it when her mouth stretched into a grin and she winked at him. Jimmy's mouth fell open

and then his eyes fell to the floor where he noticed
Charles sit up and yank the stake out of his own heart.
There was almost no blood from the wound, and he
didn't appear to be suffering. . . .

Simon had noticed the change in her too. He raised
his head and looked at the sparkling eyes and wicked
smirk. Meghann saw shock on his face—he had not
expected this.

In the same moment that he whipped around to deal
with Charles, the vampire took all the energy he had
summoned while he lay ignored on the floor and flung
it toward Meghann.

She felt the energy enter her soul, and used it to
scream out for the assistance they so desperately
needed to slaughter Simon. "Isabelle!" Meghann
screamed with all her strength—nearly shattering
Jimmy's eardrums.

He ignored the humming sound in his ears—he was
far too amazed by what he saw happen next. "Holy
shit," Jimmy muttered when Simon flew across the
room to land on the rack. Some unseen force shoved
him back down when he tried to sit up, and the slack
ropes attached themselves to his wrists and ankles.
Jimmy felt utter fury and hatred in the room, but he
sensed it wasn't directed at him—it was all focused on
Simon Baldevar and the ropes stretching his body farther apart.

Charles pulled the restraints off his friend, and she
rushed over to the tote bag. Meghann pulled on her
black shirt and jeans—no way she was standing around
looking like Simon's sex slave. Charles took out a lethal
hatchet.

"What the hell is going on?" Jimmy inquired from
his chained post. Charles stretched his hand out, and
the manacles opened. Meghann was at his side in an
instant—holding him up to prevent him from falling.

He tried to put his arms around her, but he was too weak. Together they made their way over to the rack where the machine was rapidly winding up to break every bone in Simon's body.

Charles held the hatchet over Simon's head, but Meghann restrained him. "Not so fast—I've waited far too long for this."

She leaned down, in the precise spot where Simon had whispered to Jimmy while he was on the rack, and began her own monologue. "You're not the only one who knows how to lace instruments with magical properties, Master," she taunted him while the rack stretched his limbs. "You were so eager to stab Charles you never even felt the healing potion we drenched the stake in. You dared to speak to me of overweening pride! Your ego and conceit allowed you to believe I'd betray my dearest friend and lover out of love for you. And I knew damn well you'd ignore Charles because there was no way you could pass up an opportunity to degrade me in front of Jimmy, leave us both with nothing." She smiled at the light sheen of perspiration covering Simon's body, at his clenched jaw. "Trying not to scream? How many times did Isabelle bite down on her lip to keep from giving you the satisfaction of seeing her agony? I am honored to help her destroy you. I'm sure she'll see to it that your death is slow and painful, a fitting end to your miserable existence." She kissed his cheek with mocking tenderness, then spat on him. "That's for Alcuin. I almost feel sorry for you, Master. After all those centuries, you fell in love," she said in a singsong, vicious whisper. "Actually had tender feelings for someone. But you're just not good enough for me. I have a lover— someone who makes you look like the low, vicious scum you are." She yanked his eyes open, and kissed Jimmy Delacroix on the mouth.

Now it was Jimmy who leaned down and slapped the

helpless vampire across the face. Then he gave Simon a lopsided grin. "I told you the night would end with Maggie telling you she loved me."

For the next part of her revenge, Meghann meant to drain his blood while he was in pain, then let Charles cut off his head. But when her mouth touched his neck, she felt her throat close up with tears. She had to fight to keep herself from undoing his restraints, from pulling him close and ending his pain. What on earth was wrong with her? Meghann knew—she did love him, some part of her actually had tender feelings for this evil creature. Her trembling hand fell on the pulse in his neck; then her eyes widened. Simon was not in pain at all—his jaw was clenched because he was concentrating. *Meghann, I cannot help you much longer,* a feminine voice whispered.

She backed away from the rack, trembling and pale as a ghost. "Now!" she ordered Charles.

He did not know what was making her so uneasy, but he brought the blade down to Simon's neck . . . and screamed when the thing disintegrated. The hatchet simply fell apart in his hands. The wood handle snapped in half, and the blade shattered into a thousand harmless pieces.

"Abi in malam rem, Isabelle!" Simon thundered so loudly the heavy wooden rack trembled.

Now Isabelle's presence had been banished. Meghann and Charles were all alone with a diabolical fiend they had failed to slay. And Meghann had not simply attempted to kill him—she'd reviled him with that castigating speech in front of the two people he despised most. What would happen to them now?

The steel door slammed shut, blowing out the few candles in the room. Jimmy could not see anything, but Meghann and Charles could see far more than they wished. When the ropes holding him down simply vanished, Simon sat up and instilled in the young vampires the same fear Jimmy had felt earlier when Simon opened his saffron eyes.

Meghann tried to step away from the rack, and her master's hand lashed out to grab her.

"Let her go!" Charles screamed.

Simon waved his other hand, and Charles flew off his feet, crashing into Jimmy.

"What's going on?" the mortal whispered to Charles.

Meghann watched helplessly while an evil, shadowy form sprang up from the stone floor behind Jimmy and Charles. Simon held her in an iron vise while the thing grabbed Jimmy. He could not see it but felt the pain when one specter claw mauled his cheek down to the gum. Charles was able to repel the thing when it tried to attack him, but he could not help Jimmy. Nor could he break through the malevolent force that prevented him from taking one step toward Meghann.

"Maggie!" Jimmy howled. "Help me!"

"Jimmy!" she yelled, thrashing around in a desperate attempt to break Simon's fierce grip.

Simon spun her around and backhanded her viciously enough to make her fall to the ground; then he yanked her up by the hair. A dagger flew off the stone table to land in his hand. When he put it to her cheek, Meghann felt the power within the blade—if that thing cut her, the wounds would remain forever.

"Trying not to scream?" Simon mimicked while he pressed the blade against her skin. His amber eyes blazed with fury and hurt. "I gave you my love and you attempted to use that to make a fool out of me. The only reason I do not kill you where you stand is that you wanted to cry when you thought I might be in pain. Maybe those two fools were deceived by your harsh, spiteful words, but you wanted to help me in the penultimate moment, didn't you?"

When she didn't answer, the monster that held Jimmy ran its half-seen talons across his stomach.

Don't make me ask you again, Meghann.

She glanced up at him. *Yes, I wanted to help you,* she told him.

Simon gave her a twisted grin. *Proud to the very end, my darling. God forbid those idiots should hear you admit what you feel toward me, isn't that right? Now say that aloud . . . and perhaps your lover's end will not be the excruciating torment I have in mind.*

"I wanted to help you!" she screamed. "I hated the thought of you being in pain."

Simon ran a hand over her bruised cheek. *I love you, Meghann.*

Dumbfounded, she looked up at him.

Simon saw her amazement and laughed cruelly. Then he brushed her forehead with his lips.

Simon tilted her head up, kissing her in the same gentle manner he'd used the night before. Then he pushed her away from him.

But I am outraged that you would attempt to use your amateurish talents to hurt me. I'm through spoiling you, little one. It is time for you to learn why you never want me to hate you. Go to your friends now. See how long you can stand against me before you plead for me to take you back. Perhaps I will . . . or I might just allow you the painful death your foolish conscience makes you think you want.

Simon picked her up by the hair, flinging her against Charles. They clung to each other again; neither could think of one thing they could do to save their lives or Jimmy's.

Meghann looked behind her. The shadow being had vanished, but Jimmy had fainted again. She decided to leave him unconscious. . . . There was no need to expose him to whatever Simon had in mind now.

"Meghann." For the first time, she heard Simon Baldevar address her as he did all others—with no love, just that detachment and lack of empathy that allowed him to commit any atrocity he wished. It made her shiver violently, small beads of perspiration forming on her forehead. "Truly, I hoped it would not come to this. But you leave me no other choice."

EPILOGUE

June 19, 1998

Grotesque forms whirling through the air, a manic high-pitched insane laughter no human could mimic, the sound of a thousand souls screaming in agony . . .

Meghann came back to her senses when a small hand reached out to touch her shoulder.

She looked up and saw a young boy—he couldn't be older than ten.

He gave Meghann a sheepish smile. "I'm sorry, lady, I didn't mean to scare you. I was just practicing for the Fourth." He held out the remnants of an M-80 firecracker.

She smiled back at the child and, with trembling hands, lit a cigarette. Briefly she considered the wisdom of smoking now and then decided the hell with it. "It's OK—you just startled me a little."

The kid was relieved—it was weird the way that lady's face got all pale and she jumped about a mile when his M-80 went off.

Meghann watched the boy wander off, and then she turned her gaze to the water where her dog Max was joyfully swimming in the still, cold ocean.

She looked down at her arms, still covered in goose

bumps. When was it going to get better? The other night, a streetlight had blown out, leaving her in the dark. She'd screamed and screamed for almost a full minute before getting hold of herself, managing to convince herself it wasn't the same darkness Simon had conjured.

Her senses warned her of the immortal presence near her, and she rubbed her head gingerly. Even after a month and a half, she was suffering migraine headaches whenever she tried to focus.

She turned her eyes away from the sea to identify the approaching figure. He joined her, staring at her anxiously. "Another episode?"

Meghann nodded. "They're getting worse. They come and go . . . these flashbacks. It's awful. . . . I feel like I'm right back there. I lose touch with reality and then I think I'm back there with those evil things—" Meghann couldn't go on; she wrapped her arms around her shaking torso.

The other vampire shivered too, remembering the sudden darkness that made it impossible to see, even for a vampire. Then there was the bitter cold and the foul odor that permeated the small chamber. . . . He had no idea what Simon had conjured that night.

Meghann glanced at him. "Won't you tell me now what happened?"

He shook his head. "No, Meghann. Let your mind and body heal at their own pace. You'll remember when you're ready."

Meghann took his hand. "Please tell me . . . I can't take living like this. Never knowing when those thoughts are going to attack. I think if you tell me everything it will stop. Please."

More than her words, it was the haunted look in her eyes that changed his mind. Meghann did have a right to know what happened, what they lived through. He couldn't stand seeing that pinched, drawn look on her face anymore or having to worry about what was going to trigger another flashback. But how could he explain that even more than the chaos that was unleashed, he'd been terrified by the clear lack of sanity in Simon Baldevar's eyes. He felt his heart plummet to his stomach when that monster glared at Meghann. Rage, betrayal, and what chilled him most of all . . .

Simon actually had tears in his eyes when he said his last words to Meghann. "I treated you with a tenderness I have never lavished on another. And this is how you repay me? By kicking my love for you away like something vile and nasty you would not deign to touch? You want to fight with the angels, little one? Very well."

Simon bowed his head and started chanting. It was a low, sinister sound in a language neither Charles nor Meghann was familiar with. But they did not need to know the words when the effect was so plain. There was a sudden gust of wind that made everything—including the wooden rack that easily weighed a ton—fly around the room, and tore Jimmy from their grasp.

Meghann screamed out, "My vision! My vision! No, Simon, you can't let these things walk the earth. . . . Stop them!"

And Charles thought the thing never even heard her. For one chilling moment, Simon's gold eyes blazed bright enough to be visible in the thick darkness; Charles did not see a soul or consciousness there. Even a 400-year-old vampire could not stop such an ancient deadly power from taking him over. . . .

Charles took a bemused look at the horizon and then turned back to Meghann. "You won, you know."

Meghann shook her head. "How can you say that? Lord Baldevar is alive and, well, Jimmy is—" She broke off, but not before Charles heard her voice tighten with tears. "What have I won?"

Charles took her hand. "Throughout his chanting,

when he released those evil forms, you never once
moved from my side. I know what he said to you. . . .
He thought you'd lose your nerve and beg him to help
you. But you did not cry out to him, never going to his
side."

*Meghann did more than stand by Charles—she saved his
life. As the evil grew stronger, it became plain the daemons
ruled this room. Somehow Simon had brought the Lower Astral
to their physical world and given it dominion. Now the monsters moved toward Charles and Meghann, rejoicing at the
thought of possessing the souls of vampires, glorying in the
thought of the power that would give them.*

*They tried every form of magic they knew to repel the evil
emanations but nothing worked. The icy presence was nearly
inside Charles when Meghann screamed, "The Higher Astral!"*

*Though he was holding her tight, Charles could not see his
friend. "What?"*

*"It's our only chance to repel these monsters! Let your soul
leave your body and take refuge in the Higher Astral! We'll
fool them. . . . They'll take our bodies, but our souls will be
protected."*

"But they'll destroy our bodies!"

"Would you rather give them your soul?"

*Charles knew what Meghann was telling him. . . . They
would very likely die now, but at least they would not be possessed. Before he could tell her he agreed, her body went completely limp and fell to the ground.*

*"Meghann!" he screamed. In this oppressive blackness, he
could not even find her body. Charles knew she had not been
taken over. . . . No, the daemons would glory in the strength
of their new body; she would not fall to the floor. Not knowing
if she was dead, Charles abandoned his body and took refuge
in the Astral Plane.*

*Immediately he felt peace. The evil could not chase him here.
It was impossible to describe what he saw . . . or if he saw*

*anything at all. All he knew was he felt a security he had not
known since he was a small child and his mother kissed him
good night. . . .*

"Go help Meghann."

*"Master?" he questioned. He did not see a form, nor really
hear a voice. . . . He simply felt an image.*

*"Meghann needs you . . . and you need her too. Promise
me you'll help her through this."*

*"Through what?" But the pinkish cord that bound him to
his body was yanked and he found himself traveling back to
that hellish room. . . .*

What happened? he asked himself for the ump-
teenth time. Charles came back to the chamber—his
watch informed him that he wandered the Astral for
nearly an hour—and found it an absolute shambles,
but the evil had been banished. Had Simon recovered
his sanity and exorcised the monsters, sending them
back to the dim bowels from which he called them?
Had Alcuin done his apprentices one final service before he told Charles to go back and help Meghann? Or
had some other, stronger force, maybe Fate, simply decided the monsters had no place in this world and sent
them away? They would never know.

*All Charles knew was the first thing he saw was Meghann
with a hideous wound in her head. The pincer had gone
through the top part of her skull, sticking out of the back at
an obscene angle. He yanked it from her scalp, and stared in
horror at the gaping hole. Blood and gore rushed out; he took
the ragged remains of her dress and used them to stanch the
flow.*

*Then Charles began shaking her frantically. Could a vam-
pire suffer brain damage? Meghann was insensible—she
didn't respond until he cut open his wrists and forced the blood
down her throat, keeping her in a sitting position so she
wouldn't choke. At last, she spluttered and began moaning in
pain.*

"It hurts." She mewled like a weak kitten.

Charles sagged in relief—the trauma hadn't affected her mind, and the daemons had not entered her.

Charles picked her up. "Come on, we must leave here!"

"Jimmy," she mumbled. "Where's Jimmy?"

Now Charles looked at a dog-eared, crumpled letter Meghann took out of her pocket. He knew its contents as well as she did.

Charles was so concerned about Meghann it hadn't even occurred to him to wonder where Simon and Jimmy were. Now he glanced about the destroyed chamber. Somehow he knew Simon was gone—but where was Jimmy?

He placed Meghann in a corner of the room and started searching for some kind of clue. Where was the man's body? Surely, he had not been well enough to get up and leave before them.

"Charles," Meghann whispered.

He went back to her. "Are you in pain?"

"No, not that. By the table . . . see, it looks like a letter."

Charles glanced at the overturned table, and saw that his friend was right. With a rose serving as a paperweight, there was an envelope on the ground, its white parchment sullied by the filthy floor.

Now Meghann read the cursed letter aloud again. As she read, Charles could almost see that vile bastard savoring each line as he put it on paper, knowing what it would do to Meghann, how badly it would hurt. . . .

Meghann,

You are almost enough to make me believe in the existence of my departed uncle's self-righteous, punishing god. As you yourself put it, falling in love and being spurned is a rather fitting chastisement for several lifetimes spent never caring for another person. Not that I regret one action I've taken—and that includes my decision to transform you, my reluctant consort.

As my good friend Will Shakespeare put it . . . the course of true love never did run smooth. You need not fear me, darling. I shall never again lift a hand to harm you. That would not bring me what I most desire—your love.

Therefore, until the day comes that you seek me out of your own free will, our paths will not cross. The next time you see me, Meghann, it will be because you want to.

That does not mean I will stand idly by and allow you to seek out others to share your immortality with. My dear one, if I cannot have you, then no one will. Be forewarned, little one, that your life without me shall be a lonely one. Should you be at all tempted to shrug off this part of my letter, I would strongly urge you to keep the example of James Delacroix before you.

Never fear he is quite alive. But you will take no pleasure in seeing him. For he is no longer your lover, but rather, I have transformed him into my apprentice— to replace the one you so thoughtlessly slaughtered.

> *Farewell for now, sweet child.*
>
> *All my love,*
>
> *Lord Simon Baldevar, Earl of Lecarrow*

Meghann spat on the letter. "You'll see me because you want to see me! The fiend overlooks the fact that he has Jimmy with him. . . . Of course our paths will cross again!" Angrily she punched the steel railing on the boardwalk, causing it to bend. "Goddamn him to hell!" she yelled.

Charles was relieved by the sight of her temper. Let her get angry; let her start to feel again. This was the first time he'd seen any strong emotion in her since that awful night. Charles hated to remember the piteous way Meghann had wept, how she beat her fists on the stone floor until Charles forcibly restrained her.

He'd been frightened she might harm herself, but then she cried and cried. It seemed like hours until the pain of her injury forced her to stop, and even then quiet tears still trickled down her face.

As they walked on the boardwalk, Charles took in his friend's appearance. The evil wretch had done his work well that evening—a light had forever gone out of Meghann's eyes. The wonderful sprite and funny girl he loved was no more—now her eyes were bitter and cold. But Charles told himself it was too soon to decide if this was a permanent condition—she had not even been without Jimmy two months; it was normal to grieve now.

Meghann glanced at Charles. "Why are you still alive?" The question was in no way a reproach, not an indication of disappointment that he was well while her lover lived through the hell of being Simon's slave. It was honest puzzlement.

Charles had no more answers to that than she did. "The only thing I can think of is that the fiend simply didn't have time to deal with me and Jimmy . . . so he made a choice. Which would hurt more . . . my death or Jimmy's transformation at his hands? He made his decision; then he hurried to steal Jimmy away and write that miserable letter before we could stop him." There was another possibility—one he wasn't ready to share with Meghann. Lord Baldevar had to have known she was hurt before he left the estate. Could he have left Charles alive to make sure someone could help her? Did he truly love her?

"Simon told me he knew I must have tried to console myself with the idea I'd change things if I were ever given an opportunity," she said in a quiet tone. The brief flash of rage was gone; in its place was that gray numbness that worried Charles so much. "He was right—I did tell myself how differently I'd do things if

I had a second chance. But look what happened—God gave me a chance to find love again with Jimmy. But I failed him the same way I failed Johnny Devlin—I couldn't save either of them from Simon."

"That's not true." Charles forced her to look at him—forced himself actually; he couldn't stand her haunted, shadowed eyes. "Jimmy Delacroix is alive. Maybe he is changed, but he's alive all the same. We'll find him, Meghann. And no matter what Simon has done to him, I believe we can cure him. Don't you remember that awful night? Even if it was only for a brief moment, you undid Simon's work on Jimmy with love. And you saved me too. Who knows what would have happened if I didn't travel away? And if that isn't enough for you, what about Darlene?"

Meghann was silent, but Charles thought he saw a small gleam of satisfaction in her expression. He recalled how stunned he was when Meghann pulled herself off that stone floor.

Her green eyes were absolutely steady and calm. In an awful way, he was reminded of that still quality Simon had . . . where you could not know what he was feeling or thinking behind the cold mask. Meghann looked liked that when she said quietly but emphatically, "Darlene!"

"What?" he had said dumbly.

"Darlene!" she shouted. "Jimmy's twin sister . . . I know Simon! He'll try to twist Jimmy's soul by making him kill the person he loves most of all . . . just like he did to me! We have to go upstate; we have to save Darlene."

"He can't attack Jimmy's sister tonight," Charles protested. "He has to watch over Jimmy's transformation."

"That's right," Meghann told him. "There's no way for Simon to attack Darlene tonight . . . so that's why we have to act; while he's occupied with Jimmy!"

He recalled the frenzied drive upstate, him driving while Meghann directed him. Fortunately, Charles had three pints of blood in his bag. He made Meghann take most of it, and that grisly wound began to shut. But there was still a hole in her forehead when they pulled up in front of Darlene Delacroix Parker's house.

Now Meghann laughed. It was a bit grim, somewhat rusty—but a laugh all the same. "Oh, God, Darlene looked like she'd seen a ghost. She never believed Jimmy's story about the vampire that killed Amy and Jay. Suddenly she had little choice with me standing before her with a window in my skull like the one that killed Kennedy."

Darlene came running out of the small, neat, white-frame house, her husband behind her with a hunting rifle.

The woman paled like a ghost when she saw her twin's girlfriend standing in front of her with a huge red hole in her forehead. Darlene thought she could see the other woman's brain. "Maggie?" she whispered.

"I need to talk to you," Meghann told her.

By some miracle, Darlene remained on her feet and asked her husband to go back inside. He'd been reluctant—until Charles reached into his mind.

Once he shut the screen door, Darlene asked haltingly, "Everything Jimmy said . . . was true, wasn't it?"

Meghann nodded. "You have to trust me now, Darlene."

"Where the hell is my brother?"

"Something very bad happened to him."

"Well, why didn't you help him?" Darlene asked her twin's lover. She didn't know what exactly this woman was . . . or if she was a woman at all. But Jimmy loved her—he'd been with her for six years. "Ain't that what you've been up to all this time? Helping Jimmy with that . . . mess?"

"I tried to help," Meghann said softly.

Darlene took in the incredible injury and the woman's ragged appearance, standing before her clad only in an oversize T-shirt. And she looked at the stranger with her. . . . They were both white like sheets and their eyes kept jumping around. "I guess you did try to help him. But where is he? Why are you here?"

Meghann sighed, and tried to put this situation as simply as she could. "Jimmy has been hurt . . . badly hurt and very changed. You would not recognize him as your brother. And right now, he wouldn't care that you're the sister he loves so much. . . . You'd mean nothing to him." She saw the pain on Darlene's face and tried to soften the blow. "But I don't think he'll be that way forever. I'll be able to help him again. Right now I'm helping him by keeping you safe."

Darlene did not want to know any more about this situation than she absolutely had to. That was fortunate since Meghann was not going to tell her anything. . . . The less Darlene knew, the better.

Darlene had not argued when Meghann insisted that she and her family leave their home at the crack of dawn. There was no protest when Meghann gave her the location of a fixer who would be happy to supply the family with new identities. Yes, she agreed to send her new address to Meghann at a post office box Jimmy did not know about. Reluctantly she agreed to accept the money Meghann offered to start the family's new life.

Charles grinned when he thought of where Meghann got the funds to assist Jimmy's family. She pointed out that since the deed to Simon's manor house was in her name, there was no reason for her not to sell it. She'd been lucky enough to find a buyer quickly, then gave most of the money from the sale of the estate to Darlene. Hopefully, their new identities—unknown to Jimmy—and wealth would keep them safe.

The two vampires stood guard over the family until dawn, and Darlene raised no objection when Meghann told her they would be staying in the cellar.

Charles remembered the last conversation between the two women. The car was loaded down, Darlene's children and husband ready to leave.

Before she got in the car, Darlene grabbed Meghann. "I want you to promise me something."

"Anything."

"You say something bad has changed my brother, that he might hurt us, and he wouldn't be able to help himself."

"Yes."

"Well, let me tell you something. I don't know you all that well, but I do know Jimmy just about worshiped the ground you walked on. If he's mixed up in something bad, he'll listen to you if you tell him to quit. So you swear to me that you and this guy you're with . . . you swear that you'll both use whatever you've got to help Jimmy out of this mess he's in."

Meghann grabbed Darlene back, and kissed her cheek. "I swear to you I'll bring Jimmy back."

"Meghann, how can you tell me, after all you did that night, that you failed?" She started to speak, but Charles pressed on. "You saved Darlene's life. You don't think Jimmy would thank you for that if he could? No . . . one day he will thank you for it. And look at Lord Baldevar—no matter how you enrage or resist him, he can't kill you. That gives you quite a bit of power over him. Perhaps in time we'll figure out a way to use that to our advantage."

Meghann shrugged. "Maybe he can't kill me. . . . Maybe that's as close to love as Simon Baldevar is ever going to get. But what good is it? Our strength is nothing compared to his."

"Right now that's true," Charles told her quietly. "I did not mean we could rescue Jimmy anytime soon. But in time, Meghann, we'll go home to Ballnamore. We have to go anyway—explain our master's death to the others. While we're there . . . we'll pour over every resource our mentor left behind. We'll do what that rotten fiend did and develop our power. We're vampires, Meghann, and that gives us one invaluable resource for our feud with Simon . . . time."

For a brief moment, Meghann was herself again. Her green eyes glowed with hope and anticipation. But then her eyes turned apathetic once more. "I'm afraid Simon has even managed to take that resource from me, Charles."

Charles took her hands. "Meghann, what do you mean? I was sure you were recovering over the past few weeks—you seemed stronger and I saw that depression start to alleviate. Then the past two nights—I know you've spent most of them weeping. Please tell me what's wrong. . . . Let me help you."

Meghann sat down on the cold sand. Charles perched by her, wishing there were some way to remove that tense, anxious, desperately unhappy look from her eyes.

"Charles," she said quietly, "I'm not trying to be coy, or keep things from you. It's just . . . I don't know how to tell you this. I can't seem to say the words."

Charles put his arms around her. "Take your time."

But Meghann just looked up at him with the strangest expression. He saw pain in her eyes, pain with fear, embarrassment . . . and a curious acceptance of something. Wait a minute! Now he remembered when he'd seen a look to rival hers . . . in his mortal days, when he had to tell patients they were dying. . . . Once they accepted the news, they had that same bitter resignation Meghann did.

Do you think you're dying, Meghann?

Startled, she looked up. It was very rare for her and Charles to speak to each other telepathically. . . . They usually preferred to keep their mortal ways with each other.

"I don't know," she told him softly. "I . . . I guess I should start at the beginning." She met his eyes again, and this time the embarrassment was stronger in her eyes . . . and in the blush covering her cheeks. "I never told you everything that happened between me and Simon after he killed Alcuin."

"I didn't want to embarrass you by prying," Charles said.

"I thank you for that, and I was hoping I'd never have to tell you. I wanted to forget it happened. But now—"

Charles put an arm around her. "Meghann, I told you once before—it doesn't matter what you did to stay alive. I think I know some of what's bothering you. . . . Don't forget I heard every word that fiend said to you when he thought I was unconscious. What's eating you? Are you scared that you have . . . feelings for him?"

Meghann gave a bitter laugh. "I have better things to worry about now. But as far as that goes . . . I've had a lot of time to think about it. It did gnaw at me . . . the fact that I told him I loved him, that I almost wanted to sever his bonds when he was on the rack."

"That was only him using his power as your master to do his bidding—nothing more. It's not like you're in love with him."

Meghann shrugged. "I wish that were true. But I think a part of me . . . the dark part, maybe what he put there when he transformed me . . . part of me loves him. Otherwise, he never would have gotten me to respond to him when we were alone. And that was before he forced that potion down my throat. One thing he told me . . . I see a side of him no one else does. That's probably true. . . . He is not tender to anyone else, just me."

"Is that enough for you?" Charles asked her.

"Of course not!" she replied quickly. "No, I had something far better with Jimmy. . . . Which is why the bastard is probably doing his best to warp Jimmy even as we speak. What I was trying to tell you is that Alcuin was right. . . . I can't resist Simon when I'm alone with him. When you're there, when Jimmy was with me . . . I could ignore that cord, or bond, or link, or whatever the hell it is that he uses to bind me to him."

"I think it drives Lord Baldevar insane that you can ignore it all—that he'll never have what he wants from you."

Meghann sighed. "You're wrong there. . . . Simon got precisely what he wanted from me. I told him I loved him . . . and I meant it. I think maybe that was very important; it wouldn't have worked if I didn't feel I loved him, that I wanted to belong to him in that moment."

"What wouldn't have worked? What did he do to you, Meghann?"

"After he gave me that potion, we made love."

"I guessed that."

"Did you also guess that he had me invoke the goddess while we made love?"

Charles felt something icy at the back of his neck—he shivered because he was starting to understand what Meghann was driving at.

She saw his comprehension and nodded. "I brought the goddess into my body. . . . We performed the strongest form of love magic on Beltane . . . the night for fertility." Meghann sighed again, and looked out at the black water with the crashing surf. "I thought all Simon was after that night was my soul. I had no idea he performed that rite to gain something far more tangible."

Beltane . . . lovemaking . . . invoking the goddess . . . Charles's eyes swept over his friend's body. He prayed the dark suspicion he had was wrong. He started babbling in fear and denial. "We'll rescue Jimmy, Meghann. We'll be safe from Simon at Ballnamore and we'll do as I told you, find some way to develop our strength until we're a fit match for—"

Meghann smiled sadly and put her hand over his

mouth to stem the hysterical promises. "I don't have time to develop my strength, Charles." She took one of his icy, trembling hands and placed it on her stomach. "I'm pregnant."

ABOUT THE AUTHOR

Trisha Baker lives with her family in New York. She is currently working on the sequel to CRIMSON KISS. It will be published by Pinnacle Books in 2002. Trisha loves hearing from readers; you may write to her c/o Pinnacle Books. Please include a self-addressed, stamped envelope if you wish to receive a response. You can also visit her Web site at www.crimsonkiss.org.

Feel the Seduction of
Pinnacle Horror

__**The Vampire Memoirs**
by Mara McCunniff   **0-7860-1124-6**   **$5.99US/$7.99CAN**
& Traci Briery

__**The Stake**
by Richard Laymon   **0-7860-1095-9**   **$5.99US/$7.99CAN**

__**Blood of My Blood: The Vampire Legacy**
by Karen E. Taylor   **0-7860-1153-X**   **$5.99US/$7.99CAN**

HORROR FROM PINNACLE . . .

__HAUNTED__ by Tamara Thorne
0-7860-1090-8 $5.99US/$7.99CAN

Its violent, sordid past is what draws best-selling author David Masters to the infamous Victorian mansion called Baudey House. Its shrouded history of madness and murder is just the inspiration he needs to write his ultimate masterpiece of horror. But what waits for David and his teenaged daughter at Baudey House is more terrifying than any legend; it is the dead, seducing the living, in an age-old ritual of perverted desire and unholy blood lust.

__THIRST__ by Michael Cecilione
0-7860-1091-6 $5.99US/$7.99CAN

Cassandra Hall meets her new lover at a Greenwich Village poetry reading—and sex with him is like nothing she's ever experienced. But Cassandra's new man has a secret he wants her to share: he's a vampire. And soon, Cassandra descends into a deeper realm of exotic thirst and unspeakable passion, where she must confront the dark side of her own sensuality . . . and where a beautiful rival threatens her earthly soul.

__THE HAUNTING__ by Ruby Jean Jensen
0-7860-1095-9 $5.99US/$7.99CAN

Soon after Katie Rogers moves into an abandoned house in the woods with her sister and her young niece and nephew, she begins having bizarre nightmares in which she is a small child again, running in terror. Then come horrifying visions of a woman wielding a gleaming butcher knife. Of course, Katie doesn't believe that any of it is *real* . . . until her niece and nephew disappear. Now only Katie can put an end to a savage evil that is slowly awakening to unleash a fresh cycle of slaughter and death in which the innocent will die again and again!

Call toll free **1-888-345-BOOK** to order by phone or use this coupon to order by mail.

Name_____

Address_____

City_____ State _____ Zip _____

Please send me the books I have checked above.

I am enclosing	$_____
Plus postage and handling*	$_____
Sales tax (in NY and TN)	$_____
Total amount enclosed	$_____

*Add $2.50 for the first book and $.50 for each additional book.
Send check or money order (no cash or CODs) to: **Kensington Publishing Corp., Dept. C.O., 850 Third Avenue, 16th Floor, New York, NY 10022**
Prices and numbers subject to change without notice. All orders subject to availability.
Check out our website at **www.kensingtonbooks.com**.

When Darkness Falls
Grab One of These
Pinnacle Horrors